TROUBLE IN MIND

JEFFERY DEAVER

TROUBLE IN MIND

HODDER &
STOUGHTON

First published in the United States of America in 2014 by Grand Central Publishing

First published in Great Britain in 2014 by Hodder & Stoughton
An Hachette UK company

1

Notes on previously published stories: .
'Fast', 'Game' and 'Paradice' were first published in the ebook *Triple Threat*, and
'A Textbook Case' was first published as a standalone ebook, both from Grand
Central Publishing and Hodder & Stoughton (2013).
'The Plot' previously appeared in *First Thrills*, edited by Lee Child (Forge Books, 2010).
'The Therapist' previously appeared in *Stories*, edited by Neil Gaiman and Al
Sarrantonio (HarperCollins, 2010). 'The Weapon' previously appeared in *Thriller 2*,
edited by Clive Cussler (Mira, 2009). 'The Obit' previously appeared in *The Lineup*,
edited by Otto Penzler (Little, Brown and Company, 2009). 'Bump' previously appeared
in *Dead Man's Hand*, edited by Otto Penzler (Houghton Mifflin Harcourt, 2007).
'Forever' previously appeared in *Transgressions*, edited by Ed McBain
(Forge Books, 2005). All other stories are originals.

A CIP catalogue record for this title is available from the British Library

Hardback ISBN 978 1 444 70452 5
Trade paperback ISBN 978 1 444 70453 2
Ebook ISBN 978 1 848 94921 8

Typeset in Fairfield by Palimpsest Book Production Ltd, Falkirk, Stirlingshire

Printed and bound in Great Britain by Clays Ltd, St Ives plc

Hodder & Stoughton policy is to use papers that are natural, renewable and
recyclable products and made from wood grown in sustainable forests.
The logging and manufacturing processes are expected to conform to
the environmental regulations of the country of origin.

Hodder & Stoughton Ltd
338 Euston Road
London NW1 3BH

www.hodder.co.uk

Contents

Author's Note

I began writing fiction at the ripe young age of eleven. Sometimes I claim that that first effort was a novel, since I divided my opus into chapters (two) and included a jacket with cover art that I drew myself. But there's an expression I've heard down here in North Carolina: Just 'cause your cat has a litter in the laundry basket doesn't mean the kittens are socks.

What I wrote back then, fifty years ago, was a short story, whatever I called it.

I've always had an affection for reading short fiction and I've learned much about writing from the stories of Edgar Allan Poe, Conan Doyle and Ray Bradbury, among many others. I also thoroughly enjoy writing short stories. Now, it's my entrenched belief that all storytelling has as its most important goal emotionally engaging the audience as much as possible. I don't want to come away from reading a book or seeing a film and think, Well, wasn't that interesting? I want to think: OMG, I need to calm down, take a breath, allow the stitch in my side to ease from the uncontrolled laughter or let the tears subside . . . In short, I want to be captivated by art and entertainment.

In novels, this level of intensity is accomplished by creating multi-dimensional characters and throwing each into his or her own roller-coaster subplots that are rife with reversals and escalating levels of conflicts, which are ultimately resolved. (I *hate* ambiguous endings!) In short stories, an author doesn't have the time or space to follow this formula. But short fiction still needs to captivate, to enthrall. What's one to do?

The answer is to go for the gut with a shocking twist, a surprise, the unexpected.

An example: My novel version of *Lassie* would be to tell a multilayered story about Timmy, the collie, a broken home life for the kid, and disreputable corporate interests digging wells where they shouldn't. We'd speed through these several intersecting subplots to a sweaty-palm ending where Timmy is, thank God, saved from the well and Lassie finds evidence to land the evil developers in prison.

O joyous day!

My short story version would be this: The boy's down the well. Cut to: Lassie running through the fields frantically. Cut back to: Timmy's about to drown. But then a paw reaches over the edge. The kid grabs it and is pulled out of the freezing water. Cut to: Lassie, a mile away, still chasing the squirrel she's been after for ten minutes. Back to: Timmy, outside the well, standing in front of the large wolf who just plucked him to safety and who's eyeing his main course hungrily.

Sorry, kid.

The stories in this anthology are typical of that approach. What you see isn't, I hope, what you think you're seeing.

Six of the stories are new, one Lincoln Rhyme ('A Textbook Case'), one Kathryn Dance ('Fast'), one John Pellam ('Paradice') and three stand-alones ('Game', 'The Competitors' and 'Reconciliation'), though those familiar with my older work will note that 'Game' was inspired by a short piece I did for *Esquire* magazine years ago on the Kenneth and Sante Kimes murder of New York socialite Irene Silverman. Similarly, 'Paradice' had its roots in my story 'Switchback', which appeared in the wonderful *Ellery Queen Mystery Magazine* about fifteen years ago. I'd be curious to know what any of you think of the twist that ends 'Paradice' now; it's one of my all-time favorites.

I should mention, too, that one thing I like about short stories is that they allow an author to step out of genre more easily than novels do. I believe in brand identification – a lofty corporate way of saying you must make sure your audience knows what they're getting when they buy your fiction. My readers enjoy my thrillers, so I'll continue to produce crime novels, rather than fantasy or science fiction.

Short stories, though, involve a more modest commitment on the part of readers. So I can easily slip out of category briefly with a story or two, while assuring fans that my next novel will be filled with the murder and mayhem they've come to expect from me.

Two stories in this collection, 'The Therapist' and 'Forever', are genre benders, bordering on the occult. (Or are they . . .?)

Welcome to this, the third collection of my short fiction. The first two anthologies were entitled *Twisted* and *More Twisted*. In casting about for a name for this volume, I decided to move away from that theme (What was left, anyway: *Excessively Twisted*? *Son of Twisted*?). I opted for a similar yet fresh phrase – one that clearly describes many of the characters we meet in these pages – and, some would suggest, the author as well.

I take that as a compliment.

J.D.

FAST

They were just about to see the octopus when she received a text alerting her that two hundred people were going to die in two hours.

Kathryn Dance rarely received texts marked with exclamation points – the law enforcement community tended not to punctuate with emotion – so she read it immediately. Then called her office, via speed dial three.

'Boss,' the young man's voice spilled from her iPhone.

'Details, TJ?'

Over their heads:

'Will the ticket holders for the one-thirty exhibition make their way inside, please.'

'Mom!' The little girl's voice was urgent. 'That's us.'

'Hold on a second, honey.' Then into the phone: 'Go on.'

TJ Scanlon said, 'Sorry, Boss, this's bad. On the wire from up north.'

'Mom . . .'

'Let me talk, Mags.'

'Long story short, Alameda was monitoring this domestic separatist outfit, planning an attack up there.'

'I know. Brothers of Liberty, based in Oakland, white supremacists, antigovernment. Osmond Carter, their leader, was arrested last week and they threatened retaliation if he's not released.'

'You knew that?'

'You read the statewide dailies, TJ?'

'Mean to.'

'. . . the Monterey Bay Aquarium is pleased to host the largest specimen of Enteroctopus dofleini on exhibit in the northern California area, weighing in at a hundred and twenty-one pounds! We know you're going to enjoy viewing our visiting guest in his specially created habitat.'

'Okay. What's the story?' Dance persisted into the phone as she and her children edged closer to the exhibit hall. They'd waited forty-five minutes. Who would have thought octopuses, octopi, would be such a big draw?

TJ said, 'Everybody believed they were going to hit somewhere up there, Alameda, Contra Costa, San Fran, but maybe there was too much heat. Oakland PD had a CI inside the group and he said two of their people came down here, set up something. And—'

She interrupted. '"Set up something." What does that mean?'

'An attack of some kind. He doesn't know what exactly. Maybe an IED, maybe chemical. Probably not bio but could be. But the number of victims is for sure, what I texted you. Two hundred plus or minus. That's confirmed. And whatever it is, it's up and running; the perps set it and they were headed back. The CI said four p.m. is when the attack goes down.'

Two and a half hours. A little less. Lord . . .

'No idea of the victims, location?'

TJ Scanlon offered, 'None.'

'But you said they "were" headed back.'

'Right, we caught a break. There's a chance we can nail 'em. The CI gave us the make of the car – a 2000 Taurus, light blue. CHP spotted one in Marina and went after it. The driver took off. Probably them. They lost the pursuit on surface roads. Everybody's searching the area. Bureau's coming in from the field office. Hold on, Boss. I'm getting something.'

Dance happened to glance up and see her reflection in the glass panel on the other side of which elegant and eerie sea horses floated with sublime, careless ease. Dance noted her own still gaze looking back at her, in a narrow, Cate Blanchett face, hair in a ponytail, held taut by a black-and-green scrunchy installed that morning by her ten-year-old daughter, currently champing beside her. Her mop-headed son, Wes, twelve, was detached from mother and sister. He was less intrigued by cephalopods, however big, and more by an aloof fourteen-year-old in line, a girl who should have been a cheerleader if she wasn't.

Dance was wearing jeans, a blue silk blouse and a tan quilted vest, comfortably warm. Sunny at the moment, the Monterey Peninsula could be quite fickle when it came to weather. Fog mostly.

'*Mom*, they're calling us,' Maggie said in her weegee voice, the high pitch that conveyed exasperation really well.

'One minute, this's important.'

'First, it was a second. Now it's a minute. Jeez. One one-thousand, two one-thousand . . .'

Wes was smiling toward, but not at, the cheerleader.

The line inched forward, drawing them seductively closer to the Cephalopod of the Century.

TJ came back on the line. 'Boss, yep, it's them. The Taurus's registered to the Brothers of Liberty. CHP's in pursuit.'

'Where?'

'Seaside.'

Dance glanced around her at the dim concrete and glass aquarium. It was holiday break – ten days before Christmas – and the place was packed. And there were dozens of tourist attractions like this in the area, not to mention movie theaters, churches and offices. Some schools were closed but others not. Was the plan to leave a bomb in, say, that trash can out front? She said into the phone, 'I'll be right in.' Turning to the children, she grimaced at their disappointed faces. She had a theory – possibly unfounded – that her two children were more sensitive to disappointment than other kids their age because they were fatherless . . . and because Bill had died suddenly. There in the morning, and then never again. It was so very hard for her to say what she now had to: 'Sorry, guys. It's a big problem at work.'

'Aw, Mom!' Maggie grumbled. 'This is the last day! It's going to San Diego tomorrow.' Wes, too, was disappointed, though part of this wasn't sea life but pretty cheerleaders.

'Sorry, guys. Can't be helped. I'll make it up to you.' Dance held the phone back to her ear and she said firmly to TJ, 'And tell everybody: No shooting unless it's absolutely necessary. I don't want either of them killed.'

Which brought conversation around them in the octopus line to a complete stop. Everyone stared.

Speaking to the wide-eyed blonde, Wes said reassuringly, 'It's okay. She says that a lot.'

The venue for the party was good. The Monterey Bay Seaside Motel was near the water, north of the city. And what was especially nice about this place was that unlike a lot of banquet rooms this one had large windows opening onto a stretch of beach.

Right now, Carol Messner noted, the beach had that December afternoon look to it: bleached, dusty, though the haze was mostly mist with a bit of fog thrown in. Not so focused, but, hey, a beach view beat a Highway 1 view any day, provided the sun held.

'Hal,' she said to her associate. 'You think we need more tables over there? It looks empty.'

Carol, president of the local branch of the California Central Coast Bankers' Association, was a woman in her sixties, a grandmother several times over. Although her employer was one of the larger chain banks that had misbehaved a bit a few years ago, she'd had no part of mortgage-backed securities; she firmly believed banks did good. She wouldn't have been in the business if she didn't think that. She was living proof of the beneficence of the world of finance. Carol and her husband had comfortable retirement funds thanks to banks, her daughter and son-in-law had expanded their graphic arts business and made it successful thanks to banks, her grandsons would be going to Stanford and UC-Davis next fall thanks to student loans.

The earth revolved around money, but that was a good thing – far better than guns and battleships – and she was happy and proud to be a part of the process. The diminutive, white-haired woman wouldn't have been in the business for forty-six years if she'd felt otherwise.

Hal Reskin, her second-in-command at the CCCBA, was a heavyset man with a still face, a lawyer specializing in commercial paper and banking law. He eyed the corner she pointed at and agreed. 'Asymmetrical,' he said. 'Can't have that.'

Carol tried not to smile. Hal took everything he did quite seriously and was a far better i-dotter than she. 'Asymmetrical' would be a sin, possibly mortal.

She walked up to the two motel employees who were organizing the room for the Christmas party, which would last from three to five today, and asked that they move several of the round ten-tops to cover the bald spot on the banquet room floor. The men hefted the tables and rearranged them.

Hal nodded.

Carol said, 'De-asymmetricalized.'

Her vice president laughed. Taking his tasks seriously didn't mean he was missing a sense of humor.

Hal took the room in. 'Looks good to me. Double-check the sound system. Then we'll get the decorations up.'

'The PA?' she asked. 'I tried it yesterday. It was fine.' But being the i-dotting banker that she was, Carol walked to the stage and flicked on the PA system.

Nothing.

A few more flicks of the off-on toggle.

As if that would do any good.

'This could be a problem.'

Carol followed the cord but it disappeared below the stage.

'Maybe those workers,' Hal said, peering at the microphones.

'Who?'

'Those two guys who were here a half-hour ago. Maybe before you got here?'

'No, I didn't see anybody. José and Miguel?' she asked, nodding at the men on the motel staff, now setting up chairs.

'No, other ones. They asked if this is where the banking meeting was going to be. I told them yes and they said they had to make some repairs under the stage. They were under there for a few minutes, then they left.'

She asked the two motel workers in the corner, 'Did you hear that there was a problem with the sound system?'

'No, ma'am. Maria, Guest Services, she handle everything with the microphones and all that. She said it was fine this morning. But she off now.'

'Where are those other workers?' Carol asked. After receiving blank stares, she explained what Hal had told her.

'I don't know who they'd be, ma'am. We're the ones, José and me, who set up the rooms.'

Walking toward the access door to the stage, Hal said, 'I'll take a look.'

'You know electronics?' she asked.

'Are you kidding? I set up my grandson's Kinect with his Xbox. All by my little ole lonesome.'

Carol had no idea what he was talking about but he said it with such pride she had to smile. She held open the access door as he descended beneath the stage. 'Good luck.'

Three minutes later the PA system came on with a resonant click through the speakers.

Carol applauded.

Hal appeared and dusted off his hands. 'Those guys earlier, they knocked the cord loose when they were under there. We'll have to keep an eye out, they don't do it again. I think they'll be back.'

'Really?'

'Maybe. They left a toolbox and some big bottles down there. Cleaner, I guess.'

'Okay. We'll keep an eye out.' But the workmen were gone from Carol's mind. Decorations had to be set up, food had to be arranged. She wanted the room to be as nice as possible for the two hundred CCCBA members who'd been looking forward to the party for months.

A stroke of luck . . . and good policing.

The CHP had collared the Brothers of Liberty perps.

Kathryn Dance, who'd dropped the disgruntled children off with her parents in Carmel, was standing in the weedy parking lot of an outlet mall only six miles from the California Bureau of Investigation's Monterey Office, where she worked. Michael O'Neil now approached. He looked like a character from a John Steinbeck novel, maybe Doc in *Cannery Row*. Although the uniform of the MCSO was typical county sheriff's khaki, Chief Detective O'Neil usually dressed soft – today in sports coat and tan slacks and blue dress shirt, no tie. His hair was salt-and-pepper and his brown eyes, beneath lids that dipped low, moved slowly as he explained the pursuit and collar. His physique was solid and his arms very strong – though not from working out in a gym (that was amusing to him) but from muscling salmon and other delicacies into his boat in Monterey Bay every chance he got.

O'Neil was taciturn by design and his face registered little emotion, but with Dance he could usually be counted on to crack a wry joke or banter.

Not now. He was all business.

A fellow CBI agent, massive shaved-headed Albert Stemple, stalked up and O'Neil explained to him and Dance how the perps had been caught.

The fastest way out of the area was on busy Highway 1 north, to 156, then to 101, which would take the suspected terrorists directly back to their nest in Oakland. That route was where the bulk of the searchers had been concentrating – without any success.

But an inventive young Highway Patrol officer had asked himself how would *he* leave the area, if he knew his mission was compromised. He decided the smartest approach would be to take neighborhood and single-lane roads all the way to Highway 5, several hours away. And so he concentrated on small avenues like Jacks and Oil Well and – this was the luck part – he spotted the perps near this strip mall, which was close to Highway 68, the Monterey–Salinas Highway.

The trooper had called in backup then lit 'em up.

After a twenty-minute high-speed pursuit, the perps skidded into the mall, sped around back and vanished, but the trooper decided they were trying a feint. He didn't head in the same direction they were; instead, he squealed to a stop and waited beside a Tires Plus operation.

After five excessively tense minutes, the Brothers of Liberty had apparently decided they'd misled the pursuit and sped out the way they'd come in, only to find the trooper had anticipated them. He floored the cruiser, equipped with ram bars, and totaled the Taurus. The perps bailed.

The trooper tackled and hog-tied one. The other galloped toward a warehouse area three or four hundred yards away, just as backup arrived. There was a brief exchange of gunfire and the second perp, wounded, was collared, too. Several CHP officers and a colleague of Dance's at the CBI, TJ Scanlon, were at that scene.

Now, at the outlet mall, the perp who'd been tackled, one Wayne Keplar, regarded Dance, Stemple and O'Neil and the growing entourage of law enforcers.

'Nice day for an event,' Keplar said. He was a lean man, skinny, you could say. Parentheses of creases surrounded his mouth, and his dark, narrow-set eyes hid beneath a severely straight fringe of black hair. A hook nose. Long arms, big hands, but he didn't appear particularly strong.

Albert Stemple, whose every muscle seemed to be massive, stood nearby and eyed the perp carefully, ready to step on the bug if need be. O'Neil took a radio call. He stepped away.

Keplar repeated, 'Event. Event . . . Could describe a game, you know.' He spoke in an oddly high voice, which Dance found irritating. Probably not the tone, more the smirk with which the words were delivered. 'Or could be a tragedy. Like they'd call an earthquake or a nuclear meltdown an "event". The press, I mean. They love words like that.'

O'Neil motioned Dance aside. 'That was Oakland PD. The CI's reporting that Keplar's pretty senior in the Brothers of Liberty. The other guy – the wounded one . . .' He nodded toward the warehouses. 'Gabe Paulson, he's technical. At least has some schooling in engineering. If it's a bomb, he's probably the one set it up.'

'They think that's what it is?'

'No intelligence about the means,' O'Neil explained. 'On their website they've talked about doing anything and everything to make their point.

Bio, chemical, snipers, even hooking up with some Islamic extremist group and doing a quote "joint venture".'

Dance's mouth tightened. 'We supply the explosives, you supply the suicide bomber?'

'That pretty much describes it.'

Her eyes took in Keplar, sitting on the curb, and she noted that he was relaxed, even jovial. Dance, whose position with the CBI trumped the other law enforcers, approached him and regarded the lean man calmly. 'We understand you're planning an attack of some sort—'

'Event,' he reminded her.

'Event, then, in two and a half hours. Is that true?'

"Deed it is.'

'Well, right now, the only crimes you'll be charged with are traffic. At the worst, we could get you for conspiracy and attempt, several different counts. If that event occurs and people lose their lives—'

'The charges'll be a *lot* more serious,' he said jovially. 'Let me ask you – what's your name?'

'Agent Dance. CBI.' She proffered her ID.

He smacked his lips. As irritating as his weaselly voice. 'Agent Dance, of the CBI, let me ask you, don't you think we have a few too many laws in this country? My goodness, Moses gave us *ten*. Things seemed to work pretty well back then and now we've got Washington and Sacramento telling us what to do, what not to do. Every little detail. Honestly! They don't have faith in our good, smart selves.'

'Mr Keplar—'

'Call me Wayne, please.' He looked her over appraisingly. Which cut of meat looks good today? 'I'll call you Kathryn.'

She noted that he'd memorized her name from the perusal of the ID. While Dance, as an attractive woman, was frequently undressed in the imaginations of the suspects she interviewed, Keplar's gaze suggested he was pitying her, as if she were afflicted with a disease. In her case, she guessed, the disease was the tumor of government and racial tolerance.

Dance noted the impervious smile on his face, his air of . . . what? Yes, almost triumph. He didn't appear at all concerned he'd been arrested.

Glancing at her watch: 1:37.

Dance stepped away to take a call from TJ Scanlon, updating her on the status of Gabe Paulson, the other perp. She was talking to him when O'Neil tapped her shoulder. She followed his gaze.

Three black SUVs, dusty and dinged but imposing, sped into the parking lot and squealed to a halt, red and blue lights flashing. A half-dozen men in suits climbed out, two others in tactical gear.

The largest of the men who were Brooks Brothers–clad – six two and two hundred pounds – brushed his thick graying hair back and strode forward.

'Michael, Kathryn.'

'Hi, Steve.'

Stephen Nichols was the head of the local field office of the FBI. He'd worked with Dance's husband, Bill Swenson, a bureau agent until his death. She'd met Nichols once or twice. He was a competent agent but ambitious in a locale where ambition didn't do you much good. He should have been in Houston or Atlanta, where he could free-style his way a bit further.

He said, 'I never got the file on this one.'

Don't you read the dailies?

Dance said, 'We didn't either. Everybody assumed the BOL would strike up near San Francisco, *that* bay, not ours.'

Nichols said, 'Who's he?'

Keplar stared back with amused hostility toward Nichols, who would represent that most pernicious of enemies – the federal government.

Dance explained his role in the group and what it was believed they'd done here.

'Any idea exactly what they have in mind?' another agent with Nichols asked.

'Nothing. So far.'

'There were two of them?' Nichols asked.

Dance added, 'The other's Gabe Paulson.' She nodded toward the warehouses some distance away. 'He was wounded but I just talked to my associate. It's a minor injury. He can be interrogated.'

Nichols hesitated, looking at the fog coming in fast. 'You know, I have to take them, Kathryn.' He sounded genuinely regretful at this rank-pulling. His glance wafted toward O'Neil, too, though Monterey was pretty far down on the rung in the hierarchy of law enforcement here represented, and nobody – even the sheriff himself – expected that the County would snag the bad boys.

'Sure.' Dance glanced toward her watch. 'But we haven't got much time. How many interrogators do you have?'

The agent was hesitating. 'Just me for now. We're bringing in some-body from San Francisco. He's good.'

'Bo?'

'Right.'

'He's good. But—' She tapped her watch. 'Let's split them up, Steve. Give me one of them. At least for the time being.'

Nichols shrugged. 'I guess.'

Dance said, 'Keplar's going to be the trickiest. He's senior in the organization and he's not the least shaken by the collar.' She nodded toward the perp, who was lecturing nearby officers relentlessly about the destruction of the Individual by Government – he was supplying the capitalization. 'He's going to be trickier to break. Paulson's been wounded and that'll make him more vulnerable.' She could see that Nichols was considering this. 'I think, our different styles, background, yours and mine, it'd make sense for me to take Keplar, you take Paulson.'

Nichols squinted against some momentary glare as a roll of fog vanished. 'Who's Paulson exactly?'

O'Neil answered, 'Seems to be the technician. He'd know about the device, if that's what they've planted. Even if he doesn't tell you directly, he could give something away that'd let us figure out what's going on.' The Monterey detective wouldn't know exactly why Dance wanted Keplar and not Gabe but he'd picked up on her preference and he was playing along.

This wasn't completely lost on the FBI agent. Nichols would be considering a lot of things. Did Dance's idea to split up the interrogation make sense? Did she and he indeed have different interrogation styles and background? Also, he'd know that O'Neil and Dance were close and they might be double-teaming him in some way, though he might not figure out to what end. He might have thought she was bluffing, hoping that he'd pick Wayne Keplar, because she herself wanted Gabe Paulson for some reason. Or he might have decided that all was good and it made sense for him to take the wounded perp.

Whatever schematics were drawn in his mind, he debated a long moment and then agreed.

Dance nodded. 'I'll call my associate, have Paulson brought over here.'

She gestured to the two CHP officers towering over Wayne Keplar. He was hoisted to his feet and led to Dance, O'Neil and Nichols. Albert Stemple – who weighed twice what the suspect did – took custody with a no-nonsense grip on the man's scrawny arm.

Keplar couldn't take his eyes off the FBI agents. 'Do you know the five reasons the federal government is a travesty?'

Dance wanted him to shut up – she was afraid Nichols would change his mind and drag the perp off himself.

'First, economically. I—'

'Whatever,' Nichols muttered and wandered off to await his own prisoner.

Dance nodded and Stemple escorted Keplar to a CBI unmarked Dodge and inserted him into the backseat.

Michael O'Neil would stay to supervise the crime scene here, canvassing for witnesses and searching for evidence – possibly items thrown from the car that might give them more information about the site of the attack.

As she got into her personal vehicle, a gray Nissan Pathfinder, Dance called to Nichols and O'Neil, 'And remember: We have two and a half hours. We've got to move fast.'

She pulled out her phone, briefed TJ Scanlon about Paulson and Nichols and turned on the flashing lights suctioned to her windshield.

1:52.

Dance left rubber on the concrete as she sped out of the parking lot.

Fast . . .

Albert Stemple was parked outside CBI, looking with some contempt at the press vans that were lolling near the front door. Dance parked behind him. She strode to the Dodge.

A reporter – a man with an aura of Jude Law, if not the exact looks – pushed to the barricade and thrust a microphone their way.

'Kathryn! Kathryn Dance! Dan Simmons, The True Story dot com.'

She knew him. A sensationalist reporter who oozed toward the tawdrier aspects of a story like slugs to Dance's doomed vegetable garden.

Simmons's cameraman, a squat, froggy man with crinkly and unwashed hair, aimed a fancy Sony video cam their way as if about to launch a rocket-propelled grenade.

'No comment on anything, Dan.' She and Stemple shoehorned Wayne Keplar out of the car.

The reporter ignored her. 'Can you give us your name?' Aimed at the suspect.

Keplar was all too happy to talk. He shouted out, 'The Brothers of Liberty,' and began a lecturette about how the fourth estate was in the pocket of corporate money and the government.

'Not all reporters, Wayne,' Simmons said. 'Not us. We're with you, brother! Keep talking.'

This impressed Keplar.

'Quiet,' Dance muttered, leading him toward the front door.

'And we're about to strike a blow for freedom!'

'What are you going to do, Wayne?' Simmons shouted.

'We have no comment,' Dance called.

'Well, *I* do. I've only been *arrested*,' Wayne offered energetically, with a smile, ignoring Dance and mugging for the reporter, whose disheveled photographer was shooting away with his fancy digital video camera. 'I'm not under a gag order. Freedom of speech! That's what the founders of this country believed in. Even if the people in charge now don't.'

'Let him talk, Agent!' the reporter called.

'I have no comment at this time.'

Simmons replied, 'We don't want *your* comment, Kathryn. We want Wayne's.' He then added, 'Were you hurt, Wayne? You're limping.'

'They hurt me in the arrest. That'll be part of the lawsuit.'

He hadn't been limping earlier. Dance tried to keep the disgust off her face.

'We heard there were other suspects. One's wounded and in FBI custody. The other's at large.'

Police scanners. Dance grimaced. It was illegal to hack cell phones, but anybody could buy a scanner and learn all they wanted to about police operations.

'Wayne, what do you expect to achieve by what you're doing?'

'Makin' the people aware of the overbearing government. The disrespect for the people of this great nation and—'

Dance actually pushed him through the door into the CBI Monterey headquarters, an unimpressive building that resembled one of the insurance agencies or law offices in this business park east of the airport on the way to Salinas, off Highway 68.

Simmons called, 'Kathryn! Agent Dance—'

The CBI's front door was on a hydraulic closer but she would have slammed it if she could have.

Dance turned to him. 'Wayne, I've read you your rights. You understand you have the right to an attorney. And that anything you say can and will be used against you in court.'

'Yes, ma'am.'

'Do you wish to waive your right to an attorney and to remain silent?'

'Yup.'

'You understand you can break off our interview at any time.'

'I do now. Thanks very much. Informative.'

'Will you tell us where you're planning this attack? Do that and we'll work out a deal.'

'Will you let our founder, Osmond Carter, go free? He's been illegally arrested, in contravention of his basic human rights.'

'We can't do that.'

'Then I think I'm not inclined to tell you what we've got in mind.' A grin. 'But I'm happy to talk. Always enjoy a good chin-wag with an attractive woman.'

Dance nodded to Stemple, who guided Keplar through the maze of hallways to an interrogation room. She followed. She checked her weapon and took the file that a fellow agent had put together on the suspect. Three pages were in the manila sleeve. That's all? she wondered, flipping open the file and reading the sparse history of Wayne Keplar and the pathetic organization he was sacrificing his life for.

She paused only once. To glance at her watch and learn that she had only two hours and one minute to stop the attack.

Michael O'Neil was pursuing the case at the crime scene, as he always did: meticulously, patiently.

If an idea occurred to him, if a clue presented itself, he followed the lead until it paid off or it turned to dust.

He finished jotting down largely useless observations and impressions of witnesses in front of where the trooper rammed the suspects' car. ('Man, it was totally, like, loud.') The detective felt a coalescing of moisture on his face; that damn Monterey fog – as much a local institution as John Steinbeck, Cannery Row and Langston Hughes. He wiped his face with broad palms. On the water, fishing from his boat, he didn't think anything of the damp air. Now, it was irritating.

He approached the head of his Forensic Services Unit, a dark-complexioned man, who was of Latino and Scandinavian heritage, Abbott Calderman. The CBI didn't have a crime-scene operation and the FBI's closest one was in the San Jose–San Francisco area. The MCSO provided most of the forensics for crimes in this area. Calderman's team was clustered around the still-vaporing Taurus, practically dismantling it, to find clues that could tell them about the impending attack. Officers were also examining, then bagging and tagging, the pocket litter from the two suspects – the police term for wallets, money, receipts, twenty-dollar bills (serial numbers, thanks to ATMs, revealed more than you'd think), sunglasses, keys and the like. These items would be logged and would ultimately end up at the jail where the men would be booked – Salinas – but for now the team would examine the items for information about the 'event' Wayne Keplar had so proudly referred to.

Calderman was speaking to one of his officers, who was swathed in bright blue crime-scene overalls, booties and a surgeon's shower cap.

'Michael,' the CS head said, joining the detective. 'My folks're going through the car.' A glance at the totaled vehicle, air bags deployed. 'It's real clean – no motel keys, letters or schematics.'

Rarely were perps discovered with maps in their possession with a red grease pencil X, the legend reading: 'Attack here!'

'We'll know more when we analyze the trace from the tires and the floor of the passenger compartment and the trunk. But they did find something you ought to know about. A thermos of coffee.'

'And it was still hot?'

'Right.' Calderman nodded that O'Neil caught the significance of the discovery. 'And no receipts from Starbucks or a place that sells brewed coffee.'

'So they might've stayed the night here somewhere and brewed it this morning.'

'Possibly.' Oakland was a long drive. It could take three hours or more. Finding the thermos suggested, though hardly proved, that they'd come down a day or two early to prepare for the attack. This meant there'd probably be a motel nearby, with additional evidence. Though they'd been too smart to keep receipts or reservation records.

The Crime Scene head added, 'But most important: We found three cups inside. Two in the cup holders in the front seat, one on the floor in the back, and the rear floor was wet with spilled coffee.'

'So, there's a third perp?' O'Neil asked.

'Looks that way – though the trooper who nailed them didn't see anybody else. Could've been hiding in the back.'

O'Neil considered this and called Oakland PD. He learned that the CI had only heard about Paulson and Keplar, but it was certainly possible, he decided, to ask someone else along. The snitch had severed all contact with the BOL, worried that by diming out the operation he'd be discovered and killed.

O'Neil texted Dance and let her know about the third perp, in case this would help in the interrogation. He informed the FBI's Steve Nichols, too.

He then disconnected and looked over the hundred or so people standing at the yellow police tape gawking at the activity.

The third perp . . . Maybe he'd gotten out of the car earlier, after setting up the attack but before the CHP trooper found the suspects.

Or maybe he'd bailed out here, when the Taurus was momentarily out of sight behind the outlet store.

O'Neil summoned several other Monterey County officers and a few CHP troopers. They headed behind the long building, searching the loading docks – and even in the Dumpsters – for any trace of the third suspect.

O'Neil hoped they'd be successful. Maybe the perp had bailed because he had particularly sensitive or incriminating information on him. Or he was a local contact who did use credit cards and ATM machines – whose paper trail could steer the police toward the target.

Or maybe he was the sort who couldn't resist interrogation, perhaps the teenage child of one of the perps. Fanatics like those in the Brothers of Liberty had no compunction about enlisting – and endangering – their children.

But the search team found no hint that someone had gotten out of the car and fled. The rear of the mall faced a hill of sand, dotted with succulent plants. The area was crowned with a tall chain-link fence, topped with barbed wire. It would have been possible, though challenging, to escape that way, but no footprints in the sand led to the fence. All the loading dock doors were locked and alarmed; he couldn't have gotten into the stores that way.

O'Neil continued to the far side of the building. He walked there now and noted a Burger King about fifty or sixty feet away. He entered the restaurant, carefully scanning to see if anyone avoided eye contact or, more helpfully, took off quickly.

No one did. But that didn't mean the third perp wasn't here. This happened relatively often. Not because of the adage (which was wrong) about returning to or remaining at the scene of the crime out of a subconscious desire to get caught. No, perps were often arrogant enough to stay around and scope out the nature of the investigation, as well as get the identities of the investigators who were pursuing them – even, in some cases, taking digital pictures to let their friends and fellow gangbangers know who was searching for them.

In English and Spanish he interviewed the diners, asking if they'd seen anyone get out of the perps' car behind the outlet store. Typical of witnesses, people had seen two cars, three cars, no cars, red Tauruses, blue Camrys, green Chryslers, gray Buicks. No one had seen any passengers exit any vehicles. Finally, though, he had some luck. One woman nodded in answer to his questions. She pulled gaudy eyeglasses out of her blond hair, where they rested like a tiara, and put them on, squinting as she looked over the scene thoughtfully. Pointing with her gigantic soda cup, she indicated a spot behind the stores where she'd noticed a man standing *next* to a car that could've been blue. She didn't know if he'd gotten out or not. She explained that somebody in the car handed him a blue backpack and he'd left. Her description of the men – one in combat fatigues and one in black cargo pants and a black leather jacket – left no doubt that the men in the car were Keplar and Paulson.

'Did you see where he went?'

'Toward the parking lot, I guess. I, like, didn't pay much attention.' Looking around. Then she stiffened. 'Oh . . .'

'What?' O'Neil asked.

'That's him!' she whispered, pointing to a sandy-haired man in jeans and work shirt, with a backpack over his shoulder. Even from this distance, O'Neil could see he was nervous, rocking from foot to foot, as he studied the crime scene. He was short, about five three or so, explaining why the trooper might easily miss him in the back of the Taurus.

O'Neil used his radio to call an MCSO deputy and have her get the woman's particulars. She agreed to stay here until they collared the perp so she could make a formal ID. He then pulled his badge off his neck and slipped it into the pocket of his jacket, which he buttoned, to conceal the Glock.

He started out of the Burger King.

'Mister . . . Detective,' the woman called. 'One thing . . . that backpack? You oughta know, when the guy handed it to him, they treated it real careful. I thought maybe it had something breakable in it. But now maybe I'm thinking it could be, you know, dangerous.'

'Thanks.'

It was then that the sandy-haired man glanced toward O'Neil.

And he understood.

He eased back into the crowd. Hiking the backpack higher on his shoulder, he turned and began to run, speeding between the buildings to the back of the mall. There he hesitated for only a moment, charged up the sand hill and scaled the six-foot chain-link O'Neil had surveyed earlier, shredding part of his jacket as he deftly vaulted the barbed wire.

He sprawled onto the unkempt land on the other side of the fence, also mostly sand. It was a deserted former military base, hundreds of acres.

O'Neil and two deputies approached the fence. The detective scaled it fast, tearing his shirt and losing some skin on the back of his hand as he crested the barbed wire. He leapt to the sand on the other side. He rolled once, righted himself and drew his gun, anticipating an attack.

But the perp had disappeared.

One of the deputies behind him got most of the way up the fence, but lost his grip and fell. He dropped straight down, off balance, and O'Neil heard the pop of his ankle as it broke.

'Oh,' the young man muttered as he looked down at the odd angle. He turned as pale as the fog and passed out.

The other deputy called for a medic then started up the fence.

'No!' O'Neil shouted. 'Stay there.'

'But—'

'I'll handle the pursuit. Call a chopper.' And he turned, sprinting through the sand and succulents and scrub oak and pine, dodging around dunes and stands of dry trees – behind any one of which an armed suspect could be waiting.

He hardly wanted to handle the pursuit alone but he had no choice. Just after he'd landed, he'd seen a sign lying face-up on the sand.

DANGER UXO

UNEXPLODED ORDNANCE

It featured a picture of an explosion coming up from the ground. Red years ago, the paint was now pink.

This area had been part of the military base's artillery range, and reportedly thousands of tons of shells and grenades were buried here, waiting to be cleared as soon as the Pentagon's budget allowed.

But O'Neil thought of the two hundred people who'd die in less than two hours and began to sprint along the trail that the suspect had been kind enough to leave in the sand.

The unreasonable idea occurred to him that if he took Kathryn Dance's advice – to move *fast* – he might be past the cannon shell when it detonated.

He didn't, however, think an explosion like that was something you could outrun.

*

Kinesic analysis works because of one simple concept, which Dance thought of as the Ten Commandments Principle.

Although she herself wasn't religious, she liked the metaphor. It boiled down to simply: Thou Shalt Not . . .

What came after that prohibition didn't matter. The gist was that people knew the difference between right and wrong and they felt uneasy doing something they shouldn't.

Some of this stemmed from the fear of getting caught, but still we're largely hardwired to do the right thing.

When people are deceptive (either actively misstating or failing to give the whole story) they experience stress and this stress reveals itself. Charles Darwin said, 'Repressed emotion almost always comes to the surface in some form of body motion.'

The problem for interrogators is that stress doesn't necessarily show up as nail biting, sweating and eye avoidance. It could take the form of a pleasant grin, a cheerful nod, a sympathetic wag of the head.

You don't say . . .

Well, that's terrible . . .

What a body language expert must do is compare subjects' behavior in nonstressful situations with their behavior when they might be lying. Differences between the two suggest – though they don't prove – deception. If there *is* some variation, a kinesic analyst then continues to probe the topic that's causing the stress until the subject confesses, or it's otherwise explained.

In interrogating Wayne Keplar, Dance would take her normal approach: asking a number of innocuous questions that she knew the answers to and that the suspect would have no reason to lie about. She'd also just shoot the breeze with him, no agenda other than to note how he behaved when feeling no stress. This would establish his kinesic 'baseline' – a catalog of his body language, tone of voice and choice of expressions when he was at ease and truthful.

Only then would she turn to questions about the impending attack and look for variations from the baseline when he answered.

But establishing the baseline usually requires many hours, if not days, of casual discussion.

Time that Kathryn Dance didn't have.

It was now 2:08.

Still, there was no option other than to do the best she could. She'd learned that there was another suspect, escaping through the old military ordnance storage and practice ground, with Michael O'Neil in pursuit (she knew the dangers of the base and didn't want to think of the risks to him). And the Monterey Crime Scene team was still going over the Taurus and the items that Paulson and Keplar had on them when arrested. But these aspects of the investigation had produced no leads.

Dance now read the sparse file once more quickly. Wayne Keplar was forty-four, high-school educated only, but he'd done well at school and was now one of the 'philosophers' at the Brothers of Liberty, writing many of the essays and diatribes on the group's blogs and website. He was single, never married. He'd been born in the Haight, lived in San Diego and Bakersfield. Now in Oakland. He didn't have a passport and had never been out of the country. His father was dead – killed in a Waco/Ruby Ridge-type standoff with federal officers. His mother and sister, a few years older than he, were also involved in the BOL, which despite the name, boasted members of both sexes. Neither of these family members had a criminal record.

Keplar, on the other hand, did – but a minor one, and nothing violent. His only federal offense had been graffiti-ing an armed forces recruitment center.

He also had an older brother, who lived on the East Coast, but the man apparently hadn't had any contact with Keplar for years and had nothing to do with the BOL.

A deep data mine search had revealed nothing about Keplar's and Gabe Paulson's journey here. This was typical of militia types, worried about Big Brother. They'd pay cash for as much as they could.

Normally she'd want far more details than this, but there was no more time.

Fast . . .

Dance left the folder at the desk out front and entered the interrogation room. Keplar glanced up with a smile.

'Uncuff him,' she said to Albert Stemple, who didn't hesitate even though he clearly wasn't crazy about the idea.

Dance would be alone in the room with an unshackled suspect, but she couldn't afford to have the man's arms limited by chains. Body language analysis is hard enough even with all the limbs unfettered.

Keplar slumped lazily in the gray padded office chair, as if settling in to watch a football game he had some, but not a lot of, interest in.

Dance nodded to Stemple, who left and closed the thick door behind him. Her eyes went to the large analog clock at the far end of the room.

2:16.

Keplar followed her gaze then looked back. 'You're goin' to try to find out where the . . . *event*'s takin' place. Ask away. But I'll tell you right now, it's going to be a waste of time.'

Dance moved her chair so that she sat across from him, with no furniture between them. Any barrier between interviewer and subject, even a small table, gives the perp a sense of protection and makes kinesic analysis that much harder. Dance was about three feet from him, in his personal proxemic zone – not so close as to make him stonewall, but near enough to keep him unsettled.

Except that he wasn't unsettled. At all. Wayne Keplar was as calm as could be.

He looked at her steadily, a gaze that was not haughty, not challenging, not sexy. It was almost as if he were sizing up a dog to buy for his child.

'Wayne, you don't have a driver's license.'

'Another way for the government to keep tabs on you.'

'Where do you live?'

'Oakland. Near the water. Been there for six years. Town has a bad rap but it's okay.'

'Where were you before that?'

'San Diego.'

She asked more about his personal life and travels, pretending not to know the answers. She'd left the file outside.

His responses were truthful. And as he spoke she noted his shoulders were forward, his right hand tended to come to rest on his thigh, he looked her straight in the eye when he spoke, his lips often curled into a half smile. He had a habit of poking his tongue into the interior of his cheek from time to time. It could have been a habit or could be from withdrawal – missing chewing tobacco, which Dance knew could be as addictive as smoking.

'Why'd you leave San Diego, Wayne? Weather's nicer than Oakland.'

'Not really. I don't agree with that. But I just didn't like it. You know how you get a vibration and it's just not right.'

'That's true,' she said.

He beamed in an eerie way. 'Do you? You know that? You're a firecracker, Kathryn. Yes, you are.'

A chill coursed down her spine as the near-set eyes tapped across her face.

She ignored it as best she could and asked, 'How senior are you in the Brothers of Liberty?'

'I'm pretty near the top. You know anything about it?'

'No.'

'I'd love to tell you. You're smart, Ms Firecracker. You'd probably think there're some pretty all right ideas we've got.'

'I'm not sure I would.'

A one-shoulder shrug – another of his baseline gestures. 'But you never know.'

Then came more questions about his life in Oakland, his prior convictions, his childhood. Dance knew the answers to some but the others were such that he'd have no reason to lie and she continued to rack up elements of baseline body language and verbal quality (the tone and speed of speech).

She snuck a glance at the clock.

'Time's got you rattled, does it?'

'You're planning to kill a lot of people. Yes, that bothers me. But not you, I see.'

'Ha, now you're sounding just like a therapist. I was in counseling once. It didn't take.'

'Let's talk about what you have planned, the two hundred people you're going to kill.'

'Two hundred and *change*.'

So, more victims. His behavior fit the baseline. This was true; he wasn't just boasting.

'How many more?'

'Two hundred twenty, I'd guess.'

An idea occurred to Dance and she said, 'I've told you we're not releasing Osmond Carter. That will never be on the table.'

'Your loss . . . well, not yours. Two hundred and some odd people's loss.'

'And killing them is only going to make your organization a pariah, a—'

'I know what "pariah" means. Go on.'

'Don't you think it would work to your advantage, from a publicity point of view, if you call off the attack, or tell me the location now?'

He hesitated. 'Maybe. That could be, yeah.' Then his eyes brightened. 'Now, I'm not inclined to call anything off. That'd look bad. Or tell you direct where this thing's going to happen. But you being Ms

Firecracker and all, how 'bout I give you a chance to figure it out. We'll play a game.'

'Game?'

'Twenty Questions. I'll answer honestly, I swear I will.'

Sometimes that last sentence was a deception flag. Now, she didn't think so.

'And if you find out where those two hundred and twenty souls're going to meet Jesus . . . then good for you. I can honestly say I didn't tell you. But you only get twenty questions. You don't figure it out, get the morgue ready. You want to play, Kathryn? If not, I'll just decide I want my lawyer and hope I'm next to a TV in' – he looked at the clock – 'one hour and forty-one minutes.'

'All right, let's play,' Dance said, and she subtly wiped the sweat that had dotted her palms. How on earth to frame twenty questions to narrow down where the attack would take place? She'd never been in an interrogation like this.

He sat forward. 'This'll be fun!'

'Is the attack going to be an explosive device?'

'Question one – I'll keep count. No.'

'What will it be?'

'That's question two but, sorry, you know Twenty Questions: has to be yes or no answers. But I'll give you a do-over.'

'Will it be a chemical/bio weapon?'

'Sorta cheating there, a twofer. But I'll say yes.'

'Is it going to be in a place open to the public?'

'Number three. Yes, sorta public. Let's say, there'll be public access.'

He was telling the truth. All his behavior and the pitch and tempo of voice bore out his honesty. But what did he mean by public access but not quite public?

'Is it an entertainment venue?'

'Question four. Well, not really, but there will be entertainment there.'

'Christmas related?'

He scoffed. 'That's five. Are you asking questions wisely, Ms Firecracker? You've used a quarter of them already. You could have combined Christmas and entertainment. Anyway, yes, Christmas is involved.'

Dance thought this curious. The Brothers of Liberty apparently had a religious side, even if they weren't born-again fanatics. She would have thought the target might be Islamic or Jewish.

'Have the victims done anything to your organization personally?'

Thinking police or law enforcement or government.

'Six. No.'

'You're targeting them on ideological grounds?'

'Seven. Yes.'

She asked, 'Will it be in Monterey County?'

'Number eight. Yes.'

'In the city of . . .' No, if she followed those lines of questioning, she'd use up all the questions just asking about the many towns and unincorporated areas in Monterey County. 'Will it be near the water?'

'Sloppy question. Expect better from you, Ms Firecracker. Do-over. Near the *what?*'

Stupid of her, Dance realized, her heart pounding. There were a number of bodies of water and rivers in the area. And don't ask about the ocean. Technically, Monterey wasn't on the Pacific. 'Will it be within a half mile of Monterey Bay?'

'Good!' he said, enjoying himself. 'Yes. That was nine. Almost halfway there.'

And she could see he was telling the truth completely. Every answer was delivered according to his kinesic baseline.

'Do you and Gabe Paulson have a partner helping you in the event?'

One eyebrow rose. 'Yes. Number ten. You're halfway to saving all them poor folks, Kathryn.'

'Is the third person a member of the Brothers of Liberty?'

'Yes. Eleven.'

She was thinking hard, unsure how to finesse the partner's existence into helpful information. She changed tack. 'Do the victims need tickets to get into the venue?'

'Twelve. I want to play fair. I honestly don't know. But they did have to sign up and pay. That's more than I should give you, but I'm enjoying this.' And indeed it seemed that Keplar was.

She was beginning to form some ideas.

'Is the venue a tourist attraction?'

'Thirteen. Yes, I'd say so. At least near tourist attractions.'

Now she felt safe using one of her geographical questions. 'Is it in the city of Monterey?'

'No. Fourteen.'

'Carmel?'

'No. Fifteen.'

Dance kept her own face neutral. What else should she be asking? If she could narrow it down a bit more, and if Michael O'Neil and his Crime Scene team came up with other details, they might cobble together a clear picture of where the attack would take place then evacuate every building in the area.

'How you doing there, Kathryn? Feeling the excitement of a good game? I sure am.' He looked at the clock. Dance did, too. Hell, time had sped by during this exchange. It was now 2:42.

She didn't respond to his question, but tried a different tack. 'Do your close friends know what you're doing?'

He frowned. 'You want to use question sixteen for that? Well, your choice. Yes.'

'Do they approve?'

'Yes, all of them. Seventeen. Getting all you need here, Kathryn? Seems you're getting off track.'

But she wasn't. Dance had another strategy. She was comfortable with the information she had – tourist area, near the water, a paid-for event, Christmas related, a few other facts – and with what O'Neil found, she hoped they could narrow down areas to evacuate. Now she was hoping to convince him to confess by playing up the idea raised earlier. That by averting the attack he'd still score some good publicity but wouldn't have to go to jail forever or die by lethal injection. Even if she lost the Twenty Questions game, which seemed likely, she was getting him to think about the people he was close to, friends and family he could still spend time with – if he stopped the attack.

'And family – do your siblings approve?'

'Question eighteen. Don't have any. I'm an only child. You only got two questions left, Kathryn. Spend 'em wisely.'

Dance hardly heard the last sentences. She was stunned.

Oh, no . . .

His behavior when he'd made the comment about not having siblings – a bald lie – was identical to that of the baseline.

During the entire game he'd been lying.

Their eyes met. 'Tripped up there, didn't I?' He laughed hard. 'We're off the grid so much, didn't think you knew about my family. Shoulda been more careful.'

'Everything you just told me was a lie.'

'Thin air. Whole cloth. Pick your cliché, Ms Firecracker. Had to run the clock. There's nothing on God's green earth going to save those people.'

She understood now what a waste of time this had been. Wayne Keplar was probably incapable of being kinesically analyzed. The Ten Commandments Principle didn't apply in his case. Keplar felt no more stress lying than he did telling the truth. Like serial killers and schizophrenics, political extremists often feel they are doing what's right, even if those acts are criminal or reprehensible to others. They're convinced of their own moral rectitude.

'Look at it from my perspective. Sure, we would've gotten *some* press if I'd confessed. But you know reporters – they'd get tired of the story after a couple days. Two hundred dead folk? Hell, we'll be on CNN for weeks. You can't *buy* publicity like that.'

Dance pushed back from the table and, without a word, stepped outside.

Michael O'Neil sprinted past ghosts.

The Monterey area is a place where apparitions from the past are ever present.

The Ohlone Native Americans, the Spanish, the railroad barons, the commercial fishermen . . . all gone.

And the soldiers, too, who'd inhabited Fort Ord and the other military facilities that once dotted the Monterey Peninsula and defined the economy and the culture.

Gasping and sweating despite the chill and mist, O'Neil jogged past the remnants of barracks and classrooms and training facilities, some intact, some sagging, some collapsed.

Past vehicle pool parking lots, supply huts, rifle ranges, parade grounds.

Past signs that featured faded skulls and crossed bones and pink explosions.

UXO . . .

The suspect wove through the area desperately and the chase was exhausting. The land had been bulldozed flat in the 1930s and '40s for the construction of the base but the dunes had reclaimed much of the landscape, rippled mounds of blond sand, some of them four stories high.

The perp made his way through these valleys in a panicked run, falling often, as did O'Neil because of the dicey traction – and the fast turns and stop-and-go sprinting when what looked like a potential explosives stash loomed.

O'Neil debated about parking a slug in the man's leg, though that's technically a no-no. Besides, O'Neil couldn't afford to miss and kill him.

The suspect chugged along, gasping, red-faced, the deadly backpack over his shoulder bouncing.

Finally, O'Neil heard the thud thud thud of rotors moving in.

He reflected that a chopper was the only smart way to pursue somebody through an area like this, even if it wasn't technically a minefield. The birds wouldn't trip the explosives, as long as they hovered.

And what were the odds that he himself would detonate some ordnance, mangling his legs?

What about the kids then?

What about his possible life with Kathryn Dance?

He decided that those questions were pointless. This was military ordnance. He'd end up not an amputee but a mass of red jelly.

The chopper moved closer. God, they were loud. He'd forgotten that.

The suspect stopped, glanced back and then turned right, disappearing fast behind a dune.

Was it a trap? O'Neil started forward slowly. But he couldn't see clearly. The chopper was raising a turbulent cloud of dust and sand. O'Neil waved it back. He pointed his weapon ahead of him and began to approach the valley down which the perp had disappeared.

The helicopter hovered closer yet. The pilot apparently hadn't seen O'Neil's hand gestures. The sandstorm grew fiercer. Some completely indiscernible words rattled from a loudspeaker.

'Back, back!' O'Neil called, uselessly.

Then, in front of him, he noticed what seemed to be a person's form, indistinct in the miasma of dust and sand. The figure was moving in.

Blinking, trying to clear his eyes, he aimed his pistol. 'Freeze!'

Putting some pressure on the trigger. The gun was double-action now and it would take a bit of poundage to fire the first round.

Shoot, he told himself.

But there was too much dust to be sure this was in fact the perp. What if it was a hostage or a lost hiker?

He crouched and staggered forward.

Damn chopper! Grit clotted his mouth.

Which was when a second silhouette, smaller, detached from the first and seemed to fly through the gauzy air toward him.

What was—?

The blue backpack struck him in the face. He fell backward, tumbling to the ground, the bag resting beside his legs. Choking on the sand, Michael O'Neil thought how ironic it was that he'd survived a UXO field only to be blown to pieces by a bomb the perp had brought with him.

The Bankers' Association holiday party was under way. It had started, as they always did, a little early. Who wanted to deny loans or take care of the massive paperwork of approved ones when the joy of the season beckoned?

Carol and Hal were greeting the CCCBA members at the door, showing them where to hang coats, giving them gift bags and making sure the bar and snacks were in good supply.

The place did look magical. She'd opted to close the curtains – on a nice summer day the water view might be fine but the fog had descended and the scenery was gray and gloomy. Inside, though, with the holiday lights and dimmed overheads, the banquet room took on a warm, comfy tone.

Hal was walking around in his conservative suit, white shirt and oversized Santa hat. People sipped wine and punch, snapped digital pictures and clustered, talking about politics and sports and shopping and impending vacations.

Also, a lot of comments about interest rates, the Fed, and the euro.

With bankers you couldn't get away from shop talk. Ever.

'We heard there's a surprise, Carol,' one of the members called.

'What?' came another voice.

'Be patient,' she said, laughing. 'If I told you, it wouldn't be a surprise, now would it?'

When the party seemed to be spinning along on its own, she walked to the stage and tested the PA system once again. Yes, it was working fine.

Thank goodness.

The 'surprise' depended on it. She'd arranged for the chorus from one of her grandsons' high schools to go up onstage and present a holiday concert, traditional and modern Christmas and Hanukkah songs. She glanced at her watch. The kids would arrive at about 3:45. She'd heard the youngsters before and they were very good.

Carol laughed to herself, recalling the entertainment at last year's party. Herb Ross, a VP at First People's Trust, who'd ingested close to a quart of the 'special' punch, had climbed on the table to sing – and even worse (or better, for later water cooler stories) to act out – the entire 'Twelve Days of Christmas' himself, the leaping lords being the high point.

Kathryn Dance spent a precious ten minutes texting and talking to a number of people in the field and here at headquarters.

It seemed that outside the surreality of the interrogation room, the investigation hadn't moved well at all. Monterey's Forensic Services Unit was still analyzing trace connected with the Taurus and the suspects' pocket litter, and Abbott Calderman said they might not have any answers for another ten or fifteen minutes.

Lord, she thought.

Michael O'Neil, when last heard from, had been pursuing the third conspirator in the abandoned army base. A police chopper had lost him in a cloud of dust and sand. She'd had a brief conversation with FBI agent Steve Nichols in a nearby mobile command post, who'd said, 'This Paulson isn't saying anything. Not a word. Just stares at me. I'd like to waterboard him.'

'We don't do that,' Dance had reminded.

'I'm just daydreaming,' Nichols had muttered and hung up.

Now, returning to the interrogation room with Wayne Keplar, Dance looked at the clock on the wall.

3:10.

'Hey,' said Wayne Keplar, eyeing it briefly, then turning his gaze to Dance. 'You're not mad at me, are you?'

Dance sat across the table from him. It was clear she wasn't going to power a confession out of him, so she didn't bother with the tradecraft of kinesic interviewing. She said, 'I'm sure it's no surprise that, before, I tried to analyze your body language and was hoping to come up with a way to pressure you into telling me what you and Gabe and your other associate had planned.'

'Didn't know that about the body language. But makes sense.'

'Now I want to do something else, and I'm going to tell you exactly what that is. No tricks.'

'Shoot. I'm game.'

Dance had decided that traditional analysis and interrogation wouldn't work with someone like Wayne Keplar. His lack of affect, his fanatic's belief in the righteousness of his cause made kinesics useless. Content-based analysis wouldn't do much good either; this is body language's poor cousin, seeking to learn whether a suspect is telling the truth by considering if what he says makes sense. But Keplar was too much in control to let slip anything that she might parse for clues about deception and truth.

So she was doing something radical.

Dance now said, 'I want to prove to you that your beliefs – what's motivating you and your group to perform this attack – they're wrong.'

He lifted an eyebrow. Intrigued.

This was a ludicrous idea for an interrogator. One should never argue substance with a suspect. If a man is accused of killing his wife, your job is to determine the facts and, if it appears that he did indeed commit murder, get a confession or at least gather enough information to help investigators secure his conviction.

There's no point in discussing the right or wrong of what he did, much less the broader philosophical questions of taking lives in general or violence against women, say.

But that was exactly what she was going to do now.

Poking the inside of his cheek with his tongue once more, thoughtful, Keplar said, 'Do you even know what our beliefs are?'

'I read the Brothers of Liberty website. I—'

'You like the graphics? Cost a pretty penny.'

A glance at the wall. 3:14.

Dance continued. 'You advocate smaller government, virtually no taxes, decentralized banking, no large corporations, reduced military, religion in public schools. And that you have the right to violent civil disobedience. Along with some racial and ethnic theories that went out of fashion in the 1860s.'

'Well, 'bout that last one – truth is, we just throw that in to get checks from rednecks and border control nuts. Lot of us don't really feel that way. But, Ms Firecracker, you done your homework, sounds like. We've got more positions than you can shake a stick at but those'll do for a start . . . So, argue away. This's gonna be as much fun as Twenty Questions. But just remember, maybe I'll talk *you* into my way of thinking, hanging up that tin star of yours and coming over to the good guys. What do you think about that?'

'I'll stay open-minded, if you will.'

'Deal.'

She thought back to what she'd read on the group's website. 'You talk about the righteousness of the individual. Agree up to a point, but we can't survive as individuals alone. We need government. And the more people we have, with more economic and social activity, the more we need a strong central government to make sure we're safe to go about our lives.'

'That's sad, Kathryn.'

'Sad?'

'Sure. I have more faith in humankind than you do, sounds like. We're pretty capable of taking care of ourselves. Let me ask you: You go to the doctor from time to time, right?'

'Yes.'

'But not very often, right? Pretty rare, hmm? More often with the kids, I'll bet. Sure, you have kids. I can tell.'

She let this go with no reaction.

3:17.

'But what does the doctor do? Short of broken bone to set, the doctor tells you pretty much to do what your instinct told you. Take some aspirin, go to bed, drink plenty of fluids, eat fiber, go to sleep. Let the body take care of itself. And ninety per cent of the time, those ideas work.' His eyes lit up. 'That's what government should do: Leave us alone ninety per cent of the time.'

'And what about the other ten per cent?' Dance asked.

'I'll give you that we need, let's see, highways, airports, national defense . . . Ah, but what's that last word? "Defense". You know, they used to call it the "War Department". Well, then some public relations fellas got involved and "War" wouldn't do any more, so they changed it. But that's a lie. See, it's not just defense. We go poking our noses into places that we have no business being.'

'The government regulates corporations that would exploit people.'

He scoffed. 'The government helps 'em do it. How many congressmen go to Washington poor and come back rich? Most of them.'

'But you're okay with some taxes?'

He shrugged. 'To pay for roads, air traffic control and defense.'

3:20.

'The SEC for regulating stocks?'

'We don't need stocks. Ask your average Joe what the stock market is and they'll tell ya it's a way to make money or put something away for your retirement fund. They don't realize that that's *not* what it's for. The stock market's there to let people buy a company, like you'd go to a used car lot to buy a car. And why do you want to buy a company? Beats me. Maybe a few people'd buy stock because they like what the company does or they want to support a certain kind of business. That's not what people want them for. Do away with stocks altogether. Learn to live off the land.'

'You're wrong, Wayne. Look at all the innovations corporations have created: the lifesaving drugs, the medical supplies, the computers . . . that's what companies have done.'

'Sure, and iPhones and BlackBerrys and laptops have replaced parents, and kids learn their family values at porn sites.'

'What about government providing education?'

'Ha! That's another racket. Professors making a few hundred thousand dollars a year for working eight months, and not working very hard at that. Teachers who can hardly put a sentence together themselves. Tell me, Kathryn, are you happy handing over your youngsters to somebody you see at one or two PTA meetings a year? Who knows what the hell they're poisoning their minds with.'

She said nothing, but hoped her face wasn't revealing that from time to time she did indeed have those thoughts.

Keplar continued, 'No, I got two words for you there. "Home schooling".'

'You don't like the police, you claim. But we're here to make sure you and your family're safe. We'll even make sure the Brothers of Liberty're free to go about their business and won't be discriminated against and won't be the victim of hate crimes.'

'Police state . . . Think on this, Ms Firecracker. I don't know what *you* do exactly here in this fancy building, but tell me true. You put your life on the line every day and for what? Oh, maybe you stop some crazy serial killer from time to time or save somebody in a kidnapping. But mostly cops just put on their fancy cop outfits and go bust some poor kids with drugs but never get to the *why* of it. What's the reason they were scoring pot or coke in the first place? Because the government and the institutions of this country failed them.'

3:26.

'So you don't like the federal government. But it's all relative, isn't it? Go back to the eighteenth century. We weren't just a mass of individuals. There was state government and they were powerful. People had to pay taxes, they were subject to laws, they couldn't take their neighbors' property, they couldn't commit incest, they couldn't steal. Everybody accepted that. The federal government today is just a bigger version of the state governments in the 1700s.'

'Ah, good, Kathryn. I'll give you that.' He nodded agreeably. 'But we think state and even *local* laws are too much.'

'So you're in favor of no laws?'

'Let's just say a lot, lot less.'

Dance leaned forward, with her hands together. 'Then let's talk about your one belief that's the most critical now: violence to achieve your ends. I'll grant you that you have the right to hold whatever beliefs you want – and not get arrested for it. Which, by the way, isn't true in a lot of countries.'

'We're the best,' Keplar agreed. 'But that's still not good enough for us.'

'But violence is hypocritical.'

He frowned at this. 'How so?'

'Because you take away the most important right of an individual – his life – when you kill him in the name of your views. How can you be an advocate of individuals and yet be willing to destroy them at the same time?'

His head bobbed up and down. A tongue poke again. 'That's good, Kathryn. Yes.'

She lifted her eyebrows.

Keplar added, 'And there's something to it . . . Except you're missing one thing. Those people we're targeting? They're not individuals. They're part of the system, just like you.'

'So you're saying it's okay to kill them because they're, what? Not even human?'

'Couldn't have said it better myself, Ms Firecracker.' His eyes strayed to the wall. 3:34.

The helicopter set down in a parking lot of the outlet mall in Seaside, and Michael O'Neil and a handcuffed suspect – no ID on him – climbed out.

O'Neil was bleeding from a minor cut on the head incurred when he scrabbled into a cluster of scrub oaks escaping the satchel bomb.

Which turned out to be merely a distraction.

No IEDs, no anthrax.

The satchel was filled with sand.

The perp had apparently disposed of whatever noxious substance it contained on one of his crosscut turns and weaves, and the evidence or bomb or other clue was lost in the sand.

The chopper's downdraft hadn't helped either.

What was most disappointing, though, was that the man had clammed up completely.

O'Neil was wondering if he was actually mute. He hadn't said a word during the chase or after the detective had tackled and cuffed him and dragged him to the helicopter. Nothing O'Neil could say – promises or threats – could get the man to talk.

The detective handed him over to fellow Monterey County Sheriff's Office deputies. A fast search revealed no ID. They took his prints, which came back negative from the field scanner, and the man was processed under a John Doe as 'UNSUB A'.

The blond woman with the big soda cup – now mostly empty – who'd spotted him in the crowd now identified him formally and she left.

The Crime Scene boss strode up to O'Neil. 'Don't have much but I'll say that the Taurus had recently spent some time on or near the beach along a stretch five miles south of Moss Landing.' Calderman explained that because of the unique nature of cooling water from the power plant at Moss Landing, and the prevailing currents and fertilizer from some of the local farms, he could pinpoint that part of the county.

If five miles could be called pinpointing.

'Anything else?'

'Nope. That's it. Might get more in the lab.' Calderman nodded to his watch. 'But there's no time left.'

O'Neil called Kathryn, whose cell phone went right to voice mail. He texted her the information. He then looked over at the smashed Taurus, the emergency vehicles, the yellow tape stark in the gray foggy afternoon. He was thinking: It wasn't unheard of for crime scenes to raise more questions than answers.

But why the hell did it have to be this one, when so little time remained to save the two hundred victims?

Hands steady as a rock, Harriet Keplar was driving the car she'd stolen from the parking lot at the outlet mall.

But even as her grip was firm, her heart was in turmoil. Her beloved brother, Wayne, and her sometime lover, Gabe Paulson, were in custody. After the bomb detonated shortly, she'd never see them again, except at trial – given Wayne's courage, she suspected he'd plead not guilty simply so he could get up on the stand and give the judge, jury and press an earful, rather than work a deal with the prosecutor.

She pulled her glasses out of her hair and regarded her watch. Not long now. It was ten minutes to the Dunes Inn, which had been their staging area. And would have been where they'd wait out the next few days, watching the news. But now, sadly, Plan B was in effect. She'd go back to collect all the documents, maps, extra equipment and remaining explosives and get the hell back to Oakland. She bet there was a goddamn snitch within the Brothers of Liberty up there – how else would the police have known as much as they did? – and Harriet was going to find him.

It was a good thing they'd decided to split up behind the outlet mall. As the Taurus had temporarily evaded the Highway Patrol trooper and skidded to a stop, Harriet in the backseat, Wayne decided they had to make sure somebody got back to the motel and ditched the evidence – which implicated some very senior people at the BOL.

She jumped out with the backpack containing extra detonators and wires and tools and phony IDs that let them get into the banquet hall where the CCCBA was having their party. Harriet had been going to hijack a car and head back to the Dunes Inn, but the asshole of a trooper had rammed Gabe and Wayne. And police had descended.

She'd slipped into a Burger King, to let the dust settle. She'd ditched the contents of the satchel, but, to her dismay, the police were spreading out and talking to everybody at the mall. Harriet decided she had to find a fall guy to take attention away from her. She'd spotted a solo shopper, a man about her height with light hair – in case the trooper had seen her in the backseat. She stuck her Glock in his ribs, pulling him behind the BK, then grabbed his wallet. She found a picture of three spectacularly plain children and made a fake call on her cell phone to an imaginary assistant, telling him to get to the poor guy's house and round up the kidlings.

If he didn't do exactly as she said, they'd be shot, oldest to youngest. His wife would be the last to go.

She got his car keys and told him to stand in the crowd. If any cops came to talk to him he was to run and if he was caught he should throw the pack at them and keep running. If he got stopped he should say nothing. She, of course, was going to dime him out – and when the police went after him she would have a chance to take his car and leave. It would have worked fine, except that goddamn detective – O'Neil was his name – had her stay put so she could formally ID the sandy-haired guy. Oh, how she wanted to get the hell out of there. But she couldn't arouse suspicion, so Harriet had cooled her heels, sucking down Diet Coke, and tried to wrestle with the anger and sorrow about her brother and Gabe.

Then O'Neil and the poor bastard had returned. She'd IDed him with a fierce glance of warning and given them some fake information on how to reach her.

And now she was in his car, heading back to the Dunes Inn.

Oh, Wayne, I'll miss you! Gabe, too.

The motel loomed. She sped into the parking lot and braked to a stop.

She was then aware of an odd vibration under her hands. The steering column. What was it?

An earthquake?

A problem with the car?

She shut the engine off but the vibration grew louder.

Leaves began to move and the dust swirled like a tornado in the parking lot.

And Harriet understood. 'Oh, shit.'

She pulled her Glock from her bag and sprinted toward the motel door, firing blindly at the helicopter as it landed in the parking lot. Several officers and, damn it, that detective, O'Neil, charged toward her. 'Drop the weapon, drop the weapon!'

She hesitated and laid the gun and her keychain on the ground. Then she dropped facedown beside them.

Harriet was cuffed and pulled to her feet.

O'Neil was approaching, his weapon drawn and looking for accomplices. A cluster of cops dressed like soldiers was slowly moving toward the motel room.

'Anyone in there?' he asked.

'No.'

'It was just the three of you?'

'Yes.'

The detective called, 'Treat it dynamic in any case.'

'How'd you know?' she snapped.

He looked her over neutrally. 'The cargo pants.'

'What?'

'You described the man in the car and said one was wearing cargo pants. You couldn't see the pants of somebody inside a car from sixty feet away. The angle was wrong.'

Hell, Harriet thought. Never even occurred to her.

O'Neil added that the man they'd believed was one of the conspirators was acting too nervous. 'It occurred to me that he might've been set up. He told me what you'd done. We tracked his car here with his GPS.' O'Neil was going through her purse. 'You're his sister, Wayne's.'

'I'm not saying anything else.' Harriet was distracted, her eyes taking in the motel room.

O'Neil caught it and frowned. He glanced down at her keychain, which held both a fob for her car and the second one.

She caught his eye and smiled.

'IED in the room!' he called. 'Everybody back! Now.'

It wasn't an explosive device, just a gas bomb Gabe had rigged in the event something like this happened. It had been burning for three minutes or so – she'd pushed the remote control the second she'd seen the chopper – but the smoke and flames weren't yet visible.

Then a bubble of fire burst through two of the windows.

Armed with extinguishers, the tactical team hurried inside to salvage what they could, then retreated as the flames swelled. One officer called, 'Michael! We spotted a box of plastic explosive detonators, some timers.'

Another officer ran up to O'Neil and showed him what was left of a dozen scorched documents. They were the floor plan for the site of the attack at the CCCBA party. He studied it. 'A room with a stage. Could be anywhere. A corporation, school, hotel, restaurant.' He sighed.

Harriet panicked, then relaxed, as she snuck a glimpse and noted that the name of the motel was on a part of the sheet that had burned to ash.

'Where is this?' O'Neil asked her bluntly.

Harriet studied it for a moment and shook her head. 'I've never seen that before. You planted it to incriminate me. The government does that all the time.'

At the Bankers' party the high-school students arrived, looking scrubbed and festive, all in uniforms, which Carol approved of. Tan slacks and blazers for the boys, plaid skirts and white blouses for the girls.

They were checking out the treats – and the boys were probably wondering if they could cop a spiked punch – but would refrain from anything until after the twenty-minute concert. The kids took their music seriously and sweets tended to clog the throat, her grandson had explained.

She hugged the blond, good-looking boy and shook the hand of the chorus director.

'Everyone, everyone!' she called. 'Take your seats.'

And the children climbed up onstage, taking their positions.

The clock in the interrogation room registered 3:51.

Dance broke off the debate for a moment and read and sent several text messages, as Wayne Keplar watched with interest.

3:52.

'Your expression tells me the news isn't good. Not making much headway elsewhere?'

Kathryn Dance didn't respond. She slipped her phone away. 'I'm not finished with our discussion, Wayne. Now, I pointed out you were hypocritical to kill the very people you purport to represent.'

'And I pointed out a hole a mile wide with that argument.'

'Killing also goes against another tenet of yours.'

Wayne Keplar said calmly, 'How so?'

'You want religion taught in school. So you must be devout. Well, killing the innocent is a sin.'

He snickered. 'Oh, please, Ms Firecracker. Read the Bible sometime: God smites people for next to nothing. Because somebody crosses Him or to get your attention. Or because it's Tuesday, I don't know. You think everybody drowned in Noah's flood was guilty of something?'

'So al-Qaeda's terrorist tactics are okay?'

'Well, al-Qaeda itself – 'cause they want the strongest government of all. It's called a theocracy. No respect for individuals. But their tactics? Hell, yes. I admire the suicide bombers. If I was in charge, though, I'd reduce all Islamic countries to smoking nuclear craters.'

Kathryn Dance looked desperately at the clock, which showed nearly 3:57.

She rubbed her face as her shoulders slumped. Her weary eyes pleaded. 'Is there anything I can say to talk you into stopping this?'

3:58.

'No, you can't. Sometimes the truth is more important than the individuals. But,' he added with a sincere look. 'Kathryn, I want to say that I appreciate one thing.'

No more Ms Firecracker.

'What's that?' she said in a whisper, eyes on the clock.

'You took me seriously. That talk we just had. You disagree, but you treated me with respect.'

4 p.m.

Both law officer and suspect remained motionless, staring at the clock.

A phone in the room rang. She leaned over and hit the speaker button fast. 'Yes?'

The staticky voice, a man's. 'Kathryn, it's Albert. I'm sorry to have to tell you . . .'

She sighed. 'Go on.'

'It was an IED, plastic of some sort . . . We don't have the count yet. Wasn't as bad as it could be. Seems the device was under a stage and that absorbed some of the blast. But we're still looking at fifteen or so dead, maybe fifty injured . . . Hold on. CHP's calling. I'll get back to you.'

Dance disconnected, closed her eyes briefly then glared at Keplar. 'How *could* you?'

Wayne frowned; he wasn't particularly triumphant. 'I'm sorry, Kathryn. This is the way it had to be. It's a war out there. Besides, score one for your side – only fifteen dead. We screwed up.'

Dance shivered in anger. But she calmly said, 'Let's go.'

She rose and knocked on the door. It opened immediately and two large CBI agents came in, also glaring. One reshackled Keplar's hands behind him, hoping, it seemed, for an excuse to Taser the prisoner. But the man was the epitome of decorum.

One agent muttered to Dance, 'Just heard, the death count's up to—'

She waved him silent, as if denying Keplar the satisfaction of knowing the extent of his victory.

She led the prisoner out the back of CBI, toward a van that would ultimately transport him to the Salinas lockup.

'We'll have to move fast,' she told the other agents. 'There're going to be a lot of people who'd like to take things into their own hands.'

The area was largely deserted. But just then Dan Simmons, the blogger who'd pestered Dance earlier, the Jude Law lookalike, peered around the edge of the building as if he'd been checking every few minutes to see if they'd make a run for it this way. Simmons hurried toward them, along with his unwashed cameraman.

Dance ignored him.

Simmons asked, 'Agent Dance, could you comment on the failure of law enforcement to stop the bombing in time?'

She said nothing and kept ushering Keplar toward the van.

'Do you think this will be the end of your career?'

Silence.

'Wayne, do you have anything to say?' the blog reporter asked.

Eyes on the camera lens, Keplar called, 'It's about time the government started listening to people like Osmond Carter. This never would have happened if he hadn't been illegally arrested!'

'Wayne, what do you have to say about killing innocent victims?'

'Sacrifices have to be made,' he called.

Simmons called, 'But why these particular victims? What's the message you're trying to send?'

'That maybe bankers shouldn't be throwing themselves fancy holiday parties with the money they've stolen from the working folk of this country. The financial industry's been raping citizens for years. They claim—'

'Okay, hold it,' Dance snapped to the agents flanking Keplar, who literally jerked him to a stop.

Dance was pulling out a walkie-talkie. 'Michael, it's Kathryn, you read me?'

'Four by four. We've got six choppers and the entire peninsula com network standing by. You're patched in to all emergency frequencies. What do you have?'

'The target's a party – Christmas, I'd guess – involving bankers, or savings and loan people, bank regulators, something like that. It *is* a bomb and it's under the stage in that room you texted me about.'

Wayne Keplar stared at her, awash in confusion.

A half-dozen voices shot from her radio, variations of 'Roger . . . Copy that . . . Checking motels with banquet rooms in the target zone, south of Moss Landing . . . Contacting all banks in the target zone.'

'What is this?' Keplar raged.

Everyone ignored him.

A long several minutes passed, Dance standing motionless, head down, listening to the intersecting voices through the radio. And then: 'This is Major Rodriguez, CHP. We've got it! Central Coast Bankers' Association, annual Christmas party, Monterey Bay Seaside Motel. They're evacuating now.'

Wayne Keplar's eyes grew wide as he stared at Dance. 'But the bomb . . . ' He glanced at Dance's wrist and those of the other officers. They'd all removed their watches, so Keplar couldn't see the real time. He turned to an agent and snapped, 'What the hell time is it?'

'About ten to four,' replied Dan Simmons, the reporter.

He blurted to Dance, 'The clock? In the interrogation room?'

'Oh,' she said, guiding him to the prisoner transport van. 'It was fast.'

A half-hour later Michael O'Neil arrived from the motel where the bankers' party had been interrupted.

He explained that everyone got out safely, but there'd been no time to try to render the device safe. The explosion was quite impressive. The material was probably Semtex, Abbott Calderman had guessed, judging from the smell. The Forensic Services head explained to O'Neil that it was the only explosive ever to have its own FAQ on the Internet, which answered questions like: Was it named after an idyllic, pastoral village? (yes). Was it mass produced and shipped throughout the world, as the late President Václav Havel claimed? (no). And was Semtex the means by which its inventor committed suicide? (not exactly – yes, an employee at the plant did blow himself up intentionally, but he had not been one of the inventors).

Dance smiled as O'Neil recounted this trivia.

Steve Nichols of the FBI called and told her they were on the way to the CBI to deliver the other suspect, Gabe Paulson. He explained that since she'd broken the case, it made sense for her to process all the suspects. There would be federal charges – mostly related to the explosives – but those could be handled later.

As they waited in the parking lot for Nichols to arrive, O'Neil asked, 'So, how'd you do it? All I know is you called me about three, I guess, and told me to get choppers and a communications team ready. You hoped to have some details about the location of the attack in about forty-five minutes. But you didn't tell me what was going on.'

'I didn't have much time,' Dance explained. 'What happened was I found out, after wasting nearly an hour, that Keplar was kinesics-proof. So I had to trick him. I took a break at three and talked to our technical department. Seems you can speed up analog clocks by changing the voltage and the frequency of the current in the wiring. They changed the current in that part of the building so the clock started running fast.'

O'Neil smiled. 'That was the byword for this case, remember. You said it yourself.'

*And remember: We have two and a half-hours. We've got to move fast
. . .*

Dance continued, 'I remembered when we got to CBI, Keplar started lecturing Dan Simmons about his cause.'

'Oh, that obnoxious reporter and blogger?'

'Right. I called him and said that if he asked Keplar why he picked those particular victims, I'd give him an exclusive interview. And I called you to set up the search teams. Then I went back into the interrogation. I had to make sure Keplar didn't notice the clock was running fast so I started debating philosophy with him.'

'Philosophy?'

'Well, Wikipedia philosophy. Not the real stuff.'

'Probably real enough nowadays.'

She continued, 'You and the Crime Scene people found out that it was probably a bomb and that it was planted in a large room with a stage. When the clock hit four in the interrogation room, I had Albert call me and pretend a bomb had gone off and killed people but the stage had absorbed a lot of the blast. That was just enough information so that Keplar believed it had really happened. Then all I had to do was perp walk him past Simmons, who asked why those particular victims. Keplar couldn't keep himself from lecturing.'

'Sure was close.'

True. Ten minutes meant the difference between life and death for two hundred people, though fate sometimes allowed for even more narrow margins.

One of the FBI's black SUVs now eased to a stop beside Dance and O'Neil.

Steve Nichols and another agent climbed out and helped their shackled prisoner out. A large bandage covered much of his head and the side of his face. O'Neil stared at him silently.

The FBI agent said, 'Kathryn, good luck with this fellow. Wish you the best but he's the toughest I've ever seen – and I've been up against al-Qaeda and some of the Mexican cartel drug lords. They're Chatty Cathy compared with him. Not a single word. Just sits and stares at you. He's all yours.'

'I'll do what I can, Steve. But I think there's enough forensics to put everybody away for twenty years.'

The law enforcers said goodbye and the feds climbed into the Suburban, then sped out of the CBI lot.

Dance began to laugh.

So did the prisoner.

O'Neil asked, 'So what's going on?'

Dance stepped forward and undid the cuffs securing the wrists of her associate, TJ Scanlon. He removed the swaddling, revealing no injuries.

'Thanks, Boss. And by the way, those're the first words I've said in three hours.'

Dance explained to O'Neil, 'Gabe Paulson's in a lot more serious condition than I let on. He was shot in the head during the takedown and'll probably be in a vegetative state for the rest of his life. Which might not be that long. I knew Nichols'd wanted to have a part of the case – and for all we knew at that point he had primary jurisdiction. I wanted to interrogate the only suspect we had – Keplar – so I needed to give Nichols someone. TJ volunteered to play Paulson.'

'So you just deceived the FBI.'

'Technically. I know Steve. He's a brilliant agent. I'd trust him with anything except an interrogation with a deadline like this.'

'Three hours, Boss,' TJ said, rubbing his wrists. 'Did I mention not speaking for three hours? That's very hard for me.'

O'Neil asked, 'Won't he find out, see the pictures of the real Paulson in the press?'

'He was pretty bandaged up. And like I said, it may come back to haunt me. I'll deal with it then.'

'I thought I was going to be waterboarded.'

'I told him not to do that.'

'Well, he didn't share your directive with *me*. I think he would have liked to use cattle prods, too. Oh, and I would've given you up in five seconds, Boss. Just for the record.'

Dance laughed.

O'Neil left to return to his office in Salinas and Dance and TJ entered the CBI lobby, just as the head of the office, Charles Overby, joined them. 'Here you are.'

The agents greeted the paunchy man, who was in his typical work a day outfit: slacks and white shirt with sleeves rolled up, revealing tennis- and golf-tanned arms.

'Thanks, Kathryn. Appreciate what you did.'

'Sure.'

'You were in the operation, too?' Overby asked TJ.

'That's right. FBI liaison.'

Overby lowered his voice and said approvingly, 'They don't seem to want a cut of the action. Good for us.'

'I did what I could,' TJ said. Then the young man returned to his office, leaving Dance and her boss alone.

Overby turned to Dance. 'I'll need a briefing,' he said, nodding toward the reporters out front. A grimace. 'Something to feed to *them*.'

Despite the apparent disdain, though, Overby was in fact looking forward to the press conference. He always did. He loved the limelight and would want to catch the 6 p.m. local news. He'd also hope to gin up interest in some national coverage.

Dance put her watch back on her wrist and looked at the time. 'I can give you the bare bones, Charles, but I've got to see a subject in another matter. It's got to be tonight. He leaves town tomorrow.'

There was a pause. 'Well, if it's critical . . .'

'It is.'

'All right. Get me a briefing sheet now and a full report in the morning.'

'Sure, Charles.'

He started back to his office and asked, 'This guy you're meeting? You need any backup?'

'No thanks, Charles. It's all taken care of.'

'Sure. 'Night.'

'Goodnight.'

Heading to her own office, Kathryn Dance reflected on her impending mission tonight. If Overby had wanted a report on the attempted bombing for CBI headquarters in Sacramento or follow-up interrogations, she would have gladly done that, but since he was interested only in press releases, she decided to stick to her plans.

Which involved a call to her father, a retired marine biologist who worked part-time at the aquarium. She was going to have him pull some strings to arrange special admission after hours for herself and the children tonight.

And the 'subject' she'd told Overby she had to meet tonight before he left town? Not a drug lord or a terrorist or a confidential informant . . . but what was apparently the most imposing cephalopod ever to tour the Central Coast of California.

GAME

One Year Ago

The worst fear is the fear that follows you into your own home.

Fear you lock in with you when you latch the door at night.

Fear that cozies up to you twenty-four hours a day, relentless and arrogant, like cancer.

The diminutive woman, eighty-three years old, white hair tied back in a jaunty ponytail, sat at the window of her Upper East Side townhouse, looking out over the trim street, which was placid as always. But she herself was not. She was agitated and took no pleasure in the view she'd enjoyed for thirty years. The woman had fallen asleep last night thinking about the She-Beast and the He-Beast and she'd awakened thinking about them. She'd thought about them all morning and she thought about them still.

She sipped her tea and took some small pleasure in the sliver of autumn sunlight resting on her hands and arms. The flicker of gingko leaves outside, silver green, silver green. Was that all she had left? Minuscule comforts like this? And not very comforting at that.

Fear . . .

Sarah Lieberman hadn't quite figured out their game. But one thing was clear: Taking over her life was the goal – like a flag to be captured.

Three months ago Sarah had met the Westerfields at a fund-raiser held at the Ninety-second Street Y. It was for a Jewish youth organization, though neither the name nor appearance of the two suggested that was their religious or ethnic background. Still, they had seemed right at home and referred to many of the board members of the youth group as if they'd been friends for years. They'd spent a solid hour talking to Sarah alone, seemingly fascinated with her life in the 'Big Apple' (John's phrase) and explaining how they'd come here from Kansas City to 'consummate' (Miriam's) several business ventures John had set up. 'Real estate. That's my game. Ask me again and I'll tell you the same.'

They'd had dinner at Marcel's the next night, on Madison, with John dominating the five-foot-tall woman physically and Miriam doing the same conversationally, flanking Sarah in a booth in the back. She'd wanted her favorite table, which had room for three (yet was usually occupied by one) at the window. But the Westerfields had insisted, and why not? They'd made clear this was their treat.

The two were charming, informed in a Midwest, CNN kind of way, and enthusiastically curious about life in the city – and about her life in particular. Their eyes widened when they learned that Sarah had an apartment on the ground floor of the townhouse she owned on Seventy-fifth Street. Miriam asked if it was available. They'd been looking for a place to stay. The Mandarin Oriental was, Miriam offered, too expensive.

The garden apartment was on the market but was priced high – to keep out the riffraff, she'd said, laughing. But she'd drop it to fair market value for the Westerfields.

Deal.

Still, Sarah had learned about the world from her husband, a businessman who had successfully gone up against Leona Helmsley at one point. There were formalities to be adhered to and the real estate management company did their due diligence. They reported the references in the Midwest attested to the Westerfields' finances and prior history.

There was, of course, that one bit of concern: It seemed a bit odd that a fifty-something-year-old mother and a son in his late twenties would be taking an apartment together, when neither one seemed disabled. But life circumstances are fluid. Sarah could imagine situations in which she might find herself living with a family member not a husband. Maybe Miriam's husband had just died and this was temporary – until the emotional turbulence settled.

And Sarah *certainly* didn't know what to make of the fact that while the garden apartment featured three bedrooms, when she and Carmel had brought tea down as the two tenants moved in, only *one* bedroom seemed to be put to that purpose. The other two were used for storage.

Odd indeed.

But Sarah thought the best of people, always had. The two had been nice to her and, most important, treated her like an adult. It was astonishing to Sarah how many people thought that once you reached seventy or eighty you were really an infant.

That you couldn't order for yourself.

That you didn't know who Lady Gaga was.

'Oh, my,' she'd nearly said to one patronizing waitress. 'I've forgotten how this knife works. Could you cut up my food for me?'

For the first weeks the Westerfields seemed the model tenants. Respectful of landlady and premises, polite and *quiet*. That was important to Sarah, who'd always been a light sleeper. She didn't see much of them.

Not at first.

But soon their paths began to cross with more and more frequency. Sarah would return from a shopping trip with Carmel or from a board meeting or luncheon at one of the nonprofits she was involved with and there would be Miriam and John on the front steps or, if the day was cool or wet, in the tiny lobby, sitting on the couch beside the mailboxes.

They brightened when they saw her and insisted she sit with them. They pelted her with stories and observations and jokes. And they could be counted on to ask questions relentlessly: What charities was she involved in, any family members still alive, close friends? New to the area, they asked her to recommend banks, lawyers, accountants, investment advisors, hinting at large reserves of cash they had to put to work soon.

A one-trick puppy, John pronounced solemnly: 'Real estate is the way to go.'

It's also a good way to get your balls handed to you, son, unless you're very, very sharp. Sarah had not always been a demure, retiring widow.

She began to wonder if a Nigerian scam was looming, but they never pitched to her. Maybe they were what they seemed: oddballs from the Midwest, of some means, hoping for financial success here and an entrée into a New York society that had never really been available to people like them – and that people like them wouldn't enjoy even if they were admitted.

Ultimately, Sarah decided, it was their style that turned her off. The charm of the first month faded.

Miriam, also a short woman though inches taller than Sarah, wore loud, glittery clothes that clashed with her dark-complexioned, leathery skin. If she didn't focus, she tended to speak over and around the conversation, ricocheting against topics that had little to do with what you believed you were speaking about. She wouldn't look you in the eye and she hovered close. Saying, 'No, thanks,' to her was apparently synonymous with, 'You betcha.'

'This big old town, Sarah,' Miriam would say, shaking her head gravely. 'Don't . . . you get tuckered out, 'causa it?'

And the hesitation in that sentence hinted that the woman was really going to say 'Don't it tucker you out?'

John often wore a shabby sardonic grin, as if he'd caught somebody trying to cheat him. He was fleshy big, but strong, too. You could imagine his grainy picture in a newspaper above a story in which the word 'snapped' appeared in a quote from a local sheriff.

If he wasn't grumbling or snide, he'd be snorting as he told jokes, which were never very funny and usually bordered on being off-color.

But avoiding them was gasoline on a flame. When they sensed she was avoiding them they redoubled their efforts to graze their way into her life, coming to her front door at any hour, offering presents and advice . . . and always the questions about her. John would show up to take care of small handyman tasks around Sarah's apartment. Carmel's husband, Daniel, was the building's part-time maintenance man, but John had befriended him and took over on some projects to give Daniel a few hours off here and there.

Sarah believed the Westerfields actually waited, hiding behind their own door, listening for the sound of footsteps padding down the stairs – and ninety-four-pound Sarah Lieberman was a very quiet padder. Still, when she reached the ground-floor lobby, the Westerfields would spring out, tall son and short mother, joining her as if this were a rendezvous planned for weeks.

If they steamed up to her on the street outside the townhouse, they attached themselves like leeches and no amount of 'Better be going' or 'Have a good day now' could dislodge them. She stopped inviting them into her own two-story apartment – the top two floors of the townhouse – but when they tracked her down outside they would simply walk in with her when she returned.

Miriam would take her groceries and put them away and John would sit forward on the couch with a glass of water his mother brought him and grin in that got-you way of his. Miriam sat down with tea or coffee for the ladies and inquired how Sarah was feeling, did she ever go out of town, did you read about that man a few years ago, Bernie Madoff? Are you careful about things like that, Sarah? I certainly am.

Oh, Lord, leave me alone . . .

Sarah spoke to the lawyer and real estate management agent and learned there was nothing she could do to evict them.

And the matter got worse. They'd accidentally let slip facts about Sarah's life that they shouldn't have known. Bank accounts she had, meetings she'd been to, boards she was on, meetings with wealthy bankers. They'd been spying. She wondered if they'd been going through her mail – perhaps in her townhouse when John was sitting on the couch, babysitting her, and his mother was in Sarah's kitchen making them all a snack.

Or perhaps they'd finagled a key to her mailbox.

Now, *that* would be a crime.

But she wondered if the police would be very interested. Of course not.

And then a month ago, irritation became fear.

Typically they'd poured inside after her as she returned from shopping alone, Carmel Rodriguez having the day off. Miriam had scooped the Food Emporium bags from her hand and John had, out of 'courtesy,' taken her key and opened the door.

Sarah had been too flustered to protest – which would have done little good anyway, she now knew.

They'd sat for fifteen minutes, water and tea at hand, talking about who knew what, best of friends, and then Miriam had picked up her large purse and gone to use the toilet and headed for Sarah's bedroom.

Sarah had stood, saying she'd prefer the woman use the guest bathroom, but John had turned his knit brows her way and barked, 'Sit down. Mother can pick whichever she wants.'

And Sarah had, half thinking she was about to be beaten to death.

But the son slipped back to conversation mode and rambled on about yet another real estate deal he was thinking of doing.

Sarah, shaken, merely nodded and tried to sip her tea. She knew the woman was riffling through her personal things. Or planting a camera or listening device.

Or worse.

When Miriam returned, fifteen minutes later, she glanced at her son and he rose. In eerie unison, they lockstepped out of the apartment.

Sarah searched but she couldn't find any eavesdropping devices and couldn't tell if anything was disturbed or missing – and that might have been disastrous; she had close to three-quarters of a million dollars in cash and jewelry tucked away in her bedroom.

But they'd been up to no good – and had been rude and frightening. It was then that she began to think of them as the He-Beast and She-Beast.

Sycophants had given way to tyrants.

They'd become Rasputins.

The Beasts, like viruses, had infected what time Sarah had left on this earth and were destroying it – time she wanted to spend simply and harmlessly: visiting with those she cared for, directing her money where it would do the most good, volunteering at charities, working on the needlepoints she loved so much, a passion that was a legacy from her mother.

And yet those pleasures were being denied her.

Sarah Lieberman was a woman of mettle, serene though she seemed and diminutive though she was. She'd left home in Connecticut at eighteen, put herself through college in horse country in northern Virginia working in stables, raced sailboats in New Zealand, lived in New Orleans at a time when the town was still honky-tonk, then she'd plunged into Manhattan and embraced virtually every role that the city could offer – from Radio City Music Hall dancer to Greenwich Village Bohemian to Upper East Side philanthropist. At her eightieth birthday party, she'd sung a pretty good version of what had become her theme song over the years: 'I'll Take Manhattan'.

That steely spirit remained but the physical package to give it play was gone. She was an octogenarian, as tiny and frail as that gingko leaf outside the parlor window. And her *mind*, too. She wasn't as quick; nor was the memory what it had been.

What could she do about the Beasts?

Now, sitting in the parlor, she dropped her hands to her knees. Nothing occurred to her. It seemed hopeless.

Then, a key clattered in the lock. Sarah's breath sucked in. She assumed that somehow the Beasts had copied her key and she expected to see them now.

But, no. She sighed in relief to see Carmel return from shopping.

Were tears in her eyes?

'What's the matter?' Sarah asked.

'Nothing,' the woman responded quickly.

Too quickly.

'Yes, yes, yes . . . But if something *were* the matter, give me a clue, dear.'

The solid housekeeper carried the groceries into the kitchen, making sure she didn't look her boss's way.

Yes, crying.

'There's nothing wrong, Mrs Sarah. Really.' She returned to the parlor. Instinctively, the woman straightened a lace doily.

'Was it him? What did he do?'

John . . . the He-Beast.

Sarah knew he was somehow involved. Both Miriam and John disliked Carmel, as they did most of Sarah's friends, but John seemed contemptuous of the woman, as if the housekeeper mounted a campaign to limit access to Sarah. Which she did. In fact several times she had actually stepped in front of John to keep him from following Sarah into her apartment. Sarah had thought he'd been about to hit the poor woman.

'Please, it's nothing.'

Carmel Rodriguez was five feet, six inches tall and probably weighed 180 pounds. Yet the elderly woman now rose and looked up at her housekeeper, who'd been with her for more than a decade. 'Carmel. Tell me.' The voice left no room for debate.

'I got home from shopping? I was downstairs just now?'

Statements as questions – the sign of uncertainty. 'I came back from the store and was talking to him and then Mr John—'

'Just John. You can call him John.'

'John comes up and, just out of nowhere, he says, did I hear about the burglary?'

'Where?'

'The neighborhood somewhere. I said I didn't. He said somebody broke in and stole this woman's papers. Like banking papers and wills and deeds and bonds and stocks.'

'People don't keep stocks and bonds at home. The brokerage keeps them.'

'Well, he told me she got robbed and these guys took all her things. He said he was worried about you.'

'Me?'

'Yes, Mrs Sarah. And he didn't want to make you upset but he was worried and did I know where you kept things like that? Was there a safe somewhere? He said he wanted to make sure they were protected.' The woman wiped her face. Sarah had thought her name was Carmen at first, as one would think, given her pedigree and appearance. But, no, her mother and father had named her after the town in California, which they dreamed of someday visiting.

Sarah found a tissue and handed it to the woman. This was certainly alarming. It seemed to represent a new level of invasiveness. Still, John Westerfield's probing was constant and familiar, like a low-grade fever, which Carmel had her own mettle to withstand.

No, something else had happened.

'And?'

'No, really. Just that.'

Sarah herself could be persistent, too. 'Come, now . . .'

'He . . . I think it was maybe a coincidence. Didn't mean anything.'

Nothing the She-Beast and the He-Beast did was a coincidence. Sarah said, 'Tell me anyway.'

'Then he said,' the woman offered, choking back a sob, 'if I didn't tell him, he wouldn't be able to protect you. And if those papers got stolen, you'd lose all your money. I'd lose my job and . . . and then he said my daughter might have to leave her high school, Immaculata.'

'He said that?' Sarah whispered.

Carmel was crying harder now. 'How would he know she went there? Why would he find that out?'

Because he and his mother did their homework. They asked their questions like chickens pecking up seed and stones.

But now, threatening Carmel and her family?

'I got mad and I said I couldn't wait until the lease is up and he and his mother went away forever! And he said oh, they weren't going anywhere. They checked the law in New York and as long as they pay the rent and don't break the lease they can stay forever. Is that true, Mrs Sarah?'

Sarah Lieberman said, 'Yes, Carmel, it is true.' She rose and sat down at the Steinway piano she'd owned for nearly twenty years. It had been a present from her second husband for their wedding. She played a few bars of Chopin, her favorite composer and, in her opinion, the most keyboard-friendly of the great classicists.

Carmel continued, 'When he left he said, "Say hi to your family for me, Carmel. Say hi to Daniel. You know, your husband, he's a good carpenter. And say hi to Rosa. She's a pretty girl. Pretty like her mother."' Carmel was shivering now, tears were flowing.

Sarah turned from the piano and touched the maid on the shoulder. 'It's all right, dear. You did the right thing to tell me.'

The tears slowed and finally stopped. A Kleenex made its way around her face.

After a long moment Sarah said, 'When Mark and I were in Malaysia – you know he was head of a trade delegation there?'

'Yes, Mrs Sarah.'

'When we were there for that, we went to this preserve.'

'Like a nature preserve?'

'That's right. A nature preserve. And there was this moth he showed us. It's called an Atlas moth. Now, they're very big – their wings are six or eight inches across.'

'That's big, *sí.*'

'But they're still moths. The guide pointed at it. "How can it defend itself? What does it have? Teeth? No. Venom? No. Claws? No." But then the guide pointed out the markings on this moth's wings. And it looked just like a snake's head! It was exactly like a cobra. Same color, everything.'

'Really, Mrs Sarah?'

'Really. So that the predators aren't sure whether it would be safe to eat the moth or not. So they usually move on to something else and leave the moth alone.'

Carmel was nodding, not at all sure where this was going.

'I'm going to do that with the Westerfields.'

'How, Mrs Sarah?'

'I'll show them the snake head. I'm going to make them think it's too dangerous to stay here and they should move out.'

'Good! How are you going to do that?'

'Did I show you my birthday present?'

'The flowers?'

'No, this.' Sarah took an iPhone from her purse. She fiddled with the functions, many of which she had yet to figure out. 'My nephew in Virginia gave it to me. Freddy. He's a good man. Now, this phone has a recorder in it.'

'You're going to record them, doing that? Threatening you?'

'Exactly. I'll email a copy to my lawyer and several other people. The Westerfields'll have to leave me alone.'

'But it might not be safe, Mrs Sarah.'

'I'm sure it won't be. But it doesn't look like I have much choice, do I?'

Then Sarah noticed that Carmel was frowning, looking away.

The older woman said, 'I know what you're thinking. They'll just go find somebody else to torture and do the same thing to them.'

'Yes, that's what I was thinking.'

Sarah said softly, 'But in the jungle, you know, it's not the moth's job to protect the whole world, dear. It's the moth's job to stay alive.'

Present Day

'You want me to find somebody?' the man asked the solemn woman sitting across from him. 'Missing person?'

The Latina woman corrected solemnly, '*Body*. Not somebody. A body.'

'Excuse me?'

'A body. I want to know where a body is. Where it's buried.'

'Oh.' Eddie Caruso remained thoughtfully attentive but now that he realized the woman might be a crackpot he wanted mostly to get back to his iPad, on which he'd been watching a football – well, *soccer* – match currently under way in Nigeria. Eddie loved sports. He'd played softball in his middle-school days, Little League and football, well, *gridiron*, in high school and then, being a skinny guy, he'd opted for billiards and pool in college (to raise tuition while, for the most part, avoiding bodily harm). But the present sport of his heart was soccer.

Okay, *football*.

But he was also a businessman and crackpots could be paying clients, too. He kept his attention on the substantial woman across his desk, which was bisected by a slash of summer light reflected off a nearby Times Square high-rise.

'Okay. Keep going, Mrs Rodriguez.'

'Carmel.'

'Car*mel*?'

'Carmel.'

'A body, you were saying.'

'A murdered woman, a friend.'

He leaned forward, now intrigued. Crackpot clients could not only pay well. They also often meant *Game* – a term coined by sportsman Eddie Caruso; it was hard to define. It meant basically the interesting, the weird, the captivating. Game was that indefinable aspect of love and business and everything else, not just sports, that kept you engaged, that got the juices flowing, that kept you off balance.

People had Game or they didn't. And if not, break up.

Jobs had Game or they didn't. And if not, quit.

Another thing about Game. You couldn't fake it.

Eddie Caruso had a feeling this woman, and this case, had Game.

She said, 'A year ago, I lost someone I was close to.'

'I'm sorry.'

The iPad went into sleep mode. When last viewed, a winger for Senegal had been cutting through the defense, trying to open a way to goal. But Caruso let the sleeping device lie. The woman was clearly distraught about her loss. Besides, Senegal wasn't going to score.

'Here.' Carmel opened a large purse and took out what must've been fifty sheets of paper, rumpled, gray, torn. Actual newspaper clippings, too, which you didn't see much, as opposed to computer printouts, though there were some of those, too. She set them on his desk and rearranged them carefully. Pushed the stack forward.

'What's this?'

'News stories about her, Sarah Lieberman. She was the one murdered.'

Something familiar, Caruso believed. New York is a surprisingly small town when it comes to crime. News of horrific violence spreads fast, like a dot of oil on water, and the hard details seat themselves deep in citizens' memories. The Yuppie Murderer. The Subway Avenger. The Wilding Rape. Son of Sam. The Werewolf Slasher.

Caruso scanned the material fast. Yes, the story came back to him. Sarah Lieberman was an elderly woman killed by a bizarre couple – a mother and son pair of grifters from the Midwest. He saw another name in the stories, one of the witnesses: that of the woman sitting in front of him. Carmel had been Sarah's housekeeper, and Carmel's husband, Daniel, the part-time maintenance man.

She nodded toward the stack. 'Read those, read that. You'll see what I'm talking about.'

Generally Caruso didn't spend a lot of time in the free initial consulting session. But then it wasn't like he had much else going on.

Besides, as he read, he knew instinctively, this case had Game written all over it.

Here's Eddie Caruso: a lean face revealing not-unexpected forty-two-year-old creases, thick and carefully trimmed dark blond hair, still skinny everywhere, except for a belly that curls irritatingly over the belt hitching up Macy's sale Chinese-made somewhat wool slacks. A dress shirt, today blue of color, light blue like the gingham that infected the state fairs Caruso worked as a boy to make money for cars and dates and eventually college.

Rhubarb pie, cobbler, pig shows, turkey wings, dunk-the-clown.

That was where he came from.

And this is where he is: not the FBI agent he dreamed of being, nor the disillusioned personal injury lawyer he was, but a pretty good private investigator, which suits his edgy, ebullient, Game-addicted personality real well.

The actual job description is 'security consultant'.

Nowadays, everybody cares about security. They don't care about investigating. Why should they? A credit card and the Internet make us all Sam Spades.

Still, Eddie Caruso likes to think of himself as a PI.

Caruso has a scuffed, boring, nondescript office in a building those same adjectives apply to, Forty-sixth near Eighth – decorated (office, not building) with close to twenty pictures he himself has taken with a very high-speed Canon of athletes in action. You'd think he was a sports lawyer. The building features mostly orthodontists, plastic surgeons, accountants, one-man law firms and a copy shop. That's one great thing about New York: Even in the Theater District, the Mecca of all things artistic, people need teeth and boobs fixed up, their taxes paid and résumés exaggerated. Next door is a touristy but dependable restaurant of some nebulous Middle Eastern–Mediterranean affiliation; it excels at the grilled calamari. Caruso, who lives in Greenwich Village and who often walks the three miles to work (to banish the overhang of gut), likes the five-story bathwater-gray building, the location, too. Though if the city doesn't stop digging up the street in front of the building Caruso may just write a letter.

Which he'll never get around to, of course.

Now, Eddie Caruso finished reading the account of the murder, well, *skimming* the account of the murder, and pushed the material back toward Carmel.

Yep, Game . . .

Sarah Lieberman's story had indeed interested Caruso, as Mrs Rodriguez here had suggested. Sarah's itinerant younger days, a bit of a rebel, her settling into life in New York City quite easily. She seemed to be irreverent and clever and to have no patience for the pretense that breeds in the Upper East Side like germs in a four-year-old's nose. Caruso decided he would have liked the woman.

And he was mightily pissed off that the Westerfields had beat her to death with a hammer, wrapped the body in a garbage bag, and dumped her in an unmarked grave.

It seemed that mother and son had met Sarah at a fund-raiser and saw a chance to run a grift. They recognized her as a wealthy, elderly vulnerable woman with no family, living alone. A perfect target. They leased the apartment on the ground floor of her Upper East Side townhouse and began a relentless campaign to take control of her life. She had finally had enough and one morning in July, a year ago, tried to record them threatening her. They'd caught her in the act, though, and forced her to sign a contract selling them the townhouse for next to nothing. Then they zapped her with a Taser and bludgeoned her to death.

That afternoon Carmel returned to the townhouse from shopping and found her missing. Knowing that the Westerfields had been asking about her valuables and that Sarah was going to record them threatening her, the housekeeper suspected what had happened. She called the police. Given that – and the fact that a routine search revealed the Westerfields had a criminal history in Missouri and Kansas – officers responded immediately. They found some fresh blood in the garage. That was enough for a search warrant. Crime Scene found the Taser with Sarah's skin in the barbs, a hammer with John's prints and Sarah's blood and hair, and duct tape with both Sarah's and Miriam's DNA. A roll of garbage bags, too, three of them missing.

The clerk from a local spy and security shop verified the Taser had been bought, with cash, by John Westerfield a week earlier. Computer forensic experts found the couple had tried to hack into Sarah's financial accounts – without success. Investigators did, however, find insurance documents covering close to seven hundred thousand dollars in cash and jewelry kept on her premises. Two necklaces identified as Sarah's were found in Miriam's jewelry box. All of the valuables had been stolen.

The defense claimed that drug gangs had broken in and killed her. Or, as an alternative, that Sarah had gone senile and went off by herself on a bus or train.

Juries hate lame excuses and it took the Lieberman panel all of four hours to convict. The two were sentenced to life imprisonment. The farewell in the courtroom – mother and son embracing like spouses – made for one real queasy photograph.

Carmel now said to Eddie Caruso, 'I kept hoping the police would find her remains, you know?'

John's car had been spotted several days before Sarah disappeared in New Jersey, where he was reportedly looking at real property for one of his big business deals, none of which ever progressed past the daydreaming phase. It was assumed the body had been dumped there.

Carmel continued, 'I don't know about her religion, the Jewish one, but I'm sure it's important to be buried and have a gravestone and have people say some words over you. To have people come and see you. Don't you think, Mr Caruso?'

He himself didn't think that was important but he now nodded.

'The problem is, see, this is a simple death.'

'Simple?' The woman sat forward, brows furrowing a bit.

'Not to make little of it, understand me,' Caruso added quickly, seeing the dismay on her face. 'It's just that it's open and shut, you know? Nasty perps, good evidence. No love children, no hidden treasure that was never recovered, no conspiracy theories. Fast conviction. With a simple death, people lose interest. The leads go cold real fast. I'm saying, it could be expensive for me to take on the case.'

'I could pay you three thousand dollars. Not more than that.'

'That'd buy you about twenty-five hours of my time.' On impulse he decided to waive expenses, which he marked up and made a profit on.

Before he went further, though, Caruso asked, 'Have you thought this through?'

'What do you mean?'

'Well, it was a terrible crime but justice's been done. If I start searching, I may have to ask you things – you'll have to relive the incident. And, well, sometimes when people look into the past, they find things they wish they hadn't.'

'What could that be?'

'Maybe there'd be no way to recover the body, even if I find it. Maybe it was . . . let's say disrespected when it was disposed of.'

Carmel had *not* considered this, he could tell. Clients rarely did. But she said, 'I want to say a prayer at her grave, wherever it is. I don't care about anything else.'

Caruso nodded and pulled a retainer agreement from his credenza. They both signed it. Also, on whim, he penned in a discounted hourly rate. He'd seen pictures of her three children when she'd opened her purse to get her driver's license number for the agreement. They were teenagers and the parents were surely facing the horror of college expenses.

You're a goddamn softy, he told himself.

'All right,' he said to her. 'Let me keep these and I'll get to work. Give me your home and cell numbers.'

A hesitation. 'Email please. Only email.' She wrote it down.

'Sure. Not call?'

'No, please don't. See, I mentioned to my husband I was thinking about doing this and he said it wasn't a good idea.'

'Why?'

She nodded at the news clippings. 'It's in there somewhere. There was a man maybe working for the Westerfields, the police think. Daniel's worried he'd find out if we started looking for the body. He's probably dangerous.'

Glad you mentioned it, Caruso thought wryly. 'Okay, I'll email.' He rose.

Carmel Rodriguez stepped forward and actually hugged him, tears in her eyes.

Caruso mentally bumped his fee down another twenty-five, just to buy her a little more of his time.

When she'd gone he booted up the iPad just to see what he'd missed sportswise. The match was over. Senegal had won five zip.

Five?

A BBC announcer, beset by very un-BBC enthusiasm, was gushing, '*Some of the most spectacular goals I have ever seen in all my years—*'

Caruso shut the device off. He pulled the stack of clippings closer, to take more notes – and to read up in particular on the Westerfields' possible accomplice.

He was reflecting that in all his years as a privately investigating security consultant, he'd been in one pushing match that lasted ten seconds. Not one real fight. Caruso did have a license to carry a pistol and he owned one but he hadn't touched his in about five years. He believed the bullets had turned green.

He wondered if he would in fact be in danger.

Then decided, so be it. Game had to come with a little risk. Otherwise it wasn't Game.

NYPD Detective Lieutenant Lon Sellitto dropped into his chair in his Major Cases office, One Police Plaza. Dropped, not sat. Rumpled – the adjective applied to both the gray suit and the human it encased – he looked with longing affection at a large bag from Baja Express he'd set on his excessively cluttered desk. Then at his visitor. 'You want a taco?'

'No, thanks,' Caruso said.

The portly cop said, 'I don't get the cheese or the beans. It cuts the calories way down.'

Eddie Caruso had known Sellitto for years. The detective was an all right guy, who didn't bust the chops of private cops, as long as they didn't throw their weight around and sneak behind the backs of the real Boys in Blue. Caruso didn't. He was respectful.

But not sycophantic.

'You'll guarantee that?' Caruso asked.

'What?'

'No beans, so you're not going to fart. I don't want to be here if you're gonna fart.'

'I meant I don't get the *refried* beans. I get the regular beans, black beans or whatever the hell they are. They're a lot less calories. "Fried" by itself is not a good word when you're losing weight. "Refried"? Think how fucking bad that is. But black beans're okay. Good fiber, tasty. But, yeah, I fart when I eat 'em. Like any Tom, Dick and Harry. Everybody does.'

'Can we finish business before you indulge?'

Sellitto nodded at a slim, limp NYPD case file. 'We will, 'cause sorry to say, the quote business ain't going to take that long. The case is over and done with and it wasn't much to start with.'

Out the window you could catch a glimpse of the harbor and Governors Island. Caruso loved the view down here. He'd thought from time to time about relocating but then figured the only real estate he could afford in this 'hood would come with a view even worse than his present one in Midtown, which was a few trees and a lot of sunlight, secondhand – bounced off that Times Square high-rise.

The detective shoved the file Caruso's way. The Sarah Lieberman homicide investigation. 'That was one fucked-up twosome, the perps.' Sellitto winced. 'They ick me out. Mother and son, with *one* bed in the townhouse. Think about it.'

Caruso would rather not.

Sellitto continued. 'So your client wants to know where the Dysfunctional Family dumped the body?'

'Yep, she's religious. You know.'

'No, I don't.'

'I don't either. But that's the way of it.'

'I looked through it fast.' Sellitto offered a nod toward the file. 'But the best bet for the corpse is Jersey.'

'I read that in the *Daily News*. But there were no specifics.'

Sellitto grumbled, 'It's in the file. Somewhere near Kearny Marsh.'

'Don't know it.'

'No reason to. Off Bergen Avenue. The name says it all.'

'Kearny?'

Sellitto's round face cracked a smile. 'Ha, you're funny for a private dick. Why don't you join the force? We need people like you.'

'Marsh, huh?'

'Yeah. It's all swamp. Serious swamp.'

Caruso asked, 'Why'd they think there?'

'Ran John Westerfield's tags. They had him at a toll booth on the Jersey Turnpike. He got off at the Two-Eighty exit and back on again a half-hour later. Security footage in the area showed the car parked in a couple places by the Marsh. He claimed he was checking out property to buy. He said he was this real estate maven. Whatever maven is. What's that word mean?'

'If we were in a Quentin Tarantino movie,' Caruso said, 'this's where I'd start a long digression about the word "maven".'

'Well, it isn't and I don't know what the fuck you're talking about.'

Sellitto definitely had Game.

Caruso flipped through the smaller folder inside the bigger one. The smaller was labeled *John Westerfield*. Many of the documents were his own notes and records, and a lot of them had to do with real estate, all the complex paperwork that rode herd on construction in Manhattan: foundation-pouring permits, crane permits, street-access permissions. Interestingly – and incriminatingly – these were all multimillion-dollar projects that John couldn't possibly have engaged in without Sarah Lieberman's money.

'Good policing. When was Westerfield in Jersey?'

'I don't know. A couple days before she disappeared.'

'*Before?* Was there a toll record of him being there *after* she disappeared?'

'No. That's where the grassy knoll effect comes in.'

'The . . .?'

'Dallas. Kennedy assassination. The other gunman.'

'I don't believe there was one. It was Oswald. Alone.'

'I'm not arguing that. My point is that the Westerfields probably *did* have an accomplice. He's the one who got rid of the body. In *his* car. So there was no record of Westerfield returning to Jersey.'

'Yeah, my client mentioned there might've been somebody else. Why would he be the one who dumped the body, though?'

Sellitto tapped the file. 'Just after they killed her – Crime Scene knew the time from the blood – the Westerfields were seen in public so they'd have an alibi. They would've hired somebody to dump the body. Probably somebody connected.'

'Organized crime?'

'What "connected" means.'

'I know that. I'm just saying.'

Sellitto said, 'We think some low-grade punk. The Westerfields had connections with mob folks in Kansas City and they must've tapped some affiliate here.'

'Like Baja Fresh. Mobster franchises.'

Sellitto rolled his eyes, maybe thinking Caruso wasn't as clever as he'd first thought. The detective said, 'The Westerfields stole three-quarters of a million from Mrs Lieberman, cash and jewelry. They would've paid this guy from that.'

Caruso liked it that Sellitto called her Mrs Lieberman. Respect. That was good, that was part of Game. 'Any leads to him?'

'No, but he was after the fact and nobody in the DA's office gave a shit really. They had the doers. Why waste resources.' Sellitto finally gave in. He opened the lunch bag. It did smell pretty good.

Caruso began, 'The couple—'

'They're mother and son, I wouldn't call 'em a couple.'

'The couple, they say anything about the third guy?'

Sellitto looked at Caruso as if he'd gotten stupid himself. 'Remember, it was gangbangers who killed her. Or she decided to take a cruise and forgot to tell anybody. To the quote couple, there was no third guy.'

'So I go searching in Jersey. Where exactly is this Kearny Marsh?' Sellitto nodded at the file.

Caruso took it and retreated to a corner of Sellitto's office to read.

'One thing,' the detective said.

Caruso looked up, expecting legalese and disclaimers.

The detective nodded at the bowl of black beans he was eating. 'Stay at your own risk.'

Hopeless.

Eddie Caruso stood about where John Westerfield's green Mercedes had been parked as the man had surveyed the area, looking for the best place to hide a body.

There was no way he could find where Sarah Lieberman had been buried.

Before him were hundreds of acres of marshland, filled with brown water, green water, gray water, grass, cattails and mulberry trees. A trillion birds. Gulls, ducks, crows, hawks and some other type – tiny, skittish creatures with iridescent blue wings and white bellies; they were living in houses on poles stuck at the shoreline.

New Jersey housing developments, Eddie Caruso reflected. But he didn't laugh at his own cleverness because he was being assaulted by suicidal and focused mosquitoes.

Slap.

And in the distance the crisp magnificence of Manhattan, illuminated by the midafternoon sun.

Slap.

The water was brown and seemed to be only two or three feet deep. You could wrap a body in chicken wire, add a few weights, and dump it anywhere.

He wasn't surprised searchers hadn't found her brutalized corpse.

And there was plenty of land, too – in which it would be easy to dig a grave. It was soupy and he nearly lost his Ecco.

He wiped mud off his shoe as best he could and then speculated: How much would it cost to hire a helicopter with some sort of high-tech radar or infrared system to detect corpses? A huge amount, he guessed. And surely the body was completely decomposed by now. Was there any instrumentation that could find only bones in this much territory? He doubted it.

A flash of red caught his eye.

What's that?

It was a couple of people in a canoe.

New Jersey Meadowlands Commission was printed on the side.

Eddie Caruso's first thought was, of course: Meadowlands. May the Giants have a better season next year.

His second thought was: Shit.

This was *government* land, Caruso realized.

Meadowlands Commission . . .

John Westerfield claimed he'd come here to look into a real estate deal. But that was a lie. There'd be no private development on protected wetlands. And using the toll road, which identified him? He'd done that *intentionally.* To lead people off. Not being the brightest star in the heavens, he and his mother had probably figured they couldn't get convicted if the body was never found. So they'd left a trail here to stymie the police.

In fact, they'd buried Sarah Lieberman someplace else entirely.

Where . . .?

Eddie Caruso thought back to the police file in Lon Sellitto's office. He believed he knew the answer.

An hour and a half later – thank you very much, New York City traffic – Caruso parked his rental illegally. He was sure to incur a ticket, if not a tow, here near City Hall, since it was highly patrolled. But he was too impatient to wait to find a legal space.

He found his way to the Commercial Construction Permits Department.

A slow-moving clerk with an impressive do of dreadlocks surrounding her otherwise delicate face looked over his requests and disappeared. For a long, long time. Maybe coffee breaks had to be taken at exact moments or forfeited forever. Finally, she returned with three separate folders.

'Sign for these.'

He did.

'Can I check these out?'

'No.'

'But the thing is—'

She said reasonably, 'You can read 'em, you can memorize 'em, you can copy 'em. But if you want copies you gotta pay and the machines say they take dollar bills but nobody's been able to get it to take a dollar bill in three years. So you need change.'

'Do you have—?'

'We don't give change.'

Caruso thanked her anyway and returned to a cubicle to read the files.

These were originals of permits issued to three construction companies that were building high-rises on the Upper East Side not far from Sarah Lieberman's townhouse. Caruso had found copies of these in John Westerfield's police file, the one that Sellitto let him look through. They'd been discovered in the man's desk. John had claimed to be involved in real-estate work, so who would have thought twice about finding these folders? No one did.

But Eddie Caruso had.

Because why would John Westerfield have copies of permits for construction of buildings he'd had nothing to do with?

There was only one reason, which became clear when Caruso had noted that these three permits were for pouring foundations.

What better way to dispose of a body than to drop it into a pylon about to be filled with concrete?

But which building was it? Eddie Caruso's commitment to Carmel Rodriguez was to find out *exactly* where Sarah Lieberman had been buried.

As he looked down at the permits he suddenly realized how he could find out.

He copied the first pages of all three permits, after getting change from another customer because, yeah, his dollars'd all been rejected by the temperamental Xerox machine. Then, returning to the cubicle, he carefully – and painfully – worked the industrial-sized staples from the paper and replaced the originals with the copies.

This was surely a misdemeanor of some kind, but he'd developed quite an affection for Mrs Carmel Rodriguez (he had dropped his rate by another twenty-five dollars an hour). And, by the by, he'd come to form an affection for the late Mrs Sarah Lieberman, too. Nothing was going to stop him from learning where the poor woman was resting in peace.

To his relief, the clerk missed the theft, and with a sincere smile Caruso thanked her and wandered outside.

Lord be praised, there was no ticket and in a half-hour he was parked outside the private forensic lab he sometimes used. He hurried inside and paid a premium for expedited service. Then he strolled down to the waiting room, where to his delight, he found a new capsule coffee machine.

Eddie Caruso didn't drink coffee much and he never drank tea. But he loved hot chocolate. He had recipes for eighty different types and you needed recipes – you couldn't wing it. (And you *never* mixed that gray-brown powder from an envelope with hot water, especially envelopes that contained those little fake marshmallows like dandruff.)

But the Keurig did a pretty good job, provided you chocked the resulting cocoa full of Mini-Moo's half-and-half, which Eddie Caruso now did. He sat back to enjoy the frothy beverage, flipping through a *Sports Illustrated*, which happened to describe the Nigeria–Senegal match as the Game of the Century.

In ten minutes, a forensic tech – a young Asian woman in a white jacket and goggles around her neck – joined him. He'd been planning on asking her out for some time. Three years and four months, to be exact. He hadn't been courageous, or motivated, enough to do so then. And he wasn't now.

She said, 'Okay, Eddie, here's what we've got. We've isolated identifiable prints of six individuals on the permit documents from the city commission you brought me.'

Technicians were always soooo precise.

'Two of them, negative. No record in any commercial or law enforcement database. One set is yours.' She regarded him with what might pass for irony, at least in a forensic tech, and said, 'I can report that you are not in any criminal databases either. It is likely, however, that that might not be the case much longer if the police find out how you came to be in possession of an original permit, which by law has to remain on file with the city department in question.'

Precise . . .

'Oh,' Eddie said offhandedly, 'I found 'em on the street. The permits.'

No skipped beats. She continued, 'I have to tell you none are John Westerfield's.'

This was a surprise and a disappointment.

'But I could identify one other person who touched the documents. We got his prints from military records.'

'Not criminal?'

'No.'

'Who is he?'

'His name's Daniel Rodriguez.'

It took five seconds.

Carmel's husband.

Sometimes when people look into the past, they find things they wish they hadn't . . .

Whatever you call your profession, security or investigation, you need to be as professional as any cop.

Eddie Caruso was now in his office, number crunching what he'd found, not letting a single fact wander away or distort.

Was this true? Could Daniel Rodriguez be the third conspirator, the one who'd actually disposed of Sarah Lieberman's body?

There was no other conclusion.

He'd worked in Sarah's building and would have been very familiar with John and Miriam Westerfield. And they had known that Daniel, with three girls approaching college age, would need all the money he could get. He was involved in the trades and would know his way around construction sites. He probably even had friends in the building whose foundation was now Sarah Lieberman's grave.

Finally, Daniel hadn't wanted his wife to pursue her plan to find out where Sarah's body was. He claimed this was because it was dangerous. But, thinking about it, Caruso decided that was crazy. The odds of the other guy finding out were minimal. No, Daniel just didn't want anybody looking into the case again.

And whatta I do now? Caruso wondered.

Well, there wasn't much choice. All PIs are under an obligation to inform the police if they're aware of a felon at large. Besides, anybody who'd participated, however slightly, in such a terrible crime had to go to jail.

Still, was there anything he could do to mitigate the horror that Carmel and their daughters would feel when he broke the news?

Nothing occurred to him. Tomorrow would be a mass of disappointment.

Still, he had to be sure. He needed as much proof of guilt as a cop would. That's what Game required: resolution, good or bad. Game is never ambiguous.

He assembled some of his tools of the trade. And then decided he needed something else. After all, a man who can toss the body of an elderly woman into a building site can just as easily kill someone who's discovered he did that. He unlocked the box containing his pistol, nothing sexy, just a revolver, the sort you didn't see much any more.

He found the bullets, too. They weren't green. Which meant, Eddie Caruso assumed, that they still worked.

The next day Caruso rented an SUV with tinted windows and spent hours following Daniel. It was boring and unproductive, as ninety-nine per cent of tailing usually is.

On the surface, round Daniel Rodriguez was a harmless, cheerful man, who seemed to joke a lot and seemed to get along with the construction crews he worked with. Eddie Caruso had expected – and half hoped – to find him selling crack to schoolkids. If that had been the case, it would have been easier to report him to the police.

And easier to break the news to his wife and daughters? Caruso wondered. No. Nothing could relieve the sting of that.

Daniel returned home to his small but well-kept house in Queens. Caruso cruised past slowly, parked up the block and stepped outside, making his way to a park across the street, dressed like anybody else in the casual, residential neighborhood – shorts and an Izod shirt, along with sunglasses and a baseball cap. He found a bench and plopped down, pretending to read his iPad, but actually observing the family through the device's video camera.

Apple had revolutionized the PI business.

The weather was nice and the Rodriguez family cooked out, with Daniel the chef and Carmel and their daughters his assistants. Several neighbors joined them. Daniel seemed to be a good father. Caruso wasn't recording his words but much of what he said made the whole family laugh.

A look of pure love passed between husband and wife.

Shit, Caruso thought, sometimes I hate this job.

After the barbecue and after the family had been shuffled off to the house, Daniel remained outside.

And something set off an alarm within Caruso: Daniel Rodriguez was scrubbing a grill that no longer needed scrubbing.

Which meant he was stalling. On instinct, Caruso rose and ducked into some dog-piss-scented city bushes. It was good he did. The handyman looked around piercingly, making certain no one was watching. He casually – too casually – disappeared into the garage and came out a short time later, locking the door.

That mission, whatever it was, smelled funky to Caruso. He gave it two hours, for dark to descend and quiet to lull the neighborhood. Then he pulled on latex gloves and broke into the garage with a set of lock-picking tools, having as he often did at moments like this an imaginary conversation with the arresting officer. No, sir, I'm not committing burglary – which is breaking and entering with intent to commit a felony. I'm committing trespass only – breaking and entering with intent to find the truth.

Not exactly a defense under the New York State penal code.

Caruso surveyed the jam-packed garage. A systematic search could take hours, or days. The man was a carpenter and handyman so he had literally tons of wood and plasterboard and cables and dozens of tool chests. Those seemed like natural hiding places but they'd also be the first things stolen if anybody broke in, so Caruso ignored them.

He stood in one place and turned in circles, like a slow-motion radar antenna, looking from shelf to shelf, relying on the fuzzy illumination of the streetlight. He had a flashlight but he was too close to the house to use it.

Finally he decided: the likeliest place one would hide something was in the distant, dusty corner, in paint cans marred with dried drips of color. Nobody'd steal used paint.

And bingo.

In the third and fourth he found what he suspected he would: stacks and stacks of twenties. Also two diamond bracelets.

All, undoubtedly, from Sarah's safe-deposit box. This was his payment from the Westerfields for disposing of the body. They hadn't mentioned him, of course, at trial because he had enough evidence to sink them even deeper – probably enough to get them the death penalty.

Caruso took pictures of the money and jewelry with a low-light camera. He didn't end his search there, though, but continued to search through all the cans. Most of them contained paint. But not all. One, on the floor in the corner, held exactly what he needed to figure out Sarah Lieberman's last resting place.

'Come in, come in,' Eddie said to Carmel Rodriguez, shutting off the TV.

The woman entered his office and glanced around, squinting, as if he'd just decorated the walls with the sports pictures that had been there forever. 'My daughter, Rosa, she plays soccer.'

'That's my favorite, too.' Eddie sat down, gesturing her into a seat across from the desk. She eased cautiously into it.

'You said you found something.'

The PI nodded solemnly.

Most of Eddie Caruso's work involved finding runaways, running pre-employment checks and outing personal injury lawsuit fakers, but he handled domestics, too. He'd had to deliver news about betrayal and learned there were generally three different reactions: explosive anger, wailing sorrow or weary acceptance, the last of which was usually accompanied by the eeriest smile of resignation on the face of the earth.

He had no idea how Carmel would respond to what she was about to learn.

But there was no point in speculating. It was time to let her know.

'This is going to be troubling, Carmel. But—'

She interrupted. 'You told me there might be things you found that I might not like.'

He nodded and rose, walking to his other door. He opened it and gestured.

She frowned as her husband walked into the room.

The man gave her a sheepish grin and then looked back at the carpet as he sat next to her.

'Daniel! Why are you here?'

Caruso sat back in his office chair, which was starting to develop the mouse squeak that seemed to return once a month no matter how much WD-40 was involved. He whispered, 'Go ahead, Daniel. Tell her.'

He said nothing for a minute and Carmel asked pointedly, 'Is this about Mrs Sarah? Is this about what happened to her?'

The round-faced man nodded. 'Okay, honey, Carmel—'

'Tell me,' the housekeeper said briskly.

'I haven't been honest with you.' Eyes whipping toward her, then away. 'You remember last year you told me the Westerfields wanted you to find Mrs Sarah's papers?'

'Yes. And when I said no they threatened, sort of threatened our daughter.'

'They did the same to me. They said they couldn't trust you, you were too good. They wanted me to help them.'

'You?' she whispered.

'Yes, baby. Me! Only it wasn't just find the papers. They . . .'

'What? What did they want?'

'Miriam told me Sarah didn't have long to live anyway.'

'"Anyway".' What do you mean "anyway"?'

'She said Sarah had cancer.'

'She wasn't sick! She was healthier than that bitch Miriam,' Carmel spit out.

'But they said she was. And she'd told them she'd cut us out of her will. We'd get nothing. They said, if I help them now, if she died now, they could make sure we had lots of money.'

'Helped them out.' Carmel eyed her husband coolly. 'You mean, helped them kill her.'

'They said she was greedy. Why should she have so much and people like them, and us, have nothing? It was unfair.'

'And you didn't tell me? You didn't tell anybody they were dangerous?'

'I did tell somebody.'

'Who? Not the police, you didn't.'

Daniel looked at Eddie Caruso, who picked up the remote control and hit ON.

The TV, on which a webcam sat, came to life with a Skype streaming image.

On the screen an elderly woman's face gazed confidently and with some humor at the couple in the chairs, and Eddie Caruso. 'Hello, Carmel,' Sarah Lieberman said. 'It's been a long time.'

What Eddie Caruso had found in the last paint can in the Rodriguezes' garage was a letter from Sarah to Daniel with details of where she'd be spending the rest of her life – a small town near Middleburg, Virginia, with her widower nephew Frederick. Information about how to get in touch with her if need be, where she would be buried and the name of certain discreet jewelers whom he could contact to sell the bracelets Sarah had given him, along with suggestions about how to carefully invest the cash she'd provided, too.

He'd confronted the handyman this morning and while the letter seemed plausible, Caruso had insisted they both contact Sarah Lieberman this morning. She'd told them what had happened and was now telling the same story to her housekeeper.

The simple death he'd described to Carmel Rodriguez was anything but.

'I'm so sorry, Carmel . . . I'm sorry I couldn't tell you. You remember that day in July, just a year ago? I was going to take the phone Freddy gave me and record them?'

'Yes, Mrs Sarah.'

'After you left, I started to go down there. But I met Daniel on the stairs.' Her gaze shifted slightly, taking in the handyman. 'He had me come back to my apartment and he told me what they'd just said – that the Beasts wanted him to help kill me. He said they had it all planned. There was nothing anybody could do to stop them.'

'Why not go to the police?' Carmel demanded.

Sarah replied, 'Because at worst they'd get a few years in jail for conspiracy. And then they'd be out again, after somebody else. I started thinking about what I told you. Remember the moth?'

'The big moth you and your husband saw in Malaysia. With the wings that look like a snake.'

'That's right. But I decided: one way to protect yourself is to disguise yourself as a snake. The other way is to *be* the snake itself. I fight back. I couldn't kill them but I could make it look like they killed *me*. I didn't ask Daniel to help me, but he wanted to.'

'I was so mad at them and worried about you and about Rosa! John hinted that he'd been watching her, watching our daughter!'

Sarah said, 'The Westerfields were very accommodating. John already had the Taser and the tape and the garbage bags.' She gave a wry laugh. 'Think of all the money I'll waste at Beacon Brothers Funeral Home here – that damn expensive casket. There are so many cheaper ways to go.'

Daniel said, 'We pretended to forge a contract selling the building to them and then took all of the jewelry and cash Mrs Sarah had in the apartment. She kept some and gave me a very generous amount.'

'And in my will I left Freddy here' – Sarah glanced to the side of the sunroom she sat in, apparently where her other co-conspirator, her nephew, sat –'all my personal belongings. Probate took a little while but six months later everything was delivered here. Ah, but back to the scene of the crime, eh, Daniel?'

He winced and looked at Carmel. 'When the Westerfields were out and you were shopping, we both went downstairs. I put on gloves and took one of John's hammers and Mrs Sarah cut herself. We got her blood on it and some hairs, too. And put some duct tape on her mouth for a minute and we added some of Miriam's hairs. I rubbed her toothbrush on it, for the DNA. Sarah stuck herself with the sharp points on that Taser. We hid those things in their apartment, then I tried to hack into Mrs Sarah's banking accounts from Miriam's computer.'

'I used to watch *CSI*,' Sarah said. 'I know how these things work.'

'I left the city permits and maps in John's office.' Daniel started to laugh then reined in when he saw his wife staring at him in dismay. 'I was going to say it was funny because we thought the permits would be obvious. But the police missed those entirely; they thought she *had* been buried in New Jersey. But they missed it; it was Mr Caruso who figured out about the foundations.'

Sarah said, 'And I took the train down here. I've had to lead a pretty quiet life – they call it staying off the grid, right, Freddy?'

A man's voice, 'That's right, Aunt Sarah.'

'But I love it in Virginia. It's so peaceful. I lived here a long time ago and I'd always thought I'd come back to spend my last years in horse country.'

Daniel now turned to Carmel. 'I'm sorry, love. I couldn't tell you!' he said. 'This was a crime, what Mrs Sarah and I did. Putting those people in jail. I wanted to, I wanted to tell you a hundred times. I couldn't let you get involved.'

Carmel was regarding her husband. 'And the money . . . You said you were opening an account for the girls' school . . . And you always had those fifty-dollar bills. I always wondered.'

Sarah said, 'He risked a lot to save me. I was very appreciative.' Her voice faded. 'And now I think it's time for my nap. I'd invite you to come down but it's probably not a good idea for either of you to visit a dead woman, I'm afraid.'

'Oh, Mrs Sarah.'

'Goodbye, Carmel.'

Both women held their hands up in waves of farewell and Eddie Caruso, a good judge of timing, clicked the TV off.

Caruso said goodbye to the family, suspecting there would be more discussion of the events between husband and wife on the way home. He thought about lowering the bill yet more, but decided against it. After all, he'd done the job, and the case had had more or less a happy ending.

Even if it was entirely unexpected.

But that's another thing about Game, maybe what really defines a person or event as Game or not: You never know ahead of time how it's going to turn out.

Speaking of which . . .

Eddie Caruso propped up his iPad and typed on the keyboard. He was just in time to see Tottenham versus Everton. Fantastic.

You could never lose with Premier League football.

Well, *soccer*.

BUMP

Hat in hand.

There was no other way to describe it.

Aside from the flashy secretary, the middle-aged man in jeans and a sports coat was alone, surveying the glassy waiting room, which overlooked Century City's Avenue of the Stars. No, not that one, with the footprints in concrete (that was Hollywood Boulevard, about five miles from here). This street was an ordinary office park of hotels and high-rises, near an okay shopping center and a pretty-good TV network.

Checking out the flowers (fresh), the art (originals), the secretary (a wannabe, like nine-tenths of the other help in LA).

How many waiting rooms had he been in just like this, over his thirty-some years in the industry? Mike O'Connor wondered.

He couldn't even begin to guess.

O'Connor was now examining a purple orchid, trying to shake the thought: Here I am begging, hat in hand.

But he couldn't.

Nor could he ditch the adjunct thought: This is your last goddamn chance.

A faint buzz from somewhere on the woman's desk. She was blond, and O'Connor, who tended to judge women by a very high standard, his wife, thought she was attractive enough. Though, this being Hollywood, attractive enough for what? was a legitimate question and sadly the answer to that was: not enough for leading roles. A pretty character actress, walk-ons. We're in the toughest business on the face of the earth, baby, he thought to her.

She put down the phone. 'He'll see you now, Mr O'Connor.' She rose to get the door for him.

'That's okay. I'll get it . . . Good luck.' He'd seen her reading a script.

She didn't know what he meant.

O'Connor closed the door behind him and Aaron Felter, a fit man in his early thirties, wearing expensive slacks and a dark gray shirt without a tie, rose to greet him.

'Mike. My God, it's been two years.'

'Your dad's funeral.'

'Right.'

'How's your mom doing?'

'Scandal. She's dating! A production designer over on the Universal lot. At least he's only five years younger. But he wears an earring.'

'Give her my best.'

'Will do.'

Felter's father had been a director of photography for a time on O'Connor's TV show in the eighties. He'd been a talented man and wily . . . and a voice of reason in the chaotic world of weekly television.

They carried on a bit of conversation about their own families – neither particularly interested, but such was the protocol of business throughout the world.

Then because this wasn't just business, it was Hollywood, the moment soon arrived when it was okay to cut to the chase.

Felter tapped the packet of material O'Connor had sent. 'I read it, Mike. It's a real interesting concept. Tell me a little more.'

O'Connor knew the difference between 'it's interesting' and 'I'm interested'. But he continued to describe the proposal for a new TV series in more depth.

Michael O'Connor had been hot in the late seventies and eighties. He'd starred in several prime-time dramas – featuring a law firm, an EMT facility and, most successfully, the famous Homicide Detail. The show lasted for seven seasons, which was a huge success.

It had been a great time. O'Connor, a UCLA film grad, had always been serious about acting, and *Homicide Detail* was cutting-edge TV. It was gritty, was shot with handheld cameras, and the writers (O'Connor co-wrote scripts from time to time) weren't afraid to blow away a main character occasionally or let the bad guy get off. An LAPD detective, who became a good friend of O'Connor's, was the show consultant and he worked them hard to get the details right. The shows dealt with religion, abortion, race, terrorism, sex, anything. 'Cutting-edge story-telling, creativity on steroids' was the *New York Times*'s assessment of the show, and those few words meant more to O'Connor than the Emmy nomination (he lost to an actor from *Law & Order*, a thoroughly noble defeat).

But then the series folded and it was drought time.

He couldn't get work – not the kind of work that was inspired and challenging. His agent sent him scripts with absurd premises or that were hackneyed rip-offs of his own show, or sitcoms, which he had no patience or talent for. And O'Connor collected his residual checks (and signed most of them over to the Ivy League schools his daughters attended) and kept trying to survive in a town where he'd actually heard someone say of *Richard III*, 'You mean it was a play, too?'

But O'Connor was interested in more than acting. He had a vision. There's a joke in Hollywood that, when looking for a project to turn into a film or series, producers want something that's completely original and yet has been wildly successful in the past. There is, however, some truth to that irony. And for years O'Connor had it in mind to do a project that was fresh but still was rooted in television history: each week a different story, with new characters. Like TV from the 1950s and '60s: *Alfred Hitchcock Presents, Playhouse 90, The Twilight Zone*. Sometimes drama, sometimes comedy, sometimes science fiction.

He'd written a proposal and the pilot script and then shopped *Stories* all over Hollywood and to the BBC, Sky and Channel 4 in England, as well – but everyone passed. The only major producer he hadn't contacted was Aaron Felter, since the man's dad and O'Connor had been friends and he hadn't wanted to pressure him unfairly. Besides, Felter wasn't exactly in the stratosphere himself. His various production companies had backed some losing TV and film projects recently and he couldn't afford to take any risks.

Still, O'Connor was desperate.

Hence, hat in hand.

Felter nodded, listening attentively as O'Connor pitched his idea. He was good; he'd done it many times in the past year.

There was a knock and a large man, dressed similarly to Felter, walked into the office without being formally admitted. His youth and the reverential look he gave to Felter told O'Connor immediately he was a production assistant – the backbone of most TV and film companies. The man, with an effeminate manner, gave a pleasant smile to O'Connor, long enough of a gaze to make him want to say, I'm straight, but thanks for the compliment.

The PA said to Felter, 'He passed.'

'He what?'

'Yep. I was beside myself.'

'He said he was in.'

'He's not in. He's out.'

The elliptical conversation – probably about an actor who'd agreed to do something but backed out at the last minute because of a better offer – continued for a few minutes.

As they dealt with the emergency, O'Connor tuned out and glanced at the walls of the man's office. Like many producers' it was covered with posters. Some were of the shows that Felter had created. Others were of recent films – those starring Mark Wahlberg, Kate Winslet, Ethan Hawke, Tobey Maguire, Keira Knightley. And, curiously, some were of films that O'Connor remembered fondly from his childhood, the great classics like *The Guns of Navarone, The Dirty Dozen, The Magnificent Seven, Bullitt.*

The actor remembered that he and Felter's dad would sometimes hang out for a beer after the week's shooting for *Homicide Detail* had wrapped. Of course, they'd gossip about the shenanigans on the set, but they'd also talk about their shared passion: feature films. O'Connor recalled that often young Aaron would join them, their conversations helping to plant the seeds of the boy's future career.

Felter and the bodybuilder of a production assistant concluded their discussion of the actor crisis. The producer shook his head. 'Okay, find somebody else. But I'm talking one day, tops.'

'I'm on it.'

Felter grimaced. 'People make a commitment, you'd think they'd stick to it. Was it different back then?'

'Back then?'

'The *Homicide Detail* days?'

'Not really. There were good people and bad people.'

'The bad ones, fuck 'em,' Felter summarized. 'Anyway, sorry for the interruption.'

O'Connor nodded.

The producer rocked back in a sumptuous leather chair. 'I've got to be honest with you, Mike.'

Ah, one of the more-often-used rejections. O'Connor at least gave him credit for meeting with him in person to deliver the bad news; Felter had a staff of assistants, like Mr America, who could've called and left a message. He could even just have mailed back the materials. O'Connor had included a self-addressed, stamped envelope.

'We just couldn't sell episodic TV like this nowadays. We have to go with what's hot. People want reality, sitcoms, traditional drama. Look at *Arrested Development*. Brilliant. But they couldn't keep it afloat.' Another tap of O'Connor's proposal for *Stories*. 'This is groundbreaking. But to the industry now, that word scares 'em. It's like it's literal: an earthquake. Natural disaster. Everybody wants formula. Syndicators want formula, stations want formula, the audience, too. They want a familiar team, predictable conflicts. White guy, black guy, hot chick, Asian guy who knows computers. The way of the world, Mike.'

'So you're saying that *Entourage* is just *The Honeymooners* with the F word.'

'Naw, I'd say more *Leave It to Beaver*. A family, you know. But, yeah, that's exactly what it is. Hell, Mike, I wish I could help you out. My dad, rest his soul, loved working on your show. He said you were a genius. But we've gotta go with the trends.'

'Trends change. Wouldn't you like to be part of a new one?'

'Not really.' Felter laughed. 'And you know why? Because I'm a coward. We're all cowards, Mike.'

O'Connor couldn't help but smile himself.

On his show, O'Connor had played a *Columbo* kind of cop. Sharp, nothing got by him. Mike Olson the cop on *Homicide Detail* wasn't a lot different from Mike O'Connor the actor. He looked Felter over carefully. 'What else?'

Felter placed his hands on his massive glass desk. 'What can I say? Come on, Mike. You're not a kid any more.'

'This is no industry for old men,' he'd say, paraphrasing William Butler Yeats's line from 'Sailing to Byzantium'.

In general men have a longer shelf life than women in TV and films, but there are limits. Mike O'Connor was fifty-eight years old.

'Exactly.'

'I don't want to star. I'll play character from time to time, just for the fun of it. We'll have a new lead every week. We could get Damon or DiCaprio, Scarlett Johansson, Cate Blanchett. People like that.'

'Oh, you can?' Felter wryly responded to the enviable wish list.

'Or the youngster of the month. Up-and-coming talent.'

'It's brilliant, Mike. It's just not saleable.'

'Well, Aaron, I've taken up enough of your time. Thanks for seeing me. I mean that. A lot of people wouldn't have.'

They chatted a bit more about family and local sports teams and then O'Connor could see that it was time to go. Something in Felter's body language said he had another meeting to take.

They shook hands. O'Connor respected the fact that Felter didn't end the conversation with 'Let's get together sometime.' When people in his position said that to people in O'Connor's, the lunch dates were invariably canceled at the last minute.

O'Connor was at the door when he heard Felter say, 'Hey, Mike. Hold on a minute.'

The actor turned and noted the producer was looking at him closely with furrowed brows: O'Connor's flop of graying blond hair, the broad shoulders, trim hips. Like most professional actors – whether working or not – Mike O'Connor stayed in shape.

'Something just occurred to me. Take a pew again.' Nodding at the chair.

O'Connor sat and observed a curious smile on Felter's face. His eyes were sparkling.

'I've got an idea.'

'Which is?'

'You might not like it at first. But there's a method to my madness.'

'Sanity hasn't worked for me, Aaron. I'll listen to madness.'

'You play poker?'

'Of course I play poker.'

O'Connor and Diane were sitting on the patio of their house in the hills off Beverly Glen, the winding road connecting West Hollywood and Beverly Hills to the San Fernando Valley. It was a pleasant house, but modest. They'd lived here for years and he couldn't imagine another abode.

He sipped the wine he'd brought them both out from the kitchen.

'Thanks, lover,' she said. Diane, petite, feisty and wry, was a real estate broker and she and O'Connor had been together for thirty years, with never an affair between them, a testament to the fact that not all Hollywood marriages are doomed.

She poured more wine.

The patio overlooked a pleasant valley – now tinted blue at dusk. Directly beneath them was a gorgeous house. Occasionally film crews would disappear inside, the shades would be drawn, then the crews would emerge five hours later. This part of California was the number-one producer of pornography in the world.

'So, here's what Felter's proposing,' he told her. 'Celebrity poker.'

'Okay,' Diane said dubiously. 'Go on.' Her voice was yawning.

'No, no. I was skeptical at first, too. But listen to this. It's apparently a big deal. For one thing it airs during Sweeps Week.'

The week during which the networks presented the shows with the biggest draw to suck up the viewership rating points.

'Really?'

'And it's live.'

'Live TV?'

'Yep.' O'Connor went on to explain the premise of *Go For Broke*.

'So it's live, sleazy reality TV. What makes it any different?'

'Have some more wine,' was O'Connor's answer.

'Uh-oh.'

O'Connor explained that what set *Go For Broke* apart from typical celebrity poker shows was that on this one the contestants would be playing with their own money. Real money. Not for charity contributions, like the usual celeb gambling programs.

'What?'

'Aaron's view is that reality TV isn't real at all. Nobody's got anything to lose. *Survivor, Fear Factor* . . . there's really no risk. The people who climb walls or walk on girders're tethered and they've got spotters everywhere. And eating worms isn't going to kill you.'

Savvy businesswoman Diane O'Connor said, 'Get back to the "our own money" part.'

'The stakes are a quarter million. We come in with that.'

'Bullshit.'

'Nope. It's true. And we play with cash on the table. No chips. Like riverboat gamblers.'

'And the networks're behind it?'

'Huge. The ad budget alone's twenty-five million. National print, TV, radio, transit ads . . . everything. The time slot for the first show is after *Central Park West,* and on Thursday it's right after *Hostage.*'

CPW was the hottest comedy since *Friends*, and *Hostage* was the season's biggest crime drama, a 24-kind of action show.

'Okay, it's big. And we can probably get our hands on the money, but we can't afford for you to lose it, Mike. And even if you win, okay, you make a million dollars. We could do that in a couple of years in the real estate market. So, what's in it for you?'

'Oh, it's not about the money. It has nothing to do with that.'

'Then what's it about?'

'The bump.'

'The bump? What is that? A Hollywoodism?'

'Of course,' he said. 'Why use a dozen words to express yourself exactly when you can use a buzzword?'

He explained to his wife, in a slightly censored fashion, what Aaron Felter had told him earlier: 'Mike, buddy, a bump is a leg-up. It's getting recognized on the media radar. It's grabbing the limelight. A bump means you're fuckable. A bump gets your name in the trades and *Entertainment Tonight*. You haven't had a bump for years. You need one.'

O'Connor had asked Felter, 'So you're saying that if I'm in this game, I get a bump?'

'No, I'm saying if you win the game, you get a bump. Will it get you a housekeeping deal at a studio? I don't know. But it'll open doors. And I'll tell you if you win, I promise I'll take your proposal for *Stories* to the people I've got deals with. Again, am I promising they'll green-light it? No, but it'll get me in the front door.'

He now said to Diane, 'All the contestants're like me. At a certain level, but not where we want to be. They're from a cross section of entertainment industries, music, acting, stand-up comedy.'

The woman considered this for a long time, looking over the blue hills, the porn house, the pale evening stars. 'This is really your last chance to get *Stories* on, isn't it?'

'I'd say that's right.'

Then, to his disappointment, Diane was shaking her head and rising. Without a word she walked into the kitchen. O'Connor was upset. He loved her. And, more important, he trusted her. Mike O'Connor might've played the tough, blunt Detective Mike Olson on TV, but emotionally he was the antithesis of the cop. He'd never do anything to hurt his wife. And he resolved that, seeing Diane's negative reaction, he'd call Felter immediately and back out.

She returned a moment later with a new bottle of Sonoma chardonnay.

'You don't want me to do it, do you?' he asked.

'I'll answer that with one question.'

He speculated: Where would they get the money, what about the girls' tuition, would they have to hit their retirement funds?

But, it turned out, she was curious about something else. She asked, 'Does a full house beat a flush?'

'Uhm, well . . .' He frowned.

Diane withdrew from her pocket something she'd apparently collected when she'd gone into the kitchen for the wine: a deck of Bicycle playing cards. 'I can see you need some practice, son.'

And cracked the wrapper on the deck.

The bar was on Melrose, one of those streets in West Hollywood where you can see celebs and people who want to be celebs, and people who, whether they're celebs or not, are just absolutely fucking beautiful.

Sammy Ralston was checking some of them out now – the women at least – and looking for starlets. He watched a lot of TV. He watched now in his small place in Glendale. And he'd watched a lot Inside, too, though the Chicano inmates dictated what you saw, which during the day was mostly Spanish-language soaps, which weren't so bad, 'cause you got a lot of tits, but at night they watched weird shows he couldn't figure out. (Though everybody watched *CSI*, which he had a soft spot for, seeing as how it was physical evidence – from one of his cigarettes – that landed him Inside in the first place after the B and E at a Best Buy warehouse.)

He looked up and saw Jake walk through the door, shaved head, inked forearms. Huge. A biker. He wore a leather jacket with *Oakland* on the back. Say no more. He stood above Ralston. Way above. 'Why'd you get a table?'

'I don't know. I just did.'

'Because you wanted some faggot chicken wings, or what?'

'I don't know. I just did.' The repetition was edgy. Ralston was small but he didn't put up with much shit.

Jake shrugged. They moved to the bar. Jake ordered a whiskey, double, which meant he'd been here before and knew they were small pours.

He drank half the glass down, looked around and said in a soft voice, 'Normally I wouldn't fuck around with a stranger but I'm in a bind. I've got a thing going down and my man – nigger out of Bakersfield – had to get the fuck out of state. Now, here's the story. Joey Fadden—'

'Sure, I know Joey.'

'I know you know Joey. Why I'm here. Lemme finish. Jesus. Joey said you were solid. And I need somebody solid, from your line of work.'

'Windows?'

'Your other line of fucking work.'

Ralston actually had two. One was washing windows. The other was breaking into houses and offices and walking off with anything saleable. People thought that people who boosted merch went for valuable things. They didn't. They went for saleable things. Big difference. You have to know your distribution pipeline, a fence had once told him.

'And you understand that if we can't come to an agreement here and anything goes bad later, me or one of my buddies from up north'll come visit you.'

The threat was like the fine print in a car contract. It had to be included but nobody paid it much mind.

'Yeah, yeah. Fine. Go ahead.'

'So. What it is. I heard from Joey about a month ago this TV crew did a story at Lompoc. Life in prison, some shit like that, I don't know. And the crew got this hard-on to hang with the prisoners.'

'Macho shit, sure.' Ralston'd seen this before. People from the Outside feeling this connection with people Inside.

'So Joey heard them talking about this TV poker show some asshole producer is doing. It's planned for Vegas, but in a hotel, not a real casino. And they don't use chips. They use real cash. The buy-in's supposedly two-fifty K.'

'Shit. Cash? What's the game?' Ralston loved poker.

'Fuck, I don't know. Old Maid. Or Go Fish. I don't fucking lose my money at cards. So I'm thinking, if it's not a casino, security won't be so tight. Might be something to think about.' Jake ordered another whiskey. 'Okay. So I check out the prison show and get some names. And one of the gaffers—'

'Yeah, what is that? I've heard of them.'

'Electrician. Can I finish? He's a biker, too, from Culver City. And he's a little loose in the mouth when he's had a few and so I get the details. First of all, this's a live show.'

'What's that mean?'

'Live? They don't record it ahead of time.'

'They do that?' Ralston thought everything was recorded.

'So it's a big surprise who wins.'

'That's not a bad idea for a show. I mean, I'd watch it.' Ralston peeled the label off his beer. It was a nervous habit. Jake noticed him and he stopped.

'Well, you can tell 'em you fucking approve, or you can shut up and listen. My point is that they'll have a mil and a half in small bills on the set. And we'll know exactly when and exactly where. So Joey speaks for you and I thought you might be interested. You want in, you get twenty points.'

'It's not a casino's money, but there'll still be armed guards.'

'Last time I looked 7-Elevens don't have that kind of money in their fucking cash registers.'

'Guns involved, I'd be more interested for thirty.'

'I could go twenty-five.'

Sammy Ralston said he'd have to think about it.

Which meant only one thing: getting a call through to Lompoc. After he and Jake adjourned he managed to get Joey Fadden, doing three to five for GTA, hard because a weapon was involved. By virtue of the circumstances, their conversation was convoluted, but the most important sentence was a soft, 'Yeah, I know Jake. He's okay.'

Which was all Ralston needed.

And they proceeded to talk about the sports teams and how much they both lamented the name change of the San Francisco 49ers' home to 'Monster Park'.

The site of the game was the Elysium Fields Resort and Spa on the outskirts of Vegas.

On Wednesday morning, the day of the show, the contestants assembled in one of the hotel's conference rooms. It was a curious atmosphere – the typical camaraderie of fellow performers, with the added element that each one wanted to take a quarter-million dollars away from the others. The mix was eclectic:

Stone T, a hip-hop artist, whose real name, O'Connor learned from the bio that Felter had prepared for the press, was Emmanuel Evan Jackson. He had been a choirboy in Bethany Baptist Church in South Central, had put himself through Cal State, performing at night, and then got into the LA rap, ska and hip-hop scene. Stone was decked out like a homie from Compton or Inglewood – drooping JNCO jeans, Nikes, a vast sweatshirt, and bling. All of which made it jarring to hear him say things like, 'It's a true pleasure to meet you. I've admired your work for a long time.' And: 'My wife is my muse, my Aphrodite. She's the one whom I dedicate all my songs to.'

O'Connor was surprised to see Brad Kresge was one of the contestants. He was a bad boy of West Hollywood. The lean, intense-eyed kid was a pretty good actor in small roles – never with a major lead – but it was his personal life that had made the headlines. He'd been thrown out of clubs for fighting, had several DUI arrests and he'd done short time in LA County for busting up a hotel room, as well as the two security guards who'd come to see what the fuss was about. He seemed cheerful enough at the moment, though, and was attentive to the emaciated blonde hanging on his arm – despite the fact that Aaron Felter had asked that the contestants attend this preliminary meeting alone, without partners or spouses.

Kresge was unfocused and O'Connor wondered if he was stoned. He wore his hat backward and the sleeves of his wrinkled shirt rolled up, revealing a tat that started with a Gothic letter F. The rest of the word disappeared underneath the sleeve but nobody doubted what the remaining letters were.

Sandra Glickman was the only woman in the game. She was a stand-up comic originally from New York but who lived out here now. She worked the Laugh Factory and Caroline's and appeared occasionally on Comedy Central on TV. O'Connor had seen her once or twice on TV. Her routines were crude and funny ('Hey, you guys out there'll be interested to know I'm bisexual; buy me something and I'll have sex with you.'). O'Connor had learned that she'd gone to Harvard on a full scholarship and had a master's degree in advanced math. She'd started doing the comedy thing as a lark before she settled down to teach math or science. That had been six years ago and comedy had won over academia.

Charles Bingham was a familiar face from TV and movies, though few people knew his name. Extremely tanned, fit, in his early sixties, he wore a blue blazer and tan slacks, dress shirt and tie. His dyed blond hair was parted perfectly down the side and it was a fifty-fifty chance that the coif was a piece, O'Connor estimated. Bingham was a solid character player and that character was almost always the same: the older ex-husband of the leading lady, the co-worker or brother of the leading man, a petty officer in a war movie – and usually one of the first to get killed in battle.

He'd been born Charles Brzezinski, the rumor was. But so what? O'Connor's own first name was still legally Maurice.

The big surprise in the crowd was Dillon McKennah. The handsome thirtysomething was a big-screen actor. He'd be the one real star at the table. He'd been nominated for an Oscar for his role in a Spielberg film and everybody was surprised he'd lost. He'd been called the New James Dean. But his career had faltered. He'd made some bad choices recently: lackluster teen comedies and a truly terrible horror film – in which gore and a crashing soundtrack substituted, poorly, for suspense. Even on his most depressed days, O'Connor could look at himself in the mirror and say that he'd never taken on a script he didn't respect. McKennah mentioned that he was working on a new project, though he gave no details. But every actor in Hollywood was engaged in a 'new project', just like every writer had a script 'in development'.

They drank coffee, ate from the luxurious spread of breakfast delicacies and chatted, generally playing type: Stone T was hip. Sandra cracked jokes. Bingham smiled vacantly, stiff and polite. Kresge was loud. McKennah was Matt Damon in *Good Will Hunting*. And O'Connor was the strong silent sort.

As the conversation continued, O'Connor was surprised to find how lucky he was to be here. Apparently, when word went out about *Go For Broke*, close to five thousand people had contacted Aaron Felter's office, either directly or through their agents.

Everybody wanted the bump.

Now, the door of the conference room swung open and Aaron Felter entered.

'Okay, all, how you doing? . . . Hey, Sandy, caught your act on Sunset this weekend.'

The woman comic gave him a thumbs-up. 'Were you that fucking heckler?'

'Like I'd spar against you? Am I nuts?'

'Yo, Aaron, can we drink?' asked Brad Kresge. 'On the set, I mean. I play better that way.'

'You can do whatever you want,' Felter told him. 'But you break any cameras – or any heads – you pay for 'em.'

'Fucking funny.'

When coffee cups were refilled and the bagel table raided again, Felter sat on the edge of the table in the front of the room. 'Now, folks. Today's the day. I want to run through the plan. First, let's talk about the game itself.' He asked a young man into the room. The slim guy was the professional dealer Felter had flown in from Atlantic City. He sat down at the table and – after awing them with his incredible dexterity – went through protocol and rules of the game they'd be playing, Texas Hold 'Em.

This was one of the simplest of all poker games (selected, O'Connor guessed, not because of the contestants, but because of the audience, so they could follow the play). There was no ante; the players to the dealer's left would place blind bets before the deal – a small blind from the player to the immediate left and then a large blind, twice that amount, from the player on *his* left to create a pot. Each player then was dealt two hole cards, which nobody else could see, and then placed bets or folded, based on those cards. The amount of the blinds would be set ahead of time.

Then came the flop: three community cards dealt face-up in the middle of the table. Betting commenced again and two more community cards were dealt face-up, making five. Traditional rules of poker applied to the betting process: checking – choosing not to bet – as well as seeing, raising or calling someone at the showdown.

When that occurred, players used their two hole cards plus any three of the five face-up board cards to make the best hand they could.

'Now, one thing we're not doing,' Felter announced. 'No hidden cameras.'

Most televised poker shows featured small cameras that allowed the audience and commentators to see each player's hole cards. The systems were tightly controlled and the games usually recorded ahead of time so there was no risk of using that information to cheat in real time, but that wasn't Felter's concern. A born showman, he wanted the tension of live drama: 'What's the excitement if the audience knows what everybody's hand is? I want people at home to be on the edge of their seats. Hell, I want them to fall off their seats.'

'Now remember, you're live. Don't pick your nose or grab your crotch.'

'Can I grab somebody else's crotch?' Glickman asked.

McKennah and, despite the blonde on his arm, Kresge raised their hands.

Everyone laughed.

'And,' Felter continued, 'you'll be miked, so if you whisper, "Fuck me", we'll bleep it but your mother's going to know you said something naughty. Now, I want laughs and sighs and banter. We'll have three cameras on close-ups and medium angles and one camera on top showing the board. No sunglasses.' This was directed to Brad Kresge, who was always wearing them. 'I want expression. Cry, look exasperated, laugh, get pissed off. This is a poker game but first and foremost it's TV! I want the audience engaged . . . Any questions?'

There were none and the contestants dispersed.

On his way to join Diane for a swim before the show, Mike O'Connor was trying to recall what was familiar about Felter's speech.

Then he remembered: it was out of some gladiator film, when the man who was in charge gave his before-the-games pep talk, reminding the warriors that though most of them were about to die, they should go out and put on the best show they could.

Sammy Ralston and Jake were in a bar up the street from Elysium Fields Spa.

Jesus, it was hot.

'Why Nevada?' Ralston asked. 'Why the desert? They oughta put casinos where the weather's nicer.' Ralston was sweating like crazy. Jake wasn't. Big guy like that and he wasn't sweating. What was that about?

The biker said, 'If the weather's nice people stay outside and don't gamble. If the weather's shitty, they stay inside and do. That's not rocket science.'

Oh. Made sense.

Ralston fed a quarter into the minislot at the end of the bar and Jake looked at him like, you want to throw your money away, go ahead. He lost. He fed another quarter in and lost again.

The two men had spent the last few days checking out the Elysium Fields. It was one of those places that dated from the fifties and was pretty nice, but also sort of shabby. It reminded Ralston of his grandmother's apartment's décor in Paramus, New Jersey. A lot of yellows, a lot of mirrors that looked like they had bad skin conditions, a lot of fading white statuettes.

Jake, with his tats and biker physique, stood out big-time, so he'd done most of the behind-the-scenes information gathering, from press releases and a few discreet calls to his union contact on the studio back lot. He'd learned that the TV show would be shot in the grand ballroom. At the beginning of the show, armed guards would give each player a suitcase containing his buy-in, which would sit on a table behind his chair. He'd take what he needed from it to play.

'Gotta be a big suitcase, I'd guess.'

'No. Two fifty takes up shit. If it's in twenties or bigger.'

'Oh.' Ralston supposed Jake would know this. The most he himself had ever boosted in cash was about $2,000. But that was in quarters and he pulled his back out, schlepping it from the arcade to his car.

After the initial episode tonight was over, the money went back in the suitcases of the players who hadn't gone bust. The guards would take it to the hotel's safe for the night.

As for the surveillance of the Elysium Fields, Ralston had done most of that. He had his window-washing truck and his gear here, so he was virtually invisible. All contractors were. He'd learned that the ballroom was in a separate building. The guards would have to wheel the money down a service walk about sixty feet or so to get to the safe. Ralston had found that the walk was lined with tall plants, a perfect place to hide to jump out and surprise the guards. They'd overpower, cuff and duct tape them, grab the suitcases and flee to the opposite lot.

He and Jake discussed it and they decided to act tonight, after the first round of games; tomorrow, after the finale, there'd be more people around and they couldn't be sure if the money would be returned to the safe.

The plan sounded okay to both men, but Jake said, 'I think we need some kind of, you know, distraction. These security people around here. They're pros. They're going to be looking everywhere.'

Ralston suggested setting off some explosion on the grounds. Blow up a car or pull the fire alarm.

But Jake didn't like that. 'Fuck, as soon as anybody hears that they'll know something's going down, the money'll have guards all over it.' Then the biker blinked and nodded. 'Hey, you noticed people getting married around here a lot?'

'Yeah, I guess.'

'And everybody getting their pictures taken?'

Ralston caught on. 'All those flashes, yeah. You mean, blind 'em somehow with a camera?'

Jake nodded. 'But we walk up with a camera, the guards'd freak.'

'How about we get one of those flashes you see at weddings. The remote ones.'

'Yeah. On tripods.'

'We get one of those, set it up about halfway along the walk. When they're nearby we flash it. They'll be totally fucking blinded. We come up behind. They won't fucking know what hit them. I like it. Think we can find something like that around here?'

'Probably.'

The men paid for their beers and stepped out into the heat.

'Oh, one thing?'

'Yeah?' Jake grunted.

'What about . . . you know?'

'No, I don't fucking know until you tell me.'

'A piece. I don't have a piece.'

Jake laughed. 'I'm curious. You ever used one?'

'Fuck, yes.' In fact, no, he'd never fired a gun, not on a job. But he was pissed that Jake seemed to be laughing at him about it.

When they were in the window-washing truck, Jake grabbed his canvas backpack from behind the seat. He opened it up for Ralston to see. There were three pistols inside.

'Take your pick.'

Ralston chose the revolver. It had fewer moving parts and levers and things on the side. With this one he wouldn't have to ask Jake how it worked.

The banquet hall where *Go For Broke* was being shot was huge and it was completely packed.

The place was also decked out like every TV set that Mike O'Connor had ever been on: a very small portion – what the camera saw – was sleek and fashionably decorated. The rest was a mess: scaffolding, bleachers, cameras, wires, lights. It looked like a factory.

The contestants had finished with hair and makeup (except Kresge: 'You get me the way I am, leave me the fuck alone') and the sound man had wired them – mikes to their chests and plugs to their ears. They were presently in the greenroom, making small talk. O'Connor noted the costumes. Sandra Glickman was low-cut and glittery; Kresge was still in his hat-backward, show-the-tats mode. Stone T was subdued South Central and had gotten Felter's okay to wear Ali G goggles, not nearly as dark as sunglasses; you could get a good look at his eyes (for the 'drama' when he won a big pot or ended up busted, presumably). Charles Bingham was in another blazer and razor-creased gray slacks. He wore a tie, but an ascot wouldn't've been out of place. Dillon McKennah wore the de rigueur costume of youthful West Hollywood, an untucked striped blue-and-white shirt over a black T-shirt and tan chinos. His hair was spiked up in a fringe above his handsome face.

O'Connor had been dressed by Diane in 'older man sexy'. Black sports coat, white T-shirt, jeans and cowboy boots. 'Gunfight at the O.K. Corral,' she'd whispered and kissed him for luck. 'Go break a thumb.'

The production assistant – not the big gay fellow from LA, but a young nervous brunette – stood in the greenroom's doorway, clutching a clipboard, a massive radio on her hip. She listened to the voice of the director from the control room and kept glancing at her watch.

Television was timed to the tenth of a second.

Suddenly she stiffened. 'All right, everybody, please. We're on in three.' She then rounded them up like cattle and headed them to the assembly point.

There, O'Connor looked at the monitor, showing what the viewers around the country would be seeing: splashy graphics and some brash music. Then the camera settled on a handsome young man – dressed similarly to Dillon McKennah – sitting at a desk, like a sports commentator. Beside him were an African-American in a suit, and a skinny white guy in a cowboy outfit.

'Good evening, I'm Lyle Westerbrook, your host for *Go For Broke*. Two exciting days of no-holds-barred poker. And joining me here are Andy Brock, three times winner of the World Championship of Poker in Atlantic City. Welcome, Andy.'

'Good to see you, Lyle.'

'And Pete Bronsky, a professional gambler from Dallas and the man who wrote *Making a Living at Cards*. Hi, Pete.'

'Back at you, Lyle.'

'This is reality TV at its most real. You are watching live, on location, six individuals who aren't playing for prestige, they aren't playing for a charity of their choice. They're playing with their own hard cash. Somebody's going to lose big – a quarter of a million dollars. And somebody's going to win – maybe as much as six times that. One and a half million dollars is going to be at play tonight. You gentlemen must know the excitement of what our contestants are feeling.'

'Oh, you bet I do, Lyle . . .'

O'Connor tuned out of the banter, realizing that this was, in fact, the big time. Millions of people would be watching them and, more important, dozens of network and studio execs would be watching the ratings.

The bump . . .

'And now, let's meet our contestants.'

They went out in alphabetical order, as the announcer made a few comments about them and their careers. O'Connor caught Diane's eye – she was in the front row – when the applause erupted at the mention of *Homicide Detail* and the character of Detective Mike Olson. Though when, like the rest of the players, he said a few words to Lyle and mentioned the phrase 'Save it for the judge', one of his signature lines from the series, not many people laughed, which told him that the APPLAUSE sign had prompted people to cheer when the name of his show was mentioned.

Welcome to the world of TV.

When they were all seated around the table, security guards brought in the cash, which had been wire transferred to a local bank yesterday. The audience murmured when the guards, rather dramatically, opened the cases and set them behind each player on a low table. (Was there an illuminated sign that urged, 'SOUND AWED'?) The guards stood back, hands near their guns, scanning the audience from behind sunglasses.

O'Connor tried not to laugh.

The dealer explained the rules again – for the audience – then with cameras hovering, sweat already dripping, the room went utterly silent. The dealer nodded to O'Connor, to his immediate left. In Texas Hold 'Em, this was the button position, which signified the initial player, since unlike in informal games the players would not be dealing; a pro would be handling that job. O'Connor pushed the small blind out onto the table, the agreed-upon $1000.

For the big blind, Kresge, to O'Connor's left, splashed the table, tossing his $2000 out carelessly – very bad form. Chugging a beer, he grinned as the dealer straightened it.

The hole cards were dealt, the top card burned – discarded – and the flop cards spun elegantly into the center of the table.

The game proceeded with nobody winning or losing big, no dramatic hands. Kresge bet hard and took some losses but then pulled back. Sandy Glickman, with the quick mind of a natural comedian (and mathematician), seemed to be calculating the odds before each bet. She increased her winnings slowly. Stone T was a middle-of-the-road player, suffering some losses and catching some wins, as did McKennah. Neither seemed like natural players. O'Connor played conservatively and continually reminded himself of the basic poker strategy he'd picked up over the years – and that Diane had helped drill into him in the last few weeks:

It's all right to fold up front. You don't have to play every hand.

Bluff rarely, if at all. Bluffing should be used appropriately and only against certain players in limited circumstances. Many professional players go for months at a time without bluffing.

Fold if you think you're going to lose no matter how much you've already put into the pot.

Always watch the cards. Texas Hold 'Em is played with a single fifty-two-card deck, and only seven cards are known to any one player: his two and the five community cards. Unlike counting cards at blackjack or baccarat, knowing those seven won't give you great insights into what the others have. But knowing the board, you can roughly calculate the odds of whether someone else has a hand that beats yours.

Most important in poker, of course, is to watch the people playing against you. Some gamblers believe in tells – gestures or expressions that suggest what people have as their hole cards. O'Connor didn't believe that there were obvious tells, like scratching your eye when you had a high pair in the hole. But he did know that people respond consistently to stimuli – he'd learned this not from his limited experience as a card player but as an empathic actor. For instance he'd noticed that Stone T's face grew still when he had a good, though not necessarily a winning, hand. File those facts away and be aware of them.

The game progressed, with Glickman and McKennah up slightly, Kresge, Stone and O'Connor down a bit. Bingham was the big loser so far. On the whole O'Connor was pleased with his performance. He was playing a solid game.

They took a commercial break and Felter walked out, dispensing water and telling everybody how pleased he was – and how favorable the initial responses were. He walked off stage and they heard the voice of God.

'Now, back to the million-dollar action,' the commentator said. Then silence. O'Connor and the others couldn't hear anything else from the host or the pros in the control booth; he wondered how they were critiquing the performances.

A new deal. The blinds were now increased: five thousand and ten. The button player pushed out the small blind, the one to his left the big. Then the hole cards were dealt.

Shit.

O'Connor hoped he hadn't muttered that out loud. (His mother *was* watching.) He had a hammer. These were the worst hole cards dealt anyone could have, an unsuited two and a seven. You can't make a straight – you're allowed only three cards from the board – and there was no chance of a flush. There was a miraculous possibility for a full house but at best it would be sevens and twos. Not terrible, but still a long shot.

He stayed in for one round of betting but Bingham and Glickman started raising each other. Kresge folded, spitting out a word that O'Connor knew the standards and practices people would bleep.

McKennah folded and then O'Connor did, too. He was mentally counting the money he had left – about $220,000 – when he realized that something was going on at the table. Bingham, Glickman and Stone were engaged in battle. He sensed that Stone didn't have great cards but was already in for close to a hundred thousand. Glickman was less raucous than earlier, which told him that she might have a solid hand, and Bingham tried to appear neutral. He fondled the lapel of his blazer.

The flop cards were the jack of spades, king of diamonds, three of clubs, seven of clubs, six of hearts.

'Ma'am?' the dealer asked Glickman.

'Seventy-five thousand,' she raised, sighing. 'Think of all the eyeliner that'd buy.'

The audience laughed. In her routines she was known for excessive makeup.

Stone sighed, too. And folded.

Bingham snuck a peek at his cards again. This was a bad tell. It meant that you were double-checking to verify that you had one of the better hands, like a straight or flush. Then he looked over his money. His suitcase was empty and he had only about sixty thousand on the table.

'All in,' he said. Under standard rules of poker he could call with less than the raise, but couldn't win more than what he'd put into the pot.

O'Connor saw the older man's hands descend to his slacks; he wiped his sweaty palms. His face was still.

All eyes were on the cards.

O'Connor was sitting forward. Who won? What were the cards?

And the announcer said, 'And we'll be right back, folks, for the conclusion of this exciting day in Las Vegas.'

Agony. The next five minutes were agony.

The cards remained facedown on the table, the contestants chatted, sipped water. Kresge told a filthy joke to Glickman, who was subdued for a change and she smiled distantly. If she lost this hand she wouldn't go bust but she'd be way behind. If Bingham lost he'd be heading home.

No money, no bump.

Both Glickman and Bingham kept smiles on their faces, but you could see the tension they felt. Their overturned cards sat in front of them. The waiting was torture for O'Connor – and he had nothing to lose.

After an interminable few minutes during which beer, cars and consulting services were hawked to millions of people around the country, the action returned to the table.

The dealer said, 'Ma'am, you've been called. Would you please show your cards?'

She turned her two over and revealed the full house.

Bingham smiled stoically. 'Ah.' He displayed the ace-high flush. She'd beaten him with one hand better than his.

He rose and gave her a kiss. Then shook the others' hands.

The protocol, Aaron Felter had told them, was that anyone who went bust had to rise and leave.

Head off down the Walk of Shame, O'Connor dubbed it.

Departing this way seemed a bit ignominious, but this wasn't just poker, of course; it was the hybrid of poker on television.

I want drama . . .

The security guard displayed his empty suitcase to the table and the camera – more drama – and then deposited it in a specially built trash can.

The audience applauded furiously as Sandy raked in her cash.

After a commercial break and the ceremonial opening of a fresh deck of cards, the play continued. The remaining players were warmed up now and the betting grew more furious. On the sixth hand of this segment, Glickman, O'Connor and McKennah all folded and Stone T went one-on-one with Kresge.

Then the rapper made a bad mistake. He tried to bluff. O'Connor knew you couldn't bluff against people like Kresge – in poker or in real life. People who trash hotel rooms and smack their girlfriends don't have anything to lose. They kept raising hard and O'Connor could see that Stone was breaking the rule he had been reciting to himself all night: Don't stay in, just because you've already spent money.

Stone pushed in all his remaining stake – nearly eighty thousand – a cool smile on his lips, terror in his eyes, through Da Ali G lenses.

Kresge took his time finishing a light beer and then, with a sour smile, called the rapper.

Stone's two-pair hand was annihilated by an ace-high full house.

One more contestant was gone.

There was time on tonight's show for one more hand and it was during this round that divine retribution, in the form of Mike O'Connor, was visited upon Brad Kresge.

It was really too bad, O'Connor reflected from the vantage point of someone who happened to have the best hand he'd ever had in poker: a straight flush, jack high. As the betting progressed and Glickman and McKennah dropped out, O'Connor assumed the same mannerisms he'd witnessed in Stone T when the rapper was bluffing.

You're an actor, he told himself; so act.

Kresge was buzzed from the beer and kept raising, intent on bankrupting the old guy. The odds were minuscule that Kresge had a better hand than this, so it seemed almost unfair to drive him out of the game so easily. But O'Connor had always treated acting as a serious profession and was offended by Kresge's ego and his childish behavior, which demeaned the business. Especially after seeing the sneer on his face when he knocked Stone T out of the game, O'Connor wanted the punk gone.

Which happened all of ten seconds later.

Kresge went all in and O'Connor turned the hole cards, his eyes boring into Kresge's, as if saying: When I stay in a hotel, kid, I clean it up before I leave.

The audience applauded, as if the good gunslinger had just nailed the bad one.

Kresge grinned, finished his beer and took O'Connor's hand, trying for a vise grip, which didn't work, given O'Connor's workout regimen. The kid then sauntered off, down the Walk of Shame, as if he could actually set fire to a quarter-million dollars and have more fun.

Then the theme music came up and the host announced the winnings for the night: McKennah had $480,000. Glickman had $505,000. Mike O'Connor was the night's big winner with $515,000. Now, the control room mike went live to them and the poker experts took the stage to talk a bit about how the game had gone. The three remaining contestants chatted with them and Lyle for a few minutes.

Then, the theme once again and the red eyes on the cameras went dark.

The show was over for the night.

Exhausted and sweating, O'Connor said goodnight to the other players, the host and the experts. Aaron Felter joined them. He was excited about the initial ratings, which were apparently even better than he'd hoped. Diane joined them. They all made plans to have dinner together in the resort's dining room. O'Connor suggested that those who'd lost join them, too, but Felter said they were being taken out to the best restaurant in the city by an assistant.

O'Connor understood. It was important to keep the buzz going. And losers don't figure in that.

Diane said she'd meet them in the bar in twenty minutes; she wanted to call the girls. She headed off to the room and Felter went to talk to the line producer, while O'Connor and McKennah signed some autographs.

'Hey, buy you a beer?' McKennah asked.

O'Connor said sure and they started through the huge hall as the assistants took care of the equipment. TV and movies are as much about lights and electronics and computers as they are about acting. The two security guards were assembling the suitcases of money.

He didn't have his bump, not yet.

On the other hand, he was a quarter-million dollars richer.

Nothing wrong with that.

'Where's the bar?'

McKennah looked around. 'The main building. I think that's a shortcut. There's a walkway there.'

'Let's do it. I need a drink. Man, do I need a drink.'

Sammy Ralston felt the pistol, hot and heavy, in his back waistband. He was standing in the bushes in dark coveralls spearing trash and slipping it into a garbage bag.

On the other side of the walkway, behind other bushes, waited big Jake. The plan was that when the guards wheeling the money from the ballroom to the motel safe were halfway down the walkway, Ralston would hit the switch and flash the powerful photographer's light, which was set up at eye level. They'd tried it earlier. The flash was so bright it had blinded him, even in the well-lit hotel room, for a good ten, twenty seconds.

After the burst of light, Ralston and Jake would race up behind them, cuff the guards, then wrap duct tape around their mouths. With the suitcases of money, the men would return to the stolen van, parked thirty feet away, around the corner of the banquet facility. They'd drive a few miles away to Ralston's window-washing truck, then head back to California.

Ralston looked at his watch. The show was over and the guards would be packing up the money now.

But where were they? It seemed to be taking a lot of time. Were they coming this way, after all?

He glanced toward the door, then he saw it open.

Except that, no, it wasn't the guards at all. It was just a couple of men. A younger one in a striped shirt and an older one in a T-shirt, jeans and sports coat. They were walking along the path slowly, talking and laughing.

What the fuck were they doing here?

Oh, no. Behind them the door opened again and the guards – two of them, big and armed, of course – were wheeling the cart containing the cash suitcases along the path.

Shit. The two men in front were screwing everything up.

How was he going to handle it?

He crouched in the bushes, pulling the pistol from his pocket.

'Gotta say, man. I loved your show.'

'*Homicide Detail*? Thanks.'

'Classic TV. Righteous.'

'We had fun making it. That's the important thing. You interested in television?'

'Probably features for now.'

Meaning, O'Connor supposed, after a successful career he could 'retire' to the small screen. Well, some people had done it. Others, like O'Connor, thought TV was a medium totally separate from feature films, but just as valid.

'I saw *Town House*,' O'Connor offered.

'That piece of crap?'

O'Connor shrugged. He said sincerely, 'You did a good job. It was a tough role. The writing wasn't so hot.'

McKennah laughed. 'Most of the script was like: "SFX: Groaning as if the house itself is trying to cry for help." And "FX: blood pouring down the stairs, slippery mess. Stacey falls and is swept away." I thought it would be more like traditional horror. *The Exorcist. The Omen. Don't Look Now.* Or Howard Hawks' *The Thing*. Nineteen fifty-one and it still scares the piss out of me. Brilliant.'

They both agreed the recent British zombie movie, *28 Days Later*, was one of the creepiest things ever filmed.

'You mentioned a new project. What's it about?' O'Connor asked.

'A caper. Sort of *The Italian Job* meets *Ocean's Eleven*. Wahlberg kind of thing. Pulling the money together now. You know how that goes . . . How 'bout you?'

'TV probably. A new series.'

If I get my bump, O'Connor thought.

McKennah nodded behind him. 'That was pretty bizarre. Celebrity poker.'

'Beats *Survivor*. I don't dive off any platforms or eat anything too low on the food chain.'

'That Sandy, she's one hot chick. I'm glad she's still with us.'

McKennah wore no wedding ring; nor did Sandra Glickman. O'Connor wished them the best, though he knew that two-career relationships in Hollywood were sort of like the hammer at Texas Hold 'Em – not impossible to win with; you needed luck and lots of careful forethought.

'Oh, watch it there.' McKennah pointed to a thick wire on the sidewalk. It was curled and O'Connor had nearly caught his foot. The young actor paused and squinted at it.

O'Connor glanced at him.

McKennah explained that he was concerned about paparazzi. How they'd stalk you, even lay booby traps to catch you in embarrassing situations.

O'Connor laughed. 'Not a problem I've had for a while.'

'Damn, look.' McKennah gave a sour laugh. He walked to what the wire was attached to, a photographer's light, set up on a short tripod halfway along the path. Angrily he unplugged it and looked around. 'Some goddamn photog's around here somewhere.'

'Maybe it's part of the show.'

'Then Aaron should've told us.'

'True.'

'Oh, there're some guards.' He nodded at the security detail with the money, behind them. 'I'll tell them. Sometimes I get a little paranoid, I have to admit. But there are some crazy fucking people out there, you know.'

'Tell me about it.'

Ralston had to do something fast.

The two men had spotted the photoflash and, it seemed, had unplugged it.

And the guards were only about fifty feet behind.

What the hell could he do?

Without the flash there was no way they'd surprise the guards.

He glanced toward Jake, but the biker was hiding behind thick bushes and seemed not to have seen. And the two men were just standing beside the light, talking and now – fuck it – waiting for the guards. Assholes.

This was their last chance. Only seconds remained. Then an idea occurred to Ralston.

Hostage.

He'd grab one of the men at gunpoint and draw the guards' attention while Jake came up behind them.

No, better than that, he'd grab one and wound the other – leg or shoulder. That would show he meant business. The security guards'd drop their guns. Jake could cuff and tape them and the two men would flee. Everybody would be so busy caring for the wounded man, he and Jake could get to their truck before anybody realized which way they'd gone.

He pulled on the ski mask and, taking a deep breath, stepped fast out of the bushes, lifting the barrel toward the older of the two men, the one in the T-shirt and jacket, who gazed at him in astonishment. He aimed at the man's knee and started to pull the trigger.

O'Connor gasped, seeing the small man materialize from the bushes and aim a gun at him.

He'd never had a real gun pointed toward him – only fake ones on the set of the TV shows – and his initial reaction was to cringe and raise a protective hand.

As if that would do any good.

'No, wait!' he shouted involuntarily.

But just as the man was about to shoot, there came a flash of motion from his right, accompanied by a grunting gasp.

Dillon McKennah leapt forward and, with his left hand, expertly twisted away the pistol. With his right he delivered a stunning blow to the assailant, sending him staggering back, cradling his wrist. McKennah then moved in again and flipped the man to his belly and knelt on his back, calling for the guards. The gesture seemed a perfect karate move from an action-adventure film.

O'Connor, still too stunned to feel afraid, glanced back at the sound of footsteps running toward the parking lot. 'There's another one, too! That way!'

But the guards remained on the sidewalk, drawing their guns. One stayed with the money, looking around. The other ran forward, calling into his microphone. In less than ten seconds the walkway was filled with security guards and Las Vegas cops, too, who were apparently stationed in the hotel for the show.

Two officers jogged in the direction O'Connor indicated he'd heard fleeing footsteps.

The assailant's ski mask was off, revealing an emaciated little man in his forties, eyes wide with fear and dismay.

O'Connor watched a phalanx of guards, surrounding the money from *Go For Broke*, wheeling the cart fast into the hotel. Yet more guards arrived.

The officers who'd gone after the footsteps reported that they'd seen no one, though a couple reported a big man had jumped into a van and sped off. 'Dark, that's about all they could tell. You gentlemen all right?'

O'Connor nodded. McKennah was ashen-faced. 'Fine, yeah. But oh, man, I can't believe that. I just reacted.'

'You've got your moves down,' O'Connor told him.

'Tae kwon do. I just do it for a sport. I never thought I'd actually use it.'

'I'm glad you did. All I could see was that guy's eyes and I think he was about to pull the trigger.'

Diane came running out – word had spread quickly – and she hugged her husband and asked how he was.

'Fine. I'm fine. Just . . . I'm not even shaken. Not yet. It all happened so fast.'

A police captain arrived and supervised the arrest. When he was apprised of the circumstances the somber man shook his head. 'Gives a new meaning to the term "reality TV", wouldn't you say? Now, let's get your statements taken.'

Shaken, Aaron Felter walked into the bar and found O'Connor and Diane, McKennah and Glickman. He ordered a club soda.

'Jesus. How are you all?'

For a man who'd almost been shot, O'Connor admitted he was doing pretty well.

'It was my idea to use cash. I thought it'd play better. Man, this's my fault.'

'You can hardly blame yourself for some wacko, Aaron. Who was he?'

'Some punk from LA, apparently. Got a history of petty theft, the captain tells me. He had a partner but he got away.'

They talked about the incident and O'Connor recounted McKennah's martial arts skills. The young actor seemed embarrassed. He repeated, 'I just reacted.'

Felter said, 'I've got to say. I'm sure this fucked you up some, pardon my French,' he said, glancing at the women.

'I'm so offended,' Sandra Glickman said, frowning, 'you motherfucking cocksucker.'

They all laughed.

Felter continued, 'Are you cool going ahead with the show?'

McKennah and Glickman said they were. O'Connor said, 'Of course,' but then he caught something in the producer's eyes. 'That's not really what you're asking, is it, Aaron?'

A laugh. 'Okay. What I want to know is: If we go ahead with the show tomorrow, how are people going to react? I want your honest opinions. Should we give it some time to calm down? The dust to settle?'

'Which people?' McKennah asked. 'The audience?'

'Exactly. Are they going to think it's in bad taste. I mean somebody could've gotten hurt bad.'

O'Connor laughed. 'Excuse me, Aaron, but when have you ever known a TV show to fail because it's in poor taste?'

Aaron Felter pointed his finger at the man.

'Score one for the old guy' was the message in his eyes.

The Thursday finale of *Go For Broke* began with a description of the events of last night. But since *Entertainment Tonight* and every other quasi news program in the universe had covered the story, it made little sense to rehash the facts.

Besides, there was poker to be played.

With the same fanfare as yesterday – and five sunglass-clad guards nearby – the play among the last three contestants began.

They played for some time without any significant changes in their positions. Then O'Connor got his first good hole cards of the night. An ace and jack, both spades.

The betting began. O'Connor played it cautious, though, checking at first then matching the other bets or raising slightly.

The flop cards were another ace, a jack and a two, all varied suits.

Not bad, he thought . . .

Betting continued, with both Glickman and McKennah now raising significantly. Though he was uneasy, O'Connor kept a faint smile on his face as he matched the hundred thousand bet by McKennah.

The fourth card, the turn, went face-up smoothly onto the table under the dealer's skillful hands. It was another two.

Glickman eyed both of her opponents' piles of cash. But then she held back, checking. Which could mean a weak hand or was a brilliant strategy if she had a really strong one.

When the bet came to McKennah he slid out fifty thousand.

O'Connor raised another fifty. Glickman hesitated and then matched the hundred with a brassy laugh.

The final card went down, the river. It was an eight. This meant nothing to O'Connor. His hand was set. Two pair, aces and jacks. It was a fair hand for Texas Hold 'Em, but hardly a guaranteed winner.

But they'd be thinking he had a full house, aces and twos, or maybe even a four of a kind – in twos.

They, of course, could have powerful hands as well.

Then Glickman made her move. She pushed everything she had left into the middle of the table.

After a moment of debate McKennah folded.

O'Connor glanced into the brash comedian's eyes, took a deep breath and called her, counting out the money to match the bet.

If he lost he'd have about fifty thousand to call his own and his time on *Go For Broke* would be over.

Sandy Glickman gave a wry smile. She slid her cards facedown into the mush – the pile of discards. She said, for the microphone, 'Not many people know when I'm bluffing. You've got a good eye.' The brassy woman delivered another message to him when she leaned forward to embrace him, whispering: 'You fucked me and you didn't even buy me dinner.'

It was quiet enough that the censors didn't need to hit their magic button.

But she gave him a warm kiss and a wink before she headed off down the Walk of Shame.

About twenty minutes remained for the confrontation between the last two players, O'Connor with $623,000, McKennah with $877,000.

The young actor was in the button spot, to the dealer's left. He slid in the agreed-on small blind, ten thousand, and O'Connor counted out the big, twenty.

As the dealer shuffled expertly the two men glanced at each other. O'Connor's eyes conveyed a message. You're an okay kid and you saved my hide yesterday, but this is poker and I wouldn't be honest to myself, to you, or the game if I pulled back.

The faint glistening in McKennah's eyes said that he acknowledged the message. And said much the same in return.

It's showdown time.

Let's go for the bump.

The deals continued for a time, with neither of them winning or losing big. McKennah tried a bluff and lost. O'Connor tried a big move with three of a kind and got knocked out by a flush, which he should've seen coming.

A commercial break and then, with minutes enough for only one hand, the game resumed. A new deck of cards was shuffled. McKennah put in the small blind bet. The rules now dictated twenty-five thousand at this point, and O'Connor himself put in fifty.

Then the deal began.

O'Connor kept his surprise off his face as he glanced at the hole cards – cowboys, a pair of kings.

Okay, not bad. Let's see where we go from here.

McKennah glanced at his own cards without emotion. And his preflop bet was modest under the circumstances, fifty thousand.

Keeping the great stone face, O'Connor pushed in the same amount. He was tempted to raise, but decided not to. He had a good chance to win but it was still early and he didn't want to move too fast.

The dealer burned the top card and dealt the flop. First, a two of hearts, then the four of hearts and then the king of spades.

Suddenly O'Connor had three of a kind, with the other two board cards yet to come.

McKennah bet fifty thousand. At this point, because he himself had upped the bet, it wouldn't frighten the younger player off for O'Connor to raise him. He saw the fifty and raised by another fifty.

Murmurs from the crowd.

McKennah hesitated and saw the older actor.

The turn card, the fourth one, wasn't helpful to O'Connor, the six of hearts. Perhaps it was useless to McKennah as well. He checked.

O'Connor noted the hesitation of the man's betting and concluded he had a fair, but unspectacular hand. Afraid to drive him to fold, he bet only fifty thousand again, which McKennah saw.

They looked at each other over the sea of money as the fifth card, the river, slid out.

It was a king.

As delighted as O'Connor was, he regretted that this amazing hand – four of a kind – hadn't hit the table when more people were in the game. It was likely that McKennah had a functional hand at best and that there'd be a limit to how much O'Connor could raise before his opponent folded.

As the next round of betting progressed, they goosed the pot up a bit – another hundred and fifty thousand dollars.

Finally, concerned that McKennah would sense his overconfidence, O'Connor decided to buy time. 'Check.' He tapped the table with his knuckles.

A ripple through the audience. Why was he doing that?

McKennah looked him over closely. Then said, 'Five hundred K.'

And pushed the bet out.

The crowd gasped.

It was a bluff, O'Connor thought instantly. The only thing McKennah could have that would beat O'Connor was a straight flush. But, as Diane had made him learn over the past several weeks, the odds of that were very small.

And, damn it, he wanted his bump.

O'Connor said in a matter-of-fact voice, 'All in,' pushing every penny of his into the huge pile of cash on the table, nearly a million and a half dollars.

'Gentlemen, please show your cards.'

O'Connor turned over his kings. The crowd erupted in applause.

And they then fell completely silent when McKennah turned over the modest three and five of hearts to reveal his inside straight flush.

O'Connor let out a slow breath, closed his eyes momentarily and smiled.

He stood and, before taking the Walk of Shame, shook the hand of the man who'd just won himself one hell of a bump, not to mention more than a million dollars.

The weeks that followed the airing of *Go For Broke* were not the best of Mike O'Connor's life.

The loss of a quarter-million dollars hurt more than he wanted to admit.

More troubling, he thought he'd get some publicity. But in fact there was virtually none whatsoever. Oh, he got some phone calls. But they were mostly about the foiled robbery attempt and Dillon McKennah's rescue. He finally stopped returning the reporters' calls.

His pilot for *Stories* was now completely dead, and nobody was the least interested in hiring him for anything other than things like Viagra or Cialis commercials.

'I can't do it, honey,' he said to Diane.

And she'd laughed, saying, 'It wouldn't be truth-in-advertising anyway, not with you.'

And so he puttered around the house, painted the guest room. Played a little golf.

He even considered helping Diane sell real estate. He sat around the house and watched TV and movies from Netflix and On Demand.

And then one day, several weeks after the poker show, he happened to be playing couch potato and watching a World War II adventure film from the sixties. Mike O'Connor had seen it when it first came out, when he was just a boy. He'd loved it then and he'd loved it the times he'd seen it in the intervening years.

But now he realized there was something about it he'd missed. He sat up and remained riveted throughout the film.

Fascinating.

Long after the movie was over he continued to sit and think about it. He realized that he could identify with the people in the movie. They were driven and they were desperate.

He remembered a line from *Homicide Detail*. It had stuck with him all these years. His character, tough, rule-bending Detective Olson, had said to his sergeant, 'The man's desperate. And you know what desperation does – it turns you into a hero or it turns you into a villain. Don't ever forget that.'

Mike O'Connor rose from the couch and headed to his closet.

'Hey, Mike. How you doing? I'm sorry it didn't work out. That last hand. Phew. That was a cliff-hanger.'

'I saw the ratings,' O'Connor said to Aaron Felter.

'They weren't bad.'

Not bad? No, O'Connor thought, they were over-the-top amazing. They were close to OJ confessing on *Oprah*, with Dr Phil pitching in the psychobabble.

'So.' Silence rolled along for a moment. 'What're you up to next?'

Felter was pleased to see him, but his attitude said that a deal was a deal. This was true in Hollywood just as much as on Wall Street. O'Connor had taken a chance and lost, and the rules of business meant that his and the producer's arrangement was now concluded.

'Taking some time off. Rewriting a bit of *Stories*.'

'Ah. Good. You know what goes around comes around.'

O'Connor wasn't sure that it did. Or even what the hell the phrase meant. But he smiled and nodded.

Silence, during which the producer was, of course, wondering what exactly O'Connor was doing here.

So the actor got right down to it.

'Let me ask you a question, Aaron. You like old movies, right? Like your dad and I used to talk about.'

Another pause. Felter glanced at the spotless glass frames of his posters covering the walls. 'Sure. Who doesn't?'

A lot of people didn't, O'Connor was thinking; they liked modern films. Oh, there was nothing wrong with that. In fifty years people would be treasuring some of today's movies the way O'Connor treasured films like *Bonnie and Clyde*, *M*A*S*H* or *Shane*.

Every generation ought to like its own darlings best.

'You know, I was thinking about *Go For Broke*. And guess what it reminded me of?'

'Couldn't tell you.'

'A movie I just saw on TV.'

'Really? About a poker showdown? An old Western?'

'No. *The Guns of Navarone*.' He nodded at the poster to O'Connor's right.

'*Go For Broke* reminded you of that?'

'And that's not all. It also reminded me of *The Magnificent Seven*, *The Wild Bunch*, *The Dirty Dozen*, *Top Gun*, *Saving Private Ryan*, *Alien* . . . In fact, a lot of films. Action films.'

'I don't follow, Mike.'

'Well, think about . . . what was the word you used when we were talking about *Stories*? "Formula". You start with a group of diverse heroes and send 'em on a mission. One by one they're eliminated before the big third-act scene. Like *The Guns of Navarone*. It's a great film, by the way.'

'One of the best,' Felter agreed uncertainly.

'Group of intrepid commandos. Eliminated one by one . . . But in a certain order, of course: sort of in reverse order of their youth or sex appeal. The stiff white guy's one of the first to go – say, Anthony Quayle in *Navarone*. Or Robert Vaughn in *The Magnificent Seven*. Next we lose the minorities. Yaphet Kotto in *Alien*. Then the hotheaded young kid is bound to go. James Darren. Shouldn't he have ducked when he was facing down the Nazi with the machine gun? I would have. But, no, he just kept going till he was dead.

'That brings us to women. If they're not the leads, they better be careful, Tyne Daly in one of the *Dirty Harry* films. And even if they survive, it's usually so they can hang on the arm of the man who wins the showdown. And who does that bring us to finally? The main opponents? The older white guy versus the enthusiastic young white guy. Tom Cruise versus Nicholson. Denzel versus Gene Hackman. Clint Eastwood versus Lee Van Cleef. DiCaprio versus all the first-class passengers on *Titanic*.

'Kind of like the contestants on the show. Stodgy white guy, minority, hot-headed youth, the woman . . . Bingham, Stone, Kresge, Sandy. And after they were gone, who was left? Old me versus young Dillon McKennah.'

'I think you're pissed off about something, Mike. Why don't you just tell me?'

'The game was rigged, Aaron. I know it. You wrote your quote "reality" show like it was a classic Hollywood Western or war movie. You knew how it was going to come out from the beginning. You followed the formula perfectly.'

'And why the fuck would I do that?'

'Because I think you're trying to get a movie financing package moving with Dillon McKennah. That caper film he was talking about. He'd shot himself in the foot with *Town House* and that other crap he appeared in. He needed a bump – for both of you.'

Felter was speechless for a moment. Then he looked down. 'We talked about a few things, that's all, Dillon and me. Hell, you and I talked about *Stories*. That's my business. Oh, come on, Mike. Don't embarrass yourself. It was a fucking pissant reality show. There was no guarantee of a bump.'

'But it did get Dillon a bump. A big one. And you know why? Because of the robbery. The more I thought about it, the more I realized that was a classic Act Two reversal – according to the formula of scriptwriting.

You know how that works. Big plot twist three-quarters of the way through. *Guns of Navarone*? The young Greek girl, Gia Scala, the supposed patriot, turns out to be the traitor. She destroys the detonators. How're the commandos going to blow up the German guns now? We're sitting on the edge of our seats, wondering.'

'What does that have to do with anything?'

'The robbery, Aaron. The attempted robbery. It was all set up, too. You arranged the whole thing. That's what made it more than boring reality TV. My God, you even added a dash of *COPS*. You got the attempt and Dillon's Steven Seagal karate moves on security camera and that night it was on YouTube and every network in the country. TV at its best. You think there wasn't a human being in the country who wasn't going to turn on the second episode of *Go For Broke* and watch Dillon and me slug it out?'

'I don't know what—'

O'Connor held up a hand. 'Now, don't embarrass yourself, Aaron. On the set of *Homicide Detail*, we had an advisor, a real cop in the LAPD. He's retired now, but we're still good buddies. I talked to him and told him I had a problem. I needed to know some facts about the case. He made some calls. First of all, the gun that Sammy Ralston had? It was a fake gun. From a studio property department. The sort they use on TV sets, the sort I carried for seven years. Second, turns out that his phone records show Ralston called a prisoner, Joey Fadden, in Lompoc prison a few weeks ago. The same prisoner that you interviewed as part of that series you shot on California prisons last year. I think you paid Joey to get Ralston's name . . . Ah, ah, ah, let me finish. Gets better. Third, Ralston keeps talking about this mysterious biker named Jake who put the whole thing together and nobody knows about.'

'Jake.'

'I dug up my fake shield from the TV show and went to the bar on Melrose where Ralston said he met with Jake. I had a mug shot with me.'

'A—'

'From *Variety*. It was a picture of you and your assistant. The big one. The bartender recognized him. You got him to play the role of Jake, costume, fake tats, the whole thing . . . I just walked past his office, by the way. There're posters on his wall, too. One of them's *Brokeback Mountain*. Starring Jake Gyllenhaal. Jake. Think about it.'

Felter said nothing, but his expression was essentially: Shit.

'Dillon knew about the setup. He knew about the fake gun. That's why he took on a guy who was armed. He wasn't in any danger. It was all planned. All planned for the bump.'

O'Connor shook his head. 'I should've guessed before. I mean, the final hand, Aaron? You know how most poker games end: two guys half-comatose from lack of sleep, and one beats the other with three sixes over a pair of threes. A four-of-a-kind versus a straight flush? That only happens in the movies. That's not real life.'

'How could I rig the game?'

'Because you hired a sleight-of-hand artist as the dealer. You saw his card tricks when we met him . . . I ran him down. And I checked the tapes. There were no close-ups of his hands. I've got his name and address. Oh, and I also got the phone number of the gaming commission in Nevada.'

The man closed his eyes. Maybe he was thinking of excuses and explanations.

O'Connor almost hoped he'd say something. Which would give the actor a chance to throw out his famous tag line from the old TV series. Save it for the judge.

But Felter didn't try to excuse himself. He looked across the desk, as if it were a poker table, and he said, 'So where do we go from here?'

'To put it in terms of television, Aaron,' Mike O'Connor said, pulling several thick envelopes out of his briefcase, 'let's make a deal.'

A TEXTBOOK CASE

Physical evidence cannot be wrong; it cannot perjure itself; it cannot be wholly absent . . . Only human failure to find, study, and understand it can diminish its value.

                 – Paul L. Kirk, *Crime Investigation:*
                 Physical Evidence and the Police Laboratory

1

'The worst I've ever seen,' he whispered.

She listened to the young man's words and decided that was a bit ironic, since he couldn't have been more than mid-twenties. How many crime scenes could he have run?

But she noted, too, that his round, handsome face, crested by a crew-cut scalp, was genuinely troubled. He had a military air about him and didn't seem the sort to get flustered.

Something particularly troubling was down there – in the pit of the underground garage they stood in front of, delineated by yellow fluttering tape, the pit where the woman had been murdered early that morning.

Amelia Sachs was gearing up at the staging area outside the bland apartment building in this equally style-challenged neighborhood of Manhattan, East Twenty-sixth Street. Here were residential low-rises from the 1950s and '60s, some brownstones, restaurants that had been born Italian twenty years ago and had converted to Middle Eastern. For greenery, short, anemic trees, striving grass, tiny shrubs in huge concrete planters.

Sachs ripped open the plastic bag containing the disposable scene suit: white Tyvek coveralls, booties, head cap, cuffed nitrile gloves.

'You'll want the N95, too,' the young officer told her. His name was Marko, maybe first, probably last. Sachs hadn't bothered to find out.

'Chemical problem? Bio?' Nodding toward the pit.

The N95 was a particulate respirator that filtered out a lot of the bad crap you found at some crime scenes. The dangerous ones.

'Just, you'll want it.'

She didn't like the respirators and usually wore a simple surgical mask. But if Marko told her there was a problem inside, she'd go with it.

Worst I've ever seen . . .

Sachs continued to pull on the protective gear. She was claustrophobic and didn't like the layers of swaddling that crime-scene searchers had to put up with, but were necessary to protect them from dangerous substances at the scene. More importantly, the outfit protected the *scene* from contaminants police might throw off – their hairs, fibers, flecks of skin and other assorted trace they might cart about with them. (One man had nearly been arrested because a tomato seed had linked him to a murder – until it was discovered that the seed came from the shoe of a crime-scene officer, who'd neglected to wear booties . . . and who was soon, thanks to Lincoln Rhyme, a *former* crime-scene officer.)

Several other cars arrived, including that of the Major Cases detective lieutenant, Lon Sellitto, an unmarked Crown Victoria. The car was spotless and still dripping from the car wash. Sellitto, on the other hand, was typically disheveled. He wore an unpressed white shirt, a skewed tie and a rumpled suit, though fortunately in wrinkle-concealing navy blue (Sachs recalled that he'd worn seersucker once and never again; even he had thought he looked like tousled bed sheets). Sachs had given up trying to guess Sellitto's age. He was in that timeless mid-fifties that all detectives first-class on the NYPD seem to fall into.

He was also an institution and he caught a few awed looks from the uniforms now as he pushed his way through the crowd of gawkers and with some difficulty, considering his weight, ducked under the yellow tape.

He joined Sachs and Marko, who wasn't particularly awed but clearly respectful.

'Detective.'

Sellitto didn't have any idea who he was but nodded back. He said to Sachs, 'How is he?'

Which would mean only one 'he'.

'Fine. Been back for two days. Actually wanted to come to the scene.'

Lincoln Rhyme, the former head of the NYPD Crime Scene operation and now a forensic consultant, had been undergoing a series of medical procedures to improve his condition – he was a quadriplegic, largely paralyzed from the neck down because of an accident while searching a scene years ago.

Sellitto said a sincere, 'No shit. Wanted to come. God bless him.'

Sachs gave the man a wry look. She was considerably younger and a more junior detective. But she didn't let a lot pass – from anyone. Sellitto caught the glance. 'Did that sound condescending?'

She lifted an eyebrow, meaning, 'Yep. And if Rhyme heard you say it, the reply would not be pretty.'

'Well, fuck. Good for him anyway.' He focused on the off-white apartment, the water stains on the walls, the mismatched windows, the dented air conditioners underneath them, the sad grass, sick or dying from city dogs more than from the cool air. Still, even an air-shaft studio would cost two thousand and change. When Sachs was not staying with Rhyme she was at her place in Brooklyn. Big. And it had a garden. The month was September and she'd just harvested the last crop of veggies, beating the frost by twenty-four hours.

Sachs tucked her abundant red hair up under the Tyvek cap and Velcroed closed the coveralls over her jeans and tight wool sweater. The suit fit snugly. Marko watched, somewhat discreetly. Sachs had been a fashion model before joining the NYPD. She got followed by a lot of eyes.

'Chance of the scene being hot?' she asked Marko.

It was rare for perps to stick around a murder scene and target investigators, but not unheard of.

'Doubt it,' the young officer responded. 'But . . .'

Made sense for him to hedge when it came to a scene that was apparently so horrific.

Before suiting up, Sachs had drawn and set her Glock pistol aside. She now wiped it down with an alcohol swab to remove trace and slipped it into the pocket of the coveralls. If she needed the weapon, she could get to it quickly, even fire through the cloth, if need be. That was good about Glocks. No external safeties, double action. You pointed and pulled.

Any chance of it being hot? . . .

And what the hell was so bad about the scene? How had the poor woman died? And what had happened to her before . . . or after?

She guessed it was a sado-sexual killing.

Sellitto said to Marko, 'What's the story, Officer?'

He looked back and forth from the older detective to Sachs as he gave the story. 'I'm assigned to Crime Scene in Queens, HQ, sir. I had some advanced training at the academy this morning so I was heading there, when I heard the call.'

The NYPD Academy on Twentieth Street at Second Avenue.

'Dispatch said any available. I was two blocks away so I responded. I had gear with me and I suited up before I went in.' Marko, too, was dressed in a Tyvek crime-scene outfit, minus the head covering.

'Good thinking.'

'I wouldn't have waited but the dispatch said the report was a body, not an injured victim.'

Crime scenes were always a compromise. Contamination with outside trace and obliterating important evidence could hamper or even ruin an investigation, but first responders' priority is saving lives or collaring perps who were still present. Marko had acted right.

'I looked at the scene fast then called in.'

Two other crime-scene people from the Queens headquarters had just arrived in the RRV – rapid response vehicle – containing evidence collection gear. The man and woman climbed out, she Asian, he Latino. He opened the back and they, too, got their gear. 'Hey, Marko,' he called, 'how'd you beat us? Take a chopper over here?'

The young officer gave a faint smile. But it was clear he was still troubled, presumably by what he'd seen inside.

Sellitto asked Marko, 'You know any of the players yet?'

'Just, her boyfriend called it in. That's all I know.'

The older detective said, 'I'll talk to him and get a canvass team going. You handle the scene, Amelia. We'll rendezvous back at Lincoln's.'

'Sure.'

'Detective Rhyme's going to be on the case?' Marko asked.

Rhyme was decommissioned – he'd been a detective captain – but in policing, like the military, titles tended to stick.

'Yeah,' Sellitto muttered. 'We're running it out of there.' Rhyme's townhouse was often the informal command post for cases that Sellitto drew or picked.

Marko said, 'I missed my class already. At the academy. Any chance I could stay and help out?'

Apparently the horror of the scene wasn't going to deter him.

Sellitto said, 'Detective Sachs's lead Crime Scene. Up to her.'

One of the biggest problems in law enforcement was getting enough people to help in an investigation. And you could *never* have enough crime-scene searchers. She said, 'Sure, appreciate it.' She nodded toward the entrance to the parking garage beneath the building. 'I'll take the ramp and the scene itself. You and those other teams handle the—'

Marko interrupted. 'Secondary and tertiary scenes. Entrance and egress points. I took Detective Rhyme's course.'

He said this proudly.

'Good. Now tell me exactly where the vic is.'

'Go down the ramp two levels. She's on the bottom one at the back. The only car there.' He paused. 'Can't miss it.'

Worst . . .

'Okay. Now, get to those scenes.'

'Yes'm, Detective. We'll get on the grid.'

Sachs nearly smiled. He'd slung the last word out like a greeting among initiates in a secret club. Walking the grid . . . It was Rhyme's coined phrase for searching a scene in the most comprehensive way possible, covering every square inch – twice.

Marko joined his colleagues.

'Hey, you're a ma'am now, Amelia.'

'It was just an 'm. Don't make me older than I feel.'

'You could be his . . . older sister.'

'Funny.' Then Sachs said, 'Get a bio on the vic, too, Lon. As much as you can.'

For some years now she had worked with Lincoln Rhyme, and under his tutelage she'd become a fine crime-scene searcher and a solid forensic analyst. But her first skill and love in policing was people – a legacy from her father, who was an NYPD patrol officer all his life. She loved the psychology of crime, which Lincoln Rhyme tended to disparage as the 'soft' side of policing. But Sachs believed that sometimes the physical evidence didn't lead you to the perp's doorstep. Sometimes you needed to look closely at the people involved, at their passions, their fears, their motives. All the details of their lives.

Sellitto hulked off, gesturing Patrol Division officers to join him, and they huddled to arrange for canvass teams.

Sachs opened a vinyl bag and withdrew a high-def video camera rig. As she'd done with her weapon, she wiped this down, too, with the alcohol swabs. She slipped the lightweight unit over the plastic cap encasing her head. The small camera sat just above her ear and a nearly invisible stalk mike arced toward her mouth. Sachs clicked the video and audio switches and winced when loud static slugged her eardrum. She adjusted it.

'Rhyme, you there?'

A moment of clatter. 'Yes, yes, you there, you at the scene? Are you on the grid, Sachs? Time's wasting.'

'Just got here. I'm ready to go. How are you feeling?'

'Fine, why wouldn't I be?'

A three-hour microsurgery operation a couple of days ago?

She didn't answer.

'What's that light? Jesus, it's bright.'

She'd glanced at the sky and a slash of morning sun would have blasted into the video camera and onto the high-def monitor Rhyme would be looking at. 'Sorry.'

In a gloved hand Sachs picked up the evidence collection bag – a small suitcase – and a flashlight, and began walking down the ramp into the garage.

She was glancing at her feet. Odd.

Rhyme caught it, too. 'What'm I looking at, Sachs?'

'Trash.' The ramp was filthy. A nearby Dumpster was on its side and the dozen garbage bags inside had been pulled out and ripped open. The contents covered the ground.

It was a mess.

'Hard to hear you, Sachs.'

'I'm wearing an N95.'

'Chemical, gas?'

'That first responding told me it was a good idea.'

'It's really dark,' the criminalist then muttered.

The video camera automatically went to low-light mode – that greenish tint from spy movies and reality TV – but there were limits to how much bits and bytes could convey.

Eyes, too, for that matter. It *was* dark. She noted the bulbs were missing. She paused.

'What?' he asked.

'The bulbs aren't just missing, Rhyme. Somebody took them out and broke them. They're shattered.'

'If our doer's behind it, that means he probably isn't from the building. He doesn't know where the switch is and didn't want to take the time to find it.'

Count on Rhyme to come to conclusions like that . . . from a mere wisp of an observation.

'But why broken?'

'Maybe just being cautious. Tough to get prints or lift other trace from a shattered bulb. Hmm, he could be a smart one.'

Rhyme, Sachs was pleased to note, was in a good mood. The medical treatments – complicated, expensive and more than a little risky – were going well. He'd regained significant movement in both arms and hands. Not sensation; nothing would bring that back, at least not as medical science stood nowadays, but he was far less dependent than he had once been and that meant the world to a man like Lincoln Rhyme.

She finally had to resort to her flashlight. She clicked on the long Maglite and continued past a dozen parked cars, some of whose owners were undoubtedly furious that they had not been allowed to use their vehicles, because of the minor inconvenience of a murder near where they'd parked. But, on the other hand, there'd also be plenty who'd do whatever they could to help nail the suspect.

Nothing teaches you human nature like being a cop.

Sachs felt a ping of the arthritis pain that plagued her in her knees, and slowed. She then stopped altogether, not because of joint discomfort, but because of noises. Creaks and taps. A door closed – an interior door, not a car. It seemed a long way off, but she couldn't tell. The walls muffled and confused sounds.

Footsteps?

She turned suddenly, nearly swapping flashlight for Glock.

No, just dripping water, from a pipe. Water dribbled down the incline, mixing with the papers and other trash on the floor; there was even more garbage here.

'Okay, Rhyme,' she said. 'I'm almost at the bottom level. She and her car're around that corner.'

'Go on, Sachs.'

She realized she'd stopped. She was uneasy. 'I just can't figure out all this garbage.'

Sachs began walking again, slowly making her way to the corner, paused, set down the suitcase and drew her gun. In the flashlight beam was a faint haze. She lifted the mask off, inhaled and coughed. There was pungency to the air. Paint maybe, or chemicals. And smoke. She found the source. Yes, some newspapers were smoldering in the corner.

That's what Marko had been referring to.

'Okay, I'm going into the scene, Rhyme.'

Thinking of Marko's words.

The worst . . .

Weapon up, she turned the corner and aimed the powerful wide-angle beam of the flashlight at the victim and her vehicle.

Sachs gasped. 'Oh, Jesus, Rhyme. Oh, no . . .'

2

At 4 p.m. Amelia Sachs walked into Lincoln Rhyme's townhouse on Central Park West.

Rhyme found himself glaring toward her – partly because of the powerful autumn light streaming in from the open door behind her, partly because of his impatience.

The crime-scene search had taken forever, six and a half hours to be precise, the longest for a single scene he could remember.

Sachs had told him that the young officer who'd been first response reported it was the worst scene he'd ever come across. Partly, he meant that the victim had died a horrific, sadistic death. But equally he was referring to the complete contamination of the scene.

'I've never seen anything like it,' Sachs had told Rhyme through the microphone. And gazing at the high-def screen, he had to admit that he hadn't either. Every square inch of the area – from the ramp to the garage floor to the victim's car and surrounding area – was obliterated, covered with trash. And painted, powdered, coated with liquids, dusted with dirt and powders.

It was actually hard to locate the victim herself for all the mess.

Rhyme now piloted his red Storm Arrow wheelchair to the front door, through which Sachs was carrying a large carton filled with evidence collection bags. She explained that the first responder, a crime-scene officer named Marko, and she had sped here in their private vehicles – his an SUV. Rhyme noted that the vehicle was loaded to the gunwales with cartons of evidence. Young man, picking up a massive carton, had a military air about him. He did a double take when he saw Rhyme. He nodded.

Rhyme ignored him, focusing on the astonishing quantity of evidence. Sachs's ancient Ford was filled, too. He didn't see how she'd been able to drive it.

'Christ,' he muttered.

Lincoln Rhyme had a handsome face, hair a bit long for NYPD regulation, but that mattered not at all since he was no longer NYPD. His nose was prominent, his lips full, though they grew thin quickly, like irises dilating in light, when he was displeased, which occurred with some frequency, given his impatience and pole-vault high standards for crime-scene work. A pink scar was visible at the base of his throat; it resembled a bullet wound but in fact it was from the ventilator tube, which had kept him alive after the accident.

A breath of autumn wind blew through the open door and a comma of black hair tickled his forehead. He clumsily lifted his right hand to brush it away, a gesture that would have been impossible several years ago, when he'd been completely paralyzed below the neck. Those little things – the inability to scratch an itch, the impossibility of feeding oneself, the incessant *nag* of the condition – were what wore you down, more than the broader consequences of cataclysmic injury. At the moment, his left arm was bandaged to his body; he'd had additional surgery to give that limb the same awkward, but miraculous, skill as the right.

His brown eyes squinting at the curbside, Rhyme lost count of the boxes Marko was unloading. He spun around in his chair and steamed back toward the townhouse's parlor. 'Thom! Thom!'

The man he was shouting for was practically in sotto voce distance, ten feet away, though not quite in sight. 'I'm right here, you don't need to—'

'We have to *do* something with this,' Rhyme said as his caregiver appeared. The young man was today wearing what he usually did on the job: dress slacks, tan today, a dark blue shirt and a floral tie.

'Hi, Amelia.'

Sachs was coming through the front door.

'Thom.' He took the box from her and she headed out for another shipment.

Rhyme glanced from the carton to Thom Reston's face. 'Look at that! And look outside. We need to find places to organize it. Everything in the den . . . it has to go!'

'I'll clear some space.'

'We can't clear it. We have to empty it. I want everything gone.'

'All right.' The aide took off the yellow kitchen gloves he was wearing and began sliding furniture out of the room.

The den was what served as the living room for the townhouse; the other room that had been intended for social liaisons in the Victorian era, the parlor, Rhyme had converted to a forensics lab, as extensive as those in many medium-sized towns. Rhyme was by no means wealthy, but he'd received a good settlement when he'd been injured and he charged a lot for his forensic consulting activities. Much of the income went right back into his company and he had bought as many forensic 'toys' as he could afford (that's how Amelia Sachs had referred to them, after seeing his eyes light up when there'd been a new acquisition; to Rhyme they were simply tools).

'Mel!' Rhyme was shouting again.

This time he was speaking to his associate, who was at an evidence examination station in the parlor. NYPD Detective Mel Cooper, blond though balding and nerdish, was Rhyme's number-one lab man.

Cooper had arrived three hours ago from Queens, where he both worked, at the police department's Crime Scene headquarters, and lived. He would handle much of the lab work in what was being called the Unsub 26 homicide case, so named because the killer, an unknown subject, had killed the victim on East Twenty-sixth Street. Cooper had ready sheets of sterile examination paper covering work surfaces, friction ridge equipment to find latent prints, microscopes, scales, the density gradient unit, and the dozens of other tools of the trade needed for forensic analysis.

He, too, was staring at the increasing piles of collection bags, boxes and jars that Sachs, Marko, and now Thom were carting in and trying to find a place for.

'This is from *one* scene?'

'Apparently,' Rhyme said.

'And it wasn't a mass disaster?' This was the quantity of evidence that resulted from plane crashes and bomb blasts.

'One unsub, one vic.'

Cooper glanced around the parlor and into the hallway in dismay. 'You remember that line in *Jaws*, Lincoln? They're after the shark.'

'Shark,' Rhyme said absently.

'The big shark. They get their first glimpse of it – it's really big – and one of them says, "I think we're going to need a bigger boat". That's us.'

'Boat?'

'*Jaws*. The movie.'

'I never saw it,' Rhyme muttered.

The murder weapon was about the only easy part of the analysis: it was the victim's car.

The killer had snuck up behind and hit her, probably with a piece of rock or cinderblock, hard enough to stun, but not kill, her. He'd then taped her eyes, mouth, feet and arms and dragged her behind the car. Then Unsub 26 had started the Prius and backed it onto her abdomen, leaving it there. The Toyota is front heavy, with the rear weight about 530 kilos, Rhyme had learned. Only one wheel was resting on the victim, which would have cut down some of the pressure, but the medical examiner said the internal damage was devastating. Still, it took her close to an hour to die – mostly from shock and bleeding.

But apart from the COD determination, Rhyme and his team had made no other evidentiary discoveries. In fact, all they'd been able to do was catalog the evidence, everyone chipping in: Sachs, Cooper and Marko. Even Thom was helping.

Lon Sellitto arrived.

Oh, Lord no . . .

Rhyme had to laugh, though bitterly, seeing that the big detective was carrying yet another massive box of evidence collection bags.

'Not more?' asked a dismayed Mel Cooper; usually he was the epitome of detached calm.

'They found another exit route.' The big detective handed off the box to Marko. 'But this should be the end of it.' Then he frowned as he looked around at the hundreds of collection and sample bags lining the walls throughout the first floor of the townhouse. 'I don't have any idea what the fuck's going on here.'

But Lincoln Rhyme did.

'Oh, what's going on, Lon, is our unsub's smart. He's *brilliant*.' Rhyme looked around. 'I say "he", but remember, we keep open minds. It could be a she, too. Never make assumptions.'

'He, she or it,' Sellitto muttered. 'I still don't get it.'

The criminalist continued, 'You know Locard's Principle?'

'Sorta.'

'How about you, Marko?'

The young officer blinked and answered, as if reciting. A hundred years ago, he said, the famed French criminalist Edmond Locard developed a theory: In every crime there is an exchange of evidence between the perpetrator and the victim or the scene. The trace elements swapped may be extremely minuscule but they always exist and in most cases can lead to the perp if the investigator has the intelligence and resources to discover them.

'Close enough. Well, at the scene' – Rhyme's hand rose unsteadily and he pointed at the pictures Sachs had shot of the victim's body and that Cooper had printed out – 'we know the unsub left something of himself. He *had* to. Locard's Principle is never wrong. But, you see, he *knew* he'd leave something.'

Sachs said, 'And rather than trying to clean up all traces of himself afterward, he did the opposite. He covered up many clues as to who he is, why he's doing this, what he has planned next.'

Brilliant . . .

Too much evidence instead of too little.

Rhyme had to admit he felt a grudging admiration for the unsub. Last year, he had appeared in a documentary on the A&E network, about a woman's conviction for homicide in Florida. She had been sentenced to life on the basis of evidence that turned out to have been tainted – the crime-scene officer had first searched the site of the homicide and then the suspect's house, accidentally depositing a tiny paint chip from the murder site on the woman's clothes as he gathered them in her house. This chip placed her at the scene and the jury convicted. A review of forensic evidence collection procedures revealed that the officer had been told to use the same gloves in searching both scenes, as a money-saving measure. In a second trial, the woman was found not guilty.

Rhyme had been on the show to discuss the benefits and the risks of evidence in investigations. He'd commented that all it took was one or two minuscule bits of trace or foreign objects to throw a case off entirely.

In *this* situation, Unsub 26 had managed to taint the scene with thousands of smokescreens.

Rhyme glanced at Cooper. 'How long before we can get started?'

'Still be an hour or two just to categorize everything.'

'Ah.' He wasn't pleased.

Sachs asked Sellitto, 'What'd you and the canvassing teams find out about the vic?'

'Okay,' the detective said, pulling out his notebook, 'her name was Jane Levine, thirty-one. Assistant marketing manager for a brokerage firm downtown. No criminal history. She'd been going out with her boyfriend for seven, eight months. He was the guy who reported her missing then found the body. I talked to him for a while but then he lost it. I mean, totally.'

Rhyme noticed Sachs's abundant lips tighten at this news and he guessed her reaction was how not only the loss but witnessing the horror would affect the man for the rest of his life: that last searing image of his lover dying under such unthinkable circumstances. Rhyme knew that Sachs struggled with the human side of crime – not, as one would think, pushing it away. Rather, she embraced the horror and wanted to keep it raw. She believed it made her a more empathetic and, therefore, a better cop.

Though he took the opposite approach – remaining aloof – this was one of the things he loved her for.

He turned his attention back to Sellitto, who was continuing his discussion. 'Now, I checked. He's alibi'd out, the boyfriend.' Family and acquaintances are the number-one suspects – and the number-one guilty perps – in homicides. Sellitto continued, 'He was in Connecticut with his parents last night. He got back in the city about eight this morning and went to her apartment. We data mined him. Wits, tickets and security cams confirm he was there when she died. GPS, too. He's clean.'

That young crime-scene guy asked, 'Rape, Detective?'

'Nothing sexual, no. No robbery. She still had her keys, wallet, purse, jewelry.'

Sachs asked, 'Any former boyfriends, stalkers?'

'According to the boyfriend and her sister, over the last couple years she went out with one guy from work, one guy from her health club, one guy from church. Real casual. The sister said they all ended okay and there were no hard feelings. Anyway the last one she broke up with was about six months ago just before she met the current guy.'

The detective continued, 'No organized crime connection, not surprising, and she wasn't a whistleblower or witness. I can't find a motive at all.'

Rhyme didn't much care for motive. His theory was that why people killed was largely irrelevant. A paranoid schizophrenic could kill someone because he believed that person was part of the advance guard from a planet in Alpha Centauri bent on capturing the world. What got him convicted was his prints on the knife, not his mad thinking.

'Well, that tells us *something*, right?' Rhyme asked, grimacing. 'If there's no boyfriend-done-it, rapist-done-it, mugger-done-it scenario, I'm thinking it's a psycho.' He happened to be looking at the young crime-scene officer. 'Oh, I know they don't use that word any more. But it's a lot more felicitous than "individual displaying antisocial personality disorder traits".'

Marko nodded, obviously having no idea what to think about that pronouncement.

It was Sellitto who explained, 'What Linc's saying is that he could be a serial doer. Meaning he's going to strike again.'

'You think so, sir?' the young man asked.

'If that's the case it also means he's picking victims at random. And somewhere in that morass' – a nod toward the mountains of evidence – 'is the answer to who the next one's going to be.'

3

Mel Cooper was wrong.

It took nearly seven more hours to finish just categorizing the evidence. At three fifteen in the morning they decided to knock off for the night.

Sachs stayed with Rhyme, as she did three or four nights a week, and Cooper slept in the guest room. Sellitto returned to his house, where his partner, Rachel, whom he described as his 'Better Other', was waiting for him. Marko headed back to his home, wherever that might be.

By nine the next morning the team, minus the young c-s officer, was back.

As in every case they worked, Rhyme asked for a whiteboard chart listing the evidence. Sachs did the honors. She moved stiffly to the board. Rhyme noted the hitch in her leg; she suffered from arthritis and the extended search in a damp, subterranean garage had taken its toll. Once or twice, reaching to the top to start a new entry, she winced.

Finally she finished – all three boards in Rhyme's parlor were required. And that was just to list what the teams had found. There was no analysis at all, much less insightful deductions that could be made about sources, or inferences as to prospective victims.

Everyone in the room fell silent and stared.

Unsub Twenty-Six Homicide

- Location: 832 E. 26th Street
- Victim: Jane Levine, thirty-one
- COD: Internal injuries from weight of vehicle
- TOD: Approximately 4:00 a.m.

- General notes:
    - Robbery not motive
    - No sexual assault
    - Victim was not a known witness, no one appeared to be delivering 'messages'
    - No drug or other illegal or organized crime connection
    - No known enemies
    - Present boyfriend has alibi
    - Dated casually men met through work, health club, church
    - No bad breakups or stalkers
    - Appears to be a random crime, likely a serial perpetrator
- Evidence:
    - Approximately 82 pounds of household trash, covering auto ramp to garage and floor of garage, probably from Dumpster in apartment building
    - Duct tape
        - used to subdue victim
        - four nearly empty rolls located, probably taken from trash
            - to be determined if one was the source of the tape used on victim
    - Hair, some naturally detached from follicles, some cut
        - approximately 930 separate samples
        - human, animal? To be determined
    - Shattered cinderblock
        - one piece used to strike victim from behind
        - all the pieces were spray painted, obscuring evidence (see paint below)
    - Newspapers, magazines, direct mail pieces, apparently from trash and recycling bins; used, many items handled; therefore containing friction ridge prints

- Plastic spoons, forks, knives, food containers, beverage cups, coffee cartons, all used
  - 185 samples
  - DNA, to be determined
- Swabs of human and/or animal organic materials, revealed by alternative light source
  - saliva, semen, plasma, sweat, vaginal fluids?
  - possibly delivered to the scene via strewing trash and medical waste
  - 742 swabs taken from different locations
  - DNA, to be determined
- Fibers, cloth
  - 439 samples
- Fibers, nylon
  - 230 samples
- Fibers, metal
  - 25 samples
- Paint
  - used throughout the site, presumably to obscure actual evidence
  - oil-based spray
  - cans located, nearly empty, suggesting they were found in trash, rather than purchased
  - eight to ten friction ridge prints on each can
- Latex gloves, used
  - 48 separate L/R hand gloves
  - DNA, to be determined
  - Friction ridge prints, to be determined
- Dirt, dust
  - approximately two pounds in total
  - indeterminate number of sources
  - at least 12 main variations in composition
- Food crumbs
  - 34 samples
- Leaves
  - 249 collected
  - from approximately 27 known trees/bushes

- 73 unidentified
- Grass, lawn
  - 376 samples
- Grass, decorative
  - 64 samples
- Excrement
  - human/animal, to be determined
  - DNA, to be determined
- Light bulbs
  - from parking garage
  - removed, then shattered
- Powdered substances
  - 214 samples
  - non-narcotic
  - possibly over-the-counter medicine, pulverized
  - laundry detergent
    - eight different brands
- Liquid substances still liquid or dried residue
  - bleach
  - ammonia
  - dish soap
  - alcohol
  - water
  - soft drinks
  - coffee
  - gasoline
  - milk
- Organic tissue
  - 346 samples
  - human/animal, to be determined
  - DNA, to be determined
  - could be food
- Fingernail clippings
- Bones
  - 42 samples
  - human/animal, to be determined (apparently animal)
  - DNA, to be determined

- could be food
- some definitely fish bones, chicken or other fowl
- Footprints
  - 23, male and female, 18 different sizes, five associated with the victim's shoes
  - prints of feet in crime scene, surgical booties
- Vapors in crime scene
  - small fire set in corner, newspapers, possibly to obscure smell of the unsub's aftershave or other odor
  - spray paint fumes
- Disposable cigarette lighters
  - 18 separate lighters found
  - probably taken from trash – most empty of butane
  - 64 friction ridge prints

Rhyme barked, 'The chart reads like the table of contents in my goddamn book.'

Several years ago Rhyme had written a textbook, *A Comprehensive Guide to Evidence Collection and Analysis*, which was a best-seller, at least in the law enforcement community if not in the *Times*.

Sachs: 'I don't know where to start, Rhyme.'

Well, guess what? Rhyme thought. I don't either. He was recalling another passage in the book.

While every scene will contain at least *some* transferred evidence from the perpetrator, it may never be discovered, as a practical matter, because of budget and time constraints. Similarly, there may be too much evidence obscuring the relevant clues, which will similarly render effective analysis impossible.

'It's even more brilliant than I thought,' the criminalist mused. 'Getting most of what he used in the crime from the trash – covered with other people's prints. And contaminating the scene with, literally, pounds of trace and other garbage. For things he couldn't obscure – he could hardly bring a dozen shoes with him or somebody else's fingers – he wore booties and gloves.'

Sachs said, 'But those can't be his gloves, all the latex ones. He wouldn't leave them behind.'

'Probably not. But we can't afford *not* to analyze them, can we? And he knows it.'

'I suppose not,' said Mel Cooper, as discouraged as the rest of them. Rhyme believed the tech had had a ballroom dancing date with his girlfriend of many years last night. They were competitors and apparently quite accomplished. Lincoln Rhyme did not follow dancing.

'And he . . .' Rhyme's voice faded as several thoughts came to him.

'Linc—'

Rhyme lifted his right arm and waved Sellitto silent as he continued to stare.

Finally the criminalist said excitedly, 'Think about this. This person knows evidence. And that means he knows there's a good chance he's got some trace or other clue on him that could lead us to his identity or to the next victim he's got in mind.'

'Right,' Lon Sellitto said. 'And?'

Rhyme was peering at the charts. 'So what did he use the most of to contaminate the scene?'

Sachs said, 'Trash—'

'No, that was a general smokescreen. It just happened to be there. Something specific, I'm looking for.'

Cooper shoved his Harry Potter glasses higher on his nose as he read the charts. He offered, 'Fibers, hair, general trace—'

'Yes, but those are givens at every crime scene. I want to know what's *special*?'

'What's the most unique, you mean?' Sellitto offered.

'No, I don't mean that, Lon,' Rhyme said sourly. 'Because something is either unique or not. You don't have varying degrees of oneness.'

'Haven't had a grammar lesson from you lately, Lincoln. I was wondering if you'd quit the schoolmarm union.'

Drawing a smile from Thom, who was delivering coffee and pastries.

Sachs was studying the chart. She said, 'Dirt and . . . vegetation.'

Rhyme squinted. 'Yes, good. That could be it. He knew he picked up some trace either where the perp lives or works, or where he's been scoping out another victim, and he had to cover that up.'

'Which means,' Sachs said, 'a garden, park or yard?'

'I'd say yes. Soil and the greenery. That could hold the clue. It cuts the search down a bit . . . We should start there. Then anything else?' Rhyme reviewed the chart again. 'The detergent and cleansers – why'd he sprinkle or pour so many of those in the scene? We need to start working our way through those, too.' Rhyme looked around. 'That kid, Marko? Why isn't he here?'

Sachs said, 'He called. He had something he had to do back in Queens, HQ. But he'd still like to help us out if we need him. You want me to call him?'

'I do, Sachs. Fast!'

An exhausting time.

A business trip with her boss to California and back in under twenty-four hours.

Productive, necessary, but stressful.

They were now cabbing it into the city from JFK, where their flight had landed at 6 p.m. She was exhausted, a bit tipsy from the two glasses of wine, and mildly resenting the three hours that you lost flying east.

Her boss, late forties, tanned and trim, now slipped his iPhone away – he'd been making a date for tomorrow – and then turned to her with a laugh. 'Did you hear them? They really used the word "unpack".'

As in 'unpack it for us', meaning presumably explain to the network the story they'd come to pitch.

'Since when did "explain" fall off the A-list of words?'

Simone smiled. 'And the net executive? She said the concept was definitely "seismic". You know, you need a translator app in Hollywood.'

Her boss laughed and Simone eyed him obliquely. A great guy. Funny, smart, in great shape thanks to a health club regimen that bordered on the religious. He was also extremely talented, which meant extremely successful.

Oh, and single, too.

He sure was a big helping of temptation, you bet, but Simone, despite being in her mid-thirties and sans boyfriend at the moment, had success-fully corralled the baby and the lonely hormones; she could look at her boss objectively. The man's obsessive craving for detail and perfection, his intensity would drive her crazy if they were partners. Work was everything. He lived his life as if he were planning out a production. That was it: life as storyboard, pre-production, production and post. This was undoubtedly a reason his marriage hadn't worked out and why he tended to go out with somebody for only a month or two at the most.

Good luck, James, she thought. I wish you the best.

Not that he'd ever actually asked you out, Simone reflected wryly.

The cab now approached her neighborhood – Greenwich Village. For

Simone, there was no other place to live in New York City. It was, truly, a village. A neighborhood.

The cab dropped her at Tenth Street. 'Hmm,' her boss said, looking out the window at two men, constructed like bodybuilders, kissing passionately as they stood on the steps of the building next to hers.

He said, 'Not that there's anything wrong with that.' The famous line from *Seinfeld*.

Simone smiled, then looked at the main kisser. What a waste.

Then she said goodnight to her boss and stepped out of the cab, grabbed her suitcase from the trunk. She paused to let a stocky homeless woman wheel her packed grocery cart past – filled with everything but groceries, of course. Simone thought about giving her some change. But then she reflected, Why do I think the woman's homeless? Maybe she's an eccentric millionaire.

She climbed the stairs to her apartment, smelling that odd aroma of the building, which defied description, as did many of the buildings here. What on earth was it?

Eau de Old New York Apartment.

Insecticide, takeout Chinese, takeout curry, ancient wood, Lysol, damp brick, cooked onions.

Her cat more or less forgave her, though he didn't have much to complain about. The kibble dish, tended to by her neighbor, was filled with manna from heaven. The water, too, was full and the radio was playing NPR, which was Ruffles's favorite. He seemed to enjoy the pledge drives as much as *This American Life*.

Simone checked messages – nothing urgent there, though she noted no caller-ID-blocked numbers. She'd had a lot of those recently. Telemarketers, of course.

She then unpacked and assembled a laundry pile. Simone had never returned from a trip without doing her laundry the night she was back.

Clothes cooties, she called it.

Thanks, Mom.

Simone pulled her sweats on, gathered up the clothes and a cheerful orange bottle of Tide. She took the back stairway, which led to the basement laundry and storage rooms. Simone descended from the second floor to the first and then started down the steps that would take her to the basement. This stairwell was dark, though there was some illumination from downstairs, the laundry room presumably, or maybe the storeroom. She flicked the switch several times. Then squinted and noted that the bulb was missing and not just – it had fallen to the stairs and shattered.

It was at this point that Simone started feeling uneasy.

But she continued, walking carefully to avoid as much of the broken glass as she could in her Crocs. On the basement level, another bulb was broken, too.

Creeping me out.

Okay, that's it. Hell with OCD issues. I'll do the laundry tomorrow.

Then squinted and saw, with some relief, that she'd have to wait anyway. There was a sign on the laundry-room door. *Out of Order.* The sign was battered and torn. She'd never seen it before; when the washers or dryers weren't working, Henry had always just handwritten a sign, informing the tenants when they could expect the machines to be up and running again.

She turned and, eager to get the hell back to Ruffles and her apartment, took one step toward the stairs.

She felt two things in serial. First, a faint chill as the door leading to the storeroom and, eventually, to the alley, opened.

And then a searing explosion of pain as the rock, the bottle, the weight of the world slammed into the back of her head.

4

Amelia Sachs skidded her maroon 1970 Ford Torino Cobra, heir to the Fairlane, to a stop at the curb in this idyllic section of Greenwich Village.

There were six blue-and-whites, mostly from the nearby Sixth Precinct, and about fifteen uniforms canvassing house to house.

In the long-odds search for Unsub 26's next victim.

She leapt out, wincing slightly at the arthritic pang. 'Hi, how're we doing?' she asked one of the detectives she knew, a tall African-American named Ronald Simpson, just ending a radio transmission.

'Amelia. We're deploying. We make it forty-eight locations in the perimeter that you and Detective Rhyme gave us. If we don't find anything, we'll expand it.'

'Sachs!' Rhyme's voice burst through her headset. No video camera – just a standard-issue Motorola with an earpiece and stalk mike. It was voice activated. Sachs needed both hands free to drive; she'd hit close to eighty on the way down here from Rhyme's townhouse. The Torino boasted 405 bhp and with an impressive 447 foot-pounds of torque. And Amelia Sachs made use of every bit of those specs.

'I'm here, Rhyme. With Ron Simpson from the Sixth.' She relayed the information the man had given her.

'Forty-eight? Hell.'

They'd hoped the two-block area would include a lot fewer apartment buildings to search than that.

But at least it was something. And it could be a lot worse. In looking for a way to narrow down the hunt for Unsub 26 or his next victim, Rhyme had come up with an interesting strategy.

Theorizing that the soil/vegetation and cleaning materials evidence held valuable leads, the question became how to analyze them quickly, given the sheer number of samples?

Hence, the call to Marko.

Who had connections in the Forensic Science Department at the Police Academy. Rhyme had asked the young man to get his professors' okay to enlist the rookies to help, with Marko supervising. Although there were hundreds of samples, because so many students were helping, each one had no more than five or ten. They were to look for the smallest samples, on the assumption that the largest quantities were materials that the unsub had intentionally flooded the scene with.

For hours there'd been no discoveries. But an hour ago Marko had called the townhouse.

'Detective Rhyme, sir?'

Rhyme didn't bother to correct him on the appellation. 'Go on.'

'We might've found something. We did what you said and prioritized everything according to quantity, then concentrated on the smallest trace. The least common was some vegetation that contained traces of urushiol.'

'The toxin in poison ivy or sumac,' Rhyme had blurted.

Sachs had wondered, as she often did, How does he *know* that?

'Yessir. And it's in poison oak, too.'

'No, forget that. You don't see it much in Manhattan. We'll stick with ivy and sumac.'

Marko had added that that vegetation was attached to bits of flower petals. They'd absorbed small amounts of glyphosate—

'An herbicide used to *kill* poison ivy and sumac.'

'Yessir,' Marko said again. 'So the perp might've spent time in a flower garden that was recently treated for the toxic plants.'

He added another discovery: 'They also found trace fragments of bovine bone dust in the soil attached to the vegetation.'

'West Village,' Rhyme had pronounced. 'Runoff, rains, rats . . . they carry all sorts of goodies from the meatpacking district, including beef bone dust.'

He'd had Sellitto start a hunt in city parks in the western part of Greenwich Village, any that had flower gardens. 'But only the ones that've been recently treated for poisonous plants.'

And the results of that search led here, to where Sachs was now standing, on West Tenth Street. The small park was surrounded by three-, four- and five-story townhouses and brownstones, nearly all of them apartments.

Rhyme had explained their find to Sellitto, who'd ordered the sweep in the area, telling the patrol officers to pay attention to laundry rooms, kitchens and storerooms, since the other category of evidence in play was domestic cleaning supplies.

'Long shot,' the detective had muttered.

'It's the only shot we've got.'

It was now 10:30 p.m. and the officers had been canvassing for half an hour.

Many citizens were reluctant to open their doors, even for police, or someone *claiming* to be police. Language was always a barrier and, even once they were admitted, the officers often had to try to survey individual units, since some buildings did not have communal laundry rooms.

Sachs watched a team storm into a brownstone. She stared; was this the site?

They came out a few minutes later, shaking their heads.

'Anything?' Rhyme asked her urgently.

'No.'

Sachs's fingers disappeared into her mass of hair and dug obsessively into her scalp. Stop it, she told herself.

Deal with the tension.

She dug some more.

The lead would only be helpful if it led to another crime in progress. If the trace led to Unsub 26's apartment and the police knocked on the door, he might open it, smile and say, 'No sir, I never heard of a Jane Levine. You have a nice night now.'

Sachs looked past the flashing lights and saw Marko, in jeans and a dress shirt, running shows. He caught her eye, gave a brief nod of recognition and then turned back to the scene, as if studying it intently for future reference. He was holding a scene suit bag. Let's hope he gets a chance to use it, she thought.

Then her radio crackled, a woman's voice. 'Portable seven-six-six-three. I've got something.'

'Go ahead,' Sachs said, identifying herself as a detective.

The patrol officer explained she was at an address a block away, on West Tenth. 'We've got an incendiary IED and victim nearby, immobilized. We need the Bomb Squad.'

'I'm on my way,' Sachs told her and began to run. Then into her mouthpiece radio: 'Got a hit, Rhyme,' she told him and, struggling to ignore the pain in her knees, sprinted faster. Marko was following, as were several other officers.

'Tell me,' Rhyme said.

'I'll know soon,' she gasped, her feet thudding on the concrete.

She was at the building in two minutes. Sellitto joined her. They met the patrol officer who'd called it in, a round Latina, on the stairs in front. The woman was visibly shaken.

'Vic down in the laundry room. There's gas fumes all over the place. I was going for her, but I was afraid I'd set off the device.'

'What kind of gas?' Rhyme asked, having heard her through Sachs's microphone.

She repeated the question for the patrolwoman.

'Gasoline. He—'

'I'm going in,' Sachs said.

'Sachs, wait—'

'It could blow at any minute,' the patrolwoman said. 'I'd wait for the Bomb Squad.'

Sellitto said, 'I've called them. They'll be here in five minutes.' The squad was based in the Sixth Precinct.

But five minutes was too long. Sachs said, 'I'm taking off the headset, Rhyme. I don't know if it could spark or not, but I'm not taking the chance.'

'Sachs, wait—'

'I'll get back to you as soon as I can.'

'Amelia,' Sellitto began.

She ignored him, too. She was debating the Tyvek suit. At the moment she had to assume the vic was still alive and could be burned to death at any minute. Forget the suit. There was no time to wait. She said to Sellitto, 'If anything happens' – she glanced toward Marko, who was running toward the brownstone – 'have him run the scene. He's good.'

'Amelia,' Sellitto barked. 'Let the Bomb Squad handle it.'

'Can't, Lon. We're out of time.'

Sachs looked down at her clothes. A wool jacket. Did that create more static sparks than any other cloth? Or fewer? She didn't know but took it off anyway. 'Where's the vic?' she asked the Latina officer.

'In the back there's a stairway. The laundry room's in the basement off the hallway to the right. But—'

Sachs sprinted into the building, calling, 'Everybody back fifty feet.'

Then she was in the dim recesses of the old building and starting down the stairs, which, unlike those at the other scene, were relatively clean, though the bulbs in the stairwell overheads were broken as well.

Her hand on her Glock, she surveyed the narrow corridor, off which were two doors: one, the laundry room where the victim was, and the other straight ahead, leading to a storeroom or the alley behind the building, Sachs guessed.

Normally she would have cleared the entire basement first, but the smell of gasoline was overwhelming – and the risk of fire imminent. She had to move fast.

Into the laundry room quickly, swinging her weapon back and forth. In the back, duct-taped to a water pipe, was a woman in her thirties, wearing sweats, the shoulders of which were covered with blood, from some wound to her head. Strands of her dark blond hair were clotted crimson. Her face was red from crying and her eyes wide with terror.

Unsub 26 had planned another prolonged killing. In this case, terror first and then pain . . . of dying from being burned to death.

On a high shelf against the wall, over her, was a plastic pail. A hole had been cut in the side and gasoline trickled out, running down the wall and pooling on the floor. The puddle was making its way to the door. And was just about to reach the hot water heater. Sachs noted it was a gas model, which meant that it had a pilot light. Any minute the gas would flow beneath it and the fumes would ignite. The resulting fireball would ignite everything and melt the plastic pail; the five or so gallons of inflamed gasoline would flow throughout the room.

She eased forward slowly. Shuffle or not? Would that create a static spark? She couldn't worry about it. She hurried to the water heater. Surveying the system, she reached up carefully and slowly. The taped woman shook her head and gave an unearthly scream. But Sachs ignored her and pulled the gas cutoff lever down.

There was a hiss and a quiet plop.

The pilot was out.

Sachs thought about removing the bucket of gas, but it was big and heavy. Moving it would surely spill some of the liquid, which might slosh onto a part of the water heater that was hot enough to ignite it.

The immediate threat was gone.

Still, though, the victim's head was shaking madly. Her eyes were wide and from her throat came high-pitched sounds, half screams, half words.

With her switchblade Sachs carefully cut the tape binding the woman to the pipe. She inspected the nasty wound on her head, looking around for something to stop the bleeding.

Another keening sound of desperation from the victim's throat. Her head waved more frantically yet.

Ah, maybe she was suffocating.

Sachs carefully eased the duct tape off her mouth and set it aside to be collected later for evidence. The victim sucked in air desperately, starting off a jag of coughing. Finally she managed, 'We have to leave! Fire!'

'It's okay, the pilot light—'

'Not that. There!' She pointed.

The pendulum of Sachs's gaze swung to the left.

What was that?

A flicker of unsteady shadow.

She dropped to her knees. Behind the washing machine was a Starbucks Frappuccino bottle with a rag stuffed in the neck. It, too, was filled with gasoline and the improvised wick was burning. The gasoline flowing down the wall was just starting to pool around it.

A Molotov cocktail.

Oh, hell, the pilot light wasn't the igniter. This bottle was.

Sachs grabbed the woman by the shoulders. They rushed the door.

And then, the explosion.

5

'Sachs!' Lincoln Rhyme was calling into his headset microphone. He was in his parlor lab, surrounded by the thousands of evidence containers. He hadn't moved much; it was difficult to maneuver.

He glanced at Thom, who was also on the phone, trying to reach someone at the command post for an update. Neither Sellitto nor Detective Ron Simpson was answering.

The report from the scene was that there'd been a huge explosion in the basement of the townhouse that Sachs had been searching. The tenants and their pets had been saved – as had the bulk of the building; the fire was mostly out. But Sachs and the intended victim, both of whom were in the laundry room, where the device was set, were unaccounted for.

Rhyme was furious with her for not waiting for the Bomb Squad.

'It's their fucking job,' he muttered, drawing a quizzical glance from his aide, who would, of course, have no idea whom he was fighting with.

He placed a call to Lon Sellitto but the detective didn't pick up.

'Goddamn it!'

Police and fire reports tumbled their way.

Oh, Jesus Christ . . .

And then, at last, 'Rhyme . . .'

'Sachs! Where are you? What happened?'

'Wait one—'

'I don't want to wait one anything. What the hell happened?' He nodded at Thom, who hung up his own on-hold call.

'We're fine. The vic and I got out the back. We just made it to the corridor before it blew.'

She went on to describe what he'd rigged.

'I wanted to collect some of the evidence, Rhyme. Anything. This time there wasn't any contamination. But I didn't have the chance.'

'You're all right?'

'Yeah, dizzy from the fumes, smoke.'

'The vic?'

'Same, dizzy, she's on oxygen. She breathed 'em for longer than I did.'

'She see anything?'

Sachs explained that, as in the homicide on Twenty-sixth Street, the perp had hit her from behind and duct-taped her, then rigged the bomb.

'Same thing, Rhyme. It was slow. Like he wanted her to think about the death she was facing. Lon's interviewing her.'

'Come on back here right away, Sachs. We just handed our unsub his first defeat and he's probably not very happy about it. And that young guy, Marko? Is he there?'

'He came over from the academy. He and I're going to walk the grid. Not that there's much to collect.'

'Well, tell him he did a competent job,' Rhyme said, and disconnected.

Though it sounded like damning with faint praise, in fact, coming from Lincoln Rhyme, it was a stellar compliment.

At midnight, Sachs, Sellitto and Cooper were in the parlor.

The opposite of the earlier scene, the site of the attempt on Tenth Street had yielded Evidence Lite; Sachs could carry all of it herself in one milk carton.

Sellitto had interviewed the victim, Simone Randall, at length. Like Jane Levine at the first crime scene, she had no enemies, certainly none who'd do something like this. She worked as an assistant in the entertainment field. She and her boss had just gotten back from a meeting on the West Coast. Simone had no clue why someone would do this to her and hadn't seen any threats when she'd arrived. She told Sachs about the other people on the street as she'd gotten out of the taxi: two guys making out and a homeless woman. Patrol officers canvassed but didn't come up with anybody. He also contacted Simone's boss, who'd dropped her off in front of her apartment, but he hadn't seen anything either, except the three people that Simone had mentioned.

The victim added that she thought she'd seen somebody watching the building with binoculars off and on for the past month, from the garden in the city park across the street, but he might just have been bird-watching.

'Where our unsub picked up his vegetative evidence and soil,' Rhyme noted.

But Simone had not seen the person clearly.

Sellitto said, 'That's it. Zip. Zilch.'

'Hell,' Rhyme muttered, wheeling back and beaching his chair on a pile of evidence envelopes containing plastic utensils. With the bits of food and drink beginning to decay, the parlor was taking on an unhealthy smell.

He didn't know when a case had frustrated him so much.

Thom surveyed his boss and said, 'I'm going to want you to get some sleep.'

'Fine,' Rhyme snapped, 'if you're "going to" want that, it means you don't want it yet.'

'Lincoln.' Thom was placid but firm, in his caregiver/mother-hen mode. The criminalist didn't feel like arguing. Besides, Thom was usually right about Rhyme's physical state, even if the criminalist didn't want to admit it. The life expectancy for those with his level of quadriplegia can be less than that of the general population, and Rhyme had Thom to thank for the fact he was still on earth . . . and relatively healthy.

And he *was* exhausted.

'Twenty minutes, please.'

'"Please,"' Thom said with mock shock. 'That didn't sound sincere.'

It wasn't.

Though as things turned out, even twenty minutes was too much.

There virtually was no evidence, nothing to analyze, no conclusions to be drawn.

And yet the unsub had been just as clever as at the earlier scene.

The fire meant there was nothing left to trace back to his home, place of work or future attacks. The fire had turned nearly everything to ash, and the water from the fire department had blended clues with extraneous materials and produced a useless black sludge. He was sure, too, that the few recognizable remnants – the Frappuccino bottle, the duct tape, the matches – would have come from the trash.

Even an analysis of the accelerant gasoline revealed it was an unbranded generic – and could have been bought in any of five hundred stations in the area.

Ah, fire, Rhyme reflected cynically.

As he'd written in his textbook:

Arson is one of the best ways to destroy trace evidence, friction ridge prints and shoe and boot prints. Investigators have to rely on evidence from entrance and exit routes and chemical analysis of the accelerant and ignition device for clues.

As for the things that might have helped – footprints along the perp's entrance and exit routes? And tool marks where he'd picked the locks? Of course, he'd worn booties and gloves – and had figured that any telltale clues would be destroyed by the firemen charging into the building, swinging axes and knocking down doors.

Which, of course, was exactly what happened.

Thom said, 'Lincoln.'

The grace period was up. It was time for bed.

Maybe something would occur to him in the morning.

6

But the dawn arrived with no brilliant insights regarding Unsub 26.

And none at midmorning . . . nor late afternoon.

They were no longer able to enlist the number-crunching forces from the Police Academy, to review the massive amounts of evidence from the scene on Twenty-sixth Street, though the head of the Crime Scene Unit agreed to dedicate some extra technicians. Marko had taken the bulk of the collected materials from Rhyme's to the labs in Queens.

But the hours rolled by and all the updates included variations on: 'There's just too much evidence.'

Clues had never failed Rhyme so badly as in this case. He'd built his whole professional life on finding the truth because of physical evidence. In fact, he was contemptuous of other forms of investigation. Witnesses lied, motives were fishy, vivid memories were completely wrong.

Locard's Principle . . .

At 6 p.m. Mel Cooper, Sachs and Rhyme were still laboring away, doing what they could with the several hundred samples that remained here in his parlor but not making any headway.

There's just too much . . .

Rhyme reached for one of the hair sample bags. 'Let's keep going with follicles and CODIS.' The consolidated database that contained DNA samples from tens of thousands of perpetrators.

But he set it down and wheeled back from a worktable. His expression must have been particularly troubled. Sachs, too, stopped her analysis of a sheet of paper, walked behind him and massaged his shoulders, which were tense as stone.

It felt nice . . .

But didn't take away the frustration.

Rhyme gazed at the largely useless evidence, trying desperately to think of a different approach. It was clear that the classic textbook procedure for running a case forensically wasn't going to work.

What else could he—?

Textbook.

'Sachs!'

'What?' She stopped the massage and walked around in front of him.

'Textbook. Think about what I've been saying for the past couple of days. My textbook.'

The evidence chart reads like the table of contents in my goddamn book . . .

Sachs was nodding. 'It's like everything he knows about evidence and crime scenes, he learned from your book.'

He pointed to the chart. 'There's a separate chapter for each of those categories of evidence collection and analysis. And I wrote sections about contamination, having too much evidence, and arson as a means to obliterate it. Somebody who bought or borrowed my text is the perp.'

'How many copies did you sell?' Cooper asked. He knew the book well; he was one of the dedicatees.

'About twenty thousand.'

'Not very helpful then.'

Rhyme considered this. 'I'm not so sure. People aren't going to curl up with it on cold winter nights like they would with Harry Potter or one of those vampire books now, are they? The vast bulk of sales would be to law enforcement. But let's put them aside for the time being – it's too obvious, too traceable. Somebody with a forensic specialty'd be the first people we'd look at.'

'We'll drop everything and get in touch with publishers and retailers.'

'How do we factor out law enforcement sales?' Cooper asked.

'Anybody with the government got a discount, so let's get a list of any customer who paid full price.'

Sachs pointed out, 'But like you just said, it could have been borrowed. It could've been bought with cash in a store, could've been stolen.'

'Maybe, but not many retail outlets carried it. Most sales were online.

As for borrowing it, just because something is unlikely is no reason not to pursue it. I don't think we have much choice anyway.'

'Time frame for the sales?' Cooper wondered.

'I'd go back a year. The sales spiked after that documentary I did on A&E; a lot of people saw it, Googled me and bought the book.' Rhyme's head was forward and he felt exhilarated. He was on the hunt and he knew his heart was pounding hard – felt the sensation in his neck and head, of course, not in his numb chest.

'Besides, I'd think emotionally you don't buy a book to help you plan a killing and then wait two years. This perp's moving fast.'

'You're sounding quite psychological, Rhyme,' Sachs said, laughing. 'That almost sounds like you're profiling him.'

A pseudoscience, he felt. But he replied with a shrug, 'Who said forensic scientists can't be *aware* of human nature? That's all. Let's get to work. Who coughed up a hundred and twenty dollars for my words of wisdom, plus shipping and handling?'

In three hours they had a rough list from the publishers, online retailers and professional bookstores. Sixty-four people in the New York area had bought the textbook in the past year, paying full price.

'Ouch,' Cooper muttered. 'Sixty-four? That's a brick wall.'

'Not at all,' Rhyme whispered, looking over the list. 'I'd say it's merely a speed bump.'

Okay, he was a catch.

Vicki Sellick probably wouldn't've thought of him that way by herself. But Joan and Alaki from work had met them for a drink earlier that night and both gave her subtle raised-eyebrows approval ratings. Joanie had whispered, 'Go, girl! You hooked a good one.'

Oh, stop . . .

But, yeah, Vicki now thought, she had.

Her date was courteous, handsome, had a great job, and on the two times that he'd stayed over, their time together had been . . . well, fantastic. They made a solid couple, politically in tune (centrist Democrats), athletic, lovers of the out-of-doors. They'd both been through tough divorces. True, he worked long hours, but so did she, a Wall Street lawyer. And he was older – in his mid-fifties, but looked much younger. Besides, Vicki, thirty-seven, had stopped using age as a definitive criterion for potential partners some years ago, one of her better decisions in the crazy world of dating.

He now steered his Jaguar to the curb in front of her apartment and, without hesitation, took her in his arms, kissing her firmly.

She had wondered if tonight would be the third time he stayed and it probably would have been, except that he had a 6 a.m. flight tomorrow on business. His assistant was out of commission for some reason or another so he had to get ready for the meeting all by himself.

But there was nothing wrong with taking things slowly.

She kissed him back even harder.

'I'm back in two days,' he whispered. 'See you then?'

'You're on.' Another kiss sealed the deal.

'I'll walk you up,' he said, nodding at her townhouse.

But she had to pick up some milk and a few things at the deli up the street, so they kissed awhile more.

She whispered, "Night, James. Call me if you can.'

'Oh, you'll hear from me,' he said softly, nuzzling her ear. She climbed out of the sports car and he sped off.

Ten minutes later, plastic bags in hand, she returned to her townhouse, a real find she'd been in for some years. She'd lucked into a duplex on the top floors of the four-story building and scraped together enough money to buy it instantly. The living space was a refuge from the chaos and demands of Wall Street law.

Up the stairs to the second floor, then the third.

Hmm, the hallway light was out here. This was curious since the maintenance in the building was great. It seemed the light bulb had fallen out and shattered. As she walked up to the fourth floor, where the entrance to her unit was, she fished in her pocket for her phone, thinking about calling him.

No, she'd wait. Get inside, take a shower, have a final glass of wine. She left the phone where it was and got her keys. Maybe—

Then the world went black and an explosion of pain soared through her head, and as she pitched forward she felt the keys being lifted from her fingers.

7

'I think I've got it,' Rhyme said, looking over the list of book sales.

Lon Sellitto had joined them and had an arrest team ready to go, if Rhyme's textbook theory panned out.

The criminalist continued, 'A week after the special aired, somebody named James Ferguson, 734 East Sixty-eighth Street, bought a copy of my book. He's not law enforcement. He ticked the box that said it was for professional research.'

'Ferguson,' Sachs said, 'sounds familiar.'

Sellitto said, 'Yeah, yeah, yeah! I interviewed him. He's Simone Randall's – the second vic's – boss. He dropped her off in a cab about a half-hour before she was attacked.'

'Data mine him, Mel. I want to know if he belongs to a health club. And, Sachs, find out the club that first victim belonged to.'

Sellitto nodded. 'Right, good call. The vic's boyfriend said she dated somebody from the club once, I think.'

In five minutes they had the answer. Both Ferguson and Jane Levine belonged to Lower Manhattan Health and Tennis Club.

'So, he's our boy. Classic serial doer. Let's find him, pick him up,' Sellitto said, and reached for his phone.

'Hold on, Lon,' Rhyme said. 'It's not as simple as that.'

And Rhyme did something he never thought he'd ever do: started reading the witness statements, ignoring the evidence charts completely.

*

I'm dying, Vicki Sellick thought.

Why . . . why?

But she had no idea who was behind this and so she didn't *know* why.

All she knew was that the asshole who'd slugged her over the head and tied her up here was trooping through the townhouse. She heard drawers opening, she heard doors closing.

Robbery?

She didn't have anything here of any real value . . .

She stanched the tears. The duct tape was snug on her mouth and if she cried any harder she'd clog her nose and suffocate.

She was lying in her big, Victorian, claw-foot bathtub, hands bound behind her, feet, also taped, dangling over the end. The lights were out and the blinds closed. It was virtually black.

Vicki screamed through the tape. A pathetic sound nobody could have heard. She was on the top floor of her townhouse. She had it to herself, and the nearest neighbor, even if she was home, was two stories below.

Then silence for a moment. Then a faint sound.

What's that? Was—?

She gasped as the door swept open and she felt a presence. The intruder, a pure shadow, moved in, paused . . . and turned the water on.

No! Vicki tried to struggle her way out but the angle and immobility from the tape made that impossible. Her attacker left, closing the door.

The icy water continued to rise.

This time Amelia Sachs was first on the scene.

And she was momentarily alone. Backup would be here soon but Rhyme had decided there was no time to wait; the perp – no longer an unsub at this point – had gone over a borderline and was moving faster. Rhyme said they had to assume another victim was about to die.

She skidded to a stop up the street from Vicki Sellick's townhouse and sprinted to the front door fast, not even feeling the twinges of arthritis. There was no question of warrants or fair warning. Time was too critical. With the butt of her Glock she shattered the window of the front door, opened it and charged inside.

The weapon before her, she ran to the top-floor apartment and kicked the door in, searching quickly. She found the victim in the bathtub – like the Prius, an innocent object rigged to kill.

She looked down. The water was nearly at Vicki's face, and her frantic thrashing was making it worse; waves splashing up her nose. She was choking and coughing, her face bright red.

Sachs grabbed the woman's blouse and pulled up hard from the water, then ripped the tape from her mouth.

'Thank you, thank you!' she sputtered. 'But be careful! He might be here.'

Out came the switchblade again, and after a few seconds of careful surgery the woman's feet and hands were free. Sachs wrapped a towel around her shoulders.

'Where?'

'I heard him two minutes ago, downstairs! I didn't get a look. He hit me from behind.'

Then a crash of glass from the hallway, near the rear of the building, a window breaking. 'What's back there?'

'Fire escape to the alley.'

Sachs ran to the window and saw the shadow of a figure, standing uncertainly looking left and right. She told Vicki to lock the bathroom door, the backup would be there any minute – she heard the sirens approaching. Then she sped down the stairs to the second floor. She, too, went through the shattered window, after checking fast for presenting threats.

The shadow was gone.

She clambered fast down the stairs. Then stopped. A brief sigh. Like most of them in the city, the fire escape didn't go all the way to the ground and she had to drop four or so feet to the cobblestoned alley, wincing in pain as she landed.

But she stayed upright and turned toward the darker part of the alley.

She got ten feet before the shadow reemerged – behind her.

She froze.

The young crime-scene officer, Marko, was squinting her way. His weapon was in his hand.

He lifted it toward Sachs, shaking his crew-cut head. On his face was a faint but definite smile – though a cold one. Of victory. Probably the expression on the face of a sniper just before he takes his shot to kill an enemy general.

8

Surprisingly silently for such a stocky man, Marko moved closer and pointed to his lips, shaking his head, meaning that she keep still.

Sachs didn't move a muscle.

Then he pointed behind her. And suddenly he shouted, 'You! Under the blankets. There're two police officers here. We're armed. Let me see your hands.'

Sachs looked to her left. She noted a homeless nest – blankets, piles of clothing, food cartons, grocery cart, empties, books and magazines. At first she didn't see anyone. But then she spotted a human form huddling in a gamy bedspread. A woman. She glanced at Marko, who nodded, and she, too, trained her weapon on the person, though she didn't have any idea what was going on.

'Let me see your hands!' he shouted.

And slowly the middle-aged figure rose, a look of fury and hatred on her face. Sachs moved forward and cuffed the suspect, who raged, 'You don't understand. You don't have any idea what he did to me. He ruined my life!'

'Yes, ma'am,' Marko said and glanced at Sachs, who read the woman her rights. Then eased her to a sitting position as she continued her rant, while the two officers searched the nest.

'How'd you make her?' Sachs asked. 'The profile Rhyme had for the perp was middle-class, lived in a nice place on the Upper West Side.'

Marko nodded. 'Homeless lady clothes, but not homeless lady shoes.'

Sachs looked. True, a torn and dirty dress. But nice Joan & Davids on her feet. Also, her face was clean and she wore makeup.

'Good catch.'

'Thank you, ma'am.'

'"Amelia" is fine.'

'Sure.'

They collected the woman's purse – and a few other items. Notably, a pistol, with which she presumably would have shot Sachs in the back if Marko hadn't gotten to the scene as quickly as he had.

Good catch . . .

They also found a well-thumbed book, sprouting Post-it notes.

A Comprehensive Guide to Evidence Collection and Analysis.

Lincoln Rhyme's textbook.

The perp was James Ferguson's ex-wife.

In this case, Lincoln Rhyme allowed, this *one* case, motive was a pretty good clue and led them to the suspect: revenge.

Ferguson, along with Sachs, Sellitto and Marko, sat in Rhyme's town-house, filling in the details of what Rhyme had deduced an hour ago. He explained that he'd gotten divorced from his wife, Linda, about a year ago. She'd grown increasingly abusive and unstable, paranoid. She'd known his career was important to him before they got married, but she'd still resented the long hours and his obsession with his TV production projects. She was also sure he was having affairs with his assistants.

He laughed bitterly. 'Twelve-hour days don't leave a lot of time or energy for that sort of thing.'

After the divorce her mental and emotional condition grew worse, he added, though it never occurred to him that she'd grow violent.

But she sure had. Coming up with a bizarre plan to get even with Ferguson by stalking and killing some of the women Ferguson dated or knew. She dressed like a homeless woman, so she wouldn't be noticed, camping out near her intended victims' apartments to get details about their lives. Then she'd attempted to murder them using as a template Rhyme's book, both to cover up any clues to her personally and also to shift the focus to Ferguson, since there was a record he'd bought a copy of the textbook.

The last step, tonight, would be to plant evidence implicating her ex-husband in Vicki Sellick's apartment. A whole chapter in Rhyme's book was about intentionally seeding evidence at a scene to establish guilt.

Rhyme glanced at his textbook, sitting in an evidence collection bag. 'Why *did* you happen to buy it?'

Ferguson explained that as a documentary TV producer he watched as many competitors' programs as he could. 'I saw the episode on A&E about that murder in Florida, where you were talking about evidence. I thought it was brilliant. I thought maybe my company could do something along those lines. So I ordered your book. But I never got around to doing the show. I went on to other things.'

'And your wife knew about the book?' Sellitto asked.

'I guess I mentioned the project to her and that I was reading it. She's been in my apartment off and on over the past year. She must've stolen it sometime when she was over.' He regarded Rhyme. 'But why *didn't* you think I was the one, like she planned?'

Rhyme said, 'I did at first. But then I decided it wouldn't've been smart for somebody to use a book that could be traced to them as a template for murder. But it'd be *very* smart for someone else to use that book. And whoever put this together was brilliant.'

'He profiled you,' Sachs said with a smile.

Rhyme grimaced.

Sellitto had then spoken to Ferguson and learned of the nasty divorce, which gave them the idea that his ex might be behind it. They learned, too, that he'd just dropped off Vicki Sellick, the woman he was dating, at her apartment.

They'd tried to call the woman but, when she hadn't picked up, Sachs and the team had sped there to see if she was in fact under attack.

'She was nuts,' Ferguson muttered. 'Insane.'

'Ah, madness and brilliance – they're not mutually exclusive,' Rhyme replied. 'I think we can agree on that.'

Then Marko rubbed his close-cropped head and laughed. 'I'm sort of surprised you didn't suspect me. I mean, think about it. I was first on the scene at the Twenty-sixth Street homicide, I knew forensics, I'd taken your course, and you could assume I'd read your book.'

Rhyme grunted. 'Well, sorry to say, kid, but you *were* a suspect. The first one.'

'Me?'

'Sure. For the reasons you just mentioned.'

Sellitto said, 'But Linc had me check you out. You were in the lab in Queens, working late, when the first vic was killed.'

'We had to check. No offense,' Rhyme said.

'It's cool, sir . . . Lincoln.'

'All right,' Sellitto muttered. 'I got paperwork to do.' He left with Ferguson, who would go downtown to dictate his statement. Marko, too, left for the night.

'That his first name or last?' Rhyme asked.

'Don't know,' Sachs replied.

An hour later, she'd finished bundling up the last of the evidence collection bags and jars and boxes for transport to the evidence storage facility in Queens.

'We'll definitely need to air the place out,' Rhyme muttered. 'Smells like an alleyway in here.'

Sachs agreed. She flung open the windows and poured them each a Glenmorangie Scotch. She dropped into the rattan chair beside Rhyme's Storm Arrow. His drink was in a tumbler, sprouting a straw. She placed it in a cup holder near his mouth. He had good movement of his right arm and hand, thanks to the surgery, but he was still learning the subtleties of control and didn't want to risk spilling valuable single-malt.

'So,' she said, regarding him with a gleam in her eye.

'You're looking coy, Sachs.'

'Well, I was just thinking. Are you finally going to admit that there's more to policing than physical evidence?'

Rhyme thought for a moment. 'No, I don't think so.'

She laughed. 'Rhyme, we closed this one because of deductions from witness statements and observations . . . and a little profiling. Evidence didn't have anything to do with it.'

'Ah,' Rhyme said, 'but there's a flaw in your logic, Sachs.'

'Which is?'

'Those deductions and observations all came from the fact that somebody bought a textbook of mine, correct?'

'True.'

'And what was the book about?'

She shrugged. 'Evidence.'

'Ergo, physical evidence was the basis for closing the case.'

'You're not going to concede this one, are you, Rhyme?'

'Do I ever?' he asked and, placing his hand on hers, enjoyed a long sip of the smoky liquor.

PARADICE

On one side was rock, dark as old bone. On the other a drop of a hundred feet.

And in front, a Ford pickup, one of those fancy models, a pleasant navy-blue shade. It cruised down the steep grade, moving slow. The driver and passenger enjoying the Colorado scenery.

Those were his choices: Rock. Air. Pickup.

Which really wasn't much of a choice at all as a means to die.

John Pellam jammed his left boot on the emergency brake again. It dropped another notch toward the floor. The pads ground fiercely and slowed the big camper not at all. He was going close to sixty.

He downshifted. Low gear screamed and the box threatened to tear apart. Don't lose the gears, he told himself. Popped the lever back up to D.

Sixty mph . . . seventy . . .

Air. Rock.

Seventy-five.

Pickup.

Choose one, Pellam thought. His foot cramped as he instinctively shoved the useless brake pedal to the floor again. Five minutes ago he'd been easing the chugging camper over Clement Pass, near Walsenburg, three hours south of Denver, admiring the stern, impressive scenery this cool spring morning. There'd been a soft hiss, his foot had gone to the floor and the Winnebago had started its free fall.

From the tinny boom box on the passenger seat Kathy Mattea sang 'Who Turned Out the Light?'

Pellam squinted as he bore down on the pickup, honking the horn, flashing his lights to warn the driver out of the way. He caught a glimpse of sunglasses in the Ford's rearview mirror. The driver, wearing a brown cowboy hat, spun around quickly to see how close the camper really was. Then turned back, hands clasped at ten to two on the wheel.

Air, pickup . . .

Pellam picked mountain. He eased to the right, thinking maybe he could brush against the rock and brush and pine, slow down enough so that when he went head-on into a tree it wouldn't kill him. Maybe.

But just as he swerved, the driver of the truck instinctively steered in the same direction – to the right, to escape onto the shoulder. Pellam sucked in an 'Oh, hell' and spun the wheel to the left.

So did the driver of the Ford. Like one of those little dances people do trying to get out of each other's way as they approach on the sidewalk. Both vehicles swung back to the right then to the left once more as the camper bore down on the blue pickup. Pellam chose to stay in the left lane, on the edge of the cliff. The pickup veered back to the right. But it was too late; the camper struck its rear end – red and clear plastic shrapnel scattered over the asphalt – and hooked on to the pickup's trailer hitch.

The impact goosed the speed up to eighty.

Pellam looked over the roof of the Ford. He had a fine view of where the road disappeared in a curve a half-mile ahead. If they didn't slow by then the two vehicles were going to sail into space in the finest tradition of hackneyed car chase scenes.

Oh, hell. That wasn't all: a new risk, a bicyclist. A woman, it seemed, on a mountain bike. She had one of those pistachio-shell-shaped helmets, in black, and a heavy backpack.

She had no clue they were bearing down on her.

For a moment the pickup wiggled out of control then straightened its course. The driver seemed to be looking back at Pellam more than ahead. He didn't see the bike.

Seventy miles an hour. A quarter-mile from the curve.

And a hundred feet from the bicyclist.

'Look out!' Pellam shouted. Pointlessly.

The driver of the pickup began to brake. The Ford vibrated powerfully. They slowed a few miles per hour.

Maybe the curve wasn't that sharp. He squinted at a yellow warning sign.

The diagram showed a 180-degree switchback. A smaller sign commanded that thou shalt take the turn at ten miles an hour.

But they'd be on the cyclist in seconds. Without a clue they were speeding toward her, she was coasting and weaving around in the right lane, avoiding rocks. And about to get crushed to death. Some riders had tiny rearview mirrors attached to their helmets. She didn't.

'Look!' Pellam shouted again and gestured.

Whether the driver saw the gesture or not Pellam couldn't say. But the passenger did and pointed.

The pickup swerved to the left. Another squeal of brakes. The camper rode up higher on the hitch. It was like a fishhook. As they raced past the bicyclist, her mouth open in shock, she wove to the side, the far right, and managed to skid to a stop.

That was one tragedy averted. But the other loomed.

They were a thousand feet from the switchback.

Pellam felt the vibrations again, from the brakes. They slowed to sixty-five then sixty. Downshift.

Five hundred feet.

They'd slowed to fifty.

Danger Sharp Curve.

Down to forty-five leisurely miles an hour.

The switchback loomed. Straight ahead, past the curve, Pellam could see nothing. No trees. No mountains. Just a huge empty space. The tourist marker at Clement Pass said the area boasted some of the most spectacular vertical drops in Colorado.

Forty miles an hour. Thirty-nine.

Maybe we'll just bring this one off.

But then the grade dropped, an acute angle, and the wedded vehicles began accelerating. Fifty, fifty-five.

Pellam took off his Ray-Bans. Swept the pens and beer bottles off the dash. Knocked the boom box to the floor. Kathy continued to sing. The song 'Grand Canyon' was coming up soon.

A hundred feet from the switchback.

With a huge scream the pickup's nose dropped. The driver had locked the brakes in a last desperate attempt to stop. Blue smoke swirled as the truck fishtailed and the rear of the camper swung to the left. But the driver was good. He turned into the skid far enough to control it but not so much that he lost control. They straightened out and kept slowing.

They were fifty feet from the edge of the switchback. The speed had dropped to fifty.

Forty-five . . .

But it wasn't enough.

Pellam threw his arms over his face, sank down into the seat.

The pickup sliced through the pointless wooden guardrail and sailed over the edge of the road, the camper just behind.

There was a loud thump as the undercarriage of the Ford uprooted a skinny tree and then a soft jolt. Pellam opened his eyes to find the vehicles rolling down a gentle ten-foot incline, smooth as a driveway, into the parking lot of the Overlook Diner, sitting in the middle of a spacious area on an outcropping of rock high above the valley floor.

With a resounding snap the camper's front bumper broke loose and fell beneath the front tires, slicing through and flattening them, a hard jolt that launched the boom box and possibly a beer bottle or two into Pellam's ear and temple.

He winced at the pain. The truck rolled leisurely through the lot and steered out of the way of the Winnebago, which hobbled on, slowing, toward the rear of the diner.

Pellam's laughter at the peaceful conclusion to the near-tragedy vanished as the camper's nose headed directly for a large propane tank.

Shit . . .

Hitting the useless brakes again, couldn't help himself, he squinted. But the dead tires slowed the camper significantly and the result of the collision was a quiet *thonk*, not the fireball that was the requisite conclusion of car chases in the sort of movies Pellam preferred not to work on.

He lowered his head and inhaled deeply for a moment. Not praying. Just lowered his head. He climbed out and stretched. John Pellam was lean of face and frame, and tall, with not-quite-trimmed dark hair. In his denim jacket, Noconas, well-traveled jeans and a black wrinkled dress shirt converted to casual wear, he resembled a cowboy, or at least was mistaken for one in places like this, though not in the low-rent district of Beverly Hills – yes, they exist – that was his mailing address. The cowboy aura he tended to perpetuate not for image but for sentiment; the story went that he was actually related to a figure from the Old West, Wild Bill Hickok.

Pellam walked stiffly toward the pickup, noting the damage wasn't terrible. Scraped paint and hitch, broken brake- and taillight.

The driver, too, shut off the engine and eased the door open.

Pellam approached. 'Look, mister, I'm really sorry. The brakes . . .'

The Stetson came off swiftly, unleashing a cascade of long chestnut hair. The woman was in her mid-thirties, petite, about five two or so. With a heart-shaped face, red lips, brows thick and dark, which, for some reason, made them wildly sensual.

The passenger-side door opened and a young man – well built in a gangly sort of way, with an anemic goatee and short ruddy hair – climbed out. A cautious smile on his face. He looked as if he wanted to apologize for the accident, though passengers were probably not the first suspects traffic officers looked at.

Pellam continued toward the driver.

She took off her own Ray-Bans.

He was thinking that her eyes were the palest, most piercing gray he'd ever seen, when she drew back and decked him with a solid right to the jaw.

A cold Colorado desert wind had come up and they were all inside the diner, the cast now including the town sheriff, fiftyish and twice Pellam's weight. His name was partially H. Werther, according to his name plate. He stood near the counter, talking to the cowgirl.

Pellam was sitting at a table while a medic who smelled of chewing tobacco worked on his jaw. Pellam was mad at himself. He'd been in more fights than he could – or cared to – count. He'd seen the squint in her eyes as he stepped close and had an idea that it was an about-to-swing squint. And all the while Pellam kept grinning like a freshman on a first date and thinking, Now, those are some extraordinary eyes.

For Christsake, you might've ducked at least.

The fist had glanced off bone and hadn't caused any serious damage, though it loosened a tooth and laid open some skin.

Six other patrons – two older couples and two single Cat-capped workers – watched with straight-faced amusement.

'She got you good,' offered the medic, in a low voice so the sheriff didn't hear.

'It was the wreck, stuff flying everywhere.' He looked out the window at the damaged Winnebago. The medic looked, too. And, okay, it didn't seem all *that* damaged. 'Things flew around.'

'Uhn,' he grunted.

'A boom box.' He decided not to mention the beer bottles.

'We're trained to look for certain contusions and abrasions. Like, for domestic situations.'

She barely tapped me, Pellam thought and wobbled the tooth again.

The driver stood with her arms crossed. The hat was back on. The brown was set off by a small green feather. She gazed back as she spoke to the sheriff; the beige-uniformed man towered over her and his weight, not insignificant, was a high percentage muscle. Probably the only peace officer in whatever town this was; Pellam had passed a welcome-to sign but that had been just as the emergency brake pad had pungently melted and he hadn't had the inclination to check out the name and population of the place where he was about to die. He guessed it was maybe a thousand souls.

As the sheriff jotted in a small notebook Pellam studied the woman. She was calm now and he thought again how beautiful she looked.

Pale eyes, dark eyebrows.

Two red knuckles on her right hand.

She and the sheriff stood next to the cash register, an old-time hand-crank model. The diner itself was a real relic, too. Aluminum trim, paint-spatter Formica countertops, black-and-white linoleum diamonds on the floor. Arterial blood red for the vinyl upholstery – booth and stool.

The man who'd been in the passenger seat of the Ford stepped out of the washroom, still wearing a cautious smile. He was dressed in dark, baggy clothes – the sort you'd see in TriBeCa or on Melrose in West Hollywood. Pellam – for whom the line between movies and reality was always a little hazy – thought immediately that he could have stepped right out of a Quentin Tarantino or Robert Rodriguez flick. He wore no-nonsense hiking boots. Clutching his backpack, he laughed nervously again. To Pellam he nodded a rueful glance – the sort soldiers might exchange when they've just survived their first firefight. His hair was cut flat on the top, short on the sides – the kind of cut Pellam associated with characters in the comic books of his childhood; he mentally dubbed the man Butch.

Was she his wife? Girlfriend, sister? She wore a wedding ring but was easily ten years older. Not that that meant anything nowadays – if it ever had. Pellam was experienced, but not particularly successful, in the esoterica of romance. His job didn't allow much room for relationships.

Or that's what he told himself.

The medic pressed a bandage on his jaw. 'You're good to go. Keep your guard up.'

'It was a—'

'Then against dangerous entertainment devices.' The man nodded a farewell to the sheriff, shoved a chaw in his mouth and left with his fix-'em-up bag.

Pellam rose unsteadily and walked toward the driver and sheriff, who said, 'Everybody, pull out some tickets for me, if you would.'

Butch said evenly, 'Yessir. Here you go.' A moment's pause as he dug through his wallet, which was thick with scraps of paper. Pellam noted his license was Illinois. Taylor was his real name. Pellam was somehow disappointed at this.

'Don't look much like you,' the sheriff said, examining the license.

'I didn't have a beard then.' Pointing to the picture. 'Or short hair.'

'Can see that. I ain't blind. Still don't look like you.'

'Well . . .' Taylor offered, for no particular purpose.

'This your current residence? Chicago?'

'For the time being. Where I get my mail.'

The sheriff took Pellam's license, too, which contained a picture that did look like him. Still, the sheriff frowned slightly, perhaps at the word on the top, California. You saw a lot of Californians in Telluride and Vail and Aspen. Probably not a lot down here in this neck of the woods.

The door opened and a woman walked in. She looked around. 'Hey, Sheriff. Everybody all right?'

Pellam squinted. It was the bicyclist they'd nearly squashed. Frizzy blond hair, massive curls. The helmet was gone. She was short and stocky. The bicycle latex revealed serious thighs. She'd taken off her sunglasses and was scanning them all with green eyes – Pellam in particular, probably because of the bandage. A spattering of sun-enhanced freckles dusted her face.

Somebody had come to pick her up. The bike was racked on the roof of an old battered car, a man in the driver's seat. Short hair, lightish colored, but Pellam couldn't make out any details of the driver. He was preoccupied with something else – the camper, it seemed.

'Lis,' the sheriff said, glancing their way. 'Fine. More or less. That Chris with you?' A nod toward the car.

'That's right.'

She explained that she was a witness, not mentioning that she'd nearly been run down. 'Happy to give a statement if you want.'

'Good of you to come forward,' Werther said. 'Most people wouldn't've.'

'I figured you'd track me down sooner or later. Didn't want to be leaving the scene of an accident.'

'Go ahead. Tell me what you saw.'

She gave a pretty accurate description. He jotted a few notes, every fifth or sixth word, it seemed. This was apparently the investigation of the year.

'That's helpful, Lis. Thanks. And why don'tcha give them one of our cards. For their insurance companies.'

A little hesitation, as if she hadn't counted on this level of attention.

She dug into a massive purse, found some cards and gave them out. Lis and Chris were the co-directors of the Southeastern Colorado Ecological Center. Seemed a little odd that such a group was based here, since vegetation was sparse and the human footprint minimal.

'Scared the you know what out of me.'

'I'm sure,' Pellam said. 'Sorry about that.'

The driver was silent. She didn't seem to care. She pulled a cell phone from her rear pocket, looked at the screen without expression. A moment later she slipped the unit back.

'Thought you guys were racing at first, but then I saw what happened. Brakes went?'

'Mine, yeah,' Pellam said.

'Good thing there was nobody in the oncoming lane.'

That was sure true. Though there hadn't been much traffic going in any direction on barren State Route 14. Not here, where it was close to a hundred miles to any kind of town.

Lis was cute and maternal. Pellam guessed her first reason for coming here was in fact to see if anyone was hurt, rather than cover her ass about leaving the scene.

'Thanks to you. And Chris,' the sheriff said, looking out the door toward the old car, a Toyota. Had to be twenty years old. The gloss was gone from the paint entirely.

Pellam played out a scenario that the group had been threatened because they protested land use or something or because they were hippies and Sheriff Werther had stood up for them.

It would have made a bad scene in a movie and it was surely not true. But that was the way Pellam's mind worked. He wrung stories from dry rocks.

The earth mother left, climbed in the car and they sped away, she and Chris.

Without a word the sheriff stepped outside to write down VINs and to radio in the details and see who was who and what was what.

The driver got a coffee, not asking if anybody else wanted any. She paid with steady hands. 'Look,' she said softly. 'I'm sorry I hit you. I wasn't thinking . . . The pickup was a birthday present. Just last week. It's got eight hundred miles on it.'

Pellam thought about making a joke that out here that meant two trips to the grocery store and one to Blockbuster.

But he didn't, mostly because she didn't sound particularly sorry she'd slugged him.

''S'okay,' he said automatically as his tongue poked the loose tooth. 'I didn't really get the impression you were out for blood.'

Though he happened to be tasting some at that moment.

He added, 'It was a boom box hit me. That's what happened.' He nodded toward the sheriff.

'Thanks. I get carried away sometimes.'

The pain was starting now. Probably more than boom box pain.

Then the issue of assault was gone and she looked impatiently at her watch.

It seemed an appropriate time for intros. Her name turned out to be Hannah Billings. 'With an h.'

A back-end h. 'I'm John Pellam. This isn't a line – but I have to say I've never met a Hannah before. Pretty name.'

It conjured up a heroine in a World War II film, a resistance fighter, wearing a tight frock, whatever a frock might be.

Taylor brushed his butch hair and said, 'It's a palindrome. Her name.'

'A . . .?'

'A word that's spelled the same backward and forward. "Madam, I'm Adam",' he said. 'I wrote an entire poem in palindromes once.'

Poem . . .

Hannah said, 'And this is Taylor . . .'

The poet filled in, 'Duke.'

More relationship mystery.

'As in *the* Duke. Being out here makes you think of old-time Westerns, doesn't it?'

Hannah had no clue what he was talking about.

How could somebody not know John Wayne?

'So everybody okay?' Taylor asked. 'That was freaky, I mean. Seeing the road doing that turn, what's it called? A . . .?'

'Switchback,' Hannah offered and dumped sugar into her coffee. 'Yeah, I'm fine. I've had worse.' As if Pellam were an afterthought. 'You?'

'I used to be a stuntman. I've had worse.'

'Stuntman.' She was curious.

Taylor, too: 'Wow. Hollywood?'

'Yep.'

'Fascinating.' He dug into his massive backpack for a notebook and wrote something down on the stained, limp pages.

Hannah muttered to him, 'Didn't quite work out the way you'd hoped, looks like.'

He shrugged. 'Not your fault.' Taylor had a bulky presence but he seemed like a pretty softhearted guy.

There was a formality between the two of them. Pellam just couldn't figure out their relationship. She had a Colorado license, he'd noted. And Taylor, Illinois. Was he a distant relative?

Taylor looked around, offering a faint laugh. 'This place is something. A real diner. It oughta be in black and white. Like an old TV show.'

Pellam quoted, '"You're moving into a land of both shadow and substance, of things and ideas . . . You've just crossed over into . . . the Twilight Zone."'

'"Controlling the vertical and the horizontal"', Taylor replied. Pellam believed that was a different show. But nodded anyway.

The woman completely ignored them. She took her coffee outside to make another cell-phone call.

Taylor, the film- and TV-loving poet, went for some coffee, too, sitting down at the counter. He smiled, more friendly than flirtatious, at one of the waitresses: the younger of the two, a slim woman in a white uniform, which was only slightly jelly-marred. Rita, if Pellam read the scripty typeface above her left breast correctly. Taylor ordered, adding, 'How 'bout this diner, isn't it totally authentic?' And, 'Man, a real piece of America.' She glanced at him as if he'd told her he'd just seen Elvis mountain biking through the pines and went off silently to pour his coffee. It arrived in a chipped white mug that must've weighed close to a pound.

Pellam watched Hannah smoking half a cigarette, quickly. She returned inside, waving her hand about her to shoo away the smoke, as if trying to get rid of the evidence. It told Pellam her husband or some other family member wanted her to give up the habit, and while she was courteous about the practice, she wasn't going to stop.

She seemed more impatient yet, staring out toward the sheriff, hunched over his cruiser calling the incident in to points unknown. Finally she joined Pellam.

'I tried to get around you,' he said.

'I know, I saw.' Again, studying the sheriff.

Pellam reflected: Pale eyes but a great tan. Dark and rich, without a single crow's foot to show for it. Taylor was tan, too, but only hands, face and part of his neck. The rest was pale as paper. It told Pellam he spent a lot of time outside but wearing most of his clothes.

Ah, he deduced: Hitchhiker. Made sense, that tan and the backpack. And those boots. Really serious boots.

But would a single woman have picked up a man who outweighed her by seventy pounds or so?

A woman with a right hook like she had was clearly somebody who could handle herself.

And as for her tan – it seemed to be everywhere. Which was, to John Pellam, an interesting matter for imaginative speculation.

The sheriff returned and looked over the threesome without suspicion or disdain. Still, he was a pro and there were questions to be asked. He asked Pellam, 'You been drinking, sir?'

Ah, welcome to Gurney.

Pellam finally scored the name of the town; it was on the sheriff's shoulder.

Hell of a name for a place. Wasn't that some kind of medical stretcher?

'Brakes went.'

'So you say. Didn't answer my question.'

'Then the answer is: No. Last drink I had was a beer . . .'

'Sure it wasn't two?' the law enforcer asked wryly.

'How's that?'

'S'all anybody ever drinks. Two beers. A fella'll tank down a fifth of Old Crow and when we pull him outa the wreck he says he's only had two beers. What they always say. Now, how many'd you really have?'

This was pretty funny, Pellam thought. As a follower of COPS, it was true.

'One beer and it was yesterday.'

'Yessir. We'll just have you breathe into our little magic box. You object to that?'

'Not at all.'

'He hasn't been drinking,' Taylor said. 'You could tell.'

It was a Lands' End knapsack he held. He kneaded it with long fingers that could have used a good scrubbing. The backs of his hands were tanned, the palms pink.

'Doesn't really matter what he seemed to you, sir. We'll let science string him up. Or not. As the case may be.'

'Then let's do it,' Pellam said agreeably.

In the end the sheriff settled for a little heel and toe walk, along the checkerboard of the diner floor, and the law enforcer was satisfied with the result. 'I just don't want to see any empties in the front of a vehicle, you understand me? I—'

'They—'

'Even if they got themselves propelled there by the quote force of the impact.'

Pellam kind of liked this sheriff and – as a stranger in a lot of towns – he'd come under some scrutiny in his day.

'And your jaw? How'd that happen?'

Pellam looked him in the eye. 'Boom box.'

'Rap?'

'What?'

'You were listening to rap on a boom box and you fell?'

'You can listen to anything on a boom box. I was listening to country.'

'And . . .?' He pointed to the bandage.

'It hit me in the face when we went off the road.'

'Okay.' Said in the way that cops always say, 'Okay'. Like they don't exactly believe you and they don't exactly not believe you. Then he took in the driver. 'You're from Hamlin. And Billings? You Ed Billings's wife?'

'That's right. You know Ed?'

'Not personal. Know some folks who've retired to one of his developments. Paso Verde.'

'That's a big one, yeah.' She looked at her watch. 'Popular.'

'And what's your story, sir?'

Taylor said, 'I'm headed to Berkeley.'

'Colorado?'

'California. Taking a poetry course there.'

'Okay.'

'I'm hitching from Denver to Hamlin.'

Hannah said, 'I was driving back from some meetings in Colorado Springs. The Ford had a flat and he fixed it for me.'

'You have business in Hamlin?' the sheriff asked.

'I'm getting the Amtrak there. To Oakland.'

'Rather than from Denver?'

'Yup.'

'You got money for the train, why're you hitchin'?' the sheriff asked.

Pellam thought these questions, while delivered pleasantly, were a bit intrusive, directed as they were to a man who, in this particular scenario, was an innocent bystander. But Taylor was happy to talk. 'The experience of it.' He gave his enthusiastic little laugh again. 'I'd hitch all the way if I had time. I mean, the whole point of life is experience. Right?'

'You're not thumbing on the interstate, are you?'

'Ramps only,' Taylor said automatically. With a grin. He'd been through this before.

The sheriff looked at Hannah, who didn't know the drill ahead of time, but caught on. She said sourly, 'I was on Fourteen when I had the flat.'

Route 14 – the highway where the pickup/camper run-in occurred.

'Okay. Now, I'm not writing anybody up.'

'Thank you, Officer,' Taylor said. Though, once again, Pellam had no clue what he might get written up for. He was acting so easygoing that Pellam knew his pack had to be drug free.

Hannah *didn't* say thanks; her beautiful but severe face gave off the message: I got rear-ended in my birthday truck. Why the hell was a citation even an issue?

Licenses and registrations were redistributed. Except Pellam's. Which the sheriff thumbed slowly. 'Now you, sir.'

'The brakes went.'

'I said I'm not citing anybody. But on that, you know you have an obligation to check your equipment.'

Pellam didn't think he'd ever looked at a brake line. He doubted he could recognize one.

'What I'm curious about is, are you making movies here?'

When the sheriff had checked the VIN on the Winnebago's dash he must have seen the Colorado Film Commission's location permit.

'That's right. I'm a location scout for a film company based in LA.'

'Really?' Hannah asked, her curiosity piqued for the first time and sour attitude on hold. Pellam got this a lot. He wondered if she'd ask for a walk-on part. He had an amusing image of her as a femme fatale; she had the right look and spirit to be a really good bad girl. Sexy, too, which was another requirement. In fact, he was scouting for a film noir at the moment, an indie titled *Paradice*.

'And you're setting it here?' she asked.

'Well, I was going to recommend it. Came across this place east of here fifteen miles or so. What's it called? Devil's . . .?'

'Playground,' Hannah said, shaking her head. 'Be a good setting for a Stephen King movie, that's about all.'

Taylor asked, 'That's near where you picked me up, right? Spooky.'

It was. The place was nestled at the base of two mountains, a huge craggy plain of pits and arroyos. Bleak as could be. But extremely photogenic.

'But I called the county supervisor this morning. He won't issue film permits.'

'Derek Westerholm?'

'That was him.'

'Hey, Hube, you just bought some land up near there, didn't you?' Rita, the young waitress, piped up. 'Near that lake?'

Hube, Pellam reflected. Hubert. No wonder he went by a solitary H.

The sheriff didn't answer.

'Let him make his movie on your property,' Rita continued. 'And, mister, I'm available, you need a leading lady.'

Taylor said earnestly, '*I'll* put you in a poem.'

Again, the Elvis-has-been-spotted look. Taylor's hitchhiking-weathered face blushed.

'Okay, that's all I need,' Werther said. 'Just get those vehicles up to the law.'

'Whatta you mean?' Hannah asked.

'No brake light, no turn signals. No backup. You can't drive without 'em.'

'You're kidding. It's still daylight.'

'Still.'

'Where?' she asked, her eyes going, for some reason, to Pellam.

The sheriff answered, 'Rudy's. 'Bout four blocks thataway. Best mechanic in town.'

'That the *only* one in town?' Pellam found himself asking.

'That's right.' The sheriff gave him the phone number from memory.

Pellam asked, 'He by any chance related to you?'

'Hah, that's funny.' The sheriff's smile might not have been real and Pellam reminded himself to watch it. He couldn't afford to spend the night in jail on suspicion of fraternizing with empties in the front seat of a vehicle.

Ten minutes later Pellam and Hannah walked into the repair shop with the world's most beautiful view.

The windows looked out over mountains to the west and north, and craggy flats – salt or sand – to the east. Now, early afternoon, the peaks were lit brilliantly, the stunning light firing off the late spring snowcap. Way in the distance he noted a particularly impressive, elegant mountain. Was it Pikes Peak? Probably not.

Hannah had driven them both here in her rear-light-challenged Ford, with an okay from Sheriff Werther. The Winnebago was gingerly towed to a spot in front of the service station and lowered to its damaged front paws.

The garage was filthy and cluttered. The owner, Rudy, came out of the bays smiling. He nodded, but from habit, didn't shake hands. His fingers were black. He wore a Carhartt brown jacket, stained beyond saving. He smiled at them in a way that was only a bit like a cat regarding a plump mouse, and started talking like they were old friends. He was rambling on about life here in Gurney, his family (one boy in the army, one girl in nursing school) and assorted relatives. 'Hube's a good man. You know, he's got a grandkid with that autism problem. It's pretty bad, needs special help a lot. Hube works two jobs. Sheriff, and security at Preston Assembly Plant. His wife, my sister—'

Pellam was content to let him go on because, he figured, the more like friends and family this seemed, the less the chance of getting robbed blind. But Hannah wasn't in the mood. She interrupted curtly, 'You mind getting to those estimates? The pickup first.'

'Well now, I'll do that.' With a crinkly-eyed look that meant he'd just added a hundred or two onto the bill.

He headed outside. So did Hannah, setting the Stetson firmly on her head, against the up-and-coming wind. She pulled her cigarettes out of her pocket but then looked at assorted open containers of liquids that might or might not be flammable. She grimaced and put the Marlboros away. She made some calls.

Pellam did, too. He told the director that he'd been in an accident, which the man responded to with more or less genuine concern. When he learned that the county would not under any circumstances issue permits, the director had a more intense reaction.

'Fuckers. Why?'

'Fragile ecosystem.'

'Fragile? You told me it was rocks and sand.'

'Joe, that's what they said. What they mean is that they don't want horny actors and slutty actresses carousing around in their county.'

'We're behind schedule, John.'

'I'll get the camper fixed and head south tomorrow.'

A sigh. 'Okay. Thanks.' The voice grew grave: 'You okay, for sure?'

Concern in tone, not in spirit.

'Fine, Joe.'

He disconnected and happened to be looking at a map of the area. The Devil's Playground seemed to be the best locale for Paradice, the fictional town where the movie was set, as well as being the film's title.

And Pellam laughed to himself, realizing that, damn, the indie was about a stranger coming to a small desert town, like Gurney, and getting into all sorts of trouble. There wasn't much of a story to go with it, but sometimes – especially in noir – all you needed was a misspelled word in the title, some hunky lead and a sexy babe and betrayal. Oh, and a fair amount of gunplay. Never forget the gunplay.

Hannah finished her own call, walked farther away from conflagration risks, and had a portion of a cigarette. Then she returned to the waiting room, staring out the window, too. She flopped down in a cracked fiberglass chair. 'I told Ed. He wasn't happy.'

Pellam got the impression she didn't much care.

'Your husband, the real estate man.'

She looked at him as if asking, You heard that before. Why ask?

'Where's Butch?' Pellam asked.

'Who?'

Oh. Right. 'Taylor.'

'Headed to this little park in the middle of town. He wanted to write a poem.'

'A poem? He's serious about that?'

Hannah continued, 'Said he'd felt inspired by the experience of being out here. In a small Western town.' She shook her head, meaning: I don't get it. 'There's nothing to experience. Not here. Dust maybe, rednecks, losers, coyotes. Hamlin's got a mall.'

Pellam wondered if the shopping center comment was delivered with the irony that seemed warranted. Apparently not.

A few minutes later the huge, bearded mechanic lumbered into the office, rearranging the grease on his fingers with a filthy rag.

'Damn shame 'bout that pickup. Needin' bodywork when you can still smell the new leather. That's always the way, ain't it? Now, miss, I got two options. First'll get you home sooner: I can remove the old bulbs – that's tricky since they're busted – and then screw in new bulbs and mount the lenses. That'll be four hundred eighty dollars. Number two, which I'd recommend, would include all that, plus the bodywork and replacing the hitch. You don't want to tow nothing with it in that present condition. Paint, too.'

'And how much is that?'

'Twenty-eight fifty.'

Hannah squinted. 'Really? I can have my guy in Hamlin do the body-work for a thousand. The hitch is fine, I'll buff off the scratches myself. And why's that even an option? Didn't your brother-in-law tell you I was in a hurry?'

'I—'

'So, we're down to option one. And let's think it through.'

'How's that?'

She continued patiently. 'You can get bulbs for six bucks a pop at NAPA, cheaper at Walmart. I need four of them. The lenses? Let's be generous. Fifty bucks each. Just need two. That's a grand total of one twenty-four in parts. Labor? Now, the bulbs *aren't* screw-mount, like you said. They're bayonet.'

Rudy's face had gone red beneath the smudges. 'Well, I meant "screw", you know, in a like general sense.'

'I'm sure you did,' Hannah muttered. Which was really a very funny line, even if she didn't seem to realize it. 'You put a glove on. Right? Stick your finger into the broken base and push and twist. You can do all four in a minute or two. Takes you another five minutes to mount the new ones. So you're basically charging me four hundred dollars for twenty minutes' work. That's a thousand dollars an hour. My lawyer doesn't charge that. Does yours?' A look at Pellam.

'I don't have a lawyer.' He did but he wasn't going to get involved in this. He was enjoying himself too much.

Silence for a moment.

'I have overheads' was the only defense Rudy could mount.

From beneath her dark, silken eyebrows, she gazed unflinchingly into his evasive eyes.

'Two fifty,' he muttered.

'One fifty.'

'Two fifty.'

'One fifty,' Hannah said firmly.

'Cash?' came the uneasy riposte.

'Cash.'

'Okay. Jesus.' The mechanic sullenly retreated into his garage to fetch the tools.

Pellam glanced at the Winnebago. He had no talent whatsoever when it came to motor vehicles, except for the uncanny ability to attract state troopers when he was speeding. Rudy was going to hose him. Maybe he should have Hannah go over the estimate.

He walked to the vending machine and bought a Moon Pie. Pellam noted the 'complimentary' coffee and thought about making a joke that it *better* say nice things about you because it looked like sludge. But Hannah just didn't seem to be the sort to share clever comments with. He bought a vending-machine instant coffee. Which wasn't terrible, with the double milk powder.

'You really picked that fellow up?' Pellam asked her after a moment. 'I clock a hundred thousand miles a year but I never pick up hitchers.'

'Even pretty women?'

'Especially them. Though I've been tempted.' A glance into her pale eyes. Then he grazed her tan.

She chose not to flirt back. 'I normally wouldn't've, but he did help me out. And I mean, really, a poet or grad student? He's about as harmless as they come.'

'Still could be pretty dangerous,' Pellam said gravely.

She looked at him with consideration.

'What if he started reciting poetry at you?'

A blink. 'Actually, he did. And it sucks.'

'You ever been to Berkeley?'

'No. I don't travel much. Not out of the state.'

Pellam had scouted for a film there. The movie was about the regents at a fictional school, which happened to look a lot like UC-B, tear-gassing protesting students in the sixties, and the rise of the counterculture. All very politically correct. The critics liked it. Unfortunately most of the people who went to see it, which was not very many, did not. Pellam thought the concept had potential, but the director had ignored his suggestions – because he was JTLS. And even though he'd been a successful director himself years ago, anyone who was Just-the-Location-Scout, like Just-the-Grip or even Just-the-Screenwriter, was bound to be ignored by God.

'He seems old to be a student.'

A shrug, a glance toward Pellam, as if she were noticing him for the first time. 'Maybe one of those perpetual college kids. Doesn't want to get into the real world. Afraid of making money.'

The Moon Pie was pretty good. He thought about offering her a bite.

But he liked it more than he liked her, despite the glance from her cool, gray eyes.

Pellam eyed a '74 Gremlin, painted an iridescent green that existed nowhere in nature. Now, that was a car with personality, whatever else you could say about it. From the tiny engine to the downright weird logo of, yes, a gremlin. He stuck his head inside. It smelled like what 1974 must have smelled like.

Rudy finished the job in jiffy time and even washed the windshield for her, though the water in the pail didn't leave it much cleaner than before.

She paid him, and the big mechanic went on to look over Pellam's Winnebago. Two flat tires, wrecked bumper, probably front-end work. Maybe the fan. Bum brakes too, of course. What landed him here in the first place. If a bit of paint and fixing some dents were going to cost Ms Hostility nearly three grand, what the hell was his estimate going to be? At least he had the production company credit card, though that would entail a complicated and thorough explanation to the accounting powers that be – and in the film business those were formidable powers indeed.

Rudy went off to do his ciphering. Pellam expected him to lick his pencil tip before he wrote, but he didn't.

'Where the hell's Taylor?' Hannah looked around with some irritation. 'I told him to meet me here.'

Pellam decided that with her impatience, edge, and taste for authentic jewelry, in quantity, a poet would not make the cut in a relationship.

Good luck to you, Ed.

'You have Taylor's number?' Pellam asked.

'No phone. He doesn't believe in them. One of those.'

He didn't know exactly what that category was, but he could figure it out. 'How big can Gurney be?' Pellam asked.

'Too big,' she said.

She was tough, but Pellam had to give her credit for some really good lines.

Rudy came back and, maybe it was Hannah's presence, but the estimate was just under three Gs. Not terrible. He said okay. Rudy explained he'd call for the parts. They'd be here in the morning. 'You'll need to get a room for the night.'

'I have one.'

'You do?'

'The camper.'

'Oh, right.' The mechanic returned to his shop.

Pellam ate some more Moon Pie and sipped coffee.

Hannah looked around the repair shop office and didn't see anything to sit on. She started to ask Pellam, 'You—'

But she was interrupted when two law enforcement vehicles, different jurisdictions, to judge from the color, pulled into the lot in front of the station. They parked. Werther got out of the first and was joined by the second car's occupant, a young Colorado state trooper, in a dark blue shirt, leather jacket and Smokey the Bear hat.

Pellam and Hannah left the shop, stepping into the windy afternoon, and joined them.

'Ms Billings, Mr Pellam, this's Sergeant Lambert from the Colorado State Patrol. He'd like to talk to you for a minute.'

Heads were nodded. No hands shaken.

Lambert wasn't as young as he seemed, looking into the weathered face up close, though he was still a decade behind Pellam. His dark eyes were still and cautious.

'You were both near Devil's Playground around ten thirty a.m. today, is that correct?'

'I was,' Pellam said. 'Around then.'

Hannah: 'Probably, yeah.'

'And the sheriff says you weren't alone.'

'No, a man was with me. Taylor . . . Duke was with me.'

'I see. Well, seems a man was murdered about that time near the Playground. On some private land near Lake Lobos.'

'Really,' Hannah said, not particularly interested.

'His name was Jonas Barnes. A commercial real estate developer from Quincy.'

Pellam pitched out the remaining Moon Pie. For some reason it just seemed like a bad idea to eat junk food pastries while being questioned about a homicide. The coffee went, too.

The trooper continued, 'He was stabbed to death. We think the killer was surprised. He started to drag him to one of the caves nearby, but somebody showed up and he fled. That tells us there was a witness. Either of you happen to see anyone around there then? Parked vehicles? Hikers, fishermen? Anything out of the ordinary?'

Hannah shook her head.

Pellam thought back. 'This was in the Devil's Playground?'

'South of there. The victim was looking over some land he was thinking of buying.'

'Where that spur to the interstate's gonna go?' This was from Rudy, who'd wandered up, doing more grease rearranging. He nodded a greeting to his brother-in-law.

'That's the place, yeah,' the trooper offered. Werther said he didn't know.

'Well, that's what I heard. Connecting Fourteen to I-Fifty-two.'

Ah, the infamous State Route 14. Pellam looked at Hannah Billings again. Her cool eyes and grim mouth didn't make her any less attractive. He'd never see her again after today, of course, but he wondered just how married was she? Women like that, that was a natural question. It asked itself.

Hannah said, 'I wasn't in the park. I had a flat about a half-mile south. It was near a café.'

'Duncan Schaeffer's place?'

She looked at the mechanic with a gaze that said, And why the hell would I know who owns it?

The trooper said, 'And the fellow who helped you with the flat? The hitchhiker? He might've seen more, since he was on foot.'

'Could be,' she offered.

'Where is he now?'

'He was downtown. He's supposed to meet me. Should've been here by now, I'd think.'

The trooper took down their information and said he'd get an update while he waited until Taylor Duke returned. With ramrod-straight posture, he returned to his car, sat down, and began to type onto his computer. Sheriff Werther finished a conversation with Rudy, who headed back to the shop. The sheriff started up the cruiser and headed off.

Pellam spotted a convenience store fifty yards up the dusty road. He could get a frozen dinner to nuke, and curl up with a whiskey and a map of southeastern Colorado to find a shooting location for *Paradice*.

He'd get something, but he was pissed he'd been denied Devil's Playground. It was perfect.

Stepping away, Hannah lit another cigarette, having some trouble getting the tobacco to stay alight in the stream of wind. He caught a glimpse of her pale eyes, her dark eyebrows, jeans tight as paint, as the flame flared. She snapped the lighter shut – a silver one, not disposable.

Madam, I'm Adam . . .

She ambled in his direction, as a fierce gust of wind pushed her starboard a few inches. As she closed in, she hung up. 'Don't get married,' she muttered. 'Ever.'

This intelligence about Ed was interesting. So was what she said next. 'We go inside?' A nod at the camper.

But when he responded, 'You bet we can,' he wasn't flirting. The damn wind had chilled him to the bone.

Once they were in the confined space, Pellam noted immediately that they both smelled of service station – a sweet and ultimately unpleasant astringent smell, courtesy of Rudy and Gurney Auto Service, *We Fix All Makes and Models, Foriegn too!! Dump your Oil HERE.*

Hannah noticed this as well and smelled her leather sleeve. 'Jesus.' She settled into the bench seat behind the tiny kitchenette table. 'Kind of homey.'

'I like it.'

Eyeing her beautiful face, to gauge if she was bored by his narrative, he told her about life on the road, what appealed to him. She did seem more or less interested. She rose, went to the cupboard. 'Vodka?'

'Whiskey.'

'Headache.' She seemed to pout.

Pellam was amused. Hurrying off into the windy afternoon to buy her vodka was just the sort of thing that the straight guy, the innocent, the mark would do for a femme fatale in a noir movie like *Paradice*. And it was generally a bad decision on all fronts.

Hannah looked him over carefully once more and then sat down on the bed, rather than the banquette. Her head dipped, her eyes locked on to his.

He asked, 'Grey Goose or Belvedere?'

Ten minutes later he'd shelled out big bucks for the premium and bought himself an extra fifth of Knob Creek, just to be safe. Two Stouffer's frozen lasagnas, too. They were both for him. He didn't think Hannah would stay around for dinner.

Don't get married. Ever.

At first he'd thought that was a warning, not an invitation. But seeing her on the bed he wasn't so sure.

The wind kept up its insistent buffeting, and Pellam walked with his head down, eyes squinted to slits. He'd spent a lot of time in deserts and it seemed to him that the grit in Colorado, Gurney in particular, was the sharpest and most abrasive. Imagination probably.

He lifted his head and oriented himself, then adjusted course. Pellam walked past an abandoned one-story building that had been a video store. You hardly saw any of these any more. As somebody in the Industry, he'd never really liked video tape or DVDs. And he didn't like streaming movies on your computer or through your TV, however gargantuan was your Samsung or Sony. There was an intimacy about going to a theater to watch a movie. Lights going down, the hush of the crowd, then experiencing the images big and loud and awash with the reactions of everyone else. That was how movies should be—

Whatever hit him weighed fifty pounds easy. It shattered the vodka and whiskey and sent Pellam tumbling into the street.

But stuntman instincts never quite go away. He rolled rather than impacted, diffusing the energy. And in a smooth motion he sprang up, flexing his right hand to see if it was broken – it wasn't. Two fists and he was ready to fight.

The assailant, however, wasn't. He was already sprinting away from the attack, through the brush. Pellam couldn't see him clearly, but he noted that it seemed the man had a backpack on.

Interesting . . .

Pellam was about to go after him, but glanced toward the camper, about a hundred feet away, and saw the body lying on the ground.

In dark clothing.

Hell, was it Hannah?

He ran forward and stopped fast.

No, it was the State Patrol trooper. He was lying on his back, one leg straight, the other up, knee crooked. His throat had been slit, deep. A lake of blood surrounded his head and neck. His holster was empty. Bootprints led from the body into the woods behind the service station.

Then a man's voice from nearby: 'Help me!'

Pellam spun around. From the repair shop Rudy staggered toward the street. He'd been stabbed or struck on the head, and blood cascaded down to his shoulder. He was staring at his hand, covered with the red liquid. 'What's this? What's this?' He was hysterical.

Pellam ran to the mechanic. The wound wasn't deep – a blow to the back of the head, it seemed. He eased the man to the ground and found a rag, filthy, but presumably saturated with enough petrochemical substances to render it relatively germ free. He pressed it against the wound.

Hannah?

Pellam ran to the camper and flung the door open.

'Any sign of—?' Hannah's question skidded to a halt as she looked him over, covered with the aromatic dregs of whiskey and vodka, which glued dust and dirt to his body.

'Jesus. What's going on?'

Pellam opened the tiny compartment beside the door. He took out his antique Colt .45 Peacemaker, a cowboy gun, and loaded it. Slipped it into his back waistband.

'Trooper's dead, Rudy's hurt. Somebody decked me. I think it was your hitchhiker. I couldn't see for sure but I think so.'

'The poet?'

'Yep.'

'You have a gun? Where'd you get a gun?'

'Wait here.'

Recalling that Taylor would have the trooper's weapon, he opened the camper door slowly and stepped into the wind.

No shots. And no sign of the man. Where would he have fled to?

He pulled out his cell phone and hit 911.

He got the operator, but five seconds later he was patched through to the sheriff himself.

Pellam didn't think that was the sort of thing that ever happened in the big city.

Ten minutes later Hannah joined him outside as Werther showed up.

Hannah Billings was not the sort of person who stayed inside when she didn't want to stay inside, whatever threats awaited.

The sheriff jumped out fast and ran to the trooper first, then saw there was nothing he could do for the man. He went to his brother-in-law, sitting on a bench in front of the service station. After a word or two with the man he returned to Hannah and Pellam. He made a radio call to see about the ambulance and to call in several other state patrol cars.

And then he pulled his weapon out and pointed it toward Pellam. He arrested him for murder.

Pellam blinked. 'You're out of your mind.'

Werther was his typical calm, the statue of reason. 'You told me you weren't where Jonas Barnes was killed this afternoon.'

'Well, I didn't *know* where he was killed. I told you as best I could.'

'Witness saw you standing over the body.'

Pellam closed his eyes and shook his head. 'No. I didn't *see* a body.'

'And it looked like you were holding a knife. Which is how Barnes died. You started to drag him away into a cave and then you realized somebody was nearby. You ran.'

'Who is this witness?'

'It was anonymous. But he described you to a T.'

Hannah said, 'It was Taylor. It had to be.'

Pellam pointed to the ground. 'Those footprints! Those're just what he was wearing. And he attacked me.'

'You say that. I didn't see it.' He looked to Hannah. 'Did you see it?'

She hesitated. 'He couldn't've done it.'

'Was he with you?'

Before she spoke Pellam said, 'No, I was just coming back from the store up there and I got jumped. Then I found them. Why would I call 911 if I was the guilty party?'

'So you wouldn't look guilty, of course.'

'Jesus Christ. Taylor's getting away.'

'Turn around and put your hands behind your back.'

Pellam turned around and gave it ten seconds for Werther to holster his weapon and get his cuffs out. He fast-drew the Colt from his waistband and touched the muzzle against the sheriff's belly, pulled out the man's Glock and flung it into bushes across the road.

The man gasped. 'Oh, Lord. Please, I got a family . . .'

'And if you want to see 'em you'll hand the cuffs to your brother-in-law.'

'I—'

Pellam stepped back and now aimed at Rudy. 'Sorry, but do it.'

The big man hesitated, looked at the gun, then at the spreading lake of blood around the trooper. He took the cuffs. 'Cuff him.' Pellam then barked, 'Now! I don't have time to wait!'

The big man said, 'I don't know how they work.'

'Mister, this's going to mean nothing but trouble for you for a long, long time.'

Pellam ignored the law enforcer and explained the cuffs to Rudy. Everyone, Hannah included, probably wondered why he knew this esoteric skill.

Motioning Rudy back, Pellam frisked Werther and found plastic hand restraints. He bound Rudy's wrists behind him. Then, pointing his Colt Hannah's way, he said, 'I'm taking your car . . . and you. You're driving.'

'Listen—'

'No, I'm tired of listening,' Pellam snapped. 'Move now!'

'Pellam,' Werther called. 'You won't get but a mile. Troopers already have roadblocks up.'

But he was gesturing Hannah into the truck. The big engine fired up and she skidded into the road, the fix-your-seatbelt light flashing but the chime disconnected. Hannah seemed like the kind of woman who couldn't be bothered with things like safety restraints.

Pellam slipped the gun away. 'Sorry. I didn't have any choice.'

'No,' she said. The word might've been a question.

'I didn't kill Barnes,' he said. 'Or anyone.'

'I didn't think you had. Why'd you kidnap me?'

'It's not a kidnap. It's a borrowing. I need your car . . . and, okay, I needed a hostage.'

She snickered bitterly.

He continued. 'The only way to prove I'm innocent is to find your goddamn poet. He's not driving out of here either. He'll be hiding out someplace. The cops'll be checking all the motels. He'll camp out somewhere. Caverns or someplace like that, I'd guess. You have any ideas?'

'Me?' she snapped, sounding insulted. 'I'm not from here. I was just passing through this fucking place when you rear-ended me. Most I've ever done in Gurney 'fore today's bought overpriced gas.'

She took a turn at nearly fifty, inducing a slight skid, which she controlled expertly. Pellam's knees banged the dash. So she could reach the pedals, she'd moved the seats all the way forward.

She was staying off the main roads.

Pellam thought for a minute. 'I've got an idea.' He dug in his pocket for a business card.

*

The office of Southeastern Colorado Ecological Center was outside Gurney in an area that looked more like ski territory than desert: pines, brush, grass and scrub oak, or low trees that looked like they ought to be called scrub oak even if they weren't. The building seemed to include offices, a small museum, and an even smaller lecture hall.

A sign announced that people could learn about the relationship between carbon dioxide and 'our green friends' next Tuesday at 6:30 p.m. Pellam supposed the audience would be local. He didn't know who'd drive from Mosby, the next town north, let alone Denver, three hours away, for entertainment like this.

'No troopers. That's the good news.' Pellam was looking over the three cars parked in the employee lot. None of them were hybrids; that was one of the ironies about the eco movement. Even many people in the field couldn't afford to practice what they preached. He counted four bicycles, though.

Inside, at the desk, he found the woman who'd been bicycling along Route 14 when Pellam had slugged the rear of Hannah's truck. Lis, of Lis and Chris.

She looked up with her official visitor-greeting grin. Then blinked as a wave of recognition descended over her. 'Today . . . the accident . . . Hey.'

And no other reaction. Pellam looked at Hannah and the meaning was, So, Werther hasn't been in touch asking her to report a kidnapper and kidnappee.

'Sorry, I forgot your names.'

'John and Hannah,' Pellam offered.

'Sure. What can I do for you? Is this about the insurance?'

'No, actually,' Hannah said, delivering the spiel they'd come up with in the car. 'We're trying to find that friend of mine? Was in the diner with me?'

'With the crew cut?'

'Right. He was talking about camping out, maybe around some caverns in the area. But my truck got fixed up sooner than I thought. I want to get back to Hamlin now. He'll want to come with me.'

'Camping, hmm? Hope he brought his long underwear. Gets cold there.'

'So there's a place you think he might be?'

Lis pulled a map out of a rack on the edge of her desk. She consulted it and pointed. 'Here, I'd bet. Just past the old quarry.'

It was about three miles or so from where they were.

'Appreciate that. Thanks.'

Pellam took the map. He noted the price was two dollars. He gave her a ten. 'Consider the rest a donation.'

'Hey, thanks.' She gave him a button that said, *Earth Lover*.

This time Pellam drove, fast and just a bit recklessly. Hannah didn't mind one bit. If anything, she seemed bored. She fished under the seat and found a small bottle of screw-top wine, the sort they give you on airplanes. She untwisted the lid with a cracking sound. She drank half. 'You want some?'

Pellam wouldn't have minded a hit of whiskey, but his Knob Creek was history and there was nothing worse than airplane wine. 'Pass.'

She finished it.

In ten minutes they were at the quarry. A chain-link fence attempted to seal it off but even a sumo wrestler could have squeezed in through the gaps.

Pellam looked at his watch. It was nearly six thirty. He checked the gun once more. Thinking he should've brought more shells. But too late for that.

'You head on back. Tell 'em you escaped.'

'How'll you get out?'

'I'll have to call our friend Werther, whatever happens. Whether I find Taylor or not I'm going to get busted. The only difference'll be how long it takes to recite the charges against me.'

Eerie as hell.

Devil's Playground had been plenty spooky but the Gurney Quarry at dusk on a windy day ran a very close second.

Of course some of that might have to do with the fact that there was possibly a killer wandering around here. There'd been one at the Playground, too, it seemed, but Pellam hadn't known it. That made a big difference. In the failing light he could just make out the austere beauty of the place, the chalky bone-white cliffs, the turquoise water at the base of the quarry going from azure to gray, the sensual curves of the black shadows of the hills.

Soon, in the dark, it would just be a maze of hiding places and traps. The wind howled mournfully over the landscape.

Thinking about Taylor. Sheriff Werther. And about Hannah. He thought about Ed some, too. He moved forward slowly, nervously thumbing the hammer of the Colt and not hearing a single boot on rock as a killer snuck up behind him.

An owl swooped low and snagged something – mouse or chipmunk – then veered off into the sky. The squeak had been loud and brief.

For half an hour, he tracked along the ground here, looking for suitable hiding places. With the cowboy gun and the ambience here, he was thinking of his ancestor. Wild Bill Hickok – James Butler; no 'William' was involved in any part of the name. The gunslinger/marshal had been murdered, shot in the back of the head by a man he'd beat at poker the day before. But what specifically Pellam was recalling was that Hickok felt bad for Jack McCall, the murderer, and gave him back some of what he'd lost.

But McCall had thought the gesture condescending, and that was the motive for the murder, not cheating, not arrogance.

A good deed.

Pellam shivered in the wind. He moved more slowly now – dusk was thick, and moonlight still an hour away. But he saw no signs of anyone.

A moment later, though, a hundred yards away, the flicker of light. From one of the large caverns near the edge of the quarry. Pellam moved quickly toward the cavern where he'd seen it, dodging rocks and scrub oak and wiry balls of tumbleweed. The cavern was in a cul-de-sac. On one side a sheer wall rose fifty feet into the air, its surface scarred and chopped by the stonecutters. On the other side, the quarry fell into blackness.

Twenty feet from the entrance to the cavern. The light seemed dimmer now.

Moving closer, listening. Moving again. Hell, it was noisy, this persistent wind. Like the slipstream roaring through the window of the Winnebago that afternoon.

Mountain, truck or air . . .

He saw nothing other than the dancing light. Was it a fire? Or a lantern?

And then: What the hell am I doing here?

A question that was never answered because at that moment a man stepped from the shadows beside him and aimed his pistol at Pellam's head.

'Drop that.'

'Can I set it down?'

'No.'

Pellam dropped the gun.

It wasn't Taylor. The man had salt-and-pepper hair. He was in his fifties, Pellam estimated, and he was wearing khaki hiking clothes. He gestured Pellam back and retrieved the Peacemaker. Into a cell phone he said, 'He's here.'

'Where is he?'

That being the hitchhiker/poet.

Though Pellam knew the answer to the question: The ramblin' man was either dead or tied up somewhere nearby.

Was this fellow in front of him, with the gun, Chris? The husband or partner of green-minded Lis, who had murdered Jonas Barnes near the Devil's Playground today – presumably because Barnes was going to rape the earth by putting in a shopping center along the spur to the interstate?

If that was the case, then he reflected that it was rather ironic that they'd nearly run her down as she was returning from her deadly mission.

And, sure enough, he heard a woman's voice. 'I'm here, it's me.'

Glancing toward the sound, Pellam realized that his theory about Barnes's demise, while logical, was in fact wrong.

The murderer was not earth-loving Lis.

It was Hannah Billings.

Pellam turned to the man with the gun and said, 'So, you must be Ed.'

'Does that thing work?' she asked her husband.

The man was looking over Pellam's Peacemaker with some admiration. 'Nice. I have a collection myself.'

Pellam had the bizarre thought that Ed Billings was going to start a genial conversation about antique firearms.

With a neutral glance Pellam's way, Ed walked into the cavern and hauled Taylor to his feet. He was tied – though not duct-taped – which would, presumably, leave a residue that crime-scene folks could detect. They were good at that. Pellam knew this from several movies he'd worked on. He'd known it, too, from an incident in his past, a manslaughter charge that had derailed his directing career and was responsible for his present vocation of location scouting. The police had been all over the evidence. Pellam's extremely expensive defense attorney hadn't bothered to try to sever the head of that testimony.

'What the hell is going on here?' he pleaded. 'Who are you?'

Pellam could picture clearly what these two had planned: Oh, damn, we got it wrong, the sheriff would announce. That Pellam fellow wasn't guilty after all. It was that weird poet who killed Jonas Barnes. A hitchhiker, what did you expect? Pellam tracked him down – to prove he was innocent – and the man jumped him. They fought, they died.

A shame.

The poor hitchhiker was as baffled as he was terrified.

Pellam nodded. 'Was it the real estate?'

Hannah was ignoring him. She was looking over the scenery, approaches, backdrops. Hell, she looked just like a cinematographer blocking out camera angles.

But Ed was happy to talk. 'Barnes had an option to buy the five hundred acres next to Devil's Playground.'

'Worth millions to whoever owned the land,' Pellam said. 'When the spur was finished.'

Ed Billings nodded. 'Fast food, gasoline and toilets. That kind of describes our country, docsn't it?'

Pellam was distracted, since the man's gun – a very efficient Glock – moved toward his abdomen, now his groin. There was no traditional safety on a Glock. You simply pointed and shot. And the trigger pull was pretty light. Pellam felt certain parts south contracting.

'But his estate could exercise the option.'

'No, we know the wife. She wasn't interested in real estate.'

Pellam said to Hannah, 'You killed Barnes but you needed a fall guy, so you picked up the hitchhiker, who would've taken the blame. It was going to be easy. Kill the real estate guy, plant some of his things on Taylor, a little DNA . . . It probably would've worked. But then – ah, got it now – then came the monkey wrench. Me.'

Hannah said, 'After Barnes was dead I saw you with that fancy video camera of yours. I was afraid you'd got me on tape.'

'And you undid my brake line.' He gave a brittle laugh. 'Sure, you know cars – the way you talked Rudy down with the brake lights incident. You were going to go through the wreckage and find the camera and tapes.'

'Except you got to the switchback faster than I thought you would and rammed into me.'

Pellam understood. 'Change of plans, sure. You decided to go for cocktails in my camper. You get the tapes when I went to the convenience store?'

'I got 'em.' She nodded, presumably at the truck, parked nearby.

'But you still needed the fall guy.' Pellam looked toward Ed Billings. 'And you showed up to kidnap Taylor, dress up in his clothes and kill the trooper.'

'Right.'

'And now I kill Taylor and he kills me. End of story.'

Hannah had lost interest in the narrative. 'Yeah,' she said. 'Shoot him. I'm bored with all this crap. I want to get home.'

Hamlin has a mall . . .

Just like the end of a Quentin Tarantino film. The filmmaker tended to fall back on the good old Mexican standoff, everybody pointing a gun at each other.

'Only one thing,' Pellam said, buying time.

'What's that?' Ed asked.

'When does she shoot *you*?'

'Me?'

'That's the scenario, situations like this. The girl sets it all up and then shifts the blame to her husband. He takes the fall and she rides off into the sunset with the money.'

A brief pause. Ed said, 'You know the flaw in that? You can only do it once. And so far we're worth more to each other alive.'

He lifted the Glock.

Which was when a series of lights came on and voices started shouting, 'Police, police! On the ground, drop the weapons!' and similar assorted cop phrases, all enthusiastically punctuated.

Pellam supposed that Sheriff Werther and the others were charging forward with their assault rifles and executing some nifty arrest procedures.

He couldn't say. At the first flash of spotlight he'd dropped to his belly and ducked. Another aspect of noir stories is that everybody has a gun and is always real eager to use it.

Fifteen minutes later Pellam was leaning against the side of Sheriff Werther's car. He handed back the tracking device – it looked like a garage door opener – that the man had slipped into his pocket at the sham arrest two hours ago, in front of the Winnebago.

'Worked pretty good,' Pellam observed.

Werther, though, winced, looking at it. 'Truth be told, seems there was only five minutes or so of battery left.'

Meaning, Pellam assumed, that if they hadn't tracked him to the quarry in that time he'd now be dead.

'Ah.'

But considering that the sheriff's plan had been thrown together quickly, it was understandable that there'd been a glitch or two.

When Pellam had been patched through to Werther after finding the trooper dead and Rudy injured, the sheriff had explained that the medical examiner had given the opinion that the man had been stabbed by someone who was short – five five or less, given the angle of the knife wounds. 'And remember, somebody'd tried to drag the body to a cave? The trooper thought it was that they'd been spotted. Fact is, I decided they just weren't strong enough.'

Those facts suggested the killer might be a woman, he explained.

Well, there were two women having something to do with the case, Werther had said: Hannah and Lis. And each of them had a male partner who could be an accomplice. So the sheriff decided to set up a trap to find out if either of them was the killer. But he needed Pellam's help. The location scout was supposed to let both Hannah and Lis know that he was searching for Taylor.

Turning himself into a fall guy.

Whoever showed up at the quarry to kill him would be the guilty party.

Taylor was at the hospital in Redding for observation. Ed Billings had whaled on him pretty bad. When he'd said goodbye to Pellam a half-hour before, he'd smiled ruefully and said, 'Hey, quite an experience, hmm?'

'Good luck with the poems,' the location scout had told him as he walked to the ambulance.

'Say,' Werther now asked Pellam, '*did* you get anybody on tape at Devil's Playground?'

Pellam gave a sour laugh. 'Not a soul.'

'Hmm, too bad. Though I don't suspect we need the evidence.'

'You've got property around there, too, don't you, Sheriff?' Pellam asked wryly.

'Oh, what Rita was saying? Yeah, I do. Vacation house that I rent out. Helps for some of the expenses my son has.'

For his autistic grandchild, Pellam recalled.

'You suspect me?' Werther asked.

'No, sir, never occurred to me.'

It had.

'Okay . . . Now, about that little matter you and I horse-traded on? It's all taken care of,' the sheriff said.

'Thanks.'

'You earned it.'

Pellam then asked for his brother-in-law's phone number.

'Rudy? He can't get your camper in shape until tomorrow.'

'This is about something else.'

Motion in the corner of his eye. Hannah Billings was being led across the parking area in front of the quarry to a squad car. She glanced his way.

A phrase came to Pellam's mind:

If looks could kill . . .

Here's Rita at the diner, her name proudly stitched on her impressive bosom.

She's doing what she does best with diligence and polite mien, and with no tolerance for nonsense from former movie directors turned location scouts, from flirtatious poets, from killers noir at heart, from saints. Anybody. She takes waitressing seriously.

Pellam wasn't in the mood for frozen so he'd arranged a private vehicle rental from Rudy (yes, the bile-green Gremlin, which was, he knew, a very underrated vehicle – it could beat the Pinto and VW Beetle hands down, at least with the optional four-speed BorgWarner).

He's finished a meatloaf dinner and orders pie with cheese. He didn't used to like this combo but, really, who shouldn't? It doesn't get any better than sweet apples and savory Kraft. He'd go for a whiskey, but that's not an option at the Overlook, so it's coffee, which is exemplary.

He gets a call on his cell. The director of *Paradice* is ecstatic that Pellam has secured a permit to shoot in Devil's Playground after all.

'How'd you do it?'

Put my life on the line to catch a femme fatale, he thinks, earning Sheriff Werther's friendship and assistance in all things governmental here.

'Just pulled some strings.'

'Ah, I love string pullers,' the director says breathily.

Pellam thinks about suggesting a new name for the film: *Devil's Playground*. But he knows in his heart that the director will never buy it – he just *loves* his misspelled title.

Fine. It's his movie, not mine.

As he ends the call Pellam feels eyes aimed his way. He looks up and believes that Rita is casting him a flirt, which is not by any means a bad thing.

Then he glances at her with a smile and sees she is, in fact, looking a few degrees past him. It's toward a young man standing beside a revolving dessert display, featuring cakes that seem three feet high. He's looking back at her. The nervous boy is handsome if pimply. He sits down at the end of the counter, isolated so he can gab a bit with her in private. He also will, Pellam knows, leave a five-dollar tip, though he can't really afford it, on a ten-dollar tab, which will both embarrass and enthrall her.

Ain't love grand?

The pie comes in for a landing and Pellam indulges. It's good, no question.

His thoughts wander. He's considering his time in Paradice, wait, no in *Gurney*, and he decides that, just like State Route 14, life sometimes is a switchback. You never know what's going to happen around the next hairpin, or who's who and what's what.

But other times the road doesn't curve at all. It's straight as a ruler for miles and miles. What you see ahead is exactly what you're going to get, no twists, no surprises. And the people you meet are just what they seem to be. The environmentalist is simply passionate about saving the earth. The hitchhiking poet is nothing more or less than a self-styled soul mate of Jack Kerouac, rambling around the country in search of who knows what. The sheriff is a hardworking pro with a conscience and a grandkid who needs particular looking after.

And the sexy cowgirl with red nails and a feather in her Stetson is exactly the bitch you pretty much knew in your heart she'd turn out to be.

THE COMPETITORS

Olympic stadiums are unlike any other structures on earth.

From the 1936 sports complex in Berlin to the 1976 Montreal games' soaring edifice, taller than the Washington Monument . . . all such stadiums exude true magnificence, each a testament to a pivotal moment in human history.

The power, though, derives less from architecture than from the spirit of competitions past and competitions to come, an energy filling the massive spaces like the cries of spectators. An Olympic stadium is where you test yourself against your fellow man. For that defines human nature.

This philosophical thought was going through the mind of Yuri Umarov as he gazed at the world's most recent Olympic stadium, brilliantly conceived to resemble a bird's nest, its image rippling in the heat.

Yuri, sitting, coated in sweat, beside the cinder track of a Beijing high school, where, along with dozens of other people – local and international – he'd been working out all morning.

Competition. Winning. Bringing glory to your countrymen.

He felt this spirit now, this energy.

Though he also felt exhausted. And the glory he sought seemed extremely elusive. His legs and side hurt from pounding along the track the hundredth time since 5 a.m. His lungs hurt from inhaling the thick air. The government here had supposedly been working to cleanse the atmosphere, but to Yuri, a country boy from the mountains, it was like training in a roomful of smokers.

He looked up and saw his mentor approach.

Gregor Dallayev, white haired, twice his age, walked briskly. Still athletic himself, the man, who sported a massive mustache, was wearing white slacks and a dark shirt with a collar. Sweat stains blossomed under his arms, but he appeared otherwise unmoved by the fierce summer heat.

He was also unmoved by Yuri's performance.

'You are sitting down,' Gregor said impatiently in Russian.

Yuri stood immediately. He took the water the man held and drank half down, then poured the rest on his head and shoulders. He was breathing harder than he needed to, trying to convince the older man that he was truly exhausted. Gregor's sharp eye studied the athlete with a look that said, 'Don't try to fool me. I've seen that before.'

'That last run was not acceptable.' He held up a stopwatch. 'Look at that time.'

Sweat clouded Yuri's eyes and he could hardly see the watch itself, much less the digital numbers.

'I was . . .' Yuri was going to come up with an excuse, a cramp, a slippery patch of cinders. But Gregor would not accept excuses from anyone. And in fact they tasted bad in Yuri's mouth, too. Such was his upbringing and training, during his nineteen years of life. 'I'm sorry.'

Gregor, though, relented, smiling. 'Beastly sun. Not like home.'

'No, sir. It's not like home at all.'

Then, as they walked back to the starting line, Gregor was once again the taskmaster. 'Do you know what your problem is?'

There were undoubtedly many of them. Yuri found it easier to say, 'No, sir.'

His mentor said softly, 'You are not seeing the second ribbon.'

'The second ribbon?'

Gregor nodded. 'In there,' he said, nodding at the stadium sitting in the hazy sun, 'in there, the best runners will not be running to break the tape with their chests at the finish line.'

'They won't?'

'No!' the mentor scoffed. 'They will not even see the tape. They won't even see the finish line. They will be concentrating on the second ribbon.'

'Where is the second ribbon, sir?'

'It is *beyond* the finish line. Maybe ten feet, maybe twenty. Maybe one.'

'I don't think I've ever seen it.'

'You don't see it, not with your eyes. You see it in here.' He touched his chest. 'In your heart.'

Yuri waited for him to finish, as he knew the older man would.

'That is the ribbon you must reach. It's the goal beyond the goal. See, inferior runners will slow as they approach the end of the race. But you won't. You will continue on faster and faster, even though you can go no faster. You must pass through the finish line as if it's not there and fly straight to the second ribbon.'

'I think I understand, sir.'

Gregor looked at him closely. 'Yes, I think you do. Tomorrow, any time over thirty seconds is failure. Your whole journey here will have been wasted. You don't wish to disgrace yourself and your country, do you?'

'Of course not, sir.'

'Good. Let's try it again. Your last run was thirty-one point two seconds. That's not enough. Now, take your mark. And this time, run for the second ribbon.'

Billy Savitch was the youngest on the American team.

In his thin nylon running suit, emblazoned with the tricolor US flag, he was wandering around the American compound, nodding hello to the athletes he knew, pausing to chat with the staff. And ignoring the flirts from the girls. Billy had no interest in them, but you could understand why they'd smile his way. He was rugged and handsome and charming. With his crew cut and sharp eyes and chiseled face he looked like a cowboy – which they still had a fair amount of in his home state of Texas.

This was the second time he'd been out of the country and the first time to the Olympics, though, of course, he watched the games every four years – in the past on the big-screen TV at his parents' house and, the last one, on his very small-screen TV, in the house that he shared with his wife and baby daughter.

And, my God, just think about it. Here he was in China, part of the most famous sporting event of the world. It was the best thing that had happened to him ever, short of being a husband and father.

Though there was a bit of a taint on the experience.

His junior status. He was just a green kid. And, as an all-star running back on his team at home, it was hard for him to be relegated to the bottom of the barrel. Not that his colleagues didn't treat him politely. It's just that they rarely even noticed him.

Tomorrow was the start of the games and he knew he'd be virtually ignored.

He shouldn't complain. But he was ambitious and had a restless streak about him – that's what had driven him here in the first place. Doing what he believed he was meant to do.

He lifted the bottle of water to his lips and drank a huge amount. He looked at his watch. In a half-hour he could get into the gym and work out. He was looking forward to it. He'd worked out for two hours yesterday and he'd work out for two hours again today. His arms were solid as steel, his legs, too.

'Savitch!'

He turned immediately, hearing the voice of the man who was responsible for his being here.

Muscular and with a narrow, etched face, Frederick Alston strode quickly over the grass. That was one thing about him. He never made you come to him. He had that kind of confidence. He could walk right up to you and you'd still feel you'd been summoned. Despite the heat, he wore a suit and tie – which he always did. Whatever the weather, whatever the occasion.

Alston stopped and looked him over. The young man didn't expect a long conversation; that wasn't Alston's way. While some directors here would micromanage and look over the shoulder of their teams, Alston didn't. If you couldn't pull your share, you were out. Just like that.

And in fact this encounter was brief.

What did surprise – no, shock – Billy, though, was the content of the short exchange.

'I think you're ready to go on the field. Are you?'

'Ready to what?'

'Are you ready to go on the field?' Alston repeated, seemingly irritated that he had to.

'Yessir.'

'Good. Tomorrow. Nine a.m.'

'Opening day?' Billy blurted.

Alston's mouth tightened. 'When is opening day?'

'Tomorrow.'

'Then I guess that's what I mean.' He started away. Then stopped. 'One thing, Savitch?'

'Yessir?'

'Don't screw up.'

'No, sir.'

And with that his only advice, Alston turned, walking away briskly, leaving the young man standing beside a practice track, sweating in sunlight as strong and hot as anything Texas had ever produced.

Ch'ao Yuan was in his forties, a solid man with lotioned hair, cut short. He was wearing a dark suit and white shirt. He was a government bureaucrat, former Communist Party official, and presently the head of security at the stadium. He was one of a half-dozen such security officers – as with all Olympics, there were dozens of venues around the city – but he knew that his was the most prestigious of the assignments. And the most stressful. The big bird nest would be *the* target for enemies, of which his country had more than a few.

Not to mention the Israelis and Americans and Iranians.

And the Iraqis . . . Oh, please.

Now, late afternoon before the first day of games, he was sitting in a modest room in one of the many temporary office buildings constructed for the Olympics. (The games, Ch'ao had learned, were partly athletic, but mostly business, which meant paperwork.)

He was sitting forward, looking over his computer on which was a decrypted email, which had been sent to him from an internal intelligence contact. He'd read it once. And now he was reading it again.

Trying to figure out where this fell on the scale of dangers.

Security for the event was, of course, intense.

There were a number of systems in place. A security fence perimeter around the stadium. Passes with computer chips embedded in them. Fingerprint detectors, iris scanners. Metal detectors, of course, as well as bomb sniffers – dogs and machines at entryways. Alarms on all the service doors. Automatic backup generators that took only thirty seconds to kick in and could support the entire power requirements of the stadium. And there were backups on those.

Ch'ao had five hundred security officers at his disposal.

He was confident of the protective measures that had been taken.

And, yet, this particular piece of intelligence bothered him more than the others.

He grimaced and when his secretary announced that his visitors were here, shut the computer screen off.

A few minutes later two men entered his office: Frederick Alston, whose American team was nearby, and his Russian counterpart, Vladimir Rudenko, whose team was across some miles away.

He'd met them weeks ago and they'd become friends, despite their different cultures and histories – 'Strange bedfellows', was the expression that Alston had used. (Which Ch'ao at first thought he'd mistranslated.)

He greeted them in what was the virtual if not official language of the Olympics, English, though both Alston and Rudenko said hello in passable Mandarin.

Ch'ao said, 'I must tell you something. I've received a communication of a security threat against either of your teams, or both.'

'Just Russian or American?' Rudenko asked.

'That's right.'

'From the Arabs?' Alston asked. He had short gray hair and smooth skin, which pocked-faced Ch'ao envied.

'No information about the source of the threat.'

Rudenko, a large but spongy man, who stood out in contrast to the lean and muscular athletes he came to China with, gave a faint laugh, 'I won't bother to ask about us; the motherland has far too many enemies.'

'What's the threat?' Alston asked.

'Not really a specific threat. It's a tip-off.'

'Tip,' Alston corrected.

'Yes,' Rudenko added. 'A tip-off is what happens in basketball, one of our favorite sports.' His wry look to Alston could mean only one thing – a reminder of the famous 1972 game and Russia's controversial win. Alston ignored the dig.

Ch'ao continued, explaining that an informant said he'd seen someone in a green Chevy taking delivery of plastic explosives yesterday. 'And *another* informant, independent of the first, said that there was going to be an attempt to target some of your players here. I don't know if they're related but it would seem so.'

'Green what?' Rudenko asked. 'Cherry?'

Ch'ao explained about the inexpensive car that was sweeping the country.

'And you don't know more than that?' Alston asked.

'No, we're checking it out now.'

The Russian chuckled. 'And there's a look in your eye, may I say *Comrade* Ch'ao, that makes me concerned.'

Ch'ao sighed and nodded. 'I'm asking you to pull your teams from tomorrow's competition until we see what's going on.'

Rudenko stared. Alston laughed. 'You can't be serious.'

'I'm afraid so.'

'It's the opening day of games. We *have* to compete. It would look very bad if we didn't.'

'Yes, and some of these players are here for only one or two events. If they don't play tomorrow, they might lose their only chance of a lifetime to compete in the Olympics.'

'Our young men and women have trained for years for this.'

'I understand the dilemma but I am concerned for the safety of your players.'

The Russian and American looked at each other. Alston said, 'I'll talk to the team. It will be their decision. But I can tell you right now how they'll vote.'

'How many threats like this have you received?' Rudenko asked.

'We've received dozens of threats. Nothing this specific, though.'

'But,' the Russian pointed out, 'that's hardly specific.'

'Still, I must strongly suggest you consider withdrawing.'

The men said their goodbyes and left the office.

An hour later Ch'ao's phone rang. He picked it up. It was Alston explaining that he'd talked to everyone on the team and the decision was unanimous. They would compete. 'We're here to play. Not to hide.'

He'd no sooner hung up than he got a call from the Russian, saying that his team, too, would be participating on opening day.

Sighing, Ch'ao hung up thinking: No wonder the Cold War lasted so long, if the Kremlin and White House back then were like these two – stubborn and foolish as donkeys.

Around 9 a.m. on the first day of the games a man bicycled up to a low dusty building near Chaoyang Park, which was, coincidentally, a venue for one of the events: the volleyball competition. The man paused, hopped off and leaned the bike against the wall. He looked up the street, filled with many such bicycles, and observed the park, where security officers patrolled.

He kept his face emotionless but, in fact, he was incensed that the Chinese had won the Olympics this year. Furious. The man was a Uyghur, pronounced Wee-gur; these were a Turkic-speaking people from the interior of China, who had long fought for their independence – mostly politically but occasionally through terrorism.

He took a pack of cigarettes from his shirt pocket and slipped his stubby finger inside. He found the key that had been hidden there when he was palmed the pack and, looking around, undid a padlock on the large door, pulled it open and stepped inside.

There he found the green car, one of the small new ones that were flooding China. He resented the car as much as the Olympics because it represented more money and trade for the country that oppressed his people.

He opened the trunk. There he found several hundred posters, urging independence for the Uyghur people. They were crude but they got the point across. He then opened another box and examined the contents, which excited him much more than the Mao-style rhetoric: thirty kilos of a yellow, clay-like substance, which gave off a pungent aroma. He stared at the plastic explosives for a long moment, then put the lids back on the boxes.

He consulted the map and noted exactly where he was to meet the man who would supply the detonators. He started the car and drove carefully out of the warehouse, not bothering to close and lock the door. He also left behind his bicycle. He felt a bit sad about that – he'd had it for a year – but, considering the direction his life was about to take, he certainly wouldn't need it any longer.

'Look at you,' said Gregor, eyeing his young protégé's training jacket and sweatpants, a Russian flag bold and clear on the shoulder. From a young age Yuri had been taught not to pay too much attention to his appearance, but today he'd spent considerable time – after warming up, of course – shaving and combing his hair.

The teenager smiled shyly, as Gregor saluted.

They were outside the stadium, near a security fence, watching the thousands of spectators head in serpentine lines toward the stadium. Near the two men, buses continued to disgorge the athletes as well, who were walking through their own entrance with their gear bags over their shoulders. Some were nervous, some jovial. All were eager.

Gregor consulted his watch. The Russian team would be taking pictures with the heads of the Olympic committee in a half-hour, just before the games began. Yuri would, of course, be there, front and center. 'You should go. But first . . . I have something for you.'

'You have, sir?'

'Yes.'

Gregor reached into his pocket and pulled out a small bag. He extracted a gold-colored strip of satin.

'Here, this is for you.'

Yuri exclaimed, 'It's the second ribbon!'

Gregor was not given to soft expressions of face but he allowed himself a faint smile. 'It is indeed.' He took it from the boy, tied a knot and slipped it over his neck.

'Now, go make your countrymen proud.'

'I will, sir.'

Gregor turned and stalked off in that distracted way of his, as if you'd slipped from his mind the instant he turned. Though Yuri knew that was never the case.

The Uyghur found the intersection he'd sought and parked the green Chevy. Ahead of him, a mile away, he could see part of the Olympic stadium. It did indeed look like a bird nest.

For vultures, he thought. Pleased with his cleverness.

Ten minutes until the man was to meet him here. He was Chinese and would be wearing black slacks and a yellow Mao jacket. The Uyghur scanned the people walking by on the streets. He hated it in Beijing. The sooner . . .

His thoughts faded as he saw motion in the rearview mirror.

Police were running toward him, pointing.

These were not your typical Beijing police, nor Olympic guards in their powder-blue jumpsuits. These were military security, in full battle gear, training machine guns his way. Shouting and motioning people off the street.

No! I've been betrayed! he thought.

He reached for the ignition.

Which was when he and the car vanished in a fraction of a second, becoming whatever a trunk full of plastic explosives turns you into.

Yuri Umarov cringed, like everyone else around him, when the bang came from somewhere south of the stadium.

The decorative lights around the stadium went out.

A few car alarms began to bleat.

And Yuri began to run.

He hurdled the security fence but the guards were, like everyone else, turning toward the explosion, wondering if a threat would follow from that direction.

Then he hit the ground in the secure zone and began running toward the stadium, sprinting for all he was worth, pounding along the concrete, then the grass.

Thirty seconds.

That was all the time, his mentor Gregor had told him, that he would have to sprint to the service door in the back of the stadium and open it up before the backup generators kicked in and the alarm systems went back online.

Breath coming fast, a machine gun firing, rocks avalanching down a mountain.

His lungs burned.

Counting the seconds: Twenty-two, twenty-one.

Not looking at his watch, not looking at the guards, the spectators.

Looking at only one thing – something he couldn't even see: the second ribbon.

Eighteen seconds, seventeen.

Faster, faster.

The second ribbon . . .

Eleven, ten, nine . . .

Then, sucking in the hot, damp air, sweat streaming, he came to the service door. He ripped a short crowbar from his pocket, jimmied the lock open and leapt into the cold, dim storeroom inside the belly of the stadium.

Six, five, four . . .

He slammed the door shut and made sure the alarm sensors aligned. *Click.*

The lights popped back on. The alarm system glowed red.

He said a brief prayer of thanks.

Yuri crouched, stretching his agonized legs, struggling to breathe in the musty air around him.

After five minutes he rose and stepped to one of the interior doors, which weren't alarmed, and he entered the brightly lit corridor. He made his way past the shops and stands. He finally stepped outside into the stadium itself, which opened below him.

It was magnificent. He was chilled at the sight.

People were once more streaming into the stadium, apparently re-assured by an announcement that the brief power outage was due to a minor technical difficulty.

Laughing to himself at the comment, Yuri oriented himself. He found the place on the stadium grounds, at the foot of the dignitaries' boxes, where the Russian team was milling about, awaiting their photo session with officials.

Wonderful, he reflected. And there was also a video camera. God willing, it would be a live transmission and would broadcast throughout the world his shout: 'Death to the Russian oppressors! Long live the Republic of Chechnya!'

He'd rehearsed the cry as many times as he had practiced his thirty-second run.

Competition. Winning. Bringing glory to your countrymen . . .

Now, Yuri knelt and unzipped his sports bag. He began slipping the detonating caps into the explosives inside and rigging them to the push-button detonator. Sprinting full out from the security fence to the stadium with the bomb armed was, as Gregor had pointed out, not a good idea.

'What was it?' Ch'ao Yuan demanded, speaking into his secure cell phone.

'We aren't sure, sir.'

'Well, somebody is sure,' Ch'ao snapped.

Because that somebody, from the public liaison office, had gone on the public address system to tell the 85,000 people in the stadium that there was no risk. It was a technical problem and it had been resolved.

Yet no one had called Ch'ao to tell *him* anything.

One of his underlings, a man who spoke Mandarin as if he'd been raised in Canton, was continuing. 'We've checked with the state power company. We can't say for certain, sir. The infrastructure . . . you know. This has happened before. Overuse of electricity.'

'So you don't know if it was a bomb or it was the half-million extra people in the city turning on their air conditioning?'

'We're looking now. There's a team there, examining the residue. They'll know soon.'

'How soon?'

'Very soon.'

Ch'ao slammed the phone shut.

Very soon . . .

He was about to make another call when a man walked into his office. Ch'ao rose. He said respectfully, 'Mr Liu.'

The man, a senior official from internal security in Beijing, nodded. 'I'm on my way to the stadium, Yuan.'

Ch'ao noted the dismissive use of his first name.

'Have you heard?'

'Nothing yet, sir.'

Liu, a long face and bristly hair, looked perplexed. 'What do you mean?'

'About the explosion, I assume. Nothing. The men are still searching the relay station. It will be—'

'No, no, no.' The man's expression was explosive. He gestured broadly with his hands. 'We have our answer.'

'Answer.'

'Yes. I have my people there now. And they found Uyghur independence posters. The terrorist was on his way to the stadium when we found him on a tip. The bomb detonated prematurely as he was being arrested.'

'Uyghur?' This made some sense. Still, Ch'ao added, 'I wasn't told.'

'Well, we're not making the information widely available as yet. We think he was going to drive the car into the crowd at the entrance. But he saw the police and detonated the bomb where it was. Or the system malfunctioned.'

'Or perhaps there was some gunfire.' Ch'ao was ever vigilant about being respectful. But he was furious at this peremptory disposition of the case. Furious, too, that, whatever the cause of the explosion, there was no witness to interrogate. And everyone knew the military security forces were quick to pull the trigger.

But Liu said calmly, 'There were no shots.' He lowered his voice. 'If the mechanism was constructed here, a malfunction is the most likely explanation.' He actually smiled. 'So the matter is disposed of.'

'Disposed of?'

'It's clear what happened.'

'But this could be part of a broader conspiracy.'

'When do the Uyghurs have broad conspiracies? They are always one man, one bomb, one bus. No conspiracy, Yuan.'

'We have to investigate. Find out where the explosives came from. Where the car came from. The informant said the targets were the Russians or the Americans. There was no mention of the Uyghurs.'

'Then the informant was wrong. Obviously.'

Before thinking, Ch'ao blurted, 'We must postpone the games.'

'What are you talking about?'

'Until we find out more.'

'Postpone the games? Are you a madman, Yuan? We were presented with a threat. We have met that threat. It is no longer a threat.' Liu often spoke as if he were reading from old-time propaganda.

'You're satisfied that there's no risk, sir?'

'The backup generators are working, are they not?'

'Yessir.'

'All the security is in place and no one was admitted through the metal detectors until the power resumed, correct?'

'Yessir. Though the systems were down for a full thirty seconds.'

'Thirty seconds,' Liu mused. 'What can happen in that time?'

In this age, 85,000 people can die, Ch'ao thought. But he could see Liu was not pleased with his attitude. He remained silent.

'Well, there we are. If something else turns up, we will have to consider it. For now the explosion was infrastructure. This evening we will announce the bombing was the result of the Uyghur movement. We'll say that there was no intent to harm anyone; the explosion was meant to be an inconvenience . . .' Liu's eyes grew focused and dark. 'And you will say nothing for the time being except infrastructure. An overloaded electrical system. After all, we still have a few things left to blame the Chairman for.'

There was a fortuitous development, Yuri noted, his bag over his shoulder, as he trooped down the endless steps toward the field.

He observed a number of American athletes were standing near the Russians, chatting and laughing.

This was perfect. The Americans had offered only lip service to the Chechen plight, being far more interested in foreign trade with Russia. In fact, back in Grozny, planning the attack, Gregor told him, they'd considered targeting Americans, too. But a dual attack was considered too difficult.

But now, Yuri was thrilled to see, he would take a number of the citizens of both countries to the grave with him.

He nodded at a guard, who gave the most perfunctory of glances at his pass and motioned him on.

Yuri stepped onto the Olympic field and made his way toward the two teams.

In his mind was a vision of the second ribbon.

Standing on the grass grounds of the Olympic field, Billy Savitch looked around him. The field had been impressive when he'd seen it upon arrival. It was even more so now.

He was near a group of American athletes. He nodded greetings.

They gave him thumbs-up, high-fives.

I'm actually on the field, he reflected. The first day of the games.

And then recalled, Don't screw up.

I'll try.

No, *trying* is what losers do.

I *won't* screw up.

The Americans were next to a large group of Russians. Most of the team, it seemed. They were waiting to have their picture taken by a Chinese photographer. There was also a video crew here and an interpreter; they were doing interviews with certain athletes.

Billy stayed close to the Americans, many of whom were walking over to their Russian competitors and shaking hands. Wishing them good luck.

Yet never shucking that certain ruthlessness of eye.

He wondered if he, too, looked ruthless.

He heard the announcer repeat that the power failure had been due to a technical problem. The evasive language of all governments. They apologized for the inconvenience.

A Russian nodded to him and said to a lean US athlete nearby, 'What's your event, my friend?'

'I'm a sprinter,' the American said. 'Hundred meters is my main event.'

'A sprinter?' The Russian looked at him with a gaze of wistfulness. 'I envy that. You are a hawk. Me, a plodding ostrich! I run long distances. When do you compete?'

'In an hour.'

'You must be impatient.'

'Yeah, some. But this isn't about me. It's about the team.'

The Russian laughed. 'Spoken like a good Communist.'

The two men laughed.

Billy joined them as he viewed another Russian athlete, slim with slicked-back dark hair, walking toward them from the stands, his bag over his shoulder. He had a pleasant smile on his face as he surveyed the field around him. He headed straight for the Russians at the photography station.

'Where are you from?' the first Russian asked Billy. 'Your voice.'

'Texas.'

'Ah. The stars at night.' The man clapped his hands four times.

Drawing another laugh from Billy.

One of the Russian coaches announced something – presumably it was time for the pictures because the men and women began clustering around the photographer. The long-distance runner said, 'Come with me, my cowboy friend. You and your colleague. I want you both in the picture, too.'

'Us?' Billy asked.

The man's eyes sparkled. 'Yes, so you'll have something to remember our victory over you.'

Yuri was twenty feet away from the dignitary box, which was draped in red in honor of the host country, and blue and white in honor of the birthplace of the games. He noted that the photographer was set up. The video camera, too. And a number of Americans were mingling with the Russians. Young men and women, happy to be here, thrilled.

If they only knew what the next few minutes would bring. A shattering explosion, ball bearings and nails tearing skin, piercing their highly tuned bodies.

He looked around. There were guards in the stands and some near the doors, but none here.

He was, as the Americans said, home free.

When he was ten feet away he'd detonate the device, he decided. That would be plenty close enough.

He swung the bag under his arm and began to unzip to pull out the detonator.

As he was doing this he glanced at someone nearby, looking at him, someone with the American team, wearing a running suit. He was a young man, blond. He was rubbing his crew-cut head.

But not only rubbing his head, Yuri realized to his shock. He was speaking into a microphone at his wrist.

His eyes met the blond American's.

Yuri froze. Then frantically began to reach into his bag for the detonator button.

Which was when the young American drew a pistol from his windbreaker, aimed it at Yuri's head. People screamed and dived for the ground.

Yuri went for the button.

He saw a flash, but not from the explosive. It was from the hand of the young American.

And then he saw nothing.

Frederick Alston and Billy Savitch were standing in the office of Security Chief Ch'ao.

Billy thought he looked a little like Jackie Chan, but he didn't think it would be a good idea to say that. You had to be careful about accidental insults over here, he'd learned.

'I'm so very grateful to you both,' Ch'ao said, rising and clasping their hands in both of his.

Billy nodded, looking like the bashful Southern boy that he was. Secretly he, too, was grateful. As the junior member of the US State Department Security Team, which Alston headed, he'd never expected to be on the front line of an operation here. He'd expected he'd continue to do what he'd been doing since he'd arrived: checking IDs, standing on rooftops with a machine gun, checking cars, sweeping bedrooms.

But Alston had had enough confidence in Billy to put him to work in the stadium.

I think you're ready to go on the field . . .

'How did you know that the man was a terrorist?' Ch'ao asked him.

'I didn't know, not at first. But I'd studied all the entrances and exits of the stadium, and players were never in the part of the stands where he was coming from. You can't get to that place from the competitors' entrance. Why would he come from that direction? And he was carrying his sports bag. None of the other players on the field had bags; they were all in the locker rooms.' Billy shrugged. 'Then I looked into his eyes. And I knew.'

'Who was he?' Alston asked.

'Yuri Umarov. Lived outside of Grozny. He came into Beijing with Gregor Dallayev last week. They've been training ever since, making the bomb, surveying the grounds and security.'

'Dallayev, sure.' Alston nodded. 'The separatist guerrilla. We think he was involved in the Moscow subway attack last year.'

'We'll be able to find out for certain,' the Chinese man said with a smile. 'He's in custody.'

Billy asked, 'What was their plan exactly?'

Ch'ao explained, 'They made connections with a cell of Uyghur terrorists and promised them thirty kilos of plastic explosive to use as they wished, as long as it disrupted the games. A Uyghur picked up the explosives at a drop site near Chaoyang Park this morning. It was that green Chevy I told you about. He drove to a meeting place not far from the stadium. We think that he believed he was meeting an intermediary to pick up detonators. But the explosive was already rigged to blow remotely. We had that tip early about explosives in a green Chevy—'

'Which Gregor called in?' Alston asked.

'Yes, I'm sure. So as soon as the Uyghur parked near the electrical relay station Gregor then made another anonymous call and reported the green car. When the police arrived, Gregor blew the car up with a remote control . . . And that took out the power station next to it.'

'So that was the point of meeting there,' Alston said. 'A cover to take out the electricity.'

'That's right. It shut down the alarm system temporarily and gave Yuri a chance to get inside.'

Alston added, 'We heard from Washington that your government wanted to end it right there – with the Uyghur's death. But you called us to say there was more of a threat. How'd you know that?'

'Just like you' – a nod at Billy Savitch – 'I didn't know. But I suspected. I play go. Do you know it?'

'Never heard of it,' Billy said. Alston, too, shook his head.

'It's our version of chess. Only better, of course.' He didn't seem to be making a joke. 'I look forward when I play the game. You must always look forward to beat your opponent at go. You must see beyond the board. Well, I looked forward today. Yes, the explosion could have been an accident. But looking forward, I believed it could be an excellent diversion.'

His phone buzzed. There was a rattle of Chinese. Ch'ao grimaced. Said something back. Hung up.

Man, they talked fast in this country, Billy thought.

'Something wrong?' Alston asked.

'I would like to ask a favor.'

'Sure.'

'There will be a man here in a few minutes. His name is Mr Liu. He . . . well, shall I say, he is *not* a forward thinker. I promised him that I would *not* alert the security forces that there might be another threat . . .'

'Politics, huh?' Alston asked.

'Precisely.'

'Fine with us.' He looked at Billy. 'Savitch here acted on his own initiative.'

'Yessir.'

'Thank you.'

Then in the distance a huge round of cheering and applause rose from the bird nest.

Ch'ao looked at his watch and then consulted a schedule. 'Ah, the first events are over. They're awarding the medals. Let me find out the results.' He made a call and spoke in that explosive way of his. He nodded, then hung up.

'Who won the gold?' Billy asked.

Ch'ao only smiled.

THE PLOT

When J.B. Prescott, the hugely popular crime novelist, died, millions of readers around the world were stunned and saddened.

But only one fan thought that there was something more to his death than what was revealed in the press reports.

Rumpled, round, middle-aged Jimmy Malloy was an NYPD detective sergeant. He had three passions other than police work: his family, his boat, and reading. Malloy read anything, but preferred crime novels. He liked the clever plots and the fast-moving stories. That's what books should be, he felt. He'd been at a party once and people were talking about how long they should give a book before they put it down. Some people had said they'd endure fifty pages, some said a hundred.

Malloy had laughed. 'No, no, no. It's not dental work, like you're waiting for the anesthetic to kick in. You should enjoy the book from page one.'

Prescott's books were that way. They entertained you from the git-go. They took you away from your job, they took you away from the problems with your wife or daughter, your mortgage company.

They took you away from everything. And in this life, Malloy reflected, there was a lot to be taken away from.

'What're you moping around about?' his partner, Ralph DeLeon, asked, walking into the shabby office they shared in the Midtown South Precinct, after half a weekend off. 'I'm the only one round here got reason to be upset. Thanks to the Mets yesterday. Oh, wait. You don't even know who the Mets are, son, do you?'

'Sure, I love basketball,' Malloy joked. But it was a distracted joke.

'So?' DeLeon asked. He was tall, slim, muscular, black – the opposite of Malloy, detail for detail.

'Got one of those feelings.'

'Shit. Last one of those *feelings* earned us a sit-down with the dep com.'

Plate glass and Corvettes are extremely expensive. Especially when owned by people with lawyers.

But Malloy wasn't paying much attention to their past collars. Or to DeLeon. He once more read the obit that had appeared in the *Times* a month ago.

J.B. Prescott, 68, author of thirty-two best-selling crime novels, died yesterday while on a hike in a remote section of Vermont, where he had a summer home.

The cause of death was a heart attack.

'We're terribly saddened by the death of one of our most prolific and important writers,' said Dolores Kemper, CEO of Hutton-Fielding, Inc., which had been his publisher for many years. 'In these days of lower book sales and fewer people reading, J.B.'s books still flew off the shelves. It's a terrible loss for everyone.'

Prescott's best known creation was Jacob Sharpe, a down-and-dirty counterintelligence agent, who traveled the world, fighting terrorists and criminals. Sharpe was frequently compared to James Bond and Jason Bourne.

Prescott was not a critical darling. Reviewers called his books 'airport time-passers', 'beach reads' and 'junk food for the mind – superior junk food, but empty calories nonetheless.'

Still, he was immensely popular with his fans. Each of his books sold millions of copies.

His success brought him fame and fortune, but Prescott shunned the public life, rarely going on book tours or giving interviews. Though a multimillionaire, he had no interest in the celebrity lifestyle. He and his second wife, the former Jane Spenser, 38, owned an apartment in Manhattan, where she was a part-time photo editor for *Styles*, the popular fashion magazine. Prescott himself, however, spent most of his time in Vermont or in the countryside of Spain, where he could write in peace.

Born in Kansas, John Balin Prescott studied English literature at the University of Iowa and was an advertising copywriter and teacher for some years while trying to publish literary fiction and poetry. He had little success and ultimately switched to writing thrillers. His first, *The Trinity Connection*, became a runaway hit in 1991. The book was on *The New York Times* Best Seller List for more than 100 weeks.

Demand for his books became so great that ten years ago he took on a co-writer, Aaron Reilly, 39, with whom he wrote 16 bestsellers. This increased his output to two novels a year, sometimes more.

'We're just devastated,' said Reilly, who described himself as a friend as well as colleague. 'John hadn't been feeling well lately. But we couldn't get him back to the city to see his doctor, he was so intent on finishing our latest manuscript. That's the way he was. Type A in the extreme.'

Last week, Prescott traveled to Vermont alone to work on his next novel. Taking a break from the writing, he went for a hike, as he often did, in a deserted area near the Green Mountains. It was there that he suffered the coronary.

'John's personal physician described the heart attack as massive,' co-author Reilly added. 'Even if he hadn't been alone, the odds of saving him were slim to nonexistent.'

Mr Prescott is survived by his wife and two children from a prior marriage.

'So what's this feeling you're talking about?' DeLeon asked, reading over his partner's shoulder.

'I'm not sure. Something.'

'Now, *there* is some evidence to get straight to the crime lab. "Something". Come on, there's some *real* cases on our plate, son. Put your mopey hat away. We gotta meet our snitch.'

'Mopey hat? Did you actually say mopey hat?'

A half-hour later, Malloy and DeLeon were sitting in a disgusting dive of a coffee shop near the Hudson docks, talking to a scummy little guy of indeterminate race and age.

Lucius was eating chili in a sloppy way and saying, 'So what happened was Bark, remember I was telling you about Bark.'

'Who's Bark?' Malloy asked.

'I *told* you.'

DeLeon said, 'He told us.'

'What Bark did was he was going to mark the bag, only he's a nimrod so he forgot which one it was. I figured it out and got it marked. That worked out okay. It's marked, it's on the truck. Nobody saw me. They had, I'd be capped.' A big mouthful of chili. And a grin. 'So.'

'Good job,' DeLeon said. And kicked Malloy under the table. Meaning: Tell him he did a good job because if you don't the man'll start to feel bad and yeah he's a little shit nimrod whatever that is but we need him.

But Malloy was remembering something. He rose abruptly. 'I gotta go.'

'I dint do a good job?' Lucius called, hurt.

But he was speaking to Jimmy Malloy's back.

Jane Prescott opened the door of the townhouse in Greenwich Village. Close to five eleven, she could look directly into Malloy's eyes.

The widow wore a black dress, closely fitted, and her eyes were red like she'd been crying. Her hair was swept back and faint gray roots showed, though Malloy recalled that she was only in her late thirties. Three decades younger than her late husband, he also recalled.

'Detective.' Hesitant, of course, looking over his ID. A policeman. She was thinking this was odd – not necessarily reason to panic, but odd.

'I recognize you,' Malloy said.

She blinked. 'Have we met?'

'In *Sharpe Edge*. You were Monica.'

She gave a hollow laugh. 'People say that, because an older man falls in love with a younger woman in the book. But I'm not a spy and I can't rappel off cliffs.'

They were both beautiful, however, if Malloy remembered the Prescott novel correctly. But he said nothing about this, she being a new widow. What he said was, 'I'm sorry for your loss.'

'Thank you. Oh, please come inside.'

The apartment was small, typical of the Village, but luxurious as diamonds. Rich antiques, original art. Even statues. Nobody Malloy knew owned statues. A peek into the kitchen revealed intimidating brushed-metal appliances with names Malloy couldn't pronounce.

They sat and she looked at him with her red-rimmed eyes. An uneasy moment later he said, 'You're wondering what a cop's doing here.'

'Yes, I am.'

'Other than just being a fan, wishing to pay condolences.'

'You could've written a letter.'

'The fact is, this is sort of personal. I didn't want to come sooner, out of respect. But there's something I'd like to ask. Some of us in the department were thinking 'bout putting together a memorial evening in honor of your husband. He wrote about New York a lot and he didn't make us cops out to be flunkies. One of them, I can't remember which one, he had this great plot line here in the city. Some NYPD rookie helping out Jacob Sharpe. It was about terrorists going after the train stations.'

'Hallowed Ground.'

'That's right. That was a good book.'

More silence.

Malloy glanced at a photograph on the desk. It showed a half-dozen people, in somber clothing, standing around a gravesite. Jane was in the foreground.

She saw him looking at it. 'The funeral.'

'Who're the other people there?'

'His daughters from his first marriage. That's Aaron, his co-writer.' She indicated a man standing next to her. Then, in the background, another, older man in an ill-fitting suit. She said, 'Frank Lester, John's former agent.'

She said nothing more. Malloy continued, 'Well, some folks in the department know I'm one of your husband's biggest fans so I got elected to come talk to you, ask if you'd come to the memorial. An appreciation night, you could call it. Maybe say a few words. Wait. 'Elected' makes it sound like I didn't want to come. But I did. I loved his books.'

'I sense you did,' she said, looking at the detective with piercing gray eyes.

'So?'

'I appreciate the offer. I'll just have to see.'

'Sure. Whatever you'd feel comfortable with.'

'You made him feel bad. He nearly got capped on that assignment.'

Malloy said to his partner, 'I'll send him a balloon basket. "Sorry I was rude to my favorite snitch." But right now I'm on to something.'

'Give me particulars.'

'Okay. Well, she's hot, Prescott's wife.'

'That's not a helpful particular.'

'I think it is. Hot . . . and thirty years younger than her husband.'

'So she took her bra off and gave him a heart attack. Murder by boob isn't in the penal code.'

'You know what I mean.'

'You mean she wanted somebody younger. So do I. So does everybody. Well, not you, 'cause nobody younger would give you the time of day.'

'And there was this feeling I got at the house. She wasn't really in mourning. She was in a black dress, yeah, but it was tighter than anything I'd ever let my daughter wear – and her red eyes? It was like she'd been rubbing them. I didn't buy the grieving widow thing.'

'You ain't marshaling *Boston Legal* evidence here, son.'

'There's more.' Malloy pulled the limp copy of Prescott's obit out of his pocket. He tapped a portion. 'I realized where my feeling came from. See this part about the personal physician?'

'Yeah. So?'

'You read books, DeLeon?'

'Yeah, I can read. I can tie my shoes. I can fieldstrip a Glock in one minute sixteen seconds. Oh, and put it back together, too, without any missing parts. What's your point?'

'You know how if you read a book and you like it and it's a good book, it stays with you? Parts of it do? Well, I read a book a few years ago. In it this guy has to kill a terrorist, but if the terrorist is murdered there'd be an international incident, so it has to look like a natural death.'

'How'd they set it up?'

'It was really smart. They shot him in the head three times with a Bushmaster.'

'That's fairly *un*natural.'

'It's natural because that's how the victim's "personal physician"' – Malloy did the quote things with his fingers – 'signed the death certificate: cerebral hemorrhage following a stroke. Your doctor does that, the death doesn't have to go to the coroner. The police weren't involved. The body was cremated. The whole thing went away.'

'Hmm. Not bad. All you need is a gun, a shitload of money and a crooked doctor. I'm starting to like these particular particulars.'

'And what's *particularly* interesting is that it was one of Prescott's books that Aaron Reilly co-wrote. *And* the wife remembered it. *That* was why I went to see her.'

'Check out the doctor.'

'I tried. He's Spanish.'

'So's half the city, in case you didn't know. We got translators, *hijo*.'

'Not Latino. *Spanish*. From Spain. He's back home and I can't track him down.'

The department secretary stuck her head in the doorway. 'Jimmy, you got a call from a Frank Lester.'

'Who'd be . . .?'

'A book agent. Worked with that guy Prescott you were talking about.'

The former agent, he recalled. 'How'd he get my number?'

'I don't know. He said he heard you were planning some memorial service and he wanted to get together with you to talk about it.'

DeLeon frowned. 'Memorial?'

'I had to make up something to get to see the wife.' Malloy took the number, a Manhattan cell phone area code, he noticed. Called. It went to voice mail. He didn't leave a message.

Malloy turned back to his partner. 'There's more. An hour ago I talked with some deputies up in Vermont. They told me that it was a private ambulance took the body away. Not one of the local outfits. The sheriff bought into the heart attack thing but he still sent a few people to the place where Prescott was hiking just to take some statements. After the ambulance left, one of the deputies saw somebody leaving the area. Male, he thinks. No description other than that, except he was carrying what looked like a briefcase or small suitcase.'

'Breakdown rifle?'

'What I was thinking. And when this guy saw the cop car, he vanished fast.'

'A pro?'

'Maybe. I was thinking that co-author might've come across some connected guys in doing his research. Or maybe it was this Aaron Reilly.'

'You got any ideas on how to find out?'

'As a matter of fact, I do.'

Standing in the dim frosted-glass corridor of a luxurious SoHo condo, Jimmy Malloy made sure his gun was unobstructed and rang the buzzer.

The large door swung open.

'Aaron Reilly?' Even though he recognized the co-author from the picture at Prescott's funeral.

'Yes, that's right.' The man gave a cautious grin.

Which remained in place, though it grew a wrinkle of surprise when the shield appeared. Malloy tried to figure out if the man had been expecting him – because Jane Prescott had called ahead of time – but couldn't tell.

'Come on inside, Detective.'

Reilly, in his late thirties, Malloy remembered, was the opposite of Jane Prescott. He was in faded jeans and a work shirt, sleeves rolled up. A Japanese product, not a Swiss, told him the time, and there was no gold dangling on him anywhere. His shoes were scuffed. He was good looking, with thick longish hair and no wedding ring.

The condo – in chic SoHo – had every right to be opulent, but, though large, it was modest and lived-in.

Not an original piece of art in the place.

Zero sculpture.

And unlike the Widow Prescott's abode, Reilly's was chockablock with books.

He gestured to the cop to sit. Malloy picked a leather chair that lowered him six inches toward the ground as it wheezed contentedly. On the wall nearby was a shelf of the books. Malloy noted one: *The Paris Deception*. 'J.B. Prescott with Aaron Reilly' was on the spine.

Malloy was struck by the word 'with'. He wondered if Reilly felt bad, defensive maybe, that his contribution to the literary world was embodied in that preposition.

And if so, did he feel bad enough to kill the man who'd bestowed it and relegated him to second-class status?

'That's one of my favorites.'

'So you're a fan, too.'

'Yep. That's why I volunteered to come talk to you. First, I have to say I really admire your work.'

'Thank you.'

Malloy kept scanning the bookshelves. And found what he'd been looking for: two entire shelves were filled with books about guns and shooting. There had to be something in one of them about rifles that could be broken down and hidden in small suitcases. They were, Malloy knew, easy to find.

'What exactly can I do for you, Detective?'

Malloy looked back. 'Just a routine matter mostly. Now, technically John Prescott was a resident of the city, so his death falls partly under our jurisdiction.'

'Yes, I suppose.' Reilly still looked perplexed.

'Whenever there's a large estate, we're sometimes asked to look into the death, even if it's ruled accidental or illness related.'

'Why would you look into it?' Reilly asked, frowning.

'Tax revenue mostly.'

'Really? That's funny. It was my understanding that only government officials had jurisdiction to make inquiries like that. In fact, I researched a similar issue for one of our books. We had Jacob Sharpe following the money – you know, to find the ultimate bad guy. The police department couldn't help him. He had to go to Revenue.'

It was an oops moment and Malloy realized he should have known better. Of course, the co-author would know all about police and law enforcement procedures.

'Unless what you're really saying is that you – or somebody – think that John's death might not have been an illness at all. It was intentional . . . But how *could* it be?'

Malloy didn't want to give away his theory about the crooked doctor. He said, 'Let's say I know you're a diabetic and if you don't get your insulin you'll die. I keep you from getting your injection, there's an argument that I'm guilty of murder.'

'And you think somebody was with him at the time he had the heart attack and didn't call for help?'

'Just speculating. Probably how you write books.'

'We're a little more organized than that. We come up with a detailed plot, all the twists and turns. Then we execute it. We know exactly how the story will end.'

'So that's how it works.'

'Yes.'

'I wondered.'

'But, see, the problem with what you're suggesting is that it would be a coincidence for this *somebody*, who wanted him dead, to be up there in Vermont at just the moment he had the attack . . . We could never get away with that.'

Malloy blinked. 'You—?'

Reilly lifted an eyebrow. 'If we put that into a book, our editor wouldn't let us get away with it.'

'Still. Did he have any enemies?'

'No, none that I knew about. He was a good boss and a nice man. I can't imagine anybody'd want him dead.'

'Well, I think that's about it,' Malloy said. 'I appreciate your time.'

Reilly rose and walked the detective to the door. 'Didn't you forget the most important question?'

'What's that?'

'The question our editor would insist we add at the end of an inter-rogation in one of the books: Where was *I* at the time he died?'

'I'm not accusing you of anything.'

'I didn't say you were. I'm just saying that a cop in a Jacob Sharpe novel would've asked the question.'

'Okay. Where were you?'

'I was here in New York. And the next question?'

Malloy knew what that was: 'Can anyone verify that?'

'No. I was alone all day. Writing. Sorry, but reality's a lot tougher than fiction, isn't it, Detective?'

'Yo, listen up,' the scrawny little man said. 'This is interesting.'

'I'm listening.' Malloy tried to look pleasant as he sat across from Lucius the snitch. Before they'd met, Ralph DeLeon reminded him how Malloy had dissed the man earlier. So he was struggling to be nice.

'I followed Reilly to a Starbucks. And she was there, Prescott's wife.'

'Good job,' DeLeon said.

Malloy nodded. The whole reason to talk to the co-author had been to push the man into action, not to get facts. When people are forced to act, they often get careless. And while Malloy had been at Reilly's apartment, DeLeon was arranging with a magistrate for a pen register – a record of phone calls to and from the co-author's phones. A register won't give you the substance of the conversation but it will tell you whom a subject calls and who's calling him.

The instant Malloy left the condo, Reilly had dialed a number.

It was Jane Prescott's. And ten minutes after that, Reilly slipped out the front door, head down, moving quickly.

And tailed by Lucius, who had accompanied Malloy to Reilly's apart-ment and waited outside.

The scrawny snitch was now reporting on that surveillance.

'Now that Mrs Prescott, she's pretty—'

Malloy broke in with, 'Hot, yeah, I know. Keep going.'

'What I was *going* to say,' the snitch offered snippily, 'before I was interrupted, is that she's pretty tough. Kind of scary, you ask me.'

'True,' Malloy conceded.

'Reilly starts out talking about you being there.' Lucius poked a bony finger at Malloy, which seemed like a dig but he let it go – as DeLeon's lifted eyebrow was instructing. 'And you were suspecting something.

And making up shit about some police procedures and estate tax or something. He thought it was pretty stupid.'

Lucius seemed to enjoy adding that. DeLeon, too, apparently.

'And the wife said, yeah, you were making up something at her place, too. About a memorial service or something. Which she didn't believe. And then she said – get this. Are you ready?'

Malloy refrained from glaring at Lucius, whose psyche apparently was as fragile as fine porcelain. He smiled. 'I'm ready.'

'The wife says that this whole problem was Reilly's fucking fault for coming up with the same idea he'd used in a book – bribing a doctor to fake a death certificate.'

He and DeLeon exchanged glances.

Lucius continued, 'And then she said, "Now we're fucked. What're you going to do about it?" Meaning Reilly. Not *you*.' Another finger at Malloy. He sat back, smugly satisfied.

'Anything else?'

'No, that was it.'

'Good job,' Malloy said with a sarcastic flourish that only DeLeon noted. He slipped an envelope to the snitch.

After Lucius left, happy at last, Malloy said, 'Pretty good case.'

'Pretty good, but not great,' the partner replied slowly. 'There's the motive issue. Okay, *she* wants to kill her husband for the insurance or the estate, and a younger man. But what's Reilly's motive? Killing Prescott's killing his golden goose.'

'Oh, I got that covered.' Malloy pulled out his BlackBerry and scrolled down to find something he'd discovered earlier.

He showed it to DeLeon.

Book News
The estate of the late J.B. Prescott has announced that his co-author Aaron Reilly has been selected to continue the author's series featuring the popular Jacob Sharpe character. Prescott's widow is presently nego- tiating a five-book contract with the author's long-time publisher, Hutton- Fielding. Neither party is talking about money at this point but insiders believe the deal will involve an eight-figure advance.

Ralph DeLeon said, 'Looks like we got ourselves a coupla perps.'

*

But not quite yet.

At 11 p.m. Jimmy Malloy was walking from the subway stop in Queens to his house six blocks away. He was thinking of how he was going to put the case together. There were still loose ends. The big pain was the cremation thing. Burning is a bitch, one instructor at the academy had told Malloy's class. Fire gets rid of nearly all important evidence. Like bullet holes in the head.

What he'd have to do is get wiretaps, line up witnesses, track down the ambulance drivers, the doctor in Spain.

It was discouraging, but it was also just part of the job. He laughed to himself. It was like Jacob Sharpe and his 'tradecraft', as he called it. Working your ass off to do your duty. And just then he saw some motion 100 feet ahead, a person. Something about the man's mannerism, his body language set off Malloy's cop radar.

A man had emerged from a car and was walking along the same street that Malloy was now on. After he'd happened to glance back at the detective, he'd stiffened and changed direction fast. Malloy was reminded of the killer in Vermont, disappearing quickly after spotting the deputy.

Who was this? The pro? Aaron Reilly?

And did he have the breakdown rifle or another weapon with him? Malloy had to assume he did.

The detective crossed the street and tried to guess where the man was. Somewhere in front of him, but where? Then he heard a dog bark and another, and he understood the guy was cutting through people's yards, back on the *other* side of the street.

The detective pressed ahead, scanning the area, looking for the logical place where the man had vanished. He decided it had to be an alleyway that led to the right, between two commercial buildings, both of them empty and dark at this time of night.

As he came to the alley, Malloy pulled up. He didn't immediately look around the corner. He'd been moving fast and breathing hard, probably scuffling his feet, too. The killer would have heard him approach.

Be smart, he told himself.

Don't be a hero.

He pulled out his phone and began to dial 911.

Which was when he heard a snap behind him. A foot on a small branch or bit of crisp leaf.

And felt the muzzle of the gun prod his back as a gloved hand reached out and lifted the phone away.

We're a little more organized than that. We come up with a detailed plot, all the twists and turns. Then we execute it. We know exactly how the story will end.

Well, Prescott's wife and co-author had done just that: come up with a perfect plot. Maybe the man on the street a moment ago was Reilly, acting as bait. And it was the professional killer who'd come up behind him.

Maybe even Jane Prescott herself.

She's pretty tough . . .

The detective had another thought. Maybe it was none of his suspects. Maybe the former agent, Frank Lester, had been bitter about being fired by his client and killed Prescott for revenge. Malloy had never followed up on that lead.

Hell, dying because he'd been careless . . .

Then the hand tugged on his shoulder slightly, indicating he should turn around.

Malloy did, slowly.

He blinked as he looked up into the eyes of the man who'd snuck up behind him.

They'd never met, but the detective knew exactly what J.B. Prescott looked like. His face was on the back jackets of a dozen books in Malloy's living room.

'Sorry for the scare,' Prescott explained, putting away the pen he'd used as a gun muzzle – ironic touch that, Malloy noted, as his heart continued to slam in his chest.

The author continued, 'I wanted to intercept you before you got home. But I didn't think you'd get here so soon. I had to come up behind you and make you think I had a weapon so you didn't call in a ten-thirteen. That would have been a disaster.'

'Intercept?' Malloy asked. 'Why?'

They were sitting in the alleyway, on the stairs of a loading dock.

'I needed to talk to you,' Prescott said. The man had a large mane of gray hair and a matching mustache that bisected his lengthy face. He looked like an author ought to look.

'You could've called,' Malloy snapped.

'No, I couldn't. If somebody had overheard or if you'd told anyone I was alive, my whole plot would've been ruined.'

'Okay, what the hell is going on?'

Prescott lowered his head to his hands and didn't speak for a moment. Then he said, 'For the past eighteen months I've been planning my own death. It took that long to find a doctor, an ambulance crew, a funeral director I could bribe. And find some remote land in Spain where we could buy a place and nobody would disturb me.'

'So you were the one the police saw walking away from where you'd supposedly had the heart attack in Vermont?'

He nodded.

'What were you carrying? A suitcase?'

'Oh, my laptop. I'm never without it. I write all the time.'

'Then who was in the ambulance?'

'Nobody. It was just for show.'

'And at the cemetery, an empty urn in the plot?'

'That's right.'

'But why on earth would you do this? Debts? Is the mob after you?'

A laugh. 'I'm worth fifty million dollars. And I may write about the mob and spies and government agents, but I've never actually met one . . . No, I'm doing this because I've decided to give up writing the Jacob Sharpe books.'

'Why?'

'Because it's time for me to try something different: publish what I first started writing, years ago, poetry and literary stories.'

Malloy remembered this from the obit.

Prescott explained quickly: 'Oh, don't get me wrong. I don't think literature's any *better* than commercial fiction, not at all. People who say that are fools. But when I tried my hand at literature when I was young, I didn't have any skill. I was self-indulgent, digressive . . . boring. Now I know how to write. The Jacob Sharpe books taught me how. I learned how to think about the audience's needs, how to structure my stories, how to communicate clearly.'

'Tradecraft,' Malloy said.

The author gave a laugh. 'Yes, tradecraft. I'm not a young man. I decided I wasn't going to die without seeing if I could make a success of it.'

'Well, why fake your death? Why not just write what you wanted to?'

'For one thing, I'd get my poems published *because* I was J.B. Prescott. My publishers around the world would pat me on the head and say, "Anything you want, J.B." No, I want my work accepted or rejected on its own merits. But more important, if I just stopped writing the Sharpe series my fans would never forgive me. Look what happened to Sherlock Holmes.'

Malloy shook his head.

'Conan Doyle killed off Holmes. But the fans were furious. He was hounded into bringing back the hero they loved. I'd be hounded in the same way. And my publisher wouldn't let me rest in peace either.' He shook his head. 'I knew there'd be various reactions, but I never thought anybody'd question my death.'

'Something didn't sit right.'

He smiled sadly. 'Maybe I'm better at making plots for fiction than making them in real life.' Then his long face grew somber. Desperate, too. 'I know what I did was wrong, Detective, but please, can you just let it go?'

'A crime's been committed.'

'Only falsifying a death certificate. But Luis, the doctor, is out of the jurisdiction. You're not going to extradite somebody for that. Jane and Aaron and I didn't actually sign anything. There's no insurance fraud because I cashed out the policy last year for surrender value. And Jane'll pay every penny of estate tax that's due . . . Look, I'm not doing this to hurt or cheat anybody.'

'But your fans . . .'

'I love them dearly. I'll always love them and I'm grateful for every minute they've spent reading my books. But it's time for me to pass the baton. Aaron will keep them happy. He's a fine writer . . . Detective, I'm asking you to help me out here. You have the power to save me or destroy me.'

'I've never walked away from a case in my life.' Malloy looked away from the author's eyes, staring at the cracked asphalt in front of them.

Prescott touched his arm. 'Please?'

Nearly a year later Detective Jimmy Malloy received a package from England. It was addressed to him, care of the NYPD.

He'd never gotten any mail from Europe and he was mostly fascinated with the postage stamps. Only when he'd had enough of looking at a tiny Queen Elizabeth did Malloy rip the envelope open and take out the contents: a book of poems written by somebody he'd never heard of.

Not that he'd heard of many poets, of course. Robert Frost. Carl Sandburg. Dr Seuss.

On the cover were some quotations from reviewers praising the author's writing. He'd apparently won awards in England, Italy and Spain.

Malloy opened the thin book and read the first poem, which was dedicated to the poet's wife.

Walking on Air

Oblique sunlight fell in perfect crimson on your face
that winter afternoon last year.
Your departure approached and, compelled to seize
your hand, I led you from sidewalk to trees
and beyond into a field of snow –
flakes of sky that had fallen to earth days ago.

We climbed onto the hardened crust, which held
our weight and, suspended above the earth,
we walked in strides as angular as the light,
spending the last hour of our time together
walking on air.

Malloy gave a brief laugh, surprised. He hadn't read a poem since school but he actually thought this one was pretty good. He liked that idea: walking on the snow, which had come from the sky – literally walking on air with somebody you loved.

He pictured John Prescott, sad that his wife had to return to New York, spending a little time with her in a snowy Vermont field before the drive to the train station.

Just then Ralph DeLeon stepped into the office, and before Malloy could hide the book, the partner scooped it up. 'Poetry.' His tone suggested that his partner was even more of a loss than he'd thought. Though he then read a few of them himself and said, 'Doesn't suck.' Then, flipping to the front, DeLeon gave a fast laugh.

'What?' Malloy asked.

'Weird. Whoever it's dedicated to has your initials.'

'No.'

DeLeon held the book open.

With eternal thanks to J.M.

'But I *know* it can't be you. Nobody'd thank you for shit, son. And if they did, it sure as hell wouldn't be eternal.'

The partner dropped the book on Malloy's desk and sat down in his chair, pulled out his phone and called one of their snitches.

Malloy read a few more of the poems and then tossed the volume on the dusty bookshelf behind his desk.

Then he, too, grabbed his phone and placed a call to the forensic lab to ask about some test results. As he waited on hold he mused that, true, Prescott's poems weren't bad at all. The man did have some skill.

But, deep down, Jimmy Malloy had to admit to himself that – given his choice – he'd rather read a Jacob Sharpe novel any day.

THE THERAPIST

One

I met her by chance, in a Starbucks near the medical building where I have my office, and I knew at once she was in trouble.

Recognizing people in distress was, after all, my profession.

I was reading over my patient notes, which I transcribe immediately after the fifty-minute sessions (often, as now, fortified by my favorite latte). I have a pretty good memory but in the field of counseling and therapy you must be 'completely diligent and tireless', the many-syllabled phrase a favorite of one of my favorite professors.

This particular venue is on the outskirts of Raleigh in a busy strip mall and, the time being 10:30 a.m. on a pleasant day in early May, there were many people inside for their caffeine fixes.

There was one empty table near me but no chair and the trim brunette, in a conservative dark blue dress, approached and asked if she could take the extra one at my table. I glanced at her round face, *Good Housekeeping* pretty, not *Vogue*, and smiled. 'Please.'

I wasn't surprised when she said nothing, didn't smile back. She just took the chair, spun it around, clattering, and sat. Not that it was a flirtation she was rejecting; my smile obviously hadn't been more than a faint pleasantry. I was twice her age and resembled – surprise, surprise – a balding, desk- and library-bound therapist. Not her type at all.

No, her chill response came from the trouble she was in. Which in turn troubled *me* a great deal.

I am a licensed counselor, a profession in which ethics rules preclude me from drumming up business the way a graphic designer or personal trainer might do. So I said nothing more, but returned to my notes, while she pulled a sheaf of papers out of a gym bag and began to review them, urgently sipping her drink but not enjoying the hot liquid. I was not surprised. I kept my head pointed straight down at my own table, but with eyes aching from oblique spying I managed to see that it was a school lesson plan she was working on. I believed it was for seventh grade.

A teacher . . . I grew even more concerned. I'm particularly sensitive to emotional and psychological problems within people who have influence over youngsters. I myself don't see children as patients – that's a specialty I've never pursued. But no psychologist can practice without a rudimentary understanding of children's psyches, where are sowed the seeds of later problems my colleagues and I treat in our adult practices. Children, especially around ten or eleven, are in particularly susceptible developmental stages and can be forever damaged by a woman like the teacher sitting next to me.

Of course, despite all my experience in this field, it's not impossible to make bum diagnoses. But my concerns were confirmed a moment later when she took a phone call. She was speaking softly at first, though with an edge in her voice, the tone and language suggesting the caller was a family member, probably a child. My heart fell at the thought that she'd have children of her own. I wasn't surprised when after only a few minutes her voice rose angrily. Sure enough, she was losing control. 'You did what? . . . I told you not to, under any circumstances . . . Were you just not listening to me? Or were you being stupid again? . . . All right, I'll be home after the conference . . . I'll talk to you about it then.'

If she could have slammed the phone down instead of pushing the disconnect button I'm sure she would have done it.

A sigh. A sip of her coffee. Then back to angrily jotting notes in the margins of the lesson plan.

I lowered my head, staring at my own notes. My taste for the latte was gone completely. I tried to consider how to proceed. I'm good at helping people and I enjoy it (there's a reason for that, of course, and one that goes back to my own childhood, no mystery there). I knew I could help her. But it wasn't as easy as that. Often people don't know they need help and even if they do they resist seeking it. Normally I wouldn't worry too much about a passing encounter like this; I'd give a person some time to figure out on their own they needed to get some counseling.

But this was serious. The more I observed, the more clear the symptoms. The stiffness of posture, the utter lack of humor or enjoyment in what she was doing with her lesson plan, the lack of pleasure from her beverage, the anger, the twitchy obsessive way she wrote.

And the eyes. That's what speaks the most, to me at least.

The eyes . . .

So I decided to give it a try. I stood to get a refill of latte and, walking back to my table, I dropped a napkin onto hers. I apologized and collected it. Then laughed, looking at her handiwork.

'My girlfriend's a teacher,' I said. 'She absolutely hates lesson plans. She's never quite sure what to do with them.'

She didn't want to be bothered, but even people in her state acknowledge some social conventions. She looked up, the troubled eyes a deep brown. 'They can be a chore. Our school board insists.'

Clumsy, but at least it broke the ice and we had a bit of a conversation.

'I'm Martin Kobel.'

'Annabelle Young.'

'Where do you teach?'

It was in Wetherby, a good-sized town in central North Carolina about an hour from Raleigh. She was here for an education conference.

'Pam, my girlfriend, teaches grade school. You?'

'Middle school.'

The most volatile years, I reflected.

'That's the age she's thinking of moving over to. She's tired of six-year-olds . . . You put a lot into that,' I said, nodding at the plan.

'I try.'

I hesitated a moment. 'Listen, kind of fortuitous I ran into you. If I gave you our phone number and you've got a few minutes – I mean, if it's no imposition – would you think about giving Pam a call? She could really use some advice. Five minutes or so. Give her some thoughts on middle school.'

'Oh, I don't know. I've only been a teacher for three years.'

'Just think about it. You seem like you know what you're doing.' I took out a business card.

Martin J. Kobel, M.S., M.S.W.
Behavioral Therapy
Specialties: Anger Management and Addiction

I wrote 'Pam Robbins' on the top along with the home phone number.

'I'll see what I can do.' She slipped the card in her pocket and turned back to her coffee and the lesson plan.

I knew I'd gone as far as I could. Anything more would have seemed inappropriate and pushed her away.

After fifteen minutes, she glanced at her watch. Apparently whatever conference she was attending was about to resume. She gave a chill smile my way. 'Nice talking to you.'

'The same,' I said.

Annabelle gathered the lesson plan and notes and stuffed them back into her gym bag. As she rose, a teenage boy eased past and jostled her inadvertently with his bulky backpack. I saw her eyes ripple with that look I know so well. 'Jesus,' she whispered to him. 'Learn some manners.'

'Hey, lady, I'm sorry—'

She waved a dismissing hand at the poor kid. Annabelle walked to the counter to add more milk to her coffee. She wiped her mouth and tossed out the napkin. Without a look back at me or anyone she pointed her cold visage toward the door and pushed outside.

I gave it thirty seconds then also stopped at the milk station. Glancing into the hole for trash, I spotted, as I'd half expected, my card, sitting next to her crumpled napkin. I'd have to take a different approach. I certainly wasn't going to give up on her. The stakes for her own well-being and of those close to her were too high.

But it would require some finesse. I've found that you can't just bluntly tell potential patients that their problems are the result not of a troubled childhood or a bad relationship, but simply because an invisible entity had latched on to their psyches like a virus and was exerting its influence.

In a different era, or in a different locale, someone might have said that the teacher was possessed by a demonic spirit or the like. Now we're much more scientific about it, but it's still wise to ease into the subject slowly.

Annabelle Young had come under the influence of a neme.

The term was first coined by a doctor in Washington, DC James Pheder was a well-known biologist and researcher. He came up with the word by combining 'negative' and 'meme', the latter describing a cultural phenomenon that spreads and replicates in societies.

I think reference to meme – m version – is a bit misleading, since it suggests something rather more abstract than what a *neme* really is. In my lengthy book on the subject, published a few years ago, I define a neme as 'a discrete body of intangible energy that evokes extreme emotional responses in humans, resulting in behavior that is most often detrimental to the host or to the society in which he or she lives'.

But 'neme' is a convenient shorthand and every therapist or researcher familiar with the concept uses it.

The word is also beneficial in that it neutrally describes a scientific, proven construct and avoids the historical terms that have muddied the truth for thousands of years. Words like ghosts, spirits, Rudolf Otto's numinous presences, revenants, Buddhism's hungry ghosts, rural countryside's white ladies, Japanese *yurei*, demons. Dozens of others.

Those fictional legends and superstitions were largely the result of the inability to explain nemes scientifically in the past. As often happens, until a phenomenon is rationally explained and quantified, folklore fills the gaps. The old belief, for instance, in spontaneous generation – that life could arise from inanimate objects – was accepted for thousands of years, supported by apparently scientific observations, for instance, that maggots and other infestations appeared in rotting food or standing water. It was only when Louis Pasteur proved via controlled, repeatable experiments that living material, like eggs or bacteria, *had* to be present for life to generate that the old view fell by the wayside.

Same thing with nemes. Framing the concept in terms of ghosts and possessing spirits was a convenient and simple fiction. Now we know better.

Growing up, I'd never heard of these things that would later be labeled nemes. It was only after a particular incident that I became aware: the deaths of my parents and brother.

You could say that my family was killed by one.

When I was sixteen we went to one of Alex's basketball games at our school. At some point my father and I hit the hot dog stand. The father of a player on the opposing team was standing nearby, sipping a Coke and watching the game. Suddenly – I can still remember it perfectly – the man underwent a transformation, instantly shifting from relaxed and benign to tense, distracted, on guard. And the eyes . . . there was no doubt that they changed. The very color seemed to alter; they grew dark, malevolent. I knew something had happened, something had possessed him, I thought at the time. I felt chilled and I stepped away from him.

Then the man suddenly grew angry. Furious. Something on the court set him off. A foul maybe, a bad call. He screamed at Alex's team, he screamed at our coach, at the ref. In his rage, he bumped against my father and dropped his soda, spilling it on his shoes. It was his fault, but he seemed to blame my father for the mishap. The men got into an argument, though my father soon realized that the man was out of control, consumed by this odd rage, and ushered us back to the bleachers.

After the game I was still troubled, but assumed the matter was over. Not so. The man followed us out into the parking lot and, screaming, bizarrely challenged my father to a fight. The man's wife was crying, pulling him back and apologizing. 'He's never behaved like this, really!'

'Shut up, bitch!' he raged, and slapped her.

Shaken, we climbed into the car and drove off. Ten minutes later, driving down I-40, we were sitting in troubled silence when a car veered over three lanes. The man from the game swerved right toward us, driving us off the road.

I remember seeing his face, twisted with anger, over the steering wheel.

In court he tearfully explained that he didn't know what happened. It was like he was possessed. That defense didn't get him very far. He was found guilty of three counts of first-degree manslaughter.

After I got out of the hospital following the crash, I couldn't get out of my head the memory of what had happened to the man. How clear it was to me that he'd changed, in a flash. It was like flipping a light switch.

I began reading about sudden changes in personality and rage and impulse. That research led eventually to the writings of Dr Pheder and other researchers and therapists. I grew fascinated with the concept of nemes, considered a theory by some, a reality by others.

As to their origin, there are several theories. I subscribe to one I found the most logical. Nemes are vestiges of human instinct. They were an integral part of the psychological makeup of the creatures in the chain that led to Homo sapiens and were necessary for survival. In the early days of humanoids, it was occasionally necessary to behave in ways we would consider bad or criminal now. To commit acts of violence, to be rageful, impulsive, sadistic, greedy. But as societies formed and developed, the need for those darker impulses faded. The governing bodies, the armies, the law enforcers, took over the task of our survival.

Violence, rage and the other darker impulses became not only unnecessary but were counter to society's interests.

Somehow – there are several theories on this – the powerful neuro impulses that motivated those dark behaviors separated from humans and came to exist as separate entities, pockets of energy, you could say. In my research I found a precedent for this migration: the same thing happened with telepathy. Many generations ago, psychic communication was common. The advent of modern communication techniques eliminated the need for what we could call extrasensory perception, though many young children still have documented telepathic skills. (However, it's interesting that with the increased use of cell phones and computers by youngsters, incidents of telepathy among young people are dramatically decreasing.)

But whatever their genealogy, nemes exist, and there are millions of them. They float around like flu viruses until they find a vulnerable person and then incorporate themselves into the psyche of their host ('incorporate' is used, rather than a judgmental term like 'infest' or 'infect', and never the theologically loaded 'possess'). If someone is impulsive, angry, depressed, confused, scared – even physically sick – nemes will sense that and make a beeline for the cerebral cortex, the portion of the brain where emotion is controlled. They usually avoid people who are emotionally stable, strong-willed, and who have high degrees of self-control, though not always.

Nemes are invisible, like electromagnetic waves, and light at the far end of the spectrum, though it's sometimes possible to tell they're nearby if you hear distortion on a cell phone, TV or radio. Usually, the host doesn't sense the incorporation itself; they only experience a sudden mood swing. Some people can outright sense them, though. I'm one of these, though there's nothing 'special' about me. It's simply like having acute hearing or good eyesight.

Do nemes think?

They do, in a way. Though 'think' is probably the wrong word. More likely they operate like insects, mostly through awareness and instinct. Survival is very strong within them, too. There's nothing immortal about nemes. When their host passes away, they seem to dissipate as well. I myself don't believe they communicate with one another, at least not in traditional ways, *our* ways, since I've never seen any evidence that they do.

This isn't to minimize the damage they can do, of course. It's significant. The rage and impulsive behavior that arise from incorporation lead to rape, murder, physical and sexual abuse, and more subtle harms such as substance overuse and verbal abuse. They also affect the physiology and morphology of the host's body itself, as a series of autopsies several years ago proved.

After my devastating personal encounter with nemes, I decided I wanted to work in a field that would help minimize the damage they could do.

So I became a therapist.

The thrust of my approach is behavioral. Once you're under the influence of a neme, you don't 'cast it out', as a (now former) practitioner unfortunately joked at a psychotherapy conference in Chicago some years ago. You treat the symptoms. I concentrate on working with my patients to achieve self-control, using any number of techniques to avoid or minimize behaviors that are destructive to them or others. In most cases it doesn't even matter that the patient knows he or she is a host for a neme (some patients are comfortable with the reality and others aren't). In any case, the methods I use are solid and well established, used by all behavioral therapists, and by and large successful.

There've been occasional defeats, of course. It's the nature of the profession. Two of my patients, in which very potent nemes had incorporated, killed themselves when they were simply unable to resolve the conflict between their goals and the neme-influenced behavior.

There's also something that's been in the back of my mind for years: risk to myself. My life has been devoted to minimizing their effectiveness and spread, and so I sometimes wonder if a neme senses that I'm a threat. This is probably according them too much credit; you have to guard against personifying them. But I can't help but think back to an incident several years ago. I was attending a psychology conference in New York City and was nearly mugged. It was curious since the young attacker was a model student at a nice high school near my hotel. He'd never been in trouble with the police. And he was armed with a long knife. An off-duty policeman happened to be nearby and managed to arrest him just as he started after me with the weapon.

It was late at night and I couldn't see clearly, but I believed, from the boy's eyes, that he was being influenced by a neme, motivated by its own sense of survival to kill me.

Probably not. But even if there was some truth to it, I wasn't going to be deterred from my mission to save people at risk.

People like Annabelle Young.

*

The day after running into her in Starbucks, I went to North Carolina State University library and did some research. The state licensing agencies' databases and ever-helpful Google revealed that the woman was thirty years old and worked at Chantelle West Middle School in Wetherby County. Interestingly, she was a widow – her husband had died three years ago – and, yes, she had a nine-year-old son, probably the target of her anger on the phone. According to information about the school where she taught, Annabelle would generally teach large classes, with an average of thirty-five students per year.

This meant that she could have a dramatic and devastating impact on the lives of many young people.

Then, too, was the matter of Annabelle's own well-being. I was pretty sure that she'd come under the influence of the neme around the time her husband died; a sudden personal loss like that makes you emotionally vulnerable and more susceptible than otherwise. (I noted, too, that she'd gone back to work around that time and I wondered if her neme sensed an opportunity to incorporate within someone who could influence a large number of equally vulnerable individuals, the children in her classes.)

Annabelle was obviously a smart woman and she might very well get into counseling at some point. But there comes a point when the neme is so deeply incorporated that people actually become accustomed or addicted to the inappropriate behaviors nemes cause. They don't *want* to change.

My assessment was that she was past this point. And so, since I wasn't going to hear from her, I did the only thing I could. I went to Wetherby.

I got there early on a Wednesday. The drive was pleasant, along one of those combined highways that traverse central North Carolina. It split somewhere outside of Raleigh and I continued on the increasingly rural branch of the two, taking me through old North Carolina. Tobacco warehouses and small industrial parts plants – most of them closed years ago but still squatting in weeds. Trailer parks, very unclosed. Bungalows and plenty of evidence of a love of Nascar and Republican party lines.

Wetherby has a redeveloped downtown, but that's just for show. I noted immediately as I cruised along the two-block stretch that nobody was buying anything in the art galleries and antique stores, and the nearly empty restaurants, I suspected, got new awnings with new names every eight months or so. The real work in places like Wetherby got done in the malls and office parks and housing developments built around new golf courses.

I checked into a motel, showered, and began my reconnaissance, checking out Chantelle Middle School. I parked around the time I'd learned classes were dismissed but didn't catch a glimpse of Annabelle Young.

Later that evening, about seven thirty, I found her house, four miles away, a modest twenty-year-old colonial in need of painting, on a cul-de-sac. There was no car in the drive. I parked under some trees and waited.

Fifteen minutes later a car pulled into the drive. I couldn't tell if her son was inside or not. The Toyota parked in the garage and the door closed. A few minutes later I got out, slipped into some woods beside the house and glanced into the kitchen. I saw her carting dishes inside. Dirty dishes from lunch or last night, I assumed. She set them in the sink and I saw her pause, staring down. Her face was turned away but her body language, even from this distance, told me that she was angry.

Her son appeared, a skinny boy with longish brown hair. *His* body language suggested that he was cautious. He said something to his mother. Her head snapped toward him and he nodded quickly. Then retreated. She stayed where she was, staring at the dishes for a moment. Without even rinsing them she stepped out of the room and swept her hand firmly along the wall, slapping the switch out. I could almost hear the angry gesture from where I was.

I didn't want to talk to her while her son was present, so I headed back to the motel.

The next day I was up early and cruised back to the school before the teachers arrived. At seven fifteen I caught a glimpse of her car arriving and watched her climb out and stride unsmilingly into the school. Too many people around and she was too harried to have a conversation now.

I returned at three in the afternoon, and when Annabelle emerged I followed her to a nearby strip mall, anchored by a Harris Teeter grocery store. She went shopping and came out a half-hour later. She dumped the plastic bags in her trunk. I was going to approach her, even though a meeting in the parking lot wasn't the most conducive to pitching my case, when I saw her lock the car and walk toward a nearby bar and grill.

At three thirty she wouldn't be eating lunch or dinner and I knew what she had in mind. People influenced by nemes often drink more than they should, to dull the anxiety and anger that come from the incorporation.

Though I would eventually work on getting her to cut down on her alcohol consumption, her being slightly intoxicated and relaxed now could be a big help. I waited five minutes and followed. Inside the dark tavern, which smelled of Lysol and onions, I spotted her at the bar. She was having a mixed drink. Vodka or gin, it seemed, and some kind of juice. She was nearly finished with her first and she waved for a second.

I sat down two stools away and ordered a Diet Coke. I felt her head swivel toward me, tilt slightly as she debated if she'd seen me before, and turn to her drink. Then the pieces fell together and she faced me again.

Without looking up I said, 'I'm a professional counselor, Ms Young. I'm here only in that capacity. To help. I'd like to talk to you.'

'You . . . you followed me here? From Raleigh?'

I made a show of leaving money for the soda to suggest that I wasn't going to stay longer than necessary, trying to put her at ease.

'I did, yes. But, please, you don't need to be afraid.'

Finally I turned to look at her. The eyes were just as I expected, narrow, cold, the eyes of somebody else entirely. The neme was even stronger than I'd thought.

'I'm about five seconds away from calling the police.'

'I understand. Please listen. I want to say something to you. And if you want me to leave I'll head back to Raleigh right now. You can choose whatever you want.'

'Say it and get out.' She took another drink.

'I specialize in treating people who aren't happy in life. I'm good at it. When I saw you the other day in Starbucks I knew you were exactly the sort of patient who could benefit from my expertise. I would like very much to help you.'

No mention of nemes, of course.

'I don't need a shrink.'

'I'm actually not a shrink. I'm a psychologist, not a doctor.'

'I don't care what you are. You can't . . . can't you be reported for this, trying to drum up business?'

'Yes, and you're free to do that. But I thought it was worth the risk to offer you my services. I don't care about the money. You can pay me whatever you can afford. I care about helping you. I can give you references and you can call the state licensing board about me.'

'Do you even have a girlfriend who's a teacher?'

'No. I lied. Which I'll never do again . . . It was that important to try to explain how I can help you.'

And then I saw her face soften. She was nodding.

My heart was pounding hard. It had been a risk, trying this, but she was going to come around. The therapy would be hard work. For both of us. But the stakes were too high to let her continue the way she was. I knew we could make significant progress.

I turned away to pull a card from my wallet. 'Let me tell you a—'

As I looked back, I took the full tide of her second drink in the face. My eyes on fire from the liquor and stinging juice, I gasped in agony and grabbed bar napkins to dry them.

'Annie, what's wrong?' the bartender snapped, and through my blurred vision I could just make out his grabbing her arm as she started to fling the glass at me. I raised my own arm to protect myself.

'What'd he do?'

'Fuck you, let go of me!' she cried to him.

'Hey, hey, take it easy, Annie. What—?'

Then he ducked as she launched the glass at *him*. It struck a row of others; half of them shattered. She was out of control. Typical.

'Fuck you both!' Screaming. She dug a bill out of her purse and flung it onto the bar.

'Please, Ms Young,' I said, 'I can help you.'

'If I see you again, I'm calling the police.' She stormed out.

'Listen, mister, what the hell d'you do?'

I didn't answer him. I grabbed some more napkins and, wiping my face, walked to the window. I saw her stride up to her son, who was standing nearby with a book bag. So this was the rendezvous spot. I wondered how often he'd had to wait outside for Mom, while she was in here getting drunk. I pictured cold January afternoons, the boy huddling and blowing breath into his hands.

She gestured him after her. Apparently there'd been something else on the agenda for after school, and, disappointed, he lifted his arms and glanced at the nearby sports store. But the shopping was not going to happen today. She stormed up and grabbed him by the arm. He pulled away. She drew back to slap him but he dutifully walked to the car. I could see him clicking on his seat belt and wiping tears.

Without a glance back at the bartender, I, too, left.

I walked to the car to head back to the motel to change. What had happened was discouraging but I'd dealt with more difficult people than Annabelle Young. There were other approaches to take. Over the years I've learned what works and what doesn't; it's all part of being a therapist.

The next morning at six I parked behind Etta's Diner, in a deserted portion of the lot. The restaurant was directly behind Annabelle's house. I made my way up the hill along a path that led to the sidewalk in her development. I had to take an oblique approach; if she saw me coming she'd never answer the door, and that would be that.

The morning was cool and fragrant with the smells of pine and wet earth. The season being spring, the sky was light even at this early hour and it was easy to make my way along the path. I wondered how different Annabelle's life had been before her husband died. How soon the neme had incorporated itself into her afterward. I suspected she'd been a vivacious, caring mother and wife, completely different from the enraged out-of-control woman she now was becoming.

I continued to the edge of the woods and waited behind a stand of camellias with exploding red blossoms. At about six thirty her son pushed out the front door, carting a heavy book bag, and strolled to the end of the cul-de-sac, presumably to catch his bus.

When he was gone, I walked to the porch and climbed the stairs.

Was I ready? I asked myself.

Always those moments of self-doubt, even though I'd been a professional therapist for years.

Always, the doubts.

But then I relaxed. My mission in life was to save people. I was good at that task. I knew what I was doing.

Yes, I was ready.

I rang the doorbell and stepped aside from the peephole. I heard the footsteps approach. She flung the door open and had only a moment to gasp at the sight of the black stocking mask I was wearing and the lengthy knife in my gloved hand.

I grabbed her hair and plunged the blade into her chest three times, then sliced through her neck. Both sides and deep, so the end would be quick.

Lord knew I didn't want her to suffer.

Two

The job of making sure that Martin Kobel was either put to death or sentenced to life in prison for the murder of Annabelle Young fell to Glenn Hollow, the Wetherby County prosecutor.

And it was a job that he had embraced wholeheartedly from the moment he got the call from county police dispatch. Forty-two years old, Hollow was the most successful prosecutor in the state of North Carolina, judged in terms of convictions won, and judged from the media since he had a preference for going after violent offenders. A mark of his success was that this was to be his last year in Wetherby. He'd be running for state attorney general in November and there wasn't much doubt he'd win.

But his grander plans wouldn't detract from his enthusiastic prosecution of the murderer of Annabelle Young. In big cities the prosecutors get cases tossed onto their desks along with the police reports. With Glenn Hollow, it was different. He had an honorary flashing blue light attached to his dash and, ten minutes after getting the call about the homicide, he was at Ms Young's house while the forensic team was still soaking up blood and taking pix.

He was now walking into the Wetherby County courthouse. Nothing Old South about the place. It was the sort of edifice you'd find in Duluth or Toledo or Schenectady. One story, nondescript white stone, overtaxed air conditioning, scuffed linoleum floors and greenish fluorescents that might engender the question, 'Hey, you feeling okay?'

Hollow was a lean man, with drawn cheeks and thick black hair close to a skullish head – defendants said he looked like a ghoul; kinder reports, that he resembled Gregory Peck in *Moby Dick*, minus the beard. He was somber and reserved and kept his personal life far, far away from professional.

He now nodded at the secretary in the ante-office of Judge Brigham Rollins's chambers.

'Go on in, Glenn.'

Inside were two big men. Rollins was mid-fifties and had a pitted face and the spiky gray hair of a crew cut neglected a week too long. He was in shirtsleeves, though noosed with a tie, of course. He wore plucky yellow suspenders that hoisted his significant tan pants like a concrete bucket under a crane. Gray stains radiated from under his arms. As usual the judge had doused Old Spice.

Sitting opposite was Ed Ringling – the circus jokes all but dead after these many years of being a defense lawyer in a medium-sized town, and, no, there was no relation. Stocky, with blondish brown hair carefully trimmed, he resembled a forty-five-year-old retired army major – not a bad deduction, since Fayetteville wasn't terribly far away, but, like the circus brothers, not true.

Hollow didn't like or dislike Ringling. The lawyer was fair though abrasive, and he made Hollow work for every victory. Which was as it should be, the prosecutor believed. God created defense lawyers, he'd said, to make sure the system was fair and the prosecution didn't cheat or get lazy. After all, there *was* that one-in-a-hundred chance that the five-foot-eight black gangbanger from Central High presently in custody wasn't the same five-foot-eight black gangbanger from Central High who actually pulled the trigger.

Judge Rollins closed a folder that he'd been perusing. He grunted. 'Tell me where we are with this one, gentlemen.'

'Yessir,' Hollow began. 'The state is seeking special circumstances murder.'

'This's about that teacher got her throat slit, right?'

'Yessir. In her house. Broad daylight.'

A grimace of distaste. Not shock. Rollins'd been a judge for years.

The courthouse was on the crook of Route 85 and Henderson Road. Through one window you could see Belted Galloway cows grazing. They were black and white, vertically striped, precise, like God had used a ruler. Hollow could look right over the judge's shoulder and see eight of them, chewing. Out the other window was a T.J. Maxx, a Barnes &

Noble and a multiplex under construction. These two views pretty much defined Wetherby.

'What's the story behind it?'

'This Kobel, a therapist. He was stalking her. They met at a Starbucks when she was in Raleigh at an educational conference. Got witnesses say he gave her his card but she threw it out. Next thing he tracked her down and shows up in Wetherby. Got into a fight at Red Robin, near Harris Teeter. She threw a drink in his face. One witness saw him park at Etta's, the diner, the morning she was killed—'

'Tonight's corned beef,' the judge said.

'They do a good job of that,' Ringling added.

True, they did. Hollow continued, 'And he hiked up into those woods behind her place. When she opened the door, he killed her. He waited till her boy left.'

'There's that, at least,' Rollins grumbled. 'How'd the boys in blue get him?'

'Unlucky for him. Busboy on a smoke break at Etta's saw him coming out of the forest, carrying some things. The kid found some blood near where he parked. Called the police with the make and model. Kobel'd tossed away the knife and mask and gloves, but they found 'em. Fibers, DNA, fingerprints on the *inside* of the gloves. People always forget that. They watch *CSI* too much . . . Oh, and then he confessed.'

'*What?*' the judge barked.

'Yep. Advised of rights, twice. Sung like a bird.'

'Then what the hell're you doing here? Take a plea and let's get some real work done.'

The judge glanced at Ringling, but the defense lawyer in turn cast his eyes on Hollow.

Rollins gripped his ceramic coffee mug and sipped the hot contents. 'What isn't who telling who? Don't play games. There's no jury to impress with your clevers.'

Ringling said, 'He's completely insane. Nuts.'

A skeptical wrinkle on the judge's brow. 'But you're saying he wore a mask and gloves?'

Most insane perps didn't care if they were identified and didn't care if they got away afterward. They didn't wear ninja or hit man outfits. They were the sort who hung around afterward and finger-painted with the blood of their victims.

Ringling shrugged.

The judge asked, 'Competent to stand trial?'

'Yessir. We're saying he was insane at the time of commission. No sense of right or wrong. No sense of reality.'

The judge grunted.

The insanity defense is based on one overriding concept in jurisprudence: responsibility. At what point are we responsible for acts we commit? If we cause an accident and we're sued in civil court for damages, the law asks, Would a reasonably prudent person have, say, driven his car on a slippery road at thirty-five miles per hour? If the jury says yes, then we're not responsible for the crash.

If we're arrested for a crime, the law asks, Did we act knowingly and intentionally to break a law? If we didn't, then we're not guilty.

There are, in fact, two ways in which the issue of the defendant's sanity arises in a criminal court. One is when the defendant is so out of it that he can't participate in his own trial. That US Constitution thing: the right to confront your accusers.

But this isn't what most people familiar with *Boston Legal* or *Perry Mason* think of as the insanity defense and, as Ed Ringling had confirmed, it wasn't an issue in *State v. Kobel*.

More common is the second sanity issue – when defense lawyers invoke various offshoots of the M'Naghten Rule, which holds that if the defendant lacked the capacity to know he was doing something wrong when he committed the crime, he can't be found guilty. This isn't to say he's going scot-free; he'll get locked up in a mental ward until it's determined that he's no longer dangerous.

This was Ed Ringling's claim regarding Martin Kobel.

But Glenn Hollow exhaled a perplexed laugh. 'He wasn't insane. He was a practicing therapist with an obsession over a pretty woman who was ignoring him. Special Circumstances. I want guilty, I want the needle. That's it.'

Ringling said to Rollins, 'Insanity. You sentence him to indefinite incarceration in Butler, Judge. We won't contest it. No trial. Everybody wins.'

Hollow said, 'Except the other people he kills when they let him out in five years.'

'Ah, you just want a feather in your cap for when you run for AG. He's a media bad boy.'

'I want justice,' Hollow said, supposing he was sounding pretentious.

And not caring one whit. Nor admitting that, yeah, he did want the feather, too.

'What's the evidence for the Looney Tunes?' the judge asked. He had a very different persona when he was in chambers compared with when he was in the courtroom, and presumably different yet at Etta's Diner, eating corned beef.

'He absolutely believes he didn't do anything wrong. He was saving the children in Annabelle's class. I've been over this with him a dozen times. He *believes* it.'

'Believes what exactly?' the judge asked.

'That she was possessed. By something like a ghost. I've looked it up. Some cult thing on the Internet. Some spirit or something makes you lose control, lose your temper and beat the crap out of your wife or kids. Even makes you kill people. It's called a neme.' He spelled it.

'Neme.'

Hollow said, 'I've looked it up, too, Judge. You can look it up. We all can look it up. Which is just what Kobel did. To lay the groundwork for claiming insanity. He killed a hot young woman who rejected him. And now he's pretending he believes in 'em to look like he's nuts.'

'If that's the case,' Ringling said gravely, 'then he's been planning ever since he was a teenager to kill a woman he met two weeks ago.'

'What's that?'

'His parents died in a car wreck when he was in high school. He had a break with reality, the doctors called it. Diagnosed as a borderline personality.'

'Like my cousin,' the judge said. 'She's awkward. The wife and I never invite her over, we can avoid it.'

'Kobel got involuntary commitment for eight months back then, talking about these creatures that possessed the driver who killed his family. Same thing as now.'

'But he had to go to shrink school,' the judge pointed out. 'He graduated. That's not crazy, in my book.'

Hollow leapt in with, 'Exactly. He has a master's in psychology. One in social work. Good grades. Sees patients. And he's written books, for God's sake.'

'One of which I happen to have with me and which I will be introducing into evidence. Thank you, Glenn, for bringing it up.' The defense lawyer opened his briefcase and dropped a ten-pound stack of 8½-by-11 sheets on the judge's desk. '*Self*-published, by the way. And written by hand.'

Hollow looked it over. He had good eyes but it was impossible to read any of the text except the title because it was in such tiny handwriting. There had to be a thousand words per page, in elegant, obsessive script.

*Biblical Evidence of malevolent
emotional ENERGY Incorporated into Psyches.*

By Martin Kobel.

© *All rights reserved*

'All rights reserved?' Hollow snorted. 'Who's gonna plagiarize this crap? And what's with the capitalization?'

'Glenn, this is one of about thirty volumes. He's been writing these things for twenty years. And it's the smallest one.'

The prosecutor repeated, 'He's faking.'

But the judge was skeptical. 'Going back all those years?'

'Okay, he's quirky. But this man is dangerous. Two of his patients killed themselves under circumstances that make it seem like he suggested they do it. Another one's serving five years because he attacked Kobel in his office. He claimed the doctor provoked him. And Kobel broke into a funeral home six years ago and was caught fucking around with the corpses.'

'What?'

'Not that way. He was dissecting them. Looking for evidence of these things, these nemes.'

Ringling said happily, 'There's another book he wrote on the autopsy. Eighteen hundred pages. Illustrated.'

'It wasn't an autopsy, Ed. It was breaking into a funeral home and fucking around with corpses.' Hollow was getting angry. But maybe it's just a neme, he thought cynically. 'He goes to conferences.'

Ringling added, 'Paranormal conferences. Wacko conferences. Full of wackos just like him.'

'Jesus Christ, Ed. The people who cop insanity pleas're paranoid schizos. They don't bathe, they take Haldol and lithium, they're delusional. They don't go to fucking Starbucks and ask for an extra shot of syrup.'

Hollow had used the F word more times today than in the past year.

Ringling said, 'They kill people because they're possessed by ghosts. That's not sane. End of story.'

The judge lifted his hand. 'You gentlemen know that when the earth was young Africa and South America were right next to each other. I mean, fifty feet away. Think about that. And here you are, same thing. You're real close, I can tell. You can work it out. Come together. There's a song about that. It's in your interest. If we go to trial, you two're doing all the work. All I'm gonna be doing is saying "sustained" and "overruled".'

'Ed, he killed that girl, a schoolteacher. In cold blood. I want him away forever. He's a danger and he's sick . . . What I can do, but only this, I'll go with life. Drop Special Circumstances. But no parole.'

The judge looked expectantly toward Ed Ringling. 'That's something.'

'I knew it'd come up,' Ringling said. 'I asked my client about it. He says he didn't do anything wrong and he has faith in the system. He's convinced there're these things, floating around, and they glom on to you and make you do bad stuff. No, we're going for insanity.'

Hollow grimaced. 'You want to play it that way, you get your expert and I'll get mine.'

The judge grumbled. 'Pick a date, gentlemen. We're going to trial. And, for Christ sake, somebody tell me what the hell is a neme?'

The *People of the State of North Carolina v. Kobel* began on a Wednesday in July.

Glenn Hollow kicked it off with a string of witnesses and police reports regarding the forensic evidence, which was irrefutable. Ed Ringling let most of it go and just got a few errant bits of trace evidence removed, which Hollow didn't care about anyway.

Another of Hollow's witnesses was a clerk from Starbucks in Raleigh, who testified about the business card exchange. (Hollow noted the troubled looks on the faces of several jurors and people in the gallery, leaving them wondering, he supposed, about the wisdom of affairs and other indiscreet behavior in places with observant baristas.)

Other witnesses testified about behavior consistent with stalking, including several who'd seen Kobel in Wetherby in the days before the murder. Several had seen his car parked outside the school where Annabelle Young taught. If there's any way to put your location on record it's to be a middle-aged man parked outside a middle school. Eight concerned citizens gave the police his tag number.

The busboy at Etta's Diner gave some very helpful testimony with the help of a Spanish translator.

As for Kobel himself, sitting at the defense table, his hair was askew and his suit didn't fit right. He frantically filled notebook after notebook with writing like ant tracks.

Son of a bitch, thought Hollow. It was pure performance, orchestrated by Edward Ringling, Esq, of course, with Martin Kobel in the role of schizophrenic. Hollow had seen the police interview video. On screen the defendant had been well scrubbed, well spoken and no twitchier than Hollow's ten-year-old Lab, known to take naps in the middle of tornados.

Any other case, the trial would've been over with on the second day – with a verdict for the People, followed by a lengthy appeal and an uncomfortable few minutes while the executioner figured out which was the better vein, right arm or left.

But there was more, of course. Where the real battle would be fought.

Ringling's expert psychiatrist testified that the defendant was, in his opinion, legally insane and unable to tell the difference between right and wrong. Kobel honestly believed that Annabelle Young was a threat to students and her son because she was infested by a neme, some spirit or force that he truly believed existed.

'He's paranoid, delusional. His reality is very, very different from ours,' was the expert's conclusion.

The shrink's credentials were good and since that was about the only way to attack him, Hollow let him go.

'Your honor,' Ringling next said. 'I move to introduce defense exhibits numbers one through twenty-eight.'

And wheeled up to the bench – literally, in carts – Kobel's notebooks and self-published treatises on nemes, more than anybody could possibly be interested in.

A second expert for the defense testified about these writings. 'These are typical of a delusional mind.' Everything Kobel had written was typical of paranoid and delusional individuals who had lost touch with reality. He stated that there was no scientific basis for the concept of neme. 'It's like voodoo, it's like vampires, werewolves.'

Ringling tried to seal the deal by having the doctor read a portion from one of these 'scientific treatises', a page of utterly incomprehensible nonsense. Judge Rollins, on the edge of sleep, cut him off. 'We get the idea, counselor. Enough.'

On cross-examination, Hollow couldn't do much to deflate this testimony. The best he could do was: 'Doctor, do you read Harry Potter?'

'Well, as a matter of fact, yes, I have.'

'The fourth was my favorite. What was yours?'

'Uhm, I don't know really.'

'Is it possible,' the prosecutor asked the witness, 'that those writings of Mr Kobel are merely attempts at writing a novel? Some big fantasy book.'

'I . . . I can't imagine it.'

'But it's possible, isn't it?'

'I suppose. But I'll tell you, he'll never sell the movie rights.'

Amid the laughter, the judge dismissed the witness.

There was testimony about the bizarre autopsy, which Hollow didn't bother to refute.

Ed Ringling also introduced two of Kobel's patients, who testified that they had been so troubled by his obsessive talk about these ghosts or spirits inhabiting their bodies that they quit seeing him.

And then Ringling had Kobel himself take the stand, dressed the part of the madman in his premeditatedly wrinkled and dirty clothes, chewing his lip, looking twitchy and weird.

This idea – insane in its own right – was a huge risk, because on cross-examination Hollow would ask the man point-blank if he'd killed Annabelle Young. Since he'd confessed once, he would have to confess again – or Hollow would read the sentence from his statement. Either way the jury would actually hear the man admit the crime.

But Ringling met the problem head-on. His first question: 'Mr Kobel, did you kill Annabelle Young?'

'Oh, yes, of course I did.' He sounded surprised.

A gasp filled the courtroom.

'And why did you do that, Mr Kobel?'

'For the sake of the children.'

'How do you mean that?'

'She was a teacher, you know. Oh, God! Every year, thirty or forty students, impressionable young people would come under her influence. She was going to poison their minds. She might even hurt them, abuse them, spread hatred.' He closed his eyes and shivered.

And the Academy Award for best performance on the part of a crazed murder suspect goes to . . .

'Now, tell me, Mr Kobel, why did you think she would hurt the children?'

'Oh, she'd come under the influence of a neme.'

'That's what we heard a little about earlier, right? In your writings?'

'Yes, in my writings.'

'Could you tell us, briefly, what a neme is?'

'You could call it an energy force. Malevolent energy. It attaches to your mind and it won't let go. It's terrible. It causes you to commit crimes, abuse people, fall into rages. A lot of temper tantrums and road rage are caused by nemes. They're all over the place. Millions of them.'

'And you were convinced she was possessed?'

'It's not possession,' Kobel said adamantly. 'That's a theological concept. Nemes are purely scientific. Like viruses.'

'You think they're as real as viruses?'

'They are! You have to believe me! They are!'

'And Ms Young was being influenced by nemes.'

'One, just one.'

'And was going to hurt her students.'

'And her son. Oh, yes, I could see it. I have this ability to see nemes. I had to save the children.'

'You weren't stalking her because you were attracted to her?'

Kobel's voice cracked. 'No, no. Nothing like that. I wanted to get her into counseling. I could have saved her. But she was too far gone. The last thing I wanted to do was kill her. But it was a blessing. It really was. I had to.' Tears glistened.

Oh, brother . . .

'Prosecution's witness.'

Hollow did the best he could. He decided not to ask about Annabelle Young. Kobel's murdering her was no longer the issue in this case. The whole question was Kobel's state of mind. Hollow got the defendant to admit that he'd been in a mental hospital only once, as a teenager, and hadn't seen a mental health professional since then. He'd taken no antipsychotic drugs. 'They take my edge off. You have to be sharp when you're fighting nemes.'

'Just answer the question, please.'

Hollow then produced Kobel's tax returns for the past three years.

When Ringling objected, Hollow said to Judge Rollins, 'Your honor, a man who files a tax return is of sound mind.'

'That's debatable,' said the ultraconservative judge, drawing laughter from the courtroom.

Oh, to be on the bench, thought Glenn Hollow. And maybe after a few years' stint as the attorney general I will be.

Rollins said, 'I'll let 'em in.'

'These are your returns, aren't they, sir?'

'I guess. Yes.'

'They indicate you made a fair amount of money at your practice. About forty thousand dollars a year.'

'Maybe. I suppose so.'

'So despite those other two patients who testified earlier, you must have a much larger number of patients you treat regularly and who are satisfied with your services.'

Kobel looked him in the eyes. 'There're a lot of nemes out there. Somebody's gotta fight 'em.'

Hollow sighed. 'No further questions, your honor.'

The prosecutor then called his own expert, a psychiatrist who'd examined Kobel. The testimony was that, though quirky, he was not legally insane. He was well aware of what he was doing, that he was committing a crime when he killed the victim.

Ringling asked a few questions, but didn't belabor the cross-examination.

Toward the end of the day, during a short break, Glenn Hollow snuck a look at the jury box; he'd been a prosecutor and a trial lawyer for a long time and was an expert not only at the law but at reading juries.

And, goddamn it, they were reacting just the way Ed Ringling wanted them to. Hollow could tell they hated and feared Martin Kobel, but because he was such a monster and the things he was saying were so bizarre, he couldn't be held to the jury's standards of ethics and behavior. Oh, Ringling had been smart. He wasn't playing his client as a victim; he wasn't playing him as somebody who'd been abused or suffered a traumatic childhood (he barely referred to the deaths of Kobel's parents and brother).

No, he was showing that this *thing* at the defense table was not even human.

Like his expert said, 'Mr Kobel's reality is not *our* reality.'

Hollow stretched his skinny legs out in front of him and watched the tassels on his loafers lean to the side. I'm going to lose this case, he thought. I'm going to lose it. And that son of a bitch'll be out in five or six years, looking for other women to stalk.

He was in despair.

Nemes . . . shit.

Then the judge turned away from his clerk and said, 'Mr Hollow? Shall we continue with your rebuttal of Mr Ringling's affirmative defense?'

It was then that a thought occurred to the prosecutor. He considered it for a moment then gasped at where the idea led.

'Mr Hollow?'

'Your honor, if possible, could we recess until tomorrow? The prosecution would appreciate the time.'

Judge Rollins debated. He looked at his watch. 'All right. We'll recess until nine a.m. tomorrow.'

Glenn Hollow thanked the judge and told his young associates to gather up the papers and take them back to the office. The prosecutor rose and headed out the door. But he didn't start sprinting until he was well out of the courthouse; he believed that you never let jurors see anything but your dignified self.

At a little after nine the next morning, Glenn Hollow rose to his feet. 'I'd like to call to the stand Dr James Pheder.'

'Objection, your honor.' Ed Ringling was on his feet.

'Reasons?'

'We received notice of this witness last night at eight p.m. We haven't had adequate time to prepare.'

'Where were you at eight?'

Ringling blinked. 'Well, your honor, I . . . the wife and I were out to dinner.'

'At eight *I* was reading documents in this case, Mr Ringling. And Mr Hollow was – obviously – sending you notices about impending witnesses. Neither of us were enjoying the buffet line at House O' Ribs.'

'But—'

'Think on your feet, counselor. That's what you get paid those big bucks for. Objection overruled. Proceed, Mr Hollow.'

Pheder, a dark-complexioned man with a curly mop of black hair and a lean face, took the oath and sat.

'Now, Mr Pheder, could you tell us about your credentials?'

'Yessir. I have degrees in psychology and biology from the University of Eastern Virginia, the University at Albany and Northern Arizona University.'

'All of which are accredited four-year colleges, correct?'

'Yes.'

'And what do you do for a living?'

'I'm an author and lecturer.'

'Are you published?'

'Yessir. I've published dozens of books.'

'Are those self-published?'

'Nosir. I'm with established publishing companies.'

'And where do you lecture?'

'All over the country. At schools, libraries, bookstores, private venues.'

'How many people attend these lectures?' Hollow asked.

'Each one is probably attended by four to six hundred people.'

'And how many lectures a year do you give?'

'About one hundred.'

Hollow paused and then asked, 'Are you familiar with the concept of neme?'

'Yessir.'

'Is it true that you coined that term?'

'Yessir.'

'What does it refer to?'

'I combined the words "negative" and "meme". "Negative" is just what it sounds like. "Meme" is a common phenomenon in society, like a song or catchphrase, that captures the popular imagination. It spreads.'

'Give us the gist of the concept of neme, that's n-e-m-e, if you would.'

'In a nutshell?'

'Oh, yessir. I got C's in science. Make it nice and simple.'

Nice touch, Hollow thought of his improvisation. Science.

Pheder continued. 'It's like a cloud of energy that affects people's emotions in a destructive way. You know how you're walking down the street and you suddenly feel different? For no reason at all. Your mood swings. It could be caused by any number of things. But it might be a neme incorporating itself into your cerebrum.'

'And you say, "negative". So nemes are bad?'

'Well, bad is a human judgment. They're neutral but they tend to make us behave in ways society characterizes as bad. Take a case of swimming in the ocean. Sharks and jellyfish aren't bad; they're simply doing what nature intended, existing. But when they take a bite out of us or sting us, we call that bad. Nemes are the same. They make us do things that to them are natural but that we call evil.'

'And you're convinced these nemes are real?'

'Oh, yessir. Absolutely.'

'In your opinion, do other people believe in them?'

'Yes, many, many do.'

'Are these people scientists?'

'Some, yes. Therapists, chemists, biologists, psychologists.'

'No further questions, your honor.'

'Your witness, Mr Ringling.'

The defense lawyer couldn't, as it turned out, think on his feet, not very well. He was prepared for Hollow to introduce testimony by experts attacking his client's claim of insanity.

He wasn't prepared for Hollow to try to prove nemes were real. Ringling asked a few meaningless questions and let it go at that.

Hollow was relieved that he hadn't explored Pheder's history and credentials in other fields, including parapsychology and pseudo-science. Nor did he find the blog postings where Pheder claimed the lunar landings were staged in a film studio in Houston, or the ones supporting the theory that the Israelis and President George Bush were behind the 9/11 attacks. Hollow had particularly worried that Pheder's essay about the 2012 apocalypse might surface.

Dodged the bullet there, he thought.

Ringling dismissed the man, seemingly convinced that the testimony had somehow worked to the defense's advantage.

This concluded the formal presentations in the case and it was now time for closing statements.

Hollow had been writing his mentally even as he'd fled the courthouse yesterday, in search of Pheder's phone number.

The slim, austere man walked to the front of the jury box and, a concession to camaraderie with the panel, undid his suit jacket's middle button, which he usually kept snugly hooked.

'Ladies and gentlemen of the jury. I'm going to make my comments brief, out of respect to you and respect to the poor victim and her family. They – and Annabelle Young's spirit – want and deserve justice and the sooner you provide that justice, the better for everyone.

'The diligent law officers involved in this case have established beyond a reasonable doubt that Martin Kobel was, in fact, the individual who viciously and without remorse stabbed to death a young, vibrant school-teacher, widow and single mother, after stalking her for a week, following her all the way from Raleigh, spying on her and causing her to flee from a restaurant while she waited to meet her son after school. Those facts are not in dispute. Nor is there any doubt about the validity of Mr

Kobel's confession, which he gave freely and after being informed of his rights. And which he repeated here in front of you.

'The only issue in this case is whether or not the defendant was insane at the time he committed this heinous crime. Now, in order for the defendant to be found not guilty by reason of insanity, it must – I repeat, *must* – be proven that he did not appreciate the difference between right and wrong at the time he killed Annabelle. It must be proven that he did not understand reality as you and I know it.

'You have heard the defendant claim he killed Annabelle Young because she was infected by forces called nemes. Let's think on that for a moment. Had Mr Kobel been convinced that she was possessed by aliens from outer space or zombies or vampires maybe that argument would have some validity. But that's not what he's claiming. He's basically saying that she was infected by what he himself described as a virus . . . not one that gives you a fever and chills but one that makes you do something bad.'

A smile. 'I have to tell you when I first heard this theory, I thought to myself, Brother, that's pretty crazy. But the more I thought about it, the more I wondered if there wasn't something to it. And in the course of this trial, listening to Mr Kobel and Dr Pheder and spending all last night reading through Mr Kobel's lengthy writings, I've changed my mind . . . I too now believe in nemes.'

The gasp throughout the courtroom was loud.

'I'm convinced that Martin Kobel is right. Nemes exist. Think about it, ladies and gentlemen: What else can explain the random acts of violence and abuse and rage we find in people who were previously incapable of them?'

Yes . . . some of the jurors were actually nodding. They were with him!

Hollow's voice rose. 'Think about it! Disembodied forces of energy that affect us. *We* can't see them, but doesn't the moon's gravitation affect us? Doesn't radiation affect us? We can't see them either. These nemes are the perfect explanation for behaviors we otherwise would find impossible.

'There was a time when the concept of flight by airplane would have been considered sorcery. The same with GPS. The same with modern medical treatments. The same with light bulbs, computers, thousands of products that we now know are rooted in scientific fact but when they were first conceived would seem like black magic.'

Hollow walked close to the rapt members of the jury. 'But . . . but . . . if that's the case, if nemes exist as Mr Kobel and I believe, then that means they're part of the *real* world. They are part of *our* society, our connection with one another, for good or for bad. Then to say that Annabelle Young was infected with one is exactly the same as saying that she had a case of the flu and might infect other people. Some of those infected people, the elderly or young, could die. Which would be a shame, tragic . . . But does that mean it would be all right to preemptively murder her to save those people? Emphatically no! That's not the way the world works, ladies and gentlemen. If, as I now believe, Annabelle Young was affected by these nemes, then as a trained professional, Martin Kobel's responsibility was to get her into treatment and help her. Help her, ladies and gentlemen. Not murder her.

'Please, honor the memory of Annabelle Young. Honor the institution of law. Honor personal responsibility. Find the defendant in this case sane. And find him guilty of murder in the first degree for taking the life of a young woman whose only flaw was to be sick and whose only chance to get well and live a content and happy and productive life was snatched from her grasp by a vicious killer. Thank you.'

His heart pounding, Glenn Hollow strode to the prosecution table through an utterly quiet courtroom, aware that everyone was staring at him.

He sat. Still, no voices, no rustling. Nothing. Pin-drop time.

After what seemed like an hour, though it was probably only thirty seconds, Ed Ringling rose, cleared his throat and delivered his closing statement. Hollow didn't pay much attention. And it seemed no one else did either. Every soul in the courtroom was staring at Glenn Hollow and, the prosecutor believed, replaying in their minds what was the most articulate and dramatic closing argument he'd ever made. Turning the whole case on its ear at the last minute.

If, as I now believe, Annabelle Young was affected by these nemes, then as a trained professional, Martin Kobel's responsibility was to get her into treatment and help her. Help her, ladies and gentlemen. Not murder her.

Glenn Hollow was inherently a modest man but he couldn't help but believe he'd pulled off the coup of his career.

And so it was a surprise, to say the least, when the good men and women on the jury panel rejected Hollow's argument completely and came back with a verdict finding Martin Kobel not guilty by reason of insanity after one of the shortest deliberations in Wetherby County history.

Three

I avoided the sunroom as much as I could.

Mostly because it was full of crazy people. Lip-chewing, Haldol-popping, delusional crazies. They smelled bad, they ate like pigs at a trough, they screamed, they wore football helmets so they didn't do any more damage to their heads. As if that were possible. At my trial I was worried that I was overacting the schizo part. I shouldn't have worried. My performance in the courtroom didn't come close to being over the top.

The Butler State Hospital doesn't include the words 'for the criminally insane' in the name because it doesn't need to. Anybody who sees the place will get the idea pretty fast.

The sunroom was a place to avoid. But I'd come to enjoy the small library and this was where I'd spent most of my time in the past two months since I was committed here.

Today I was sitting in the library's one armchair, near the one window. I usually vie for the chair with a skinny patient, Jack. The man was committed because he suspected his wife of selling his secrets to the Union Army – which would've been funny except that as punishment for her crime he tortured her for six hours before killing and dismembering her.

Jack was a curious man. Smart in some ways and a true expert on Civil War history. But he'd never quite figured out the rules of the game: that whoever got into the library first got the armchair.

I'd been looking forward to sitting here today and catching up on my reading.

But then something happened to disrupt those plans. I opened this morning's paper and noticed a reference to the prosecutor in the case against me, Glenn Hollow, whose name, I joked with my attorney, Ed Ringling, sounded like a real estate development. Alarming Ringling somewhat since I wasn't sounding as crazy as he would have liked – because, of course, I'm not.

The article was about party officials pulling all support for Hollow's bid for attorney general. He'd dropped out of the race. I continued to read, learning that his life had fallen apart completely after failing to get me convicted on murder one. He'd had to step down as county prosecutor and no law firm in the state would hire him. In fact, he couldn't find work anywhere.

The problem wasn't that he'd lost the case, but that he'd introduced evidence about the existence of spirits that possessed people and made them commit crimes. It hadn't helped that he was on record as stating that nemes were real. And his expert was a bit of a crackpot. Though I still hold that Pheder's a genius. After all, for every successful invention, Da Vinci came up with a hundred duds.

In fact, Hollow's strategy *was* brilliant and had given me some very uncomfortable moments in court. Ed Ringling, too. Part of me was surprised that the jury hadn't bought his argument and sent me to death row.

These revelations were troubling and I felt sorry for the man – I never had anything personal against him – but it was when I read the last paragraph that the whole shocking implication of what happened struck home.

> Before the Kobel trial, Hollow had been a shoo-in to become the attorney general of the state. He had the best conviction record of any prosecutor in North Carolina, particularly in violent crimes, such as rape and domestic abuse. He actually won a premeditated murder case some years ago for a road rage incident, the first time any prosecutor had convinced a jury to do so.

Reading this, I felt like I'd been slugged. My God . . . My God . . . I literally gasped.

I'd been set up.

It was suddenly clear. From the moment Annabelle Young had sat next to me in Starbucks, I was being suckered into their plan. The nemes . . . they knew I'd take on the mission of trying to become her therapist. And they knew that I'd see that the neme within her was so powerful and represented such a danger to those around her that I'd have to kill her. (I'd done this before, of course; Annabelle was hardly the first. Part of being a professional therapist is matching the right technique to each patient.)

And where did the nemes pick their host? In the very county with the prosecutor who represented perhaps the greatest threat to them. A man who was winning conviction after conviction in cases of impulsive violence – locking away some of their most successful incarnations in the county: abusers, rapists, murderers . . .

Well, that answered the question that nobody had been able to answer yet: Yes, nemes communicate.

Yes, they plot and strategize. Obviously they'd debated the matter. The price to eliminate Glenn Hollow was to get me off on an insanity plea, which meant that I would be out in a few years and back on the attack, writing about them, counseling people to guard against them.

Even killing them if I needed to.

So, they'd decided that Glenn Hollow was a threat to be eliminated.

But not me. I'd escaped. I sighed, closing my eyes, and whispered, 'But not me.'

I saw a shadow fall on the newspaper on my lap. I glanced up to see my fellow patient Jack, staring down at me.

'Sorry, got the chair first today,' I told him, still distracted by the stunning understanding. 'Tomorrow . . .'

But my voice faded as I looked into his face.

The eyes . . . the eyes.

No!

I gasped and started to rise, shouting for a guard, but before I could get to my feet, Jack was on me, 'My chair, you took my chair, you took it, you took it . . .'

But then, as the razor-sharp end of the spoon he clutched slammed into my chest again and again, it seemed that the madman began to whisper something different. My vision going, my hearing fading, I thought perhaps the words slipping from his dry lips were, 'Yes you, yes you, yes you . . .'

THE WEAPON

Monday

'A new weapon.'

The slim man in a conservative suit eased forward and lowered his voice. 'Something terrible. And our sources are certain it will be used this coming Saturday morning. They're certain of that.'

'Four days,' said retired Colonel James J. Peterson, his voice grave. It was now 5 p.m. on Monday.

The two men sat in Peterson's nondescript office, in a nondescript building in the suburban town of Reston, Virginia, about twenty-five miles from Washington, DC. There's a misconception that national security operations are conducted in high-tech bunkers filled with sweeping steel and structural concrete, video screens ten feet high and attractive boys and babes dressed by Armani.

This place, on the other hand, looked like an insurance agency.

The skinny man, who worked for the government, added, 'We don't know if we're talking conventional, nuke or something altogether new. Probably mass destruction, we've heard. It can do quote "significant" damage.'

'Who's behind this weapon? Al-Qaeda? The Koreans? Iranians?'

'One of our enemies. That's all we know at this point . . . So, we need you to find out about it. Money is no object, of course.'

'Any leads?'

'Yes, a good one: an Algerian who knows who formulated the weapon. He met with them last week in Tunis. He's a professor and journalist.'

'Terrorist?'

'He doesn't seem to be. His writings have been moderate in nature. He's not openly militant. But our local sources are convinced he's had contact with the people who created the weapon and plan to use it.'

'You have a picture?'

A photograph appeared as if by magic from the slim man's briefcase and slid across the desk like a lizard.

Colonel Peterson leaned forward.

Tuesday

Chabbi music drifted from a nearby café, lost intermittently in the sounds of trucks and scooters charging frantically along the commercial streets of Algiers.

The driver of the white van, a swarthy local, stifled a sour face when the music changed to American rock. Not that he actually preferred the old-fashioned, melodramatic chabbi tunes or thought they were more politically or religiously correct than Western music. He just didn't like Britney Spears.

Then the big man stiffened and tapped the shoulder of the man next to him, an American. Their attention swung immediately out the front window to a curly-haired man in his thirties, wearing a light-colored suit, walking out of the main entrance of the Al-Jazier School for Cultural Thought.

The man in the passenger seat nodded. The driver called, 'Ready,' in English and then repeated the command in Berber-accented Arabic. The two men in the back responded affirmatively.

The van, a battered Ford, sporting Arabic letters boasting of the city's best plumbing services, eased forward, trailing the man in the light suit. The driver had no trouble moving slowly without being conspicuous. Such was the nature of traffic here in the old portion of this city, near the harbor.

As they approached a chaotic intersection, the passenger spoke into a cell phone. 'Now.'

The driver pulled nearly even with the man they followed, just as a second van, dark blue, in the oncoming lane, suddenly leapt the curb and slammed directly into the glass window of an empty storefront, sending a shower of glass onto the sidewalk as bystanders gaped and came running.

By the time the crowds on Rue Ahmed Bourzina helped the driver of the blue van extricate his vehicle from the shattered storefront, the white van was nowhere to be seen.

Neither was the man in the light suit.

Wednesday

Colonel James Peterson was tired after the overnight flight from Dulles to Rome but he was operating on pure energy.

As his driver sped from Da Vinci Airport to his company's facility south of the city, he read the extensive dossier on the man whose abduction he had just engineered. Jacques Bennabi, the journalist and part-time professor, had indeed been in direct communication with the Tunisian group that had developed the weapon, though Washington still wasn't sure who the group was exactly.

Peterson looked impatiently at his watch. He regretted the day-long trip required to transport Bennabi from Algiers to Gaeta, south of Rome, where he'd been transferred to an ambulance for the drive here. But planes were too closely regulated nowadays. Peterson had told his people they *had* to keep a low profile. His operation here, south of Rome, was apparently a facility that specialized in rehabilitation services for people injured in industrial accidents. The Italian government had no clue that it was a sham, owned ultimately by Peterson's main company in Virginia: Intelligence Analysis Systems.

IAS was like hundreds of small businesses throughout the Washington, DC, area that provided everything from copier toner to consulting to computer software to the massive US government.

IAS, though, didn't sell office supplies.

Its only product was information, and it managed to provide some of the best in the world. IAS obtained this information not through high-tech surveillance but, Peterson liked to say, the old-fashioned way:

One suspect, one interrogator, one locked room.

It did this very efficiently.

And completely illegally.

IAS ran black sites.

Black site operations are very simple. An individual with knowledge the government wishes to learn is kidnapped and taken to a secret and secure facility outside the jurisdiction of the United States. The kidnapping is known as extraordinary rendition. Once at a black site the subject is interrogated until the desired information is learned. And then he's returned home – in most cases, that is.

IAS was a private company, with no official government affiliation, though the government was, of course, its biggest client. They operated three sites: one in Bogotá, Colombia, one in Thailand, and the one that Peterson's car was now approaching – the largest of the IAS sites, a nondescript beige facility whose front door stated, *Funzione Medica Di Riabilitazione*.

The gate closed behind him and he hurried inside, to minimize the chance a passerby might see him. Peterson rarely came to the black sites himself. Because he met regularly with government officials it would be disastrous if anyone connected him to an illegal operation like this. Still, the impending threat of the weapon dictated that he personally supervise the interrogation of Jacques Bennabi.

Despite his fatigue, he got right to work and met with the man waiting in the facility's windowless main office upstairs. He was one of several interrogators that IAS used regularly, one of the best in the world, in fact. A slightly built man, with a confident smile on his face.

'Andrew.' Peterson nodded in greeting, using the pseudonym the man was known by (no real names were ever used in black sites). Andrew was a US soldier on temporary leave from Afghanistan.

Peterson explained that Bennabi had been carefully searched and scanned. They'd found no GPS chips, listening devices or explosives in his body. The colonel added that sources in North Africa were still trying to find whom Bennabi had met with in Tunis but were having no luck.

'Doesn't matter,' Andrew said with a sour smile. 'I'll get you everything you need to know soon enough.'

Jacques Bennabi looked up at Andrew.

The soldier returned the gaze with no emotion, assessing the subject, noting his level of fear. A fair amount, it seemed. This pleased him. Not because Andrew was a sadist – he wasn't – but because fear is a gauge to a subject's resistance.

He assessed that Bennabi would tell him all he wanted to know about the weapon within four hours.

The room in which they sat was a dim, concrete cube, twenty feet on each side. Bennabi sat in a metal chair with his hands behind him, bound with restraints. His feet were bare, increasing his sense of vulnerability, and his jacket and personal effects were gone (they gave subjects a sense of comfort and orientation). Andrew now pulled a chair close to the subject and sat.

Andrew was not a physically imposing man, but he didn't need to be. The smallest person in the world need not even raise his voice if he has power. And Andrew had all the power in the world over his subject at the moment.

'Now,' he said in English, which he knew Bennabi spoke fluently, 'as you know, Jacques, you're many miles from your home. None of your family or colleagues knows you're here. The authorities in Algeria have learned of your disappearance by now – we're monitoring that – but do you know how much they care?'

No answer. The dark eyes gazed back, emotionless.

'They don't. They don't care at all. We've been following the reports. Another university professor gone missing. So what? You were robbed and shot. Or the Jihad Brothership finally got around to settling the score for something you said in class last year. Or maybe one of your articles upset some Danish journalists . . . and they kidnapped and killed you.' Andrew smiled at his own cleverness. Bennabi gave no reaction. 'So. No one is coming to help you. You understand? No midnight raids. No cowboys riding to the rescue.'

Silence.

Andrew continued, unfazed, 'Now, I want to know about this weapon you were discussing with your Tunisian friends.' He was looking carefully at the eyes of the man. Did they flicker with recognition? The interrogator believed they did. It was like a shout of acknowledgment. Good.

'We need to know who developed it, what it is and who it's going to be used against. If you tell me you'll be back home in twenty-four hours.' He let this sink in. 'If you don't . . . things won't go well.'

The subject continued to sit passively. And silently.

That was fine with Andrew; he hardly expected an immediate confession. He wouldn't want one, in fact. You couldn't trust subjects who caved in too quickly.

Finally he said, 'Jacques, I know the names of all your colleagues at the university and the newspaper where you work.'

This was Andrew's talent – he had studied the art of interrogation for years and knew that people could much more easily resist threats to themselves than to their friends and family. Andrew had spent the past two days learning every fact he could about people close to Bennabi. He'd come up with lists of each person's weaknesses and fears. It had been a huge amount of work.

Over the next few hours Andrew never once threatened Bennabi himself; but he was ruthless in threatening his colleagues. Ruining careers, exposing possible affairs, questioning an adoption of a child . . . Even suggesting that some of his friends could be subject to physical harm.

A dozen specific threats, two dozen, offering specific details: names, addresses, offices, cars they drove, restaurants they enjoyed.

But Jacques Bennabi said not a word.

'You know how easy it was to kidnap you,' Andrew muttered. 'We plucked you off the street like picking a chicken from a street vendor's cage. You think your friends are any safer? The men who got you are back in Algiers, you know. They're ready to do what I say.'

The subject only stared back at him.

Andrew grew angry for a moment. He cleared his raw throat and left the room, had a drink of water, struggled to calm down.

For three more hours he continued the interrogation. Bennabi paid attention to everything Andrew said, it seemed, but he said nothing.

Goddamn, he's good, Andrew thought, struggling not to reveal his own frustration. He glanced at his watch. It had been nearly nine hours. And he hadn't uncovered a single fact about the weapon.

Well, it was time to get serious now.

He scooted the chair even closer.

'Jacques, you're not being helpful. And now, thanks to your lack of cooperation, you've put all your friends at risk. How selfish can you be?' he snapped.

Silence.

Andrew leaned close. 'You understand that I've been restrained, don't you? I had hoped you'd be more cooperative. But apparently you're not taking me seriously. I think I have to prove how grave this matter is.'

He reached into his pocket. He pulled out a printout of a computer photograph that had been taken yesterday.

It showed Bennabi's wife and children in the front yard of their home outside Algiers.

Thursday

Colonel Peterson was in his hotel room in the center of Rome. He was awakened at 4 a.m. by his secure cell phone.

'Yes?'

'Colonel.' The caller was Andrew. His voice was ragged.

'So, what'd he tell you?'

'Nothing.'

The colonel muttered, 'You just tell me what he said and *I'll* figure out if it's important. That's *my* job.' He clicked the light on and fished for a pen.

'No, sir, I mean he didn't say a single word.'

'Not a . . . word?'

'Over sixteen hours. Completely silent. The entire time. Not one goddamn word. Never happened in all my years in this business.'

'Was he getting close to breaking, at least?'

'I . . . No, I don't think so. I even threatened his family. His children. No reaction. I'd need another week. And I'll have to make good on some of the threats.'

But Peterson knew they were already on shaky ground by kidnapping somebody who was not a known terrorist. He wouldn't dare kidnap or endanger the professor's colleagues, let alone his family.

'No,' the colonel said slowly. 'That's all for now. You can get back to your unit. We'll go to phase two.'

The woman was dressed conservatively, a long-sleeved blouse and tan slacks. Her dark blond hair was pulled back and she wore no jewelry.

Since Bennabi wasn't culturally or religiously conservative, worked with women at the University and had actually written in favor of women's rights, Peterson decided to use Claire for the second interrogator. Bennabi would view her as an enemy, yes, but not as an inferior. And, since it was known that Bennabi had dated and was married, with several children, he was clearly a man with an appreciation of attractive women.

And Peterson knew that Claire was certainly that.

She was also an army captain, in charge of a prisoner of war operation in the Middle East – though at the moment she, too, was on a brief leave of absence to permit her to practice her own skills as an interrogator — skills very different from Andrew's but just as effective in the right circumstances.

Peterson now finished briefing her. 'Good luck,' he added.

And couldn't help reminding her that it was now Thursday and the weapon would be deployed the day after tomorrow.

In perfect Arabic, Claire said, 'I must apologize, Mr Bennabi . . . *Jacques*. May I use your first name?' She was rushing into the cell, a horrified look on her face.

When Bennabi didn't reply, she switched to English. 'Your first name? You don't mind, do you? I'm Claire. And let me offer you my deepest apologies for this terrible mistake.'

She walked behind him and took the hand restraints off. There was little risk. She was an expert at aikido and tae kwon do and could easily have defended herself against the weak, exhausted subject.

But the slim man, eyes dark from lack of sleep, face drawn, simply rubbed his wrists and offered no threatening gestures.

Claire pressed the button on the intercom. 'Bring the tray in, please.'

A guard wheeled it inside: water, a pot of coffee and a plate of pastry and candy, which she knew from his file Bennabi was partial to. She sampled everything first, to show nothing was spiked with poison or truth serum. He drank some water but when she asked, 'Coffee, something to eat?' he gave no response.

Claire sat down, her face distraught. 'I'm so terribly sorry about this. I can't begin to describe how horrified we are . . . Let me explain. Someone — we don't know who — told us that you'd met with some people who are enemies of our country.' She lifted her hands. 'We didn't know who you were. All we heard was that you were sympathetic to these enemies and that they had some plans to cause huge destruction. Something terrible was going to happen. Imagine what we felt when we heard you were a famous professor . . . and an advocate of human rights!

'No, someone gave us misinformation about you. Maybe accidental.' She added coyly, 'Maybe they had a grudge against you. We don't know. All I can say is we reacted too quickly. Now, first, let me assure you that whatever threats Andrew made, nothing has or will happen to your colleagues or family . . . That was barbaric what he suggested. He's been disciplined and relieved of duty.'

No response whatsoever.

Silence filled the room and she could hear only her heartbeat, as she tried to remain calm, thinking of the weapon and the hours counting down until it was used.

'Obviously this is a very awkward situation. Certain officials are extremely embarrassed about what's happened and are willing to offer, what we could call, reparation for your inconvenience.'

He continued to remain silent but she could tell he was listening to every word.

She scooted the chair closer and sat, leaning forward. 'Mr Bennabi . . . Jacques, I have been authorized to transfer one hundred thousand euros into an account of your choice – that's tax-free money – in exchange for your agreement not to sue us for this terrible error.'

Claire knew that he made the equivalent of fifteen thousand euros as a professor and another twenty as a journalist.

'I can order all of this done immediately. Your lawyer can monitor the transaction. All you have to do is sign a release agreeing not to sue.'

Silence.

Then she continued with a smile, 'And one more small thing . . . I myself have no doubt that you have been wrongly targeted but . . . the people who have to authorize the payments, they want just a little more information about the people you met with. The ones in Tunis. They just wish to be reassured that the meeting was innocent. *I* know it was. If I had my way I'd write you a check now. But they control the money.' A smile. 'Isn't that the way the world works?'

Bennabi said nothing. He stopped rubbing his wrists and sat back.

'They don't need to know anything sensitive. Just a few names, that's all. Just to keep the money men happy.'

Is he agreeing? she wondered. Is he disagreeing? Bennabi was different from anybody she'd ever interrogated. Usually by now subjects were already planning how to spend the money and telling her whatever she wanted to know.

When he said nothing she realized: He's negotiating. Of course.

A nod. 'You're a smart man . . . And I don't blame you one bit for holding out. Just give us a bit of information to verify your story and I can probably go up to a hundred fifty thousand euros.'

Still no response.

'I'll tell you what. Why don't you name a figure? Let's put this all behind us.' Claire smiled coyly again. 'We're on your side, Jacques. We really are.'

Friday

At 9 a.m. Colonel Jim Peterson was in the office of the rehabilitation center, sitting across from a large, dark-complexioned man, who'd just arrived from Darfur.

Akhem asked, 'What happened with Claire?'

Peterson shook his head. 'Bennabi didn't go for the money. She sweetened the pot to a quarter-million euros.' The colonel sighed. 'Wouldn't take it. In fact, he didn't even say no. He didn't say a word. Just like with Andrew.'

Akhem took this information with interest but otherwise unemotionally – as if he were a surgeon called in to handle an emergency operation that was routine for him but that no one else could perform. 'Has he slept?'

'Not since yesterday.'

'Good.'

There was nothing like sleep deprivation to soften people up.

Akhem was of Middle Eastern descent, though he'd been born in America and was a US citizen. Like Peterson he'd retired from the military. He was now a professional security consultant – a euphemism for mercenary soldier. He was here with two associates, both from Africa. One white, one black.

Peterson had used Akhem on a half-dozen occasions, as had other governments. He was responsible for interrogating a Chechen separatist to learn where his colleagues had stashed a busload of Moscow schoolchildren last year.

It took him two hours to learn the exact location of the bus, the number of soldiers guarding them, their weapons and pass codes.

No one knew exactly how he'd done it. No one wanted to.

Peterson wasn't pleased he'd had to turn to Akhem's approach to interrogation, known as extreme extraction. Indeed, he realized that the Bennabi situation raised the textbook moral question on using torture: You know a terrible event is about to occur and you have in custody a prisoner who knows how to prevent it. Do you torture or not?

There were those who said, no, you don't. That it is better to be morally superior and to suffer the consequences of letting the event occur. By stooping to the enemy's techniques, these people say, we automatically lose the war, even if we militarily prevail.

Others said that it was our enemies who'd changed the rules; if they tortured and killed innocents in the name of their causes we had to fight them on their own terms.

Peterson had now made the second choice. He prayed it was the right one.

Akhem was looking at the video of Bennabi in the cell, slumped in a chair, his head cocked to the side. He wrinkled his nose and said, 'Three hours at the most.'

He rose and left the office, gesturing his fellow mercenaries after him.

But three hours came and went.

Jacques Bennabi said nothing, despite being subjected to one of the most horrific methods of extreme extraction.

In waterboarding, the subject is inverted on his back and water poured into his nose and mouth, simulating drowning. It's a horrifying experience . . . and also one of the most popular forms of torture because there's no lasting physical evidence – provided, of course, that the victim doesn't in fact drown, which happens occasionally.

'Tell me!' Akhem raged as the assistants dragged Bennabi to his feet, pulling his head out of the large tub. He choked and spit water from under the cloth mask he wore.

'*Where* is the weapon? *Who* is behind it? Tell me.'

Silence, except for the man's coughing and sputtering.

Then to the assistants: 'Again.'

Back he went onto the board, his feet in the air. And the water began to flow once more.

Four hours passed, then six, then eight.

Himself drenched, physically exhausted, Akhem looked at his watch. It was now early evening. Only five hours until Saturday – when the weapon would be deployed.

And he hadn't learned a single fact about it. He could hardly hide his astonishment. He'd never known anybody to hold out for this long. That was amazing in its own right. But more significant was the fact that Bennabi had not uttered a single word the entire time. He'd groaned, he's gasped, he'd choked, but not a single word of English or Arabic or Berber had passed his lips.

Subjects *always* begged and cursed and lied or offered partial truths to get the interrogators at least to pause for a time.

But not Bennabi.

'Again,' Akhem announced.

Then, at 11 p.m., Akhem sat down in a chair in the cell, staring at Bennabi, who lolled, gasping, on the waterboard. The interrogator said to his assistants, 'That's enough.'

Akhem dried off and looked over the subject. He then walked into the hallway outside the cell and opened his attaché case. He extracted a large scalpel and returned, closing the door behind him.

Bennabi's bleary eyes stared at the weapon as Akhem walked forward.

The subject leaned away.

Akhem nodded. His assistants took Bennabi by the shoulders, one of them gripping his arm hard, rendering it immobile.

Akhem took the subject's fingers and leaned forward with the knife.

'Where is the weapon?' he growled. 'You don't have any idea of the pain you'll experience if you don't tell me! Where is it? Who is behind the attack? Tell me!'

Bennabi looked into his eyes. He said nothing.

The interrogator moved the blade closer.

It was then that the door burst open.

'Stop,' cried Colonel Peterson. 'Come out here into the hallway.'

The interrogator paused and stood back. He wiped sweat from his forehead. The three interrogators left the cell and joined the colonel in the hallway.

'I just heard from Washington. They've found out who Bennabi was meeting with in Tunis. They're sending me the information in a few minutes. I want you to hold off until we know more.'

Akhem hesitated. Reluctantly he put the scalpel away. Then the large man stared at the video screen, on which was an image of Bennabi sitting in the chair, breathing heavily, staring back into the camera.

The interrogator shook his head. 'Not a word. He didn't say a single word.'

Saturday

At 2 a.m., on the day the weapon would be deployed, Colonel Jim Peterson was alone in the office at the rehabilitation center, awaiting the secure email about the meeting in Tunis. Armed with that information, they would have a much better chance to convince Bennabi to give them information.

Come on, he urged, staring at his computer.

A moment later it complied.

The computer pinged and he opened the encrypted email from the skinny government man he'd met with in his Reston, Virginia, office on Monday.

Colonel: We've identified the people Bennabi met with. But it's not a terrorist cell; it's a human rights group. Humanity Now. We double-checked and our local contacts are sure they're the ones who're behind the weapon. But we've followed the group for years and have no – repeat – no indication that it's a cover for a terrorist organization. Discontinue all interrogation until we know more.

Peterson frowned. He knew Humanity Now. Everybody believed it to be a legitimate organization.

My God, was this all a misunderstanding? Had Bennabi met with the group about a matter that was completely innocent?

What've we done?

He was about to call Washington and ask for more details when he happened to glance at his computer and saw that he'd received another email – from a major US newspaper. The header: *Reporter requesting comment before publication.*

He opened the message.

Colonel Peterson. I'm a reporter with the New York Daily Herald. I'm filing the attached article in a few hours with my newspaper. It will run there and in syndication in about two hundred other papers around the world. I'm giving you the opportunity to include a comment, if you like. I've also sent copies to the White House, the Central Intelligence Agency and the Pentagon, seeking their comments, too.

Oh, my God. What the hell is this?

With trembling hands the colonel opened the attachment and – to his utter horror – read:

ROME, May 22 – A private American company, with ties to the US government, has been running an illegal operation south of the city, for the purpose of kidnapping, interrogating and occasionally torturing citizens of other countries to extract information from them.

The facility, known in military circles as a black site, is owned by a Reston, Virginia, corporation, Intelligence Analysis Services, Inc., whose corporate documents list government security consulting as its main purpose.

Italian business filings state that the purpose of the Roman facility is physical rehabilitation, but no requisite government permits for health care operations have been obtained with respect to it. Further, no licensed rehabilitation professionals are employed by the company, which is owned by a Caribbean subsidiary of IAS. Employees are US and other non-Italian nationals with backgrounds not in medical science but in military and security services.

The operation was conducted without any knowledge on the part of the Italian government and the Italian ambassador to the United States has stated he will demand a full explanation as to why the illegal operation was conducted on Italian soil. Officials from the Polizia di Stato and the Ministero della Giustizia likewise have promised a full investigation.

There is no direct connection between the US government and the facility outside of Rome. But over the course of the past week, this reporter conducted extensive surveillance of the rehabilitation facility and observed the presence of a man identified as former Colonel James Peterson, the president of IAS. He is regularly seen in the company of high-ranking Pentagon, CIA and White House officials in the Washington, DC area.

Peterson's satellite phone began ringing.

He supposed the slim man from Washington was calling.

Or maybe his boss.

Or maybe the White House.

Caller ID does not work on encrypted phones.

His jaw quivering, Peterson ignored the phone. He pressed ahead in the article.

The discovery of the IAS facility in Rome came about on a tip last week from Humanity Now, a human rights group based in North Africa and long opposed to the use of torture and black sites. The group reported that an Algerian journalist was to be kidnapped in Algiers and transported to a black site somewhere in Europe.

At the same time the human rights organization gave this reporter the name of a number of individuals suspected of being black site interrogators. By examining public records and various travel documents, it was determined that several of these specialists – two US military officers and a mercenary soldier based in Africa – traveled to Rome not long after the journalist's abduction in Algiers.

Reporters were able to follow the interrogators to the rehabilitation facility, which was then determined to be owned by IAS.

Slumping in his chair, Peterson ignored the phone. He gave a grim laugh, closing his eyes.

The whole thing, the whole story about terrorists, about the weapon, about Bennabi . . . it was a setup. Yes, there was an 'enemy', but it was merely the human rights group, which had conspired with the professor to expose the black site operation to the press – and the world.

Peterson understood perfectly: Humanity Now had probably been tracking the main interrogators IAS used – Andrew, Claire, Akhem and others   for months, if not years. The group and Bennabi, a human rights activist, had planted the story about the weapon themselves to engineer his kidnapping, then alerted that reporter for the New York newspaper, who leapt after the story of a lifetime.

Bennabi was merely bait – and I went right for it. Of course, he remained silent the whole time. That was his job. To draw as many interrogators here as he could and give the reporter a chance to follow them, discover the facility and find out who was behind it.

Oh, this was bad . . . this was terrible. It was the kind of scandal that could bring down governments.

It would certainly end his career. And many others'.

It might very likely end the process of black sites altogether, or at least set them back years.

He thought about calling together the staff and telling them to destroy all the incriminating papers and to flee.

But why bother? he reflected. It was too late now.

Peterson decided there was nothing to do but accept his fate. Though he did call the guards and tell them to arrange to have Jacques Bennabi transferred back home. The enemy had won. And, in an odd way, Peterson respected that.

'And make sure he arrives unharmed.'

'Yessir.'

Peterson sat back, hearing in his thoughts the words of the slim man from Washington.

The weapon . . . it can do quote 'significant' damage . . .

Except that there was no weapon. It was all a fake.

Yet, with another sour laugh, Peterson decided this wasn't exactly true.

There *was* a goddamn weapon. It wasn't nuclear or chemical or explosive but in the end was far more effective than any of those and would indeed do significant damage.

Thinking about his prisoner's refusal to speak during his captivity, thinking, too, on the devastating paragraphs of the reporter's article, the colonel reflected: The weapon was silence. The weapon was words.

The weapon was truth.

RECONCILIATION

Ransom Fells believed from a young age that he disliked his father, if not hated the man.

And was all the angrier when his dad up and died unexpectedly nearly a decade ago, before Ransom could find out for certain who the man really was and confront him. Maybe to sever ties forever, maybe to reconcile.

But, talk about second chances, at age thirty-nine Ransom Fells coincidentally found himself in circumstances that did indeed let him learn a bit more about the man.

And at the moment, he was now reflecting on these facts and thinking, too: Be careful what you wish for. Be real careful about that.

Under a gray sky, he was sitting alone in his rental Camry in a city park in Indiana. He peered absently through the windshield at a splashy army of September trees surrounding an impromptu softball field, laid out sloppily by some local teams. The lot and park were empty.

He considered again what he'd just learned about his father, things that he never could have imagined.

And he considered, too, the bigger question they raised: Could a death – violent death – ultimately (and ironically) lead to something positive, a reconciliation of sorts?

Ransom absently touched his chin and felt stubble, turned the rear-view mirror his way and gazed back at his lean face, small buttons of gray eyes, hawkish nose, full head of businessman's neatly trimmed black hair. Yes, he'd forgotten to shave. Unlike him. He flipped the mirror back, stretched and lifted his coffee cup to his lips, realized suddenly he'd ordered the cup four or five hours ago. Ice cold. Still he swallowed the sip and took another.

His father.

Impossible.

And yet . . .

Yesterday, for his job, Ransom Fells came to this area, northern Indiana, on the cusp of the country's terminally ill Industrial Belt. Chesterton was about ten miles from where he'd grown up and twenty from Gary. This was an area of the United States to which Ransom had never traveled since he left home at age fourteen with his mother and younger brother to be near her relatives in Virginia, after his parents' divorce.

He'd had a few chances to come here for business but declined. Another man at GKS Technology generally handled this part of the country.

And as for a pleasure trip to these parts? No way in hell. There were a few remaining family members nearby, but they were indistinct, distant planets in the solar system of relations.

But he wouldn't have visited even if he'd known them better. No, the reason he was a stranger was Stanford Fells, his father.

Coming here would remind Ransom way too much of those gray Saturday afternoons in the fall, when many of his high-school classmates would go to the local football games with their dads or – unimaginable to Ransom – to Soldier Field to see the Bears, on *season* tickets! Stan had taken him to one baseball game, the White Sox, and they'd left at the seventh inning stretch, because his father figured they'd seen enough. 'Seven's good as nine. You wait till the end, takes you forever to get out of the lot.'

Coming here would remind Ransom that Stan never bothered to tell his son anything about his job as a service tech for industrial power systems, which seemed really neat to the boy, who would've loved to see some of the factories Stan worked in. He never met any of his father's work buddies, never went to barbecues with their families, like the other kids talked about.

Coming here would remind him of Stan silently enduring holiday dinners for forty minutes or so and leaving before dessert and going down to the Ironworks Tavern – yeah, even on Christmas. Preferring the Ironworks to playing with the new football his son had received as a present or helping put together the train set or playing the computer game, even though it came with two controllers.

Coming here would remind him of Ransom and his little brother – Mom dozing – glancing at the curtains of their bungalow when they heard the whooshing sound of a car approaching, lights glowing on the dingy cloth. Was it Stan? Usually not.

But then yesterday fate, God, or what have you (Ransom believed in the last of that trinity only) intervened, in the incarnation of a call from his boss. 'Joey's sick, I mean fucking sick.'

'Sorry to hear that.' Ransom's heart fell. He knew what was coming.

'Yeah. Can you take over for him?'

'Where, Chicago?'

'Indiana, north.'

Wouldn't you know it, he thought angrily.

'You're from there, right? You know it?'

He debated, but in the end decided to stop being a wuss. It was hard to say no to his boss and even though GKS was weathering the bad economy you never knew what the future would hold. Besides, the money would be great and who couldn't use a little extra green? So he'd said a reluctant okay, downloaded Joey's file and read through it. He then picked up a rental car near his home in downtown Baltimore, threw the salesman's sample cases into the trunk and hit the road, growing increasingly edgy as he miled his way west on I-70.

Near Gary he turned off the interstate and wound along state routes, until he came to an intersection he hadn't seen for years, but remembered perfectly: Poindexter Road and Route 224. One sign pointed left toward Chesterton, six miles away, the other to his hometown of Marshall, four miles. He paused under a maple canopy of yellow and crimson, his head swiveling.

The pause, however, was only to let a Peterbilt stream past on the perpendicular. Once it was past, he turned decisively left and accelerated. There'd been no decision about which way to go.

Chesterton, Indiana, had a few upscale companies, like the one whose CEO he was set to see tomorrow, Hardwick Investments. He drove past it now, a two-story glass and metal structure in a groomed office park outside of town. But Hardwick was the exception. Soon he was into the *real* Chesterton, cruising by sagging and scabby one-level shipping companies, and factories making products of mysterious purpose ('Compress-ease', 'Multi-span Tensioner Plus', 'Asphalux'). Plenty of abandoned ones, too. Forty, fifty years ago, when US Steel and other heavy manufacturers were at capacity, there wasn't an empty commercial facility for miles around or an unemployed worker who didn't choose to be.

Hell of a lot different now, half ghost town.

Damn, I hate it here . . .

The Shady Grove Motel nestled in what was now better described as stump grove, thanks to Dutch elm, it looked like, but the place was otherwise pretty decent.

Ransom checked in and drove around back to his room, away from the busy road. He took a brief nap and then reviewed Joey's file again. He carefully went through his salesman sample bags, organizing the trays containing tools for cleaning and repairing computers. Everybody tended to think of computers in terms of software, forgetting they were also physical boxes with moving parts. Desktops sucked in plenty of crap, and laptops not only did the same but also got tossed around mercilessly. If not properly cleaned, a computer could conk out at any time.

Ironically, though, it was the computer world itself that was endangering GKS Tech. People were now ordering more and more of the products online.

Thank you very much, TigerDirect.

The days of the traveling salesman would be over soon.

But Ransom knew he'd find something else that would suit. He'd always landed on his feet. He'd learned that early. His father had dropped out of community college and didn't value learning for anybody in the family. And so in reaction, Ransom decided that nothing was going to stop him when it came to education. Moderately smart, he'd muscled his way through high school by being extremely persistent. Faced with little money and less support after he graduated, the teenager did the army thing for two years, which let him slingshot his way into college, George Washington, in DC, where he did very well. He foundered a bit after his discharge – Stan providing no guidance, of course – but Ransom heard back from one of his army buddies and the man hooked him up with some people in Baltimore. He took a temporary job that turned permanent. He'd never pictured himself in this line of work, but he turned out to be a natural.

Ransom Fell's ex could be wacky, with her walls of self-help books looming like glaciers in the living room of their old Baltimore apartment, but she was pretty sharp, Ransom never hesitated to admit, even to her. Beth would look at his situation with his father and diagnose that Stan Fells had not engaged in any 'life lessoning' with his son. Instead, Ransom had to rely on 'self-foundation-building', 'me-ness', and 'inner-core structuring'. Despite the language, which could get even weirder, the ideas made sense. He would have phrased it more simply: Stan taught him shit and so he had to learn to fend for himself.

Which he did.

As for his mother, sure, she was there some of the time. Sure, she tried. But she largely checked out; who wouldn't with a husband like Stan? Besides, given his upbringing, Ransom figured a boy needs a mother only until he stops sucking and gumming pureed food. When the kid's able to walk, it's time for the other half of the act to step up. Your turn, Dad. Freud was totally screwed up – you don't want to *kill* your father; you want to go hunting with him, you want him to take you to a ball game. All. Nine. Fucking. Innings.

And with that thought he realized he was sitting forward in the cheap motel chair, hovering over his salesman's cases, shoulder muscles solid as a tire.

Shouldn't've come here.

The money's good. Gotta keep the boss happy.

Doesn't matter.

Shouldn't've come.

A little after six he worked out in the motel health club. For forty minutes he slammed along the treadmill and hefted free weights – 30-pound barbells – as he worked up a good sweat despite the chill autumn air that bled into the underpopulated exercise room. These facilities were always kept cool in the motels and hotels. He was convinced it was to save money in heating costs and to discourage people from using them because of liability. A broken neck, despite the waiver, could be very, very expensive, he figured.

Ransom took a fiercely hot shower, and at 8 p.m. he dressed in tan slacks and a dark shirt, pulled on his navy blue sports jacket and headed out the door. At the front desk a fifty-something guy who looked like a lifetime front-desk clerk directed him to the Flame and Fountain, a steakhouse. He was there in five minutes. He hardly needed the restaurant's sign to find it. Out front an energetic, blue-lit water treatment surrounded an impressive plume of fire. Tacky, but the exhaust of grilled steaks was seductive.

He smiled at the hostess and passed her by. When traveling for work he never sat at tables, only the bar, which was what he did now.

Several stools away was a woman close to his age, late thirties. In front of her was a frothy drink in a martini glass with a stem the shape of a fat teardrop or skinny boob. It was that kind of bar.

Tacky . . .

Wearing a tan skirt and matching jacket, she was attractive, a little heavier than she probably would have liked, but it was sensuous weight and definitely appealed to Ransom. Voluptuous. Her hair, probably bottle blond to combat premature white, not brunette, was matte textured and had been wrestled into a taut ponytail. When he'd sat down she didn't look his way. But then she wasn't looking at anything, except the *New Yorker* she gripped with fierce fingers, tipped in iron-clad red nails.

Ransom assessed: She'd broken up or divorced about five or six months ago and had finally decided the severing was for the best and was now determined to abandon the comfort of Häagen-Dazs or Doritos for the real world. And here she was, meeting that tough challenge head-on, no safety net, as a woman alone in a bar. You needed to be vigilant, confident and constantly measuring what came your way.

Ransom didn't think he'd have the energy to handle it.

He ordered a chardonnay, which turned out to be buttery and rich. Opening *USA Today*, he asked the bartender a few business traveler's questions about the area, more making conversation than satisfying curiosity. He noticed, through his periphery, that the woman glanced his way twice then returned to the magazine. The bartender moved on, and this time when she looked toward him he noted – not directly but in the smoky mirror behind the bar – her eyes graze the ringless heart finger of his left hand.

Ransom gave it a few minutes longer then asked her politely if she'd eaten here and if so what was good.

Food is always a good intro (she'd had a decent chicken, she told him in a husky, humorous voice; but two steaks had walked by and they'd looked better). From that icebreaker there followed typical banter – careers first, of course, then glancing reference to exes and children (the former yes, the latter no, in both their cases), then sorties about TV shows and movies and media and very careful forays into politics and religion.

But still, an objective observer, fly on the wall, would note that they survived the ritual admirably, that the conversation flowed like silk and was buoyed with humor, and that Ransom and Annie had more than a little in common. The *New Yorker, NCIS, Dancing with the Stars* and the guilty pleasure of *Two and a Half Men,* now that Sheen was gone. Cabs over pinots. They shopped at Whole Foods for special occasions, IGA or Safeway normally. They each had secret indulgences: unshelled pistachios in her case, Mounds bars in his, a line that Ransom managed to deliver without a spark of lascivious intonation.

He had dinner – yes, a steak, which lived up both to her assessment and to the aromatic promise wafting through the parking lot. When he was through, he talked her into sharing dessert, over two glasses of sweet wine.

And then, pushing ten o'clock, the night concluded. As indisputable as a chime, they both knew it was time to go.

But, the question remained, go where?

That inquiry was answered as soon as they were swathed in their coats and outside in the nose-tingling chill of the evening, under a dome of staccato stars. She said in that low voice of hers, 'Walk me home? Just two blocks?'

'You bet.'

And with that the night was settled. Love, or one of its many approximations, is always determined in subtle subtext.

They walked down a street canopied by rustling leaves, washed gray of autumn color because of the missing street lights.

In the middle of a conversation about Miami, where Ransom had just been on business, she took his arm firmly. Her breast met his biceps with persistent pressure.

And sometimes, he reflected, the communications are less subtle than at others.

A moment later they heard a loud voice: 'Hey, why're you with that old, you know, guy? You want a real dick?' The words slipped and slid as if they had vertigo.

He was stepping forward from an alley. The kid was white, acne speckled and beefy. Eighteen or maybe younger. Annie tensed immediately and Ransom increased the pressure on her arm as he led her around the boy.

'I'm talking to . . . you.' His brows knitted belligerently, but it was hard to bring off ominous since he couldn't focus.

Ransom smelled beer mostly and guessed his already hearty belly would swell to double its already impressive size in five years.

'What're we going to do?' she whispered.

'Just keep walking.'

'Fucking slut. You're a fucking slut. You want a dick?'

'Go home,' Ransom said calmly. 'Get some sleep.'

'I'll fucking take you down. I will. I'll fucking do it.'

Tighter on Annie's arm, he moved to the left and then right, swerving slowly like a ship around an iceberg. The young man's eyes were swimming as he tried to follow them. Ransom decided that in the next sixty seconds the boy would jettison most of the alcohol that wasn't in his bloodstream and he wanted to make sure they weren't nearby when that happened.

The kid made a fist and stepped forward.

Ransom stopped and held up a hand, palm first. 'Think about it.'

'You asshole . . .'

'You hit me, it'll ruin your life. You'll be in jail for a year. You want to explain that to your parents? Your future employers?'

The hesitation was enough to let Ransom and Annie get a breaking-the-spell distance down the sidewalk.

'You're both fucking sluts,' he shouted.

He didn't follow.

A half-block away Annie whispered, 'Oh, that was terrible.' She was shaking. 'I thought he was going to attack us.'

'He couldn't do much damage in that condition.'

Ransom looked back. The young man staggered around the corner and the sounds of what he'd predicted a moment ago floated unpleasantly into the sharp air.

The grunt, the groan, the splash.

Thinking suddenly of his mother.

Then, naturally, of his father, whose ghost seemed to be inescapable on this trip. A loner in school, skinny, Ransom was picked on a lot. He asked his father to teach him how to fight, but the man scoffed. 'Fighting's for fools. Don't ever get into a fight. You fight, I'll whip you.'

'Why not?' young Ransom had asked, a bit confused about the apparent contradiction – and at the man's vehemence (he never spanked the boys).

But his father had offered a cool look that meant the conversation was over and made another phone call, lighting a cigarette. Ransom didn't get it at the time but he later decided that the reason he couldn't teach him self-defense was that he was all bluster. A coward.

And just like with schooling, Ransom made sure he didn't follow his father's path in this area either; his training in the army saw to that.

'You all right?' Annie asked.

'Fine.' She'd be thinking he was tense about the real-life confrontation with the punk, not the remembered one with Stan.

She laughed. 'I thought you were going to deck him.' She squeezed his arm. 'With those muscles you could have.'

'We'll let somebody else teach him a lesson . . . Forgive me for not defending your honor.'

'He called you a slut, too,' Annie reminded.

Ransom frowned broadly. 'Hey, that's right. And you didn't defend *mine*. I guess we're even.'

Another husky laugh.

They arrived at her apartment.

She unlocked the front gate. He turned to her.

'So, is it goodnight?' Annie asked. Confident, prepared for rejection, prepared for the opposite.

Ransom read the signs. 'No, it's not goodnight,' he said firmly.

He had learned over the years – and not, of course, from his father – that indecision was usually a bad idea.

At 2 a.m., Ransom Fells lay in Annie's bed, staring at the ceiling.

Then at her curled body, hair hovering stiffly around her angelic, pretty face, marred only by lipstick he himself had skewed. Her breathing was low and, even as she slept, seemed sultry.

For his part, though, Ransom was anything but peaceful. His jaw was tight. He was awash in *that* feeling yet again: the darkness, the bad, the guilt.

Not remorse for sleeping with her, of course. The evening had been completely mutual. He'd enjoyed her company and she his, he could tell, and the sex was pretty damn good, too. No, Ransom's heart was foundering because he knew very well it was going to end, and he knew how, too: thanks to him. Just like with Karen six months ago and Julia a few months before that.

Ransom still carried the glum residue of how those times – and plenty of others – ended, just as he would carry around the burden of his anticipated behavior with Annie.

Why couldn't he just feel good about meeting her?

He couldn't quite say why exactly, but, given his frame of mind, given this perverse sentimental journey, Ransom chose to blame his father.

The man's distance, the failure to give his son guidance, to be a role model . . . that led to the conundrum: desperation to connect with these women, guilt when it was over.

Sometimes you just can't win.

A reluctant smile crossed his face. You come back to a place where for the first fourteen years of your life all you were aware of was your father's absence even though you were living in his house. Now, the man is dead and gone and yet he's everywhere.

Troubled thoughts finally gave way to sleep, though naturally it came packed with an anthology of troubled dreams.

In the morning, Ransom came out of Annie's bathroom, dressed, and he found her sitting up, smiling at him, the sheets ganging around her like an entourage.

Her look was pleasant and casual. And she asked, with no apparent agenda, if he wanted coffee and something to eat or had to be going. There was none of the edginess or downright bizarre behavior of some women at this stage of the liaison (like the one who had him listen to her entire playlist of Deer Tick, or the woman who got up at five to make him biscuits from scratch because he'd casually mentioned the night before at dinner that his grandmother made her own).

He told Annie he had a meeting but afterward he didn't necessarily have to scoot out of town too fast. Why didn't they talk later?

Her eyes narrowed.

Had he done something wrong?

She asked, 'Did you actually say "scoot"?'

His brow furrowed, too. 'Can that just be our secret?'

'Deal.'

She eased forward, wrapping the sheet around her, and kissed him. He gave her his phone number and then he was heading back to the Shady Grove.

As it turned out, though, his plans altered. He got a message that John Hardwick would not be back into town until late that afternoon.

Irritated at the delay, Ransom Fells considered these unexpected free hours. And suddenly he decided on bald impulse to do something inconceivable.

He'd go visit his childhood home.

*

Population 14,000.

The color of the timid sign welcoming drivers to Marshall was green, not white, which it had been when the Fells were living here, but Ransom believed the number on it was the same. Could this be true, the town had not shrunk or grown in twenty years? Or had the city elders not bothered to transpose census data?

Marshall was a town that tended to ask, Why bother?

While Chesterton lived in the shadows of US Steel, Marshall didn't even have the shabby grandeur of industry as a jewel in the crown. No looming cooling towers, no massive concrete blockhouses of refineries or smelters or assembly plants, no sweeping rusty vistas of marshaling yards (the name came from a minor nineteenth-century explorer, not railroad tracks), no faded, graffiti'd signs from the past century proclaiming its position in the economic spine of the nation.

Chesterton Makes, the Country Takes.

Even though the paraphrased words were stolen from Trenton, New Jersey, at least Chesterton could make the claim in honesty.

Not so, Marshall. Here were trash yards, smoldering tire dumps, service stations unspruced by national franchises, shopping centers surrounded by crumbling asphalt parking lots, anchored by small grocery stores not Targets or Walmarts. Pawn shops aplenty. The downtown featured mom-and-pop storefronts veiled with sun-blocking sheets of orange vinyl, shading products like office supplies, tube TVs, and girdles. The movie theater, in which Ransom had spent a lot of his youth, usually alone, was closed. What was left of the poster on the front was nearly impossible to make out, but Ransom believed it depicted a young Warren Beatty.

The land was largely flat, both in geometry and color, and the billboards and roadside signs were bleached and crackled like Chinese pottery. The only bright hues came from death – the exiting leaves of maple and oak trees.

Ransom's palms actually began to sweat when he turned the Camry off Center Street and approached his old neighborhood. Heart stuttering faster. He thought of his days in Iraq. He thought about the rifles, pistols, explosives he was comfortable with. I'm a fucking veteran of combat, Ransom reflected angrily, and my hands are shaking like a kid's.

Then he was unexpectedly passing the two-story, pale green colonial and had to brake fast. The trees – and there were a lot of them – had grown significantly in the twenty years since he'd been away (no Dutch elm here), so he hadn't recognized the place. Though he supposed the truth was that he simply had chained out so many memories of his birthplace that he couldn't really recall what it looked like.

He backed up, pulled to the curb and parked. The house was set back about thirty feet from the street across a leaf-strewn grass yard. The residences in this block dated to the 1930s and though the neighborhood would qualify as a subdivision or development, the structures were not made from cookie cutters. Each was significantly different. The Fells' family home had a number of distinctive elements, including one that Ransom now recalled very well: a small round window, pied by perpendicular strips of wood – like a telescopic gun sight.

An unwanted memory from earlier returned: His father going hunting. Alone. Stan had told his son, 'Pretty dangerous, guns. When you're older.'

Even though Jimmy and Todd and even Ellen went hunting with their fathers all the time.

Oh, and, by the way, older never made it onto the schedule.

How dangerous would a hunting expedition have been anyway? Stan never came back with a deer or pheasant; he couldn't have fired more than a dozen shots.

Ransom continued to examine the house, which was smaller than he remembered, though he knew that always happened when seeing something – or someone – from the past that you've been thinking about for some time.

He noted the sliver of kitchen window. He remembered Stan sitting at the uneven Formica table before he left for work, always wearing the same: boots, jeans and a blue denim shirt over his wife-beater T-shirt (description only; like the boys, their mother never received more than a gruff glance or sharp word from Stan). He would sip coffee and read, never making conversation. Occasionally stepping into the den and closing the door after him to make or take a call. Ransom and his brother left for school with Stan still sitting at the table over his book or magazine and coffee.

Ransom was startled by his buzzing phone. It was Annie. He let it go to voice mail then turned his attention back to the side yard where he and his brother played.

Back to the front porch, where his mother would sit outside with a glass of wine disguised as juice in a red plastic cup. A big cup.

Back to the lawn he would mow every Saturday for the allowance that he was never given but had to earn.

Waiting, waiting, waiting to feel something.

But no.

Numb.

Then a curtain moved, yellow and brown.

The time was 10 a.m., a little after, and the owner – wife, probably – or a cleaning lady might be wondering what a sedan was doing parked in front of the house, with the driver in sunglasses on an overcast day no less. Not smart. Ransom slipped the Toyota into gear and rolled up the street, turning at the corner. He stopped at an intersection and pulled out his cell phone, did some research, made a few calls. Five minutes later he continued on, toward downtown Marshall.

The Ironworks Tavern was still in existence, about a mile from the house. It was on the edge of downtown, beside a river the color of dried mustard, and near what had been an unenclosed train station, where commuters would board one of the infrequent trains to Gary or to change to a different line for Chicago.

Ransom's father never took the train, but he came to the Ironworks frequently, after he got home from work and wolfed down supper, often standing in the fluorescent-lit kitchen, and then changed into a clean shirt and headed to the Ironworks.

Ransom now parked on the diagonal in front of the tavern, twenty empty spaces surrounding an occupied three. Inside, the large room was similar to what he recalled from the one or two times he'd been here with his mother, looking for Stan when they 'happened' to be shopping nearby (though there was an IGA that was closer to home). The place would have been painted, of course, and the sports posters were of mostly existing teams. Jägermeister was for sale, as was Red Bull, according to the promotional signage. And, heaven help us, Hefeweizen was on tap. Stan, a beer drinker exclusively, wouldn't have approved.

Ransom was amused that breakfast was being served, which also would have been unheard of twenty or thirty years ago. Four saggy people at three tables forked eggs, sausage and bacon into their mouths. Cigarette packs bulged in several shirt pockets. Ransom bet that at least one or two were wondering what the consequences would be if they lit up after they finished.

Ransom picked a shaky stool at the bar and told the elderly man behind it he'd like a coffee. The stooped guy gave Ransom a careful scan. 'Just regular,' Ransom told him, eyeing a steaming glass pot. Behind the bar was an espresso machine, but it looked like it had never been used. He didn't like fancy drinks anyway.

'Yessir.'

'You're Bud Upshaw?' Ransom asked when the man brought a mug and two Mini-Moo's creamers. An old-fashioned sugar shaker eased forward as cautiously as the man's eyes.

'Yessir,' he repeated. He was about seventy-five, with a face aggressively wrinkled. His complexion was an odd shade – not tan, not ethnic, but some curious tone of dark. Ransom thought of the unfortunate river out back. He was sinewy, and where his hair had been now clustered a dozen age spots.

Ransom hadn't wanted to waste the time of coming to this part of town if the Ironworks wasn't here any longer or if there was no one on the staff from twenty years ago. His call earlier had been to the Shady Grove, where the desk clerk told him that the Ironworks was still a 'Marshall landmark' and Upshaw, the owner for three decades, was still 'chief cook and bottle washer', which happened to be one of Stan's favorite expressions.

The man was definitely uncomfortable, and at first Ransom thought it was because he was dressed in a business suit and tie and had a lawyer look about him. Reason enough to be cautious in Marshall, where credit problems carried off as much peace of mind as lung cancer did lives. But, no, it was Ransom's face that drew most of Upshaw's attention.

'You know me?'

Ransom might have seen a much younger version of the man but couldn't recall. He said, 'I don't. My father might have. My family used to live here years ago. I'm in the area on business and thought I'd stop by.'

'Father . . .' Upshaw was whispering. And some troubled thought was clearly volleying around in his mind. Then: 'When was it? That you lived here?'

'Oh, I left over twenty years ago. I was a kid.' Finally he couldn't let it go any longer: 'Something wrong?'

'Nosir. How'd you know my name? Just curious.'

'Fellow at the Shady Grove. Clerk.'

'Sure, sure, sure.' Though this didn't make Upshaw feel any better. He scanned the breakfasters uneasily and scribbled out a check for one table, then scurried to deliver it.

Then, returning to his roost behind the bar, Upshaw froze. The old man whispered, 'Stan Fells.'

'That's right. I'm Ransom, his son.'

'Uh-huh. Sure. Uh-huh.' His eyes scanned the room, and it seemed to Ransom that he was looking for help.

'There a problem?'

'I . . . No.'

Though there was. Clearly. And this intrigued Ransom a great deal.

Upshaw aggressively dunked a dishcloth and wrung it out several times. Dunked again. He continued, 'So. Your dad in the area? You going to meet him here, by any chance?'

'My father? Oh, he died nine years ago.'

'He died, what happened?' the man asked. Not an unusual question, under the circumstances, but the speedy velocity of the words was curious.

'Car crash. Sorry to have to tell you.'

Only Upshaw himself didn't seem troubled about the news. In fact, he looked positively relieved.

Upshaw nodded thoughtfully and ignored another man waving for a check. 'So, dead. He was the last.'

'The last?'

'Of the Round Table.' He gestured to a dim corner, where a booth – which was square – now sat. 'Stan, Murphy, Shep, Mr Kale. The regulars.' He fell silent as the diner approached with some irritation. He now paid, leaving coins for a tip. Upshaw didn't pay any attention.

'Car crash. Round here?'

Stan had skidded off the road into a river in Michigan, returning from a trip to Detroit. He told Upshaw this.

'Detroit,' the man whispered, as if this, too, was significant.

Intrigue hummed at a higher pitch in Ransom Fells's heart.

The dishrag went for another swim and wringing and Upshaw mopped a part of the scabby bar that needed varnish, not soapy water. The man's face revealed an odd milkshake of emotions: he was wary of Ransom, he was curious, he was relieved. It didn't make any sense. And the mystery continued as Upshaw asked, 'Your father ever mention me or the place?'

'What?' Ransom asked, amused. 'He died nearly ten years ago.'

'Just wondering.'

'And I didn't talk to him for a few years before that.'

'Oh. That must've been tough.'

Not really. Ransom was silent.

Upshaw looked up, caught the gray eyes and then down again at dishwater that was pretty much the same shade. 'Means you didn't much happen to cross paths with any of the other boys he worked with?'

This was laughable. 'No, I didn't know anybody at the company.'

'Company?'

'Bud, what's this all about?'

'Oh, nothing, sir. Just curious. You were talking about old times and I was thinking the same. Walk down memory lane,' he said with a big phony smile on his face. 'So.'

But Ransom wasn't going to put up with any crap. He was enduring this hard pilgrimage to find out about his father, and this man obviously knew something. He fired a glance the man's way and touched his arm, gentle but insistent. 'Tell me what's going on.'

Though Ransom believed he had a pretty good idea, and it made perfect sense.

A woman.

Stan had been having an affair and Upshaw knew about it. Dad had probably brought the slut here dozens of times. Maybe the bar owner was worried about shattering Ransom's memories of his dad. But to judge from the wariness in his face, he guessed that it was more likely his father had threatened him to shut up about it.

Ransom understood something else; he guessed his mother knew, too. There had to be some reason she graduated from beer to wine to vodka.

'Really, please, sir.' Voice quivering.

'You don't tell me, I'll just go through my father's address book from back then and start calling people. They'll give me some answers.' There was no address book – Ransom hadn't inherited anything but a few thousand from an insurance policy – but for his job he'd learned to bluff. He was good at it. But he hadn't meant his words as a threat, simply a prod to get the man to spill.

So he didn't understand the alarmed reaction. 'No, no, you don't want to do that!' Now, Upshaw's hybrid complexion paled. The resulting color was eerie. 'Look, let's forget it. Please.' He was begging. 'You want some breakfast? It'll be on the house, for old times' sake.'

Ransom tightened the grip on Upshaw's arm then flattened his hands on the bar, as if planting himself, never to leave until he had some answers.

Upshaw swallowed and went to get himself some coffee he didn't seem to want. He returned and fiddled with the sugar shaker, poured in what seemed like half a cup. He didn't stir it. 'You're not . . . you're not law, are you?'

'Law?'

'Police, or whatever?'

Confused, Ransom muttered, 'I'm a salesman, computer products.'

Now Upshaw's own gaze grew tight, as if he were a truth detector.

Instinct told Ransom to relent. 'Look, Bud, my dad was a mystery to me. This was his favorite hangout after he'd get home from his company. I thought you could tell me a little about who he was, what he talked about, what he did. That's all.'

Now, lapsing back to his whisper, Upshaw looked around the tavern. 'Okay, sir. Well, first of all, this wasn't a place he'd stop in after work. This *was* his office. And as for who he was, please, I'm sorry. Your father was an enforcer.'

'A what?'

'He killed people for a living.'

Bud Upshaw was leaning back, now clutching the coffee as if he was going to fling it Ransom's way and flee in the event of an attack.

But Ransom Fells simply laughed. 'You're crazy. You're out of your fucking mind.' Maybe the old guy was senile.

'No, no. I wish I was. It's true, sir.'

Not smiling any longer. 'Bullshit.' Still, though, Ransom remembered the look of relief on Upshaw's face when he learned that his father was dead. Maybe, for some reason, Upshaw had lived in fear of his father. And the old man now said with complete sincerity, 'No, it's not.'

'Tell me.'

'Mr Kale I mentioned?'

At the ghost table.

'He was Stephan Kale.'

Ransom had no clue.

'Kale was a lieutenant for Doyle back in the seventies and eighties.'

'Wait. *Bobby* Doyle?'

'You heard of him?'

'Something on A&E or the Discovery Channel.' Head of a largely Irish gang on the South Side of Chicago and in Cicero. Here, too, northern Indiana. Doyle was dead or in prison, but the outfit was still around, Ransom believed.

'Stephan Kale ran their Gary operation from here.' Upshaw waved his arms, indicating the Ironworks. 'This was sort of their unofficial office. Your dad was one of the first ones Mr Kale recruited. It was, I guess, forty years ago, maybe more. Mr Kale had him kidnap Vince Giacomo's wife, in River Forest.'

'The Mafia guy?'

'Yeah, who'd been moving into Chicago Heights, Doyle's territory. Giacomo backed off – and paid a half-million to get his wife returned. Was your dad's first job and it went so smooth he was in like Flynn after that. He and the rest of the crew would come in during the day, hang out, get their assignments. Protection money here, bombing a competitor's restaurant there, more kidnappings, drugs, and money laundering. *Sopranos* stuff. They'd come back at night and hand off the money or report about what'd happened on the job.'

'That's not killing people,' Ransom whispered firmly.

Even more quietly: 'But he did that, too. I know it. Oh, hell, yeah, I know.'

'Impossible.'

The drippy rag was gone and Upshaw was sipping his coffee, hunched over and leaning close to Ransom. 'Swear to God. Sure, they never talked about it out in the open. They weren't stupid, none of the Round Table crew was. But one day, I found out. See, there was this pipe started leaking in the utility room. I went in to fix it and I was behind the water heater, working away. And your dad and Mr Kale come in and they must've thought the room was empty because he says to your dad, "Good job with Krazinski. The DA suspects but my contact tells me they can't make a case. The coroner's gonna go with accidental. Doyle's happy about that, real happy." And your father didn't say anything. Course, he was always pretty quiet.'

So it wasn't just me, Ransom reflected. Despite the horrific nature of the conversation, Ransom was oddly pleased.

Upshaw continued, glancing cautiously around. 'Two days before, this star witness in a union embezzlement case, Leo Krazinski, died in a boating accident on Lake Michigan.'

'Jesus.'

'And then Mr Kale goes, "There's this numbers guy in Gary who's been skimming. He told Ig to go fuck himself. He needs to be gone." And then they got all quiet and they must've heard me breathing, even though I was trying not to, 'cause next thing I know I look up and there they are staring down at me. I started to cry, I'll admit it. I was blubbering like a kid. And your dad bends down and helps me up. And reaches into his pocket and takes out some Kleenex. And hands me one.'

'Yeah, he always carried that packet.' Ransom now realized they maybe weren't to wipe his nose but were to take care of fingerprints.

'And he looks at Mr Kale and he nods and I'm sure I'm dead. You know, this was it. Then Stan bends down and picks up the wrench I was using. And, what the fuck, he unscrews the L-joint I was working on. He looks at it and goes, "Your water's too hard." And he looks at me in this way, I can't describe it, just looks and hands me back the pipe. That's all he says. I got the message. Just that look, and I got the message.'

'And the numbers guy?'

'Ended up in a bad car crash two days later. Both him and his wife burned up.'

'His wife, too?' Ransom asked.

'Yeah, I guess because it looked more real, or something. So the cops wouldn't think it was murder.'

Ransom Fells closed his eyes and exhaled long.

'That's why I was so freaked out, sir, when I seen you. I didn't know why at first, I just felt somebody stepped on my grave. 'Cause you look like him, you know.'

This had always irritated Ransom.

'And, hell, when you told me who you were, I thought maybe the law was after your dad, and you and him were going around taking out witnesses. Or he'd been caught and you were here to settle the score.'

Though his thoughts were reeling, Ransom actually smiled at this. He felt a curious need to reassure the poor old guy. 'No, I just wanted to find out a little about him.'

'And, man, I sure told you more than you'd ever wanna know. I'm sorry.'

Ransom now wondered if the car crash in Pennsylvania had in fact been an accident. From the few times he'd driven with the man, Ransom knew his father was a good driver. Maybe back then, car crashes were a popular way for hit men to cover up their crimes.

Upshaw added, 'Maybe he got out of the business, I don't know. Probably did. He was a decent guy.'

'Decent?'

'Well, I mean, he never caused no trouble here. Tipped good. Never saw him drunk.' Upshaw shrugged. 'Wish I could tell you more, sir.'

Ransom pushed off the stool and asked for a coffee to go. When the old man gave it to him and Ransom had doctored it with cream just right, he laid a couple of dollars on the bar, but Upshaw handed him back the money. 'Naw, don't worry about it.'

As he walked to the door Ransom debated furiously. Yes, no?

Do it, don't.

He turned. 'Hey, Bud, did he ever mention me?'

Upshaw squinted, as if trying to wring out memories like water from the dishrag. 'Family stuff, things about home, it wasn't right to talk about them here. This was business. It was like it would disrespect the wives and kids to do that.'

'Sure.'

But when he got to the door, his hand on the knob, he heard the man call, 'Hey, wait, sir. Wait. You know, one time, I remember, Stan *did* say something. Did you go to Thoreau High?'

'Yeah.' Ransom stared back at the man.

'Well, I heard him talking about this great play in the last few minutes of a Thoreau–Woodrow Wilson game, a sixty-yard touchdown. He was smiling. He said his kid did a great job. The best play he'd ever seen.'

'He said that?'

'Yeah.'

Ransom nodded and walked outside, dropping into the front seat of the car and firing it up.

Reflecting that what Stan actually would have said was, '*the* kid', not '*his* kid'.

Ransom had never played football.

And now, four hours later, Ransom Fells was still sitting in the rental Toyota, on the meager hill that overlooked the lopsided softball field. He clutched his cool coffee and riffled through Upshaw's stories again and again.

His father a killer . . . and possibly murdered himself.

Impossible.

And yet . . .

The old man's account had seemed too specific to be made up, and his troubled face had registered genuine fear that Ransom had come to kill him. Ransom lined Upshaw's words up against the facts he remembered from his childhood:

How his father never talked about his job or introduced the family to fellow workers. How Ransom and his brother were never invited to his company. How Stan didn't want Ransom to get into fights – which might draw the police. How he rarely took the family out in public – for fear of jeopardizing them? How he regularly went hunting solo but never came back with a trophy (and what game had he *really* been after?). How his quiet, retiring manner was similar to, say, a sniper in Iraq that Ransom knew, who'd never boast about his kills and who was a craftsman who treated taking lives as simply another job.

One big question remained, however: What was Ransom's reaction to the news? He simply couldn't tell. He was too confused.

It was then that he remembered Annie had called. He listened to her message, in which she'd suggested, no commitment, if he wanted to get together that night she'd enjoy it.

He now called her back.

'Hey,' she said, recognizing the number.

'Hey to you, too.'

'How's your day been?'

If you only knew . . .

'Good. Productive.'

'I'm bored,' Annie said breathily.

'Well, have dinner with me. I'll cure you.'

'I'm quite familiar with your course of treatment, Doctor. Can you fit me in at seven?'

She really had one of the sexiest voices he'd ever heard.

'The appointment's been scheduled,' he said playfully.

He disconnected and, as he stared again at the field, an electric jolt coursed through him. Ransom Fells actually smiled.

Of all the weird ironies, learning the shocking truth about his father had suddenly put his own concerns in perspective. The edginess, the tension, the guilt he'd felt when connecting with someone like Annie vanished completely.

The sentimental journey, which he'd avoided for so many years, had paid off in a way he could never have expected.

More than he would ever have expected.

Ransom fired up the car and returned to Chesterton. He finished up his business with John Hardwick, then hurried to Annie's.

On the way he made up a phrase that was worthy of his ex.

Absentee reconciliation.

Ransom liked that. The phrase had two meanings when it came to his father: he'd reconciled with someone who was emotionally absent, even when they were living in the same house, and now who was absent physically.

An exhilarating sense of freedom coursed through him.

He parked and made his way to Annie's front door, rang the bell and heard the thump thump thump of steps as she approached. He noticed that she didn't play any games – like slowing down, or making him wait.

Then the door was opening and she pulled him inside fast, smiling and kissing him hard on the lips.

Ransom swung the door shut with his foot and held her tightly. He cradled her neck, stroking her hair teasingly.

She whispered, 'Don't you want to examine me before dinner, Doctor?'

Ransom smiled. Silently, he slipped the Smith & Wesson revolver from his pocket and touched her temple with the blunt muzzle. He slipped the index fingertip into his ear – the .38 special rounds were loud as hell.

'What's—?' she asked.

He pulled the trigger.

Still, the gunshot was stunning and numbed his hearing. It pitched Annie's head sideways so fast he wondered if the impact had also broken her neck.

She thudded to the floor like a sack of ice melt.

The house was at least fifty yards from the nearest neighbors, but gunshots are quite distinctive and he knew he didn't have much time. Pulling on latex gloves, he dropped to his knees and wiped her lips hard with a tissue to lift any DNA he might have left from the kiss. Then, with a new tissue, he wiped his own prints from the gun and nestled it in her still-quivering hand, which he then dusted with the gunshot residue from this particular lot of cartridges. He then planted around her house a half-dozen items he'd lifted from John Hardwick's house, after he'd killed the man and his wife a half-hour before: dirty socks and underwear, a toothbrush, condoms, a coffee mug. (On Hardwick's corpse he'd also planted some hairs he'd lifted from Annie's brush that morning in her bathroom, and more condoms, the same brand.)

The prepaid anonymous cell phone, whose number he'd given Annie earlier, was now scrubbed of his own prints and marked with Hardwick's;

it rested in the dead man's pocket. The police would find only one message, from Annie – the call he hadn't picked up earlier. It was 'John, hey, it's me, Annie. If you want to get together tonight, I'd love to. Only if you're up for it.'

Ransom had told her his first name was 'John'.

He stood for a minute and surveyed the house, deciding it was a righteous set.

It was easy to kill someone, of course. What was difficult was setting up a credible scenario so that the police stopped looking for suspects. In the thirty-five killings Ransom was responsible for, he usually found a person to take the rap. The police, forever overworked, were generally happy to take the obvious explanation, even if there were a few holes as to the truth of the incident.

Murder/suicide was always good.

The police would conclude that John Hardwick had been having an affair with Annie Colbert and had told her it was over. She'd gone to his house tonight when he got home from work, shot him and his wife, and then returned home, taking her own life with the same gun she'd used to kill the couple.

There were a few people who'd seen Annie and Ransom together. The drunk kid wouldn't remember anything. The bartender might, but the young man had been busy and Ransom had introduced himself as John to him as well.

Besides, Ransom Fells had a solid cover: a traveling salesman for GKS Tech, based in New Jersey. It was a front, of course, but a very elaborately documented one. And in any case Ransom would be out of this area in twenty minutes.

Then he was out the door and, sticking to bushes in the backyards of the properties here, he made toward the car, parked several blocks away.

Ransom's boss would be pleased. The clients would, too – a money-laundering operation on the East Coast trying to expand into the Midwest and meeting resistance from John Hardwick, who had his own financial game set up here.

Ransom was pleased, too. And about more than the success of the job.

Learning what he had about his father had removed one of the biggest draws in his career, one he'd wrestled with ever since joining the operation: the troubled feelings about making a living at murder, so to speak, and the guilt at killing the innocent to enhance your goal.

Could a death – violent death – ultimately (and ironically) lead to something positive, a reconciliation of sorts?

Apparently the answer was yes. Not his father's own death, but the killing that was his father's profession.

Knowing what he'd learned from the scrawny bar owner had worked a miracle. Now it was clear. He'd been born this way, his father's son, and there was nothing he could do to change.

And then another thought struck him like the shockwave from an IED.

My name!

Stan's first job had been the kidnapping of the Mafioso's wife in the western suburbs of Chicago, at which he'd made his own career . . . and made Bobby Doyle $500,000 – in *ransom*.

His father had named his firstborn son after his big break.

Ransom grinned like he hadn't done for years.

He was halfway through Ohio when he received an encrypted email and pulled over; he didn't want to read it while driving and risk a ticket. His other weapons were carefully hidden under the computer tools, but why tempt fate?

The message was from his boss at GKS Tech, thanking him for the Indiana job and asking if he was able to take on another assignment – back in his own territory of the New York area. A whistleblower was going to testify against a client – a government contractor, who'd been delivering shoddy military equipment and overcharging for it. The employee had not gone to the authorities yet but was going to do so on Monday. The client needed him dead right away.

Ransom answered that he'd handle the job.

A moment later he received another message. It said that Ransom ought to know that the target was presently at home with his wife and two teenage children and would be there all weekend until he left for the DA's office. It was possible that the entire family would be present when he killed the man. There'd probably have to be collateral damage.

Ransom typed: *That's not a problem.*

And cut and pasted the address of his victims into his GPS.

THE OBIT

MEMORANDUM

From: Robert McNulty, Chief of Department, New York City Police Department

To: Inspector Frederick Fielding
Deputy Inspector William Boylston
Captain Alonzo Carrega
Captain Ruth Gillespie
Captain Sam Morris
Sergeant Leo Williams
Lieutenant Detective Diego Sanchez
Lieutenant Detective Carl Sibiewski
Lieutenant Detective Lon Sellitto
Detective Antwan Brown
Detective Eddie Yu
Detective Peter Antonini
Detective Amelia Sachs
Detective Mel Cooper
Police Officer Ronald Pulaski

CC: Sergeant Amy Mandel

Re: Lincoln Rhyme News Release

In light of the recent tragic events, our Public Information Department has prepared the following release for news organizations around the country. As you are someone who has in the past worked with Lincoln Rhyme, we are sending you a draft of this document for review. If you wish to make any changes or additions, please send them by 1030 hours Friday to Sgt. Amy Mandel, the office of the Deputy Commissioner of Public Information, One Police Plaza, Room 1320.

Please note the time and place of the memorial service.

*** FOR IMMEDIATE RELEASE ***

New York City – Capt. Lincoln Henry Rhyme (Ret.), internationally known forensic scientist, died yesterday of gunshot wounds following an attack by a murder suspect he had been pursuing for more than a year.

The assailant, whose name is unknown but who goes by the nickname The Watchmaker, gained entrance to Capt. Rhyme's Central Park West townhouse, shot him twice and escaped. He was believed to be wounded by NYPD Detective Amelia Sachs, who was present at the time. The assailant's condition is unknown. An extensive manhunt is under way in the Metropolitan area.
Capt. Rhyme was pronounced dead at the scene.

'This is a terrible loss,' said Police Commissioner Harold T. Stanton, 'one that will be felt throughout the department, indeed throughout the entire area. Capt. Rhyme has been instrumental in bringing to justice many criminals who would not have been apprehended if not for his brilliance. The security of our city is now diminished due to this heinous crime.'

For years Capt. Rhyme had been commanding officer of the unit that supervised the NYPD Crime Scene operation.

It was, in fact, while he was searching a scene in a subway tunnel undergoing construction work that he was struck by a falling beam, which broke his spine. He was rendered a C-4 quadriplegic and paralyzed from the neck down, able to move only one finger of his left hand and his shoulders and head. Though initially on a ventilator, his condition stabilized and he was able to breathe without assistance.

He retired on disability but continued to consult as a private 'criminalist', or forensic scientist, working primarily for the NYPD, though also for the Federal Bureau of Investigation, the Department of Homeland Security, the Bureau of Alcohol, Tobacco, Firearms and

Explosives, and the Central Intelligence Agency, among others, as well as many international law enforcement agencies.

Lincoln Rhyme was born in the suburbs of Chicago. His father was a research scientist who held various positions with manufacturing corporations and at Argonne National Laboratory. His mother was a homemaker and occasional teacher. The family lived in various towns in the northern Illinois area. In high school, Capt. Rhyme was on the varsity track and field team and president of the Science Club and the Classics Club. He was valedictorian of his high-school graduating class. Capt. Rhyme was graduated from the University of Illinois at Urbana-Champaign, receiving dual degrees in chemistry and history. He went on to study geology, mechanical engineering and forensic science at the graduate level.

Capt. Rhyme turned down lucrative offers to work in the private sector or in colleges and chose instead to specialize in crime-scene work.

He said in an interview that theoretical science had no interest for him. He wanted to put his talents to practical use. 'I couldn't be a karate expert who spends all his time in the monastery or practice hall. I'd be itching to get out on the street.'

Some friends believed an incident in his past, possibly a crime of some sort, steered him to law enforcement but none was able to say what that might have been.

Capt. Rhyme attended the NYPD Police Academy in Manhattan and joined the force as an officer in the Crime Scene Unit. He quickly rose through the division and was eventually named commanding officer of the division overseeing the unit while still a captain, usually a position held by an officer with the higher rank of deputy inspector.

Capt. Rhyme took forensic science to a new level in New York City. He fought for budget increases to buy state-of-the-art equipment, evidence collection gear and computers. He personally created a number of databases of 'samplars', such as motor oils, gasoline, dirt, insects, animal droppings and construction materials, against which his officers could compare trace evidence from crime scenes and thus identify and locate the perpetrator with unprecedented speed. He would wander throughout the streets of the city at all hours and collect such materials.

He developed new approaches to searching crime scenes (for which he coined the now-common term, 'walking the grid'). He instituted the practice of using a single officer to examine scenes, believing that a solo searcher could achieve a better understanding of the crime and the perpetrator than when a group of officers was involved.

FBI Special Agent Frederick Dellray, who worked with Capt. Rhyme frequently, said, 'When it came to physical evidence, there was not a single, solitary soul in the country who was better. No, make that the world. I mean, he was the one we brought in to set up our Physical Evidence Response Team. Nobody from Washington or Quantico, nope. We picked *him*. I mean, this's a guy solved a case 'cause he found a fleck of cow manure from the eighteen hundreds. He couldn't tell you who Britney Spears is or who won *American Idol*, but, it came to evidence, that man knew f***ing everything.'

Although most senior crime-scene officers are content to leave the actual searches and lab work to underlings, Capt. Rhyme would have none of that. Even as a captain, he searched scenes, gathered samples and did much of the analysis himself.

'When we were partnered,' said Lt. Lon Sellitto, 'he was a lot of times first officer at the scene and would insist on searching it himself, even if it was hot.'

A 'hot' crime scene is one at which an armed and dangerous perpetrator might still be present.

'I remember one time,' Lt. Sellitto recalled, 'he was running a scene and the perp comes back with a gun, starts shooting. Lincoln dives under cover and returns fire but he was mad about the whole thing – every time he fired, he said, he was contaminating the scene. I told him later, "Geez, Linc, you shoot the guy, you're not gonna have to *worry* about the scene." He didn't laugh.'

When asked once about his fastidious approach to forensic work, Capt. Rhyme cited Locard's Principle, which was named after the early French criminalist, Edmond Locard, who stated that in every crime there is some exchange between the criminal and the victim, or the criminal and the scene, though the trace might be extremely difficult to find.

'Often the only thing that will stop a vicious killer is a microscopic bit of dust, a hair, a fiber, a sloughed-off skin cell, a coffee stain. If you're lazy or stupid and miss that cell or fiber, well, how're you going to explain that to the family of the next victim?'

He insisted on employees' total devotion to their job and once fired an officer for using the toilet beside the bedroom where a murder had occurred.

Still, he rewarded hard work and loyalty. A former protégé reported that on more than one occasion Capt. Rhyme would berate senior police officials to secure raises or promotions for his people or adamantly, and loudly, defend their judgments about handling cases.

In several instances Capt. Rhyme himself ordered senior police officials, reporters and even a deputy mayor arrested when their presence threatened to contaminate or interfere with a crime scene.

In addition to gathering and analyzing evidence, Capt. Rhyme enjoyed testifying in court against those whose arrests he had participated in.

Bernard Rothstein, a well-known criminal defense lawyer who has represented many organized crime figures, recalled several cases in which Capt. Rhyme testified. 'If I saw that Rhyme had done the forensic work in a case against one of my clients, I'd think, brother, I am *not* looking forward to *that* cross-examination. You can punch holes in the testimony of a lot of crime-scene cops when they get up on the stand. But Lincoln Rhyme? He'd punch holes in *you*.'

After his accident at the subway crime scene, he converted a parlor in his Central Park West townhouse into a forensic lab, one that was as well equipped as that in many small cities.

Det. Melvin Cooper, an NYPD crime-scene officer who often worked with Capt. Rhyme and did much of his laboratory work for him, recalled one of the first cases run out of his townhouse. 'It was a big homicide, and we had a bunch of evidence. We cranked up the gas chromatograph, the scanning electron microscope and the mass spectrometer. Some other instruments, too. Then I turned on a table lamp and that was the last straw. It blew out the electricity. I don't mean just his townhouse. I mean the entire block and a lot of Central Park, too. Took us nearly an hour to get back on line.'

Despite his injury, Capt. Rhyme was not active in disability rights organizations. He once told a reporter, 'How would you describe me? Six feet, white, one hundred eighty pounds, black hair, disabled. Those are all conditions that have, to a greater or lesser degree, affected my career as a criminalist. But I don't focus on any of them. My purpose in life is to find the truth behind crimes. Everything else is secondary. In other words, I'm a criminalist who, by the way, happens to be disabled.'

Ironically, largely because of this attitude, Capt. Rhyme has been held out by many advocates as an example of the new disabled movement, in which individuals are given neither to self-pity nor to exploiting or obsessing over their condition.

'Lincoln Rhyme stood for the proposition that the disabled are human beings first with the same talents and passions – and short-comings – as everyone else,' said Sonja Wente, director of the Spinal Cord Injury Awareness Center. 'He avoided both the pedestal and the soapbox.'

Capt. Rhyme himself observed in a recent interview, 'The line between the disabled and the nondisabled is shrinking. Computers, video cameras, high-definition monitors, biometric devices and voice recognition software have moved my life closer to that of somebody who's fully able-bodied, while the same technology is creating a more sedentary, housebound life for those who have no disability whatso-ever. From what I've read, I lead a more active life than a lot of people nowadays.'

Nonetheless, Capt. Rhyme did not simply accept his disability but fought hard to maintain his ability to live as normal a life as he could and, in fact, to improve his condition.

'Lincoln engaged in a daily regimen of exercises on various machinery, including a stationary bike and a treadmill,' said Thom Reston, his personal aide and caregiver for a number of years. 'I was always saying slow down, take it easy, watch your blood pressure.' The aide added, laughing, 'He ignored me.'

In fact in recent years, Reston said, the exercise paid off, and Capt. Rhyme was able to regain some use of his extremities and some sensation, a feat that spinal cord doctors described as a rare achievement.

Capt. Rhyme was not only a practicing criminalist; throughout his tenure at the NYPD, he was in demand as a teacher and lecturer. After his accident, when traveling became more difficult, he continued to lecture on occasion at John Jay College of Criminal Justice and Fordham University in New York City. He wrote about forensic issues and his articles have appeared in, among others, *Forensic Science Review*, *The New Scotland Yard Forensic Investigation Annual*, *American College of Forensic Examiners Journal*, *Report of the American Society of Crime Lab Directors* and *The Journal of the International Institute of Forensic Science*.

He authored two books: a text on forensic science, still in use by thousands of police departments and law enforcement agencies around the world, and a popular non-fiction book, *The Scenes of the Crime*, about sites in New York City where unsolved murders occurred. The book is still in print.

Capt. Rhyme was himself the subject of a series of best-selling popular novels, which recounted some of his better-known cases, including *The Bone Collector*, about a serial kidnapper; *The Stone Monkey*, recounting the hunt for a Chinese 'snakehead', or human smuggler; and *The Twelfth Card*, in which he and Det. Amelia Sachs, who worked with him often, had to investigate a crime that occurred just after the Civil War. Recently, *The Burning Wire* detailed his efforts to stop a killer who was using the New York City power grid as a murder weapon.

Publicly dismissive of the novels, he stated in interviews that he thought the books merely trivial 'entertainments', good for reading on airplanes or at the beach, but little else.

Privately, though, he was delighted to be the subject of the series, keeping an autographed set on his shelves. Visitors reported that he would often make them sit silently and listen to passages on CD he particularly liked.

'Lincoln and his ego were never far apart,' joked Mr Reston.

Capt. Rhyme was divorced from his wife, Blaine Chapman Rhyme, twelve years ago. They had no children. He is survived by his partner, Det. Sachs; his aunt Jeanette Hanson; and four cousins, Arthur Rhyme, Marie Rhyme-Sloane, Richard Hanson and Margaret Hanson.

A memorial service for Capt. Rhyme will be held at 7 p.m., Monday, at the New York Society for Ethical Culture, 2 West 64th Street, at Central Park West, New York, NY. Det. Sachs has asked that in lieu of flowers, donations be made to a charitable organization of their preference for the benefit of children with spinal cord injuries or disease.

The first floor of the townhouse on Central Park West was quiet, dark. The lights were off and little of the dusk light from outside penetrated the curtains in the east-facing room.

What had once been a quaint Victorian parlor was now filled with laboratory equipment, shelves, cabinets, office chairs, electronic devices. On examining tables were plastic and paper bags, tubes and boxes containing evidence. They were in no particular order.

The atmosphere here was of a workplace whose otherwise busy pulse had been stopped cold.

Tall, red-haired Amelia Sachs stood in the corner, beside frumpy Lon Sellitto. They both wore black suits.

Her eyes, gazing down at Lincoln Rhyme's obituary.

Sellitto glanced down at it. 'Weird, hmm?'

She gave a faint unhappy laugh, then shook her head.

'Felt exactly the same way. Hard enough to think about the *idea*, you know, without seeing it in black and white.'

'Yeah, I guess that's it.'

Sellitto looked at his watch. 'Well, it's about time.'

The hour was close to 7 p.m., Monday, when the obit announced the memorial service was about to start.

'Ready?'

'As I'll ever be.'

The two people shared a look, left the townhouse. Sachs locked the door. She glanced up at Lincoln Rhyme's darkened bedroom, outside of which the falcons nested on the ledge. She and Sellitto started down the street toward the Society for Ethical Culture, which was just a short walk away.

Amelia Sachs returned to the townhouse, accompanied by a group of other officers.

Casual observers might have thought that the cops were returning from the memorial service for a reception in the house of the deceased.

But they'd be wrong. The hour was merely seven twenty, which wouldn't have allowed nearly enough time for a proper service, even for someone as unspiritual as Lincoln Rhyme. And a closer look at the officers might reveal that they had their weapons drawn and were whispering into microphones held in hands or protruding from head-sets.

The dozen officers split into two groups, and on word from Lon Sellitto at a nearby command post, one sped through the front door, another jogged around back.

Amelia Sachs, not surprisingly, was the first one through the front door.

The lights flashed on and she crouched in the doorway, ignoring the painful griping of arthritic joints, as she trained her Glock on an astonished man in a suit and dark blue shirt, bending over an evidence table. He was surprised in the act of picking up a plastic bag in his latex-gloved fingers.

'Freeze,' Sachs barked and he did, noting undoubtedly the steadiness of her hand holding the pistol and the look in her eye that explained that she was more than prepared to fire it.

'I—'

'Hands on your head.'

The solidly built middle-aged man sighed in disgust, dropped the bag and complied. 'Look, I can explain.'

Sachs wondered how often she'd heard that in her years as a cop, at moments just like this.

'Cuff him, search him,' she barked to young, spiky-haired Ron Pulaski and the other officers on the takedown team. 'He's a cop. Remember he might have two weapons.'

They relieved the man of his service Glock and, yep, a backup in an ankle holster, then cuffed him.

'You don't understand.'

Sachs had heard that quite a bit, too.

'Detective Peter Antonini, you're under arrest for murder.' She offered up the mantra of the Miranda warning then asked, 'Do you wish to waive your right to remain silent?'

'No, I sure as hell don't.'

'There's not much he needs to say anyway,' said a new voice in the room. Lincoln Rhyme wheeled his Merits Vision Select wheelchair, gray with red fenders, out of the small elevator that connected the lab with the upstairs bedroom. He nodded at the examination table. 'Looks like the evidence tells it all.'

'You?' Antonini gasped. 'You're . . . you were dead.'

'I thought you wanted to remain silent,' Rhyme reminded him, enjoying the look of absolute astonishment on the guilty man's face.

The criminalist wheeled to the evidence table and looked over what the officers had pulled from Antonini's pocket – Baggies of hair and dirt and other trace, which he intended to substitute for the evidence that had been sitting on the table, evidence the officer believed would convict him of murder.

'You son of a bitch.'

'He keeps talking,' Rhyme said, amused. 'What's the point of Miranda?'

At which point Detective second-class Peter Antonini, attached to

Major Cases, did indeed fall silent as Sachs called Sellitto in the command van and told him about the successful takedown. He would in turn relay the news to the brass at One Police Plaza.

You were dead . . .

Rhyme's phony death and the obituary had been a last-ditch effort to solve a series of crimes that cut to the heart of the NYPD, though crimes that might have gone unnoticed if not for an offhand observation made by Ron Pulaski a week before.

The young officer was in the lab helping Sellitto and Rhyme on a murder investigation in Lower Manhattan when a supervisor called with the news that the suspect had shot himself. Rhyme found the death troubling; he wanted closure in his cases, sure, but resolution by suicide was inelegant. It didn't allow for complete explanations, and Lincoln Rhyme detested unanswered questions.

It was just then that Pulaski had frowned and said, 'Another one?'

'Whatta you mean?' Sellitto had barked.

'One of our suspects dying before he gets collared. That's happened before. Those two others, remember, sir?'

'No, I don't.'

'Tell us, Pulaski,' Rhyme had encouraged him.

'About two months ago, that Hidalgo woman, she was killed in a mugging.'

Rhyme remembered. A woman being investigated for attempted murder – beating her young child nearly to death – was found dead, killed during an apparent robbery. The evidence initially suggested Maria Hidalgo guilty of beating the child, but after her death it was found that she was innocent. Her ex-husband had had some kind of psychotic break and attacked the child. Sadly she'd died before she could be vindicated.

The other case, Pulaski had reminded him, involved an Arab-American who'd gotten into a fight with some non-Muslim men and killed one of them. Rhyme and Sellitto were looking into the politically charged case when the suspect fell in his bathtub and drowned. Rhyme later determined that a Muslim *had* killed the victim, but under circumstances that suggested manslaughter or even negligent homicide, not murder.

He, too, died before the facts came out.

'Kinda strange,' Sellitto had said, then nodded at Pulaski. 'Good thinking, kid.'

Rhyme had said, 'Yeah, *too* strange. Pulaski, do me a favor and check out if there're any other cases like those – where suspects under investigation got offed or committed suicide.'

A few days later Pulaski came back with the results: there were seven cases in which suspects died while out on bail or before they'd been officially arrested. The means of death were suicide, accident and random muggings.

Sellitto and Rhyme wondered if maybe a rogue cop was taking justice into his own hands – getting details on the progress of cases, deciding the suspects were guilty, and executing them himself, avoiding the risk that the suspects might have gotten off at trial.

The detective and Rhyme understood the terrible damage this could cause the department if true – a murderer in their midst using NYPD resources to facilitate his crimes. They talked to Chief of Department McNulty and were given carte blanche to get to the truth.

Amelia Sachs, Pulaski and Sellitto interviewed friends and family of the suspects and witnesses nearby at the time they died. From these accounts it appeared that a middle-aged white man had been seen with many of the suspects just before their deaths. Several witnesses thought the man had displayed a gold shield; he was therefore a detective. The killer clearly knew Rhyme, since three of the victims were apparently murdered while the criminalist was running their cases. He and Sachs came up with a list of white detectives, aged thirty-five to fifty-five, he'd worked with over the past six months.

They surreptitiously checked the detectives' whereabouts at the times of the killings, eventually clearing all but twelve.

Rhyme opened an official investigation into the most recent case – the fake suicide that Pulaski had commented on. The scene was pretty cold and hadn't been well preserved – being only a suicide – but Amelia Sachs came up with a few clues that gave some hope of finding the killer. A few clothing fibers that didn't match anything in the victim's apartment, tool marks that might have come from jimmying a window, and traces of unusual cooking oil. Those weren't helpful in finding the killer's identity, but a few things suggested where he might live: traces of loam-rich soil that turned out to be unique to the banks of the Hudson River, some of which contained 'white gas', kerosene used in boats.

So it was possible that the rogue cop lived near the river in Manhattan, the Bronx, Westchester or New Jersey.

This narrowed the list to four detectives: from the Bronx, Diego

Sanchez; from New Jersey, Carl Sibiewski; from Westchester, Peter Antonini and Eddie Yu.

But there the case stalled. The evidence wasn't strong enough to get a warrant to search their houses for the clothing fibers, tools, cooking oil and guns.

They needed to flush him. And Rhyme had an idea how.

The killer would know that Rhyme was investigating the suicide – it was an official case – and would know that the criminalist probably had some evidence. They decided to give him the perfect opportunity to steal it or replace it with something implicating someone else.

So Rhyme arranged his own death and had the chief send out the memo about it to a number of officers, including the four suspects (the others were told of the ploy and they agreed to play along). The memo would mention the memorial service, implying that at that time the lab would be unoccupied.

Sellitto set up a search and surveillance team outside the townhouse and, while Rhyme remained in his bedroom, Sachs and Sellitto played the good mourners and left, giving the perp a chance to break in and show himself.

Which he, oh so courteously, had done, using a screwdriver that appeared to be the same one that had left the marks on windows of prior victims' residences.

Rhyme now ordered, 'Get a warrant. I want all the clothes in his house, cooking oils and soil samples, other tools, too. And any guns. Send 'em to ballistics.'

As he was now led to the door, Peter Antonini pulled away roughly from one officer holding him and spun to face Rhyme and Sachs. 'You think the system works. You think justice is served.' His eyes were mad. 'But it doesn't. I've been a cop long enough to know how screwed up it all is. You know how many guilty people get off every day? Murderers, child abusers, wife beaters . . . I'm sick of it!'

Amelia Sachs responded, 'And what about those *innocent* ones you killed? *Our* system would have worked for them. Yours didn't.'

'Acceptable losses,' he said coolly. 'Sacrifices have to be made.'

Rhyme sighed. He found rants tedious. 'It's time you left, Detective Antonini. Get him downtown.'

The escorts led him off out the door.

'Thom, if you don't mind, it's cocktail hour. Well *past* it, in fact.'

A few moments later, as the aide was fastening a cup of single-malt

Scotch to Rhyme's chair, Lon Sellitto walked into the room. He squinted and gazed at Rhyme. 'You don't even look *sick*. Let alone dead.'

'Funny. Have a drink.'

The chunky detective pursed his lips then said, 'You know how many calories're in whiskey?'

'Less than a donut, I'll bet.'

Sellitto cocked his head, meaning good point, and took the glass Thom offered. Sachs declined, as did Pulaski.

The rumpled detective sipped Scotch. 'Chief of Department's on his way. Wants to thank you. Press officer, too.'

'Oh, great,' Rhyme muttered. 'Just what I need. A bunch of sappy-eyed *grateful* visitors. Hell. I liked being dead better.'

'Linc, got a question. Why'd you pick the Watchmaker to do the deed?'

'Because he's the only credible perp I could think of.' Rhyme had recently foiled an elaborate murder plot by the professional killer, who'd threatened Rhyme's life before disappearing. 'Everybody on the force knows he *wants* to kill me.' The criminalist took a long sip of the smoky liquor. 'And he's probably one of the few men in the world who could.'

An uneasy silence followed that sobering comment and Pulaski apparently felt the need to fill it. 'Hey, Detective Rhyme, is this all accurate?' A nod at the memo that contained his obituary.

'Of course it is,' Rhyme said as if the comment was absurd. 'It had to be – in case the killer knew something about me. Otherwise he might guess something was up.'

'Oh, sure. I guess.'

'And by the way, do you always get your superior officers' attention with "hey"?'

'Sorry. I—'

'Relax, rookie. I'm a civilian, not your superior. But it's something to ponder.'

'I'll keep it in mind, sir.'

Sachs sat next to Rhyme and put her hand on his – the right one, which had some motion and sensation. She squeezed his fingers. 'Gave me kind of a pause.' Looking down at the sheet. 'Lon and I were talking about it.'

It had given Rhyme some pause, too. He felt the breeze from death's wings nearly every day, closer than to most people. He'd learned to ignore the presence. But seeing the account in black and white was a bit startling.

'Whatta you gonna do with it?' Sellitto said, glancing down at the paper.

'Save it, of course. Such beautiful prose, such pithy journalism . . . Besides, it's going to come in handy someday.'

Sellitto barked a laugh. 'Hell, Linc, you're gonna live forever. You know what they say. Only the good die young.'

FOREVER

Mathematics is not a careful march down a well-cleared highway, but a journey into a strange wilderness, where the explorers often get lost.

– W. S. Anglin, 'Mathematics and History'

+ − < = > ÷

An old couple like that, the man thought, acting like kids.

Didn't have a clue how crazy they looked.

Peering over the boxwood hedge he was trimming, the gardener was looking at Patsy and Donald Benson on the wide back deck of their house, sitting in a rocking love seat and drinking champagne. Which they'd had plenty of. That was for sure.

Giggling, laughing, loud.

Like kids, he thought contemptuously.

But enviously, too, a little. Not at their wealth – oh, he didn't resent that; he made a good living tending the grounds of the Bensons' neighbors, who were just as rich.

No, the envy was simply that even at this age they looked like they were way in love and happy.

The gardener tried to remember when he'd laughed like that with his wife. Must've been ten years. And holding hands like the Bensons were doing? Hardly ever since their first year together.

The electric hedge trimmer beckoned but the man lit a cigarette and continued to watch them. They poured the last of the champagne into the glasses and finished it. Then Donald leaned forward, whispering something in the woman's ear, and she laughed again. She said something back and kissed his cheek.

Gross. And here they were, totally ancient. Sixties, probably. It was like seeing his own parents making out. Christ . . .

They stood up and walked to a metal table on the edge of the patio and piled dishes from their lunch on a tray, still laughing, still talking. With the old guy carrying the tray, they both headed into the kitchen, the gardener wondering if he'd drop it, he was weaving so much. But, no, they made it inside all right and shut the door.

The man flicked the butt into the grass and turned back to examine the boxwood hedge.

A bird trilled nearby, a pretty whistle. The gardener knew a lot about plants but not so much about wildlife and he wasn't sure what kind of bird made this call.

But there was no mistaking the sound that cut through the air a few seconds later and made the gardener freeze where he stood, between two flowering trees, a crimson azalea and a purple. The gunshot, coming from inside the Bensons' house, was quite distinctive. Only a moment later he heard a second shot.

The gardener stared at the huge Tudor house for three heartbeats, then, as the bird resumed its song, he dropped the hedge trimmer and sprinted back to his truck, where he'd left his cell phone.

+ − < = > ÷

The county of Westbrook, New York, is a large trapezoid of suburbs elegant and suburbs mean, parks, corporate headquarters and light industry – a place where the majority of residents earn their keep by commuting into Manhattan, some miles to the south.

Last year this generally benign-looking county of nearly 900,000 had been the site of 31 murders, 107 rapes, 1423 robberies, 1575 aggravated assaults, 4360 burglaries, 16,955 larcenies and 4130 automobile thefts, resulting in a crime rate of 3223.3 per 100,000 population, or 3.22% for these so-called 'index crimes', a standardized list of offenses used nationwide by statisticians to compare one community to another and each community to its own past performance. This year Westbrook County was faring poorly compared with last. Its year-to-date index crime rate was already hovering near 4.5% and the temper-inflaming months of summer were still to come.

These facts – and thousands of others about the pulse of the county – were readily available to whoever might want them, thanks largely to a slim young man, eyes as dark as his neatly cut and combed hair, who was presently sitting in a small office on the third floor of the Westbrook County Sheriff's Department, the Detective Division. On his door were two signs. One said, *Det. Talbot Simms.* The other read, *Financial Crimes/ Statistical Services.* The Detective Division was a large open space, surrounded by a U of offices. Tal and the support services were on one stroke of the letter, dubbed the 'Unreal Crimes Department' by everybody on the other arm (yes, the 'Real Crimes Department', though it was officially labeled *Major Crimes and Tactical Services*).

This April morning Tal Simms sat in his immaculate office, studying one of the few items spoiling the smooth landscape of his desktop: a spreadsheet – evidence in a stock scam perpetrated in Manhattan. The Justice Department and the SEC were jointly running the case, but there was a small local angle that required Tal's attention.

Absently adjusting his burgundy-and-black-striped tie, Tal jotted some notes in his minuscule, precise handwriting as he observed a few inconsistencies in the numbers on the spreadsheet. Hmm, he was thinking, a .588 that should've been a .743. Small but extremely incriminating. He'd have to—

His hand jerked suddenly in surprise as a deep voice boomed outside his door, 'It was a goddamn suicide. Waste of time.'

Erasing the errant pencil tail from the margins of the spreadsheet, Tal saw the bulky form of the head of Homicide – Detective Greg LaTour – stride through the middle of the pen, past secretaries and communications techs, and push into his own office, directly across from Tal's. With a loud *clunk*, the detective dropped a backpack on his desk.

'What?' somebody called. 'The Bensons?'

'Yeah, that was them,' LaTour called. 'On Meadowridge in Greeley.'

'Came in as a homicide.'

'Well, it fucking wasn't.'

Technically, it *was* a homicide; all non-accidental deaths were, even suicides, reflected Tal Simms, whose life was devoted to making the finest of distinctions. But to correct the temperamental Greg LaTour you had to either be a good friend or have a good reason and Tal fell into neither of these categories.

'Gardener working next door heard a coupla shots, called it in,' LaTour grumbled. 'Some blind rookie from Greeley PD responded.'

'Blind?'

'Had to be. Looked at the scene and thought they'd been murdered. Why don't the local boys stick to traffic?'

Like everyone else in the department Tal had been curious about the twin deaths. Greeley was an exclusive enclave in Westbrook and – Tal had looked it up – had never been the scene of a double murder. He wondered if the fact that the incident was a double *suicide* would bring the event slightly back toward the statistical norm.

Tal straightened the spreadsheet and his note pad, set his pencil in its holder, then walked over to the Real Crimes portion of the room. He stepped through LaTour's doorway.

'So, suicide?' Tal asked.

The hulking homicide detective, sporting a goatee and weighing nearly twice what Tal did, said, 'Yeah. It was so fucking obvious to me . . . But we got the Crime Scene boys in to make sure. They found GSR on—'

'GSR?' Tal interrupted.

'GSR. Gunshot residue. On both their hands. She shot herself first then he did.'

'How do you know?'

LaTour looked at Tal with a surprised blink. 'He was lying on top of her.'

'Oh. Sure.'

LaTour continued. 'There was a note, too. And the gardener said they were acting like teenagers – drunk on their asses, staggering around.'

'Staggering.'

'Old folks. Geezers, he said. Acting like kids.'

Tal nodded. 'Say, I was wondering – you happen to do a question-naire?'

'Questionnaire?' he asked. 'Oh, your questionnaire. Right. You know, Tal, it was just a suicide.'

Tal nodded. 'Still, I'd like to get that data.'

'Data plural,' LaTour said, pointing a finger at him and flashing a big, phony grin. Tal had once sent around a memo that included the sentence 'The data were very helpful.' When another cop corrected him Tal had said, 'Oh, *data*'s plural; *datum*'s singular.' The ensuing ragging taught him a pointed lesson about correcting fellow cops' grammar.

'Right,' Tal said wearily. 'Plural. It'd—'

LaTour's phone rang and he grabbed it. "'Lo? . . . I don't know, couple days we'll have the location . . . Naw, I'll go in with SWAT. I wanta piece of him personal . . .'

Tal looked around the office. A Harley poster. Another, of a rearing grizzly – 'Bear' was LaTour's nickname. A couple of flyblown certificates from continuing education courses. No other decorations. The desk, credenza, and chairs were filled with an irritating mass of papers, dirty coffee cups, magazines, boxes of ammunition, bullet-riddled targets, depositions, crime-lab reports, a scabby billy club. The big detective continued into the phone, 'When? . . . Yeah, I'll let you know.' He slammed the phone down and glanced back at Tal. 'Anyway. I didn't think you'd want it, being a suicide. The questionnaire, you know. Not like a murder.'

'Well, it'd still be pretty helpful.'

LaTour was wearing what he usually did, a black leather jacket cut like a sports coat and blue jeans. He patted the many pockets involved in the outfit. 'Shit, Tal. Think I lost it. The questionnaire, I mean. Sorry. You have another one?' He grabbed the phone, made another call.

'I'll get you one,' Tal said. He returned to his office, picked up a questionnaire from a neat pile on his credenza and returned to LaTour. The cop was still on the phone, speaking in muted but gruff tones. He glanced up and nodded at Tal, who set the sheet on his desk.

LaTour mouthed, Thank you.

Tal waited a moment and asked, 'Who else was there?'

'What?' LaTour frowned, irritated at being interrupted. He clapped his hand over the mouthpiece.

'Who else was at the scene?'

'Where the Bensons offed themselves? Fuck, I don't know. Fire and Rescue. That Greeley PD kid.' A look of concentration that Tal didn't believe. 'A few other guys. Can't remember.' The detective returned to his conversation.

Tal walked back to his office, certain that the questionnaire was presently being slam-dunked into LaTour's wastebasket.

He called the Fire and Rescue Department but couldn't track down anybody who'd responded to the suicide. He gave up for the time being and continued working on the spreadsheet.

After a half-hour he paused and stretched. His eyes slipped from the spreadsheet to the pile of blank questionnaires. A Xeroxed note was stapled neatly to each one, asking the responding or case officer to fill it out in full and explaining how helpful the information would be. He'd agonized over writing that letter (numbers came easy to Talbot Simms, words hard). Still, he knew the officers didn't take the questionnaire seriously. They joked about it. They joked about him, too, calling him 'Einstein' or 'Mr Wizard' behind his back.

1. Please state nature of incident:

He found himself agitated, then angry, tapping his mechanical pencil on the spreadsheet like a drumstick. Anything not filled out properly rankled Talbot Simms; that was his nature. But an unanswered questionnaire was particularly irritating. The information the forms harvested was important. The art and science of statistics not only compiles existing information but is used to make vital decisions and predict trends. Maybe a questionnaire in this case would reveal some fact, some *datum*, that would help the county better understand elderly suicides and save lives.

4. Please indicate the sex, approximate age, and apparent nationality and/or race of each victim:

The empty lines on the questions were like an itch – aggravated by hotshot LaTour's condescending attitude.

'Hey there, boss.' Shellee, Tal's firecracker of a secretary, stepped into his office. '*Finally* got the Templeton files. Sent 'em by mule train from Albany's my guess.' With massive blond ringlets and the feistiness of a truck-stop waitress compressed into a five-foot, hundred-pound frame, Shellee looked as if she'd sling out words with a twangy Alabaman accent but her intonation was pure Hahvahd Square Bostonian.

'Thanks.' He took the dozen folders she handed off, examined the numbers on the front of each and rearranged them in ascending order on the credenza behind his desk.

'Called the SEC again and they promise, promise, promise they'll have us the – Hey, you leaving early?' She was frowning, looking at her watch, as Tal stood, straightened his tie and pulled on the thin, navy-blue raincoat he wore to and from the office.

'Have an errand.'

A frown of curiosity filled her round face, which was deceptively girlish (Tal knew she had a twenty-one-year-old daughter and a husband who'd just retired from the phone company). 'Sure. You do? Didn't see anything on your calendar.'

The surprise was understandable. Tal had meetings out of the office once or twice a month at the most. He was virtually always at his desk, except when he went out for lunch, which he did at twelve thirty every day, joining two or three friends from a local university at the Corner Tap Room up the street.

'Just came up.'

'Be back?' Shellee asked.

He paused. 'You know, I'm not really sure.' He headed for the elevator.

The white-columned Colonial on Meadowridge had to be worth six, seven million. Tal pulled his Honda Accord into the circular drive, behind a black sedan, which he hoped belonged to a Greeley PD officer, somebody who might have the information he needed. Tal took the questionnaire and two pens from his briefcase, made sure the tips were retracted, then slipped them into his shirt pocket. He walked up the flagstone path to the house, the door to which was unlocked. He stepped inside and identified himself to a man in jeans and work shirt, carrying a clipboard. It was his car in the drive, he explained. He was here to meet the Bensons' lawyer about liquidating their estate and knew nothing about the Bensons or their death.

He stepped outside, leaving Tal alone in the house.

As he walked through the entry foyer and into the spacious first floor a feeling of disquiet came over him. It wasn't the queasy sense that somebody'd just died here; it was that the house was such an unlikely setting for death. He looked over the yellow-and-pink floral upholstery, the boldly colorful abstracts on the walls, the gold-edged china and prismatic glasses awaiting parties, the collection of crystal animals, the Moroccan pottery, shelves of well-thumbed books, framed snapshots on the walls and mantel. Two pairs of well-worn slippers – a man's size and a woman's – sat poignantly together by the back door. Tal imagined the couple taking turns to be the first to rise, make coffee and brave the dewy cold to collect the *New York Times* or the Westbrook *Ledger*.

The word that came to him was 'home'. The idea of the owners here shooting themselves was not only disconcerting, it was downright eerie.

Tal noticed a sheet of paper weighted down by a crystal vase and he blinked in surprise as he read it.

To our friends:

We're making this decison with great contentment in hearts, joyous in the knowldge that we'll be together forever.

Both Patsy and Don Benson had signed it. He stared at the words for a moment then wandered to the den, which was cordoned off with crime-scene tape. He stopped cold, gasping faintly.

Blood.

On the couch, on the carpet, on the wall.

He could clearly see where the couple had been when they'd died; the blood explained the whole scenario to him. Brown, opaque, dull. He found himself breathing shallowly, as if the stain were giving off toxic fumes.

Tal stepped back into the living room and decided to fill out as much of the questionnaire as he could. Sitting on a couch he clicked a pen point out and picked up a book from the coffee table to use as a writing surface. He read the title: *Making the Final Journey: The Complete Guide to Suicide and Euthanasia*.

Okay . . . I don't think so. He replaced the book and made a less troubling lap desk from a pile of magazines. He filled out some of the details, then he paused, aware of the front door opening. Footsteps sounded on the foyer tile and a moment later a stocky man in an expensive suit walked into the den. He frowned.

'Sheriff's Department,' Tal said and showed his ID, which the man looked at carefully.

'I'm their lawyer. George Metzer,' he said slowly, visibly shaken. 'Oh, this is terrible. Just terrible. I got a call from somebody in your department. My secretary did, I mean . . . You want to see some ID?'

Tal realized that a Real Cop would have asked for it right up front. 'Please.'

He looked over the driver's license and nodded, then gazed past the man's pudgy hand and looked again into the den. The bloodstains were like brown laminate on cheap furniture.

'Was there a note?' the lawyer asked, putting his wallet away.

Tal walked into the dining room. He nodded toward the note.

The lawyer looked it over, shook his head again. He glanced into the den and blinked, seeing the blood. Turned away.

Tal showed Metzer the questionnaire. 'Can I ask you a few questions? For our statistics department? It's anonymous. We don't use names.'

'Sure, I guess.'

Tal began querying the man about the couple. He was surprised to learn they were only in their mid-sixties.

'Any children?'

'No. No close relatives at all. A few cousins they never see . . . Never saw, I mean. They had a lot of friends, though. They'll be devastated.'

He got some more information, troubled he had to leave blank the questions that could only be answered by the responding officers. Tal felt he had nearly enough to process the data, but one more question needed an answer.

9. Apparent motive for the incident:

'You have any idea why they'd do this?' Tal asked.

'I know exactly,' Metzer said. 'Don was ill.'

Tal glanced down at the note again and noticed that the writing was unsteady and a few of the words were misspelled. LaTour'd said something about them drinking but Tal remembered seeing a wicker basket full of medicine bottles sitting on the island in the kitchen. He mentioned this then asked, 'Did one of them have some kind of palsy? Nerve disease?'

The lawyer said, 'No, it was heart problems. Bad ones.'

In space number 9 Tal wrote: *Illness*. Then he asked, 'And his wife?'

'No, Patsy was in good health. But they were very devoted to each other. Totally in love. She must've decided she didn't want to go on without him.'

'Was it terminal?'

'Not the way he described it to me,' the lawyer said. 'But he could've been bedridden for the rest of his life. I doubt Don could've handled that. He was so active, you know.'

Tal signed the questionnaire, folded and slipped it into his pocket.

The round man gave a sigh. 'I should've guessed something was up. They came to my office a couple of weeks ago and made a few changes to the will and they gave me instructions for their memorial service. I thought it was just because Don was going to have the surgery, you know, thinking about what would happen *if* . . . But I should've read between the lines. They were planning it then, I'll bet.'

He gave a sad laugh. 'You know what they wanted for their memorial service? See, they weren't religious so they wanted to be cremated then have their friends throw a big party at the club and scatter their ashes on the green at the eighteenth hole.' He grew somber again. 'It never occurred to me they had something like this in mind. They seemed so happy, you know? Crazy fucked-up life sometimes, huh? Anyway, I've got to meet with this guy outside. Here's my card. Call me, you got any other questions, Detective.'

Tal walked around the house one more time. He glanced at the calendar stuck to the refrigerator with two magnets in the shape of lobsters. *Newport Rhode Island* was written in white across the bright red tails. In the calendar box for yesterday there was a note to take the car in to have the oil changed. Two days before that Patsy'd had a hair appointment.

Today's box was empty. And there was nothing in any of the future dates for the rest of April. Tal looked through the remaining months. No notations. He made a circuit of the first floor, finding nothing out of the ordinary.

Except, someone might suggest, maybe the troubled spirits left behind by two people alive that morning and now no longer so.

Tal Simms, mathematician, empirical scientist, statistician, couldn't accept any such presence. But he hardly needed to in order to feel a churning disquiet. The stains of opaque blood that had spoiled the reassuring comfort of this homey place were as chilling as any ghost could be.

+ − < = > ÷

When he was studying math at Cornell ten years earlier Talbot Simms dreamed of being a John Nash, a Pierre de Fermat, an Euler, a Bernoulli. By the time he hit grad school and looked around him, at the other students who wanted to be the same, he realized two things: one, that his love of the beauty of mathematics was no less than it had ever been but, two, he was utterly sick of academics.

What was the point? he wondered. Writing articles that no one read? Becoming a professor? He could have done so easily thanks to his virtually perfect test scores and grades, but that life to him was like a Mobius strip – the twisted ribbon with a single surface that never ends. Teaching more teachers to teach . . .

No, he wanted a practical use for his skills, and dropped out of graduate school. At the time there was a huge demand for statisticians and analysts on Wall Street, and Tal joined up. In theory the job seemed a perfect fit – numbers, numbers and more numbers, and a practical use for them. But he soon found something else: Wall Street mathematics were fishy mathematics. Tal felt pressured to skew his statistical analysis of certain companies to help his bank sell financial products to the clients. To Tal, 3 was no more nor less than 3. Yet his bosses sometimes wanted 3 to *appear* to be 2.9999 or 3.12111. There was nothing illegal about this – all the qualifications were disclosed to customers. But statistics, to Tal, helped us understand life; they weren't smoke screens to help us sneak up on the unwary. Numbers were pure. And the glorious compensation he received didn't take the shame out of his prostitution.

On the very day he was going to quit, though, the FBI arrived in Tal's office – not for anything he or the bank had done, but to serve a warrant to examine the accounts of a client who'd been indicted in a stock scam. It turned out the agent looking over the figures was a mathematician and accountant. He and Tal had some fascinating discussions while the man pored over the records, armed with handcuffs, a large automatic pistol and a Texas Instruments calculator.

Here at last was a logical outlet for his love of numbers. He'd always been interested in police work. As a slight, reclusive only child he'd read not only books on logarithms and trigonometry and Einstein's theories but murder mysteries as well, Agatha Christie and A. Conan Doyle. His analytical mind would often spot the killer early in the story. He called the Bureau's personnel department. He was disappointed to learn that there was a federal government hiring freeze in effect. But, undeterred, he called the NYPD and other police departments in the metro area – including Westbrook County, where he'd lived with his family for several years before his widower father got a job teaching math at UCLA.

Westbrook, it turned out, needed someone to take over their financial crimes investigations. The only problem, the head of county personnel admitted, was that the officer would also have to be in charge of gathering and compiling statistics. But, to Tal Simms, numbers were numbers and he had no problem with the piggy-backed assignments.

One month later, Tal had kissed Wall Street goodbye and moved into a tiny though pristine Tudor house in Bedford Plains, the county seat.

There was one other glitch, however, which the Westbrook County personnel office had neglected to mention, probably because it was so obvious: to be a member of the sheriff's department financial crimes unit, he had to become a cop.

The two-month training was rough. Oh, the academic part about criminal law and procedure went fine. The challenge was the physical curriculum at the academy, which was a little like army basic training.

Tal Simms, who'd been five-foot-nine and had hovered around 153 pounds since high school, had fiercely avoided all sports except volleyball, tennis and the rifle team, none of which had buffed him up for the Suspect Takedown and Restraint course. Still, he got through it all and graduated in the top 1.4% of his class. The swearing-in ceremony was attended by a dozen friends from local colleges and Wall Street, as well as his father, who'd flown in from the Midwest, where he was a professor of advanced mathematics at the University of Chicago. The stern man was unable to fathom why his son had taken this route but, having largely abandoned the boy for the world of numbers in his early years, Simms Senior had forfeited all right to nudge Tal's career in one direction or another.

Financial crimes proved to be rare in Westbrook. Or, more accurately, they tended to be adjunct to federal prosecutions, and Tal found himself sidelined as an investigator but in great demand as a statistician.

Finding and analyzing data are more vital than the public thinks. Certainly crime statistics determine budget and staff-hiring strategies. But, more than that, statistics can diagnose a community's ills. If the national monthly average for murders of teenagers by other teenagers in neighborhoods with a mean annual income of $26,000 is .03, and Kendall Heights in southern Westbrook was home to 1.1 such killings per month, why? And what could be done to fix the problem?

Hence, the infamous questionnaire.

Now, 6:30 p.m., armed with the one he'd just completed, Tal had decided to return to his office from the Benson house. He input the information from the form into his database and placed the question-naire itself into his to-be-filed basket. He stared at the information on the screen for a moment then began to log off. But he changed his mind and went online and searched some databases.

He jumped when someone walked into his office. 'Hey, boss.' Shellee blinked. 'Thought you were gone.'

'Just wanted to finish up a few things here.'

'I've got that stuff you wanted.'

He glanced at it. The title was, 'Adjunct Reports. SEC Case 04-5432'.

'Thanks,' he said absently, staring at his printouts.

'Sure.' She eyed him carefully. 'You need anything else?'

'No, go on home . . . 'Night.' When she turned away, though, he glanced at the computer screen once more and said, 'Wait, Shell. You ever work in Crime Scene?'

'Never did. Bill watches that TV show. It's icky.'

'You know what I'd have to do to get Crime Scene to look over the house?'

'House?'

'Where the suicide happened. The Benson house in Greeley.'

'The—'

'Suicides. I want Crime Scene to check it out. But I don't know what to do.'

'Something funny about it?'

He explained, 'Just looked up a few things. The incident profile was out of range.'

'I'll make a call. Ingrid's still down there, I think.'

She returned to her desk and Tal rocked back in his chair.

The low April sun shot bars of ruddy light into his office, hitting the large, blank wall and leaving a geometric pattern on the white paint. The image put in mind the blood on the walls and couch and carpet of the Bensons' house. He pictured, too, the shaky lettering of their note.

Together forever . . .

Shellee appeared in the doorway. 'Sorry, boss. They said it's too late to twenty-one-twenty-four it.'

'To—?'

'That's what they said. They said you need to declare a twenty-one-twenty-four to get Crime Scene in. But you can't do it now.'

'Oh. Why?'

'Something about it being too contaminated now. You have to do it right away or get some special order from the sheriff himself. Anyway, that's what they told me, boss.'

Even though Shellee worked for three other detectives Tal was the only one who received this title – a true endearment, coming from her. She was formal, or chill, with the other cops in direct proportion to the number of times they asked her to fetch coffee or snuck peeks at her ample breasts.

Outside, a voice from the Real Crimes side of the room called out, 'Hey, Bear, you get your questionnaire done?' A chortle followed.

Greg LaTour called back, 'Naw, I'm taking mine home. Had front-row Knicks tickets but I figured, fuck, it'd be more fun to fill out paperwork all night.'

More laughter.

Shellee's face hardened into a furious mask. She started to turn, but Tal motioned her to stop.

'Hey, guys, tone it down.' The voice was Captain Dempsey's. 'He'll hear you.'

'Naw,' LaTour called, 'Einstein left already. He's probably home humping his calculator. Who's up for Sal's?'

'I'm for that, Bear.'

'Let's do it . . .'

Laughter and receding footsteps.

Shellee muttered, 'It just frosts me when they talk like that. They're like kids on the schoolyard.'

True, they were, Tal thought. Math whizzes know a lot about bullies on schoolyards.

But he said, 'It's okay.'

'No, boss, it's not okay.'

'They live in a different world,' Tal said. 'I understand.'

'Understand how people can be cruel like that? Well, I surely don't.'

'You know that thirty-four per cent of homicide detectives suffer from depression? Sixty-four per cent get divorced, twenty-eight per cent are substance abusers.'

'You're using those numbers to excuse 'em, boss. Don't do it. Don't let 'em get away with it.' She slung her purse over her shoulder and started down the hall, calling, 'Have a nice weekend, boss. See you Monday.'

'And,' Tal continued, 'six point three per cent kill themselves before retirement.'

Though he doubted she could hear.

+ – < = > ÷

The residents of Hamilton, New York, were educated, pleasant, reserved and active in politics and the arts. In business, too; they'd chosen to live here because the enclave was the closest exclusive Westbrook community to Manhattan. Industrious bankers and lawyers could be at their desks easily by eight o'clock in the morning.

The cul-de-sac of Montgomery Way, one of the nicest streets in Hamilton, was in fact home to two bankers and one lawyer, as well as one retired couple. These older residents, at No. 205, had lived in their house for twenty-four years. It was a 6000-square-foot stone Tudor with leaded-glass windows and a shale roof, surrounded by a few acres of clever landscaping.

Samuel Ellicott Whitley had attended law school while his wife worked in the advertising department of Gimbels, the department store near the harrowing intersection of Broadway, Sixth Avenue and Thirty-fourth

Street. He'd finished school in '57 and joined Brown, Lathrop & Soames on Broad Street. The week after he was named partner, Elizabeth gave birth to a daughter, and after a brief hiatus, resumed classes at Columbia Business School. She took a job at one of the country's largest cosmetics companies and rose to be a senior vice president.

But the lives of law and business were behind the Whitleys now and they'd moved into the life of retirement as gracefully and comfortably as she stepped into her Dior gowns and he into his Tripler's tux.

Tonight, a cool, beautiful April Sunday, Elizabeth hung up the phone after a conversation with her daughter, Sandra, and piled the dinner dishes in the sink. She poured herself another vodka and tonic. She stepped outside onto the back patio, looking out over the azure dusk crowning the hemlocks and pine. She stretched and sipped her drink, feeling tipsy and content. Ecstatic.

She wondered what Sam was up to. Just after they'd finished dinner he'd said that he had to pick up something. Normally she would have gone with him. She worried because of his illness. Afraid not only that his undependable heart would give out but that he might faint at the wheel or drive off the road because of the medication. But he'd insisted that she stay home; he was only going a few miles.

Taking a long sip of her drink, she cocked her head, hearing an automobile engine and the hiss of tires on the asphalt. She looked toward the driveway. But she couldn't see anything.

Was it Sam? The car, though, had not come up the main drive but had turned off the road at the service entrance and eased through the side yard, out of sight of the house. She squinted but with the foliage and the dim light of dusk she couldn't see who it was.

Logic told her she should be concerned. But Elizabeth was completely comfortable sitting here with her glass in hand, under a deep blue evening sky. Feeling the touch of cashmere on her skin, happy, warm . . . No, life was perfect. What could there possibly be to worry about?

$$+ \quad - \quad < \quad = \quad > \quad \div$$

Three nights of the week – or as Tal would sometimes phrase it, 42.8571% of his evenings – he'd go out. Maybe on a date, maybe to have drinks and dinner with friends, maybe to his regular poker game (the others in the quintet enjoyed his company though they'd learned it could be disastrous to play against a man who could remember cards photographically and calculate the odds of drawing to a full house like a computer).

The remaining 57.1429% of his nights he'd stay home and lose himself in the world of mathematics.

This Sunday, nearly 7 p.m., Tal was in his small library, which was packed with books but was as ordered and neat as his office at work. He'd spent the weekend running errands, cleaning the house, washing the car, making the obligatory – and ever awkward – call to his father in Chicago, dining with a couple up the road who'd made good their threat to set him up with a cousin (email addresses had been unenthusiastically exchanged over empty mousse dishes). Now, classical music playing on the radio, Tal had put the rest of the world aside and was working on a proof.

This is the gold ring mathematicians seek. One might have a brilliant insight about numbers, but without completing the proof – the formal argument that verifies the premise – that insight remains merely a theorem, pure speculation.

The proof that had obsessed him for months involved 'perfect numbers'. These are positive numbers whose divisors (excluding the number itself) add up to that number. The number 6, for instance, is perfect because it's divisible only by 1, 2 and 3 (not counting 6), and 1, 2 and 3 also add up to 6.

The questions Tal had been trying to answer: How many even perfect numbers are there? And, more intriguing: Are there any *odd* perfect numbers? In the entire history of mathematics no one has been able to offer a proof that an odd perfect number exists (or that it can't exist).

Perfect numbers have always intrigued mathematicians – theologians, too. St Augustine felt that God intentionally chose a perfect number of days – six – to create the world. Rabbis attach great mystical significance to the number 28, the days in the moon's cycle. Tal didn't consider perfect numbers in such a philosophical way. For him they were simply a curious mathematical construct. But this didn't minimize their importance to him; proving theorems about perfect numbers (or any other mathematical enigmas) might lead to other insights about math and science . . . and perhaps life in general.

He now hunched over his pages of neat calculations, wondering if the odd perfect number was merely a myth or if it was real and waiting to be discovered, hiding somewhere in the dim distance of numbers approaching infinity.

Something about this thought troubled him and he leaned back in his chair. It took a moment to realize why. Thinking of infinity reminded him of the suicide note Don and Patsy Benson had left.

Together forever . . .

He pictured the room where they'd died, the blood, the chilling sight of the grim how-to guide they'd bought. *Making the Final Journey.*

Tal stood and paced. Something wasn't right. For the first time in years he decided to return to the office on a Sunday night. He wanted to look up some background on suicides of this sort.

A half-hour later he was walking past the surprised guard, who had to think for a moment or two before he recognized him.

'Officer . . .'

'Detective Simms.'

'Right. Yessir.'

Ten minutes later he was in his office, tapping on the keyboard, perusing information about suicides in Westbrook County. At first irritated that the curious events of today had taken him away from his mathematical evening, he soon found himself lost in a very different world of numbers – those that defined the loss of life by one's own hand in Westbrook County.

$$+ \ - \ < \ = \ > \ \div$$

Sam Whitley emerged from the kitchen with a bottle of old Armagnac and joined his wife in the den.

It had been her husband arriving fifteen minutes ago, after all, driving up the back driveway for reasons he still hadn't explained.

Elizabeth now pulled her cashmere sweater around her shoulders and lit a vanilla-scented candle, which sat on the table in front of her. She glanced at the bottle in his hand and laughed.

'What?' her husband asked.

'I was reading some of the things your doctor gave you.'

He nodded.

'And it said that some wine is good for you.'

'I read that, too.' He blew some dust off the bottle, examined the label.

'That you should have a glass or two every day. But cognac wasn't on the list. I don't know how good *that* is for your health.'

Sam laughed, too. 'I feel like living dangerously.'

He expertly opened the bottle, whose cork stopper was close to disintegrating.

'You were always good at that,' his wife said.

'I never had many talents – only the important skills.' He handed her a glass of the honey-colored liquor and then he filled his. They downed the first glass. He poured more.

'So what've you got there?' she asked, feeling even warmer now, giddier, happier. She was nodding toward a bulge in the side pocket of his camel hair sports coat, the jacket he always wore on Sundays.

'A surprise.'

'Really? What?'

He tapped her glass and they drank again. He said, 'Close your eyes.'

She did. 'You're a tease, Samuel.' She felt him sit next to her, sensed his body close. There was a click of metal.

'You know I love you.' His tone overflowed with emotion. Sam occasionally got quite maudlin. Elizabeth had long ago learned, though, that among the long list of offenses in the catalog of masculine sins, sentiment was the least troublesome.

'And I love you, dear,' she said.

'Ready?'

'Yes, I'm ready.'

'Okay . . . Here.'

Another click of metal . . .

Then Elizabeth felt something in her hand. She opened her eyes and laughed again.

'What . . . Oh, my God, is this—?' She examined the key ring he'd placed in her palm. It held two keys and bore the distinctive logo of a British MG sports car. 'You . . . you found one?' she stammered. 'Where?'

'That import dealer up the road, believe it or not. Two miles from here! It's a 'fifty-four. He called a month ago but it needed some work to get in shape.'

'So that's what those mysterious calls were about. I was beginning to suspect another woman,' she joked.

'It's not the same color. It's more burgundy.'

'As if that matters, honey.'

The first car they'd bought as a married couple had been a red MG, which they'd driven for ten years until the poor thing had finally given out. While Liz's friends were buying Lexuses or Mercedes she refused to join the pack and continued to drive her Cadillac, holding out for an old MG like their original car.

She flung her arms around his shoulders and leaned up to kiss him.

Lights flashed into the window, startling them.

'Caught,' she whispered, 'just like when my father came home early on our first date. Remember?' She laughed flirtatiously, feeling just like a carefree, rebellious Sarah Lawrence sophomore in pleated skirt and Peter-Pan-collared blouse – exactly who she'd been forty-two years ago when she met this man, the one she would share her life with.

+ – < = > ÷

Tal Simms was hunched forward, examining the details of suicide, jotting notes, when the dispatcher's voice clattered though the audio monitor, which was linked to the 911 system, in the darkened detective pen. 'All units in the vicinity of Hamilton. Reports of a possible suicide in progress.'

Tal froze. He pushed back from his computer monitor and rose to his feet, staring at the speaker, as the electronic voice continued. 'Neighbor reports a car engine running in the closed garage at 405 Montgomery Way. Anyone in the vicinity, respond.'

Tal Simms looked up at the speaker and hesitated only a moment. Soon, he was sprinting out of the building. He was halfway out of the parking lot, doing seventy in his tinny auto, when he realized that he'd neglected to put his seat belt on. He reached for it but lost the car to a skid and gave up and sped toward the suburb of Hamilton on the Hudson, five miles away from the office.

You couldn't exactly call any of Westbrook County desolate, but Hamilton and environs were surrounded by native-wood parks and the estates of very wealthy men and women who liked their privacy; most of the land here was zoned five or ten acres, and some homes were on much larger tracts. The land Tal was now speeding past was a deserted mess of old forest, vines, brambles, jutting rocks. It was not far from here, he reflected, that Washington Irving had thought up the macabre tale of the Headless Horseman.

Normally a cautious, patient driver, Tal wove madly from lane to lane, laying on the horn often. But he didn't consider the illogicality of what he was doing. He pictured raspberry-brown blood in the Bensons' den, pictured the unsteady handwriting of their last note.

We'll be together forever . . .

He raced through downtown Hamilton at nearly three times the speed limit. As if the Headless Horseman himself were galloping close behind.

His gray Accord swerved down the long driveway leading to the Whitley house, bounding off the asphalt and taking out a bed of blooming azaleas.

He grimaced at the damage as he skidded to a stop in front of the doorway.

Leaping from his car, he noticed a Hamilton Village police car and a boxy county ambulance pull up. Two officers and two medical technicians jogged to meet him and they all sprinted to the garage door. He smelled fumes and could hear the rattle of a car engine inside.

As a uniformed cop banged on the door, Tal noticed a handwritten note taped to the siding.

WARNING: THE GARAGE IS FILLED WITH DANGROUS FUMES. WE'VE LEFT THE REMOTE CONTROL ON THE GROUN IN FRONT OF THE FLOWER POT. PLEASE USE IT TO THE DOOR AND LET IT AIR OUT BEFORE ENTRING.

'No!' Tal began tugging futilely at the door, which was locked from the inside. In the dark they couldn't immediately find the remote and a fireman with an axe ran to the side door and broke it open with one swing.

But they were too late.

To save either of them.

Once again it was a multiple suicide. And another husband and wife, too.

Samuel and Elizabeth Whitley were in the garage, reclining in an open convertible, an old-fashioned MG sports car. While one officer had shut off the engine and firemen rigged a vent fan, the medical techs had pulled them out of the car and rested them on the driveway. They'd attempted to revive them but it was futile. The couple had been very efficient in their planning; they'd sealed the doors, vents and windows of the garage with duct tape. Shades had been drawn, so no one could look inside and interrupt their deaths.

Talbot Simms stared at them, numb. No blood this time but the deaths were just as horrible to him – seeing the bodies themselves and noting the detachment in their planning: the thoughtfulness of the warning note, its cordial tone, the care in sealing the garage. And the underlying uneasiness; like the Bensons' note, this note was written in unsteady writing and there were misspellings – 'dangrous' – and a missing word or two: 'use it to the door . . .'

An interview of the neighbors who happened to hear the car engine's unusual rattle wasn't helpful. They'd seen nothing.

The uniformed officers made a circuit of the house, to make certain nobody else was inside and had been affected by the carbon monoxide. Tal entered, too, but hesitated at first when he smelled a strong odor of fumes. But then he realized that the scent wasn't auto exhaust but smoke from the fireplace. A glance at the brandy glasses and a dusty bottle on the table in front of a small couch. They'd had a final romantic drink together in front of a fire – and then died.

'Anybody else here?' Tal asked the cops as they returned to the main floor.

'No, it's clean. Neatest house I've ever seen. Looks like it was just scrubbed. Weird cleaning the house to kill yourself.'

In the kitchen they found another note, the handwriting just as unsteady as the warning about the gas.

TO OUR FRIENDS and FAMILY:
WE dO THIS WITH GREAT JOY IN HEARTS and WITH LOVE FOR EVERONE IN OUR FAMILY and EVERYONE WE'VE KNOWN. DON'T FEEL aNY SORROW; WE'VE NEVER bEEN HaPPIER.

The letter ended with the name, address and phone number of their attorney. Tal lifted his cell phone from his pocket and called the number.

'Hello.'

'Mr Wells, please. This is Detective Simms with the county police.'

A hesitation. 'Yes, sir?' the voice asked.

The pause was now on Tal's part. 'Mr Wells?'

'That's right.'

'You're the Whitleys' attorney?'

'That's right. What's this about?'

Tal took a deep breath. 'I'm sorry to tell you that they've . . . passed away. It was a suicide. We found your name in their note.'

'My, God, no . . . What happened?'

'How, you mean? In their garage. Their car.'

'When?'

'Tonight. A little while ago.'

'No! . . . Both of them? Not both of them?'

'I'm afraid so,' Tal replied.

There was a long pause. Finally the lawyer, clearly shaken, whispered, 'I should've guessed.'

'How's that? Had they talked about it?'

'No, no. But Sam was sick.'

'Sick?'

'His heart. It was pretty serious.'

Just like Don Benson.

More common denominators.

'His wife? Was she sick, too?'

'Oh, Elizabeth. No. She was in pretty good health . . . Does the daughter know?'

'They have a daughter?' This news instantly made the deaths exponentially more tragic.

'She lives in the area. I'll call her.' He sighed. 'That's what they pay me for . . . Well, thank you, Officer . . . What was your name again?'

'Simms.'

'Thank you.'

Tal put his phone away and started slowly through the house. It reminded him of the Bensons'. Wealthy, tasteful, subdued. Only more so. The Whitleys were, he guessed, much richer.

Glancing at the pictures on the wall, many of which showed a cute little girl who'd grown into a beautiful young woman.

He was grateful that the lawyer would be making the call to their daughter.

Tal walked into the kitchen. No calendars here. Nothing that gave any suggestion they intended to kill themselves.

He looked again at the note.

Joy . . . Never been happier.

Nearby was another document. He looked it over and frowned.

Curious. It was a receipt for the purchase of a restored MG automobile. Whitley'd paid for a deposit on the car earlier but had given the dealer the balance today.

Tal walked to the garage and hesitated before entering. But he steeled up his courage and stepped inside, glanced at the tarps covering the bodies. He located the vehicle identification number. Yes, this was the same car as on the receipt.

Whitley had bought an expensive restored antique vehicle today, driven it home and then killed himself.

Why?

There was motion in the driveway. Tal watched a long, dark gray van pull up outside. *Leighey's Funeral Home* was printed on the side. Already? Had the officers called, or the lawyer? Two men got out of the hearse and walked up to a uniformed officer. They seemed to know each other.

Then Tal paused. He noticed something familiar. He picked up a book on a table in the den. *Making the Final Journey.*

The same book the Bensons had.

Too many common denominators. The suicide book, the dangerous but not necessarily terminal heart diseases, spouses also dying.

Tal walked into the living room and found the older trooper filling out a form – not *his* questionnaire, Tal noticed, though every law enforcer in Westbrook was supposed to have them. Tal asked one of the men from the funeral home, 'What're you doing with the bodies?'

'Instructions were cremation as soon as possible.'

'Can we hold off on that?'

'Hold off?' he asked and glanced at the Hamilton officer. 'How do you mean, Detective?'

Tal said, 'Get an autopsy?'

'Why?'

'Just wondering if we can.'

'You're county,' the heavyset officer said. 'You're the boss. Only, I mean, you know – you can't do it halfway. Either you declare a twenty-one-twenty-four or you don't.'

Oh, *that*. He wondered what exactly it was.

A glance at the sports car. 'Okay, I'll do that. I'm declaring a twenty-four-twenty-one.'

'You mean twenty-one-twenty-four.'

'That's what I meant to say.'

'You sure about this?' the officer asked, looking uncertainly toward the funeral home assistant, who was frowning; even he apparently knew more about the damn 2124 than Tal did.

The statistician looked outside and saw the other man from the funeral home pull a stretcher out of the back of the hearse and walk toward the bodies.

'Yes,' he said firmly. 'I'm sure.' And tapped loudly on the window, gesturing for the man to stop.

+ − < = > ÷

The next morning, Monday, Tal saw the head of the Crime Scene Unit walk into the detective pen and head straight toward LaTour's office. He was carrying a half-dozen folders.

He had a gut feeling that this was the Whitley crime-scene report and was out of his office fast, to intercept him. 'Hey, how you doing? That about the Whitley case?'

'Yeah. It's just the preliminary. But there was an expedite on it. Is Greg in? LaTour?'

'I think it's for me.'

'You're . . .'

'Simms.'

'Oh, yeah,' the man said, looking at the request attached to the report. 'I didn't notice. I figured it was LaTour. Being head of Homicide, you know.'

A 2124, it turned out, was a declaration that a death was suspicious. Like hitting a fire alarm button, it set all kinds of activities in motion – getting Crime Scene to search the house, collect evidence, record friction ridge prints and photograph and video the scene; scheduling autopsies; and alerting the prosecutor's office that a homicide investigation case file had been started. In his five years on the job Tal had never gotten so many calls before ten o'clock as he had this morning.

Tal glanced into the captain's office then LaTour's. Nobody seemed to notice that a statistician who'd never issued a parking ticket in his life was clutching crime-scene files.

Except Shellee, who subtly blessed herself and winked.

Tal asked the crime-scene detective, 'Preliminary, you said. What else're you waiting for?'

'Phone records, handwriting confirmation of the note, and autopsy results. Hey, I'm really curious. What'd you find that made you think this was suspicious? Fits the classic profile of every suicide I've ever worked.'

'Some things.'

'Things,' the seasoned cop said, nodding slowly. 'Things. Ah. Got a suspect?'

'Not yet.'

'Ah. Well, good luck. You'll need it.'

Back in his office Tal carefully filed away the spreadsheet he'd been working on, then opened the CSU files. He spread the contents out on his desk.

We begin with inspiration, a theorem, an untested idea: There is a perfect odd number. There is a point at which *pi* repeats. The universe *is* infinite.

A mathematician then attempts to construct a proof that shows irrefutably that his position either is correct or cannot be correct.

Tal Simms knew how to create such proofs with numbers.

But to prove the theorem that there was something suspicious about the deaths of the Bensons and the Whitleys? He was at a loss and stared at the hieroglyphics of the crime-scene reports as he grew increasingly discouraged. He had basic academy training, of course, but beyond that he had no investigation skills or experience.

But then he realized that perhaps this wasn't quite accurate. He did have one talent that might help: the cornerstone of his profession as a mathematician – logic.

He turned his analytical mind to the materials on his desk as he examined each item carefully. He first picked the photos of the Whitleys' bodies. All in graphic, colorful detail. They troubled him a great deal. Still, he forced himself to examine them carefully, every inch. After some time he decided that nothing suggested that the Whitleys had been forced into the car or had struggled with any assailants.

He set the photos aside and read the documents in the reports themselves. There were no signs of any break-in, though the front door wasn't locked, so someone might have simply walked in. But with the absence of any foul play this seemed unlikely. And their jewelry, cash and other valuables were untouched.

One clue, though, suggested that all was not as it seemed. The Latents team found that both notes contained, in addition to Sam Whitley's,

Tal's and the police officers' prints, smudges that were probably from gloved hands or fingers protected by a cloth or tissue. The team had also found glove prints in the den where the couple had had their last drink, the room where the note had been found, and in the garage. It was, however, impossible to tell if they had been made before or after the deaths.

Gloves? Tal wondered. Curious.

The team had also found fresh tire prints on the driveway. The prints didn't match the MG, the other cars owned by the victims, or the vehicles driven by the police, the medical team or the funeral home. The report concluded that the car had been there within the three hours prior to death. The tread marks were indistinct, so that the brand of tire couldn't be determined, but the wheelbase meant the vehicle was a small one.

A search of the trace evidence revealed several off-white cotton fibers – one on the body of Elizabeth Whitley and one on the living-room couch – that didn't appear to match what the victims were wearing or any of the clothes in their closets. An inventory of drugs in the medicine cabinets and kitchen revealed no antidepressants. This suggested, even if tenuously, that mood problems and thoughts of suicide might not have been a theme in the Whitley house recently.

Tal rose, walked to his doorway and called Shellee in.

'Hi, boss. How was your weekend?'

'Fine,' he said absently. 'I need you to do something for me.'

'Are you—? I mean, you look tired.'

'Yes, yes, I'm fine. It's just about this case.'

'What case?'

'The suicide.'

'Oh. What—?'

'I need to find out if anybody's bought a book called *Making the Final Journey*. Then something about suicide and euthanasia.'

'A book. Sure.'

'I don't remember exactly. But *Making the Journey* or *Making the Final Journey* is the start of the title.'

'Okay. And I'm supposed to check on—?'

'If anybody bought it.'

'I mean, everywhere? There're probably a lot of—'

'For now, just in Westbrook County. In the last couple of weeks. Bookstores. And all the online booksellers, too.'

'Hey, can I be a cop?'

Tal hesitated. But then he said, 'Oh, hell, sure. You want, you can be a detective.'

'Yippee,' she said. 'Detective Shellee Bingham.'

'And if they *haven't* sold any, give them my name and tell them if they *do*, call us right away.'

'We need a warrant or anything?' Detective Shellee asked, thoughtful now.

Did they?

'Hmm. I don't know. Let's just try it without and see what they say.'

Ten minutes after she left, Tal felt a shadow over him and he looked up to see Captain Ronald Dempsey's six-foot-three form fill the doorway in his ubiquitous striped shirt, his sleeves ubiquitously rolled up.

The man's round face smiled pleasantly. But Tal thought immediately: Busted.

'Captain.'

'Hey, Tal.' Dempsey leaned against the doorjamb, looking over the desktop. 'Got a minute?'

'Sure do.'

Tal had known that they'd find out about the 2124 and was going to Dempsey with it soon, of course; but he'd hoped to wait until his proof about the suspicious suicide was somewhat further developed.

'Heard about the twenty-one-twenty-four at the Whitleys'.'

'Sure.'

'What's up with *that*?'

Tal explained about the two suicides, the common denominators.

Dempsey nodded. 'Kind of a coincidence, sure. But you know, Tal, we don't have a lot of resources for full investigations. Like, we've only got one dedicated homicide Crime Scene Unit.'

'Didn't know that.'

'And there was a shooting in Rolling Hills Estates last night. Two people shot up bad, one died. The unit was late running that scene 'cause you had them in Hamilton.'

'I'm sorry about that, Captain.'

'It's also expensive. Sending out CS.'

'Expensive? I didn't think about that.'

'Thousands, I'm talking. Crime Scene bills everything back to us. Every time they go out. Then there're lab tests and autopsies and every-thing. The ME, too. You know what an autopsy costs?'

'They *bill* us?' Tal asked.

'It's just the more we save for the county the better we look, you know.'

'Right. I guess it would be expensive.'

'You bet.' No longer smiling, the captain adjusted his sleeves. 'Other thing is, the way I found out: I heard from their daughter. Sandra Whitley. She was going to make funeral arrangements and then she hears about the autopsy. Phew . . . she's pissed off. Threatening to sue . . . I'm going to have to answer questions. So. Now, what exactly made you twenty-one-twenty-four the scene, Tal?'

He scanned the papers on his desk, uneasy, wondering where to start. 'Well, a couple of things. They'd just bought—'

'Hold on there a minute,' the captain said, holding up a finger. Dempsey leaned out the door and shouted, 'LaTour! . . . Hey, LaTour?'

'What?' came the grumbling baritone.

'Come're for a minute. I'm with Simms.'

Tal heard the big man make his way toward the Unreal Crimes side of the detective pen. The ruddy, goatee'd face appeared in the office. Ignoring Tal, he listened as the captain explained about the Whitleys' suicide.

'Another one, huh?'

'Tal declared a twenty-one-twenty-four.'

The homicide cop nodded noncommittally. 'Uh-huh. Why?'

The question was directed toward Dempsey, who turned toward Tal.

'Well, I was looking at the Bensons' deaths and I pulled up the standard statistical profile on suicides in Westbrook County. Now, when you look at all the attributes—'

'Attributes?' LaTour asked, frowning, as if tasting sand.

'Right. The attributes of the Bensons' death – and the Whitleys', too, now – they're way out of the standard range. Their deaths are outliers.'

'Out-liars? The fuck's that?'

Tal explained. In statistics an outlier was an event significantly different from a group of related events in the same category. He gave a concrete example. 'Say you're analyzing five murderers. Three perps killed a single victim each, one of them killed two victims, and the final man was a serial killer who'd murdered twenty people. To draw any meaningful conclusions from that, you need to treat the last one as an outlier and analyze him separately. Otherwise, your analysis'll be mathematically correct but misleading. Running the numbers, we see that the mean – the average – number of victims killed by each suspect is five. But that exaggerates the homicidal nature of the first four men, and underplays the last one. See what I mean?'

The frown on LaTour's face suggested he didn't. But he said, 'So you're saying these two suicides're different from most of the others in Westbrook?'

'*Significantly* different. Fewer than six per cent of the population kill themselves when they're facing a possibly terminal illness. That number drops to two point six per cent when the victim has medical insurance, and down to point nine when the net worth of the victim is over one million dollars. It drops even further when the victims are married and are in the relatively young category of sixty-five to seventy-five, like these folks. And love-pact deaths are only two per cent of suicides nationwide, and ninety-one per cent of those involve victims under the age of twenty-one . . . Now, what do you think the odds are that two heart patients would take their own lives, and their wives', in the space of two days?'

'I don't really know, Tal,' LaTour said, clearly uninterested. 'What else you got? Suspicious, I mean.'

'Okay, the Whitleys'd just bought a car earlier that day. Rare, antique MG. Why do that if you're going to kill yourself?'

LaTour offered, 'They needed a murder weapon. Didn't want a gun. Probably there was something about the MG that meant something to them. From when they were younger, you know. They wanted to go out that way.'

'Makes sense,' Dempsey said, tugging at a sleeve.

'There's more,' Tal said and explained about the gloves, the fiber, the tire tread, the smudges on the note. 'I'm thinking that somebody else was there around the time they killed themselves. Or just after.'

LaTour said, 'Lemme take a look.'

Tal pushed the report toward him. The big cop examined everything closely. Then shook his head. 'I just don't see it,' he said to the captain. 'No evidence of a break-in or struggle . . . The note?' He shrugged. 'Looks authentic. I mean, Documents'll tell us for sure but look—' He held up the Whitleys' checkbook ledger and the suicide note, side by side. The script was virtually identical. 'Smudges from gloves on paper? We see that on every piece of paper we find at a scene. Hell, half the pieces of paper *here* have smudges on them that look like smeared FRs—'

'FRs?'

'Friction ridges,' LaTour muttered. '*Fingerprints*. Smudges – from the manufacturer, stockers, getting moved around on shelves.'

'The fiber?' LaTour leaned forward and lifted a tiny white strand off Tal's suit jacket. 'This's the same type the Crime Scene found. Cotton worsted. See it all the time in clothing. The fibers at the Whitleys' could've come from anywhere. It might've come from you.' Shuffling sloppily through the files with his massive paws. 'Okay, the gloves and the tread marks? Those're Playtex kitchen gloves; I recognize the ridges. No perps ever use them because the wear patterns can be traced . . .' He held up the checkbook ledger again. 'Lookit the check the wife wrote today. To Esmeralda Costanzo, "For cleaning services". The housekeeper was in yesterday, cleaned the house wearing the gloves – maybe she even straightened up the stack of paper they used later for the suicide note, left the smudges then. The tread marks? That's about the size of a small import. Just the sort that a cleaning woman'd be driving. They were hers. Bet you any money.'

Though he didn't like the man's message, Tal was impressed at the way his mind worked. He'd made all those deductions – extremely *logical* deductions – based on a three-minute examination of the data.

'Got a case needs lookin' at,' LaTour grumbled and tossed the report onto Tal's desk. He clomped back to his office.

Breaking the silence that followed, Dempsey said, 'Hey, I know you don't get out into the field much. Must get frustrating to sit in the office all day long, not doing . . . you know . . .'

Real police work? Tal wondered if that's what the captain was hesitating to say.

'More active stuff' turned out to be the captain's euphemism. 'You probably feel sometimes like you don't fit in.'

He's probably at home humping his calculator . . .

'We've all felt that way sometimes. Honest. But being out in the field's not what it's cracked up to be. Not like TV, you know. And you're the best at what you do, Tal. Statistician. Man, that's a hard job. An important job. Let's face it' – lowering his voice – 'guys like Greg wouldn't know a number if it jumped out and bit 'em on the ass. You've got a real special talent.'

Tal weathered the condescension with a faint smile, which obscured the anger beneath his flushed face. The speech was clearly out of a personnel management training manual. Dempsey had just plugged in 'statistician' for 'traffic detail' or 'receptionist'.

'Okay, now, don't you have some numbers to crunch? We've got that mid-year assignment meeting coming up and nobody can put together a report like you, my friend.'

Monday evening's drive to the Whitleys' house took him considerably longer than the night before, since he drove the way he usually did: within the speed limit, perfectly centered in his lane (and with the belt firmly clasped this time).

Noting how completely he'd destroyed the shrubs last night, Tal parked in front of the door and ducked under the crime-scene tape. He stepped inside, smelling again the sweet, poignant scent of the wood smoke from the couple's last cocktail hour.

Inside their house – a side door was unlocked – he pulled on latex gloves he'd bought at a drugstore on the way here (thinking only when he got to the checkout lane: Damn, they probably have hundreds of these back in the detective pen). Then he began working his way through the house, picking up anything that Crime Scene had missed that might shed some light on the mystery of the Whitleys' deaths.

Greg LaTour's bluntness and Captain Dempsey's pep talk, in other words, had no effect on him. All intellectually honest mathematicians welcome the disproving of their theorems as much as the proving. But the more LaTour had laid out the evidence that the 2124 was wrong, the more Tal's resolve grew to get to the bottom of the deaths.

There *was* an odd perfect number out there, and there *was* something unusual about the deaths of the Bensons and the Whitleys; Tal was determined to write the proof.

Address books, Day-Timers, receipts, letters, stacks of papers, piles of business cards for lawyers, repairmen, restaurants, investment advisors, accountants. He felt a chill as he read one for some New Age organization, the Lotus Foundation for Alternative Treatment, tucked in with all the practical and mundane cards, evidence of the desperation of rational people frightened by impending death.

A snap of floorboard, a faint clunk. A metallic sound. It startled him. He'd parked in the front of the house; whoever'd arrived would know he was here. The police tape and crime-scene notice were clear about forbidding entry and since this was clearly not a 'case' in anybody's mind but his he doubted that the visitor was a cop.

And he realized with a start a corollary of his theorem that the Whitleys might have been murdered was, of course, that there might be a murderer, a person not at all pleased about his investigating the deaths.

He reached for his hip and realized, to his dismay, that he'd left his pistol in his desk at the office. The only suspects Tal had ever met face-to-face were benign accountants or investment bankers, and even then the confrontation was usually in court and he never carried the gun. Palms sweating, Tal looked around for something he could use to protect himself. He was in the bedroom, surrounded by books, clothes, furniture. Nothing he could use as a weapon.

He looked out the window.

A twenty-foot drop to the flagstone patio.

Was he too proud to hide under the bed?

Footsteps sounded closer, walking up the stairs. The carpet muted them but the old floorboards creaked as the intruder got closer. Maybe there was no danger. But then why hadn't the visitor announced his presence?

No, he decided, not too proud for the bed. But that didn't seem to be the wisest choice. Escape was better.

Out the window. Tal opened it, swung the leaded-glass panes outward. No grass below; just a flagstone deck dotted with booby traps of patio furniture.

He heard the metallic click of a gun. The steps grew closer, making directly for the bedroom.

Okay, jump. He glanced down. Aim for the padded lawn divan. You'll sprain your ankle but you won't get shot.

He put his hand on the windowsill, was about to boost himself over when a voice filled the room, a woman's voice. 'Who the hell're you?'

Tal turned fast, observing a slim blond woman in her mid or late thirties, eyes narrow. She was smoking a cigarette and putting a gold lighter back into her purse – the metallic sound he'd assumed was a gun. There was something familiar – and troubling – about her and he realized that, yes, he'd seen her face – in the snapshots on the walls. 'You're their daughter.'

'Who are you?' she repeated in a gravelly voice.

'You shouldn't be in here. It's a crime scene.'

'You're a cop. Let me see some ID.' She glanced at his latex-gloved hand on the window, undoubtedly wondering what he'd been about to do.

He offered her the badge and identification card.

She glanced at them carefully. 'You're the one who did it?'

'What?'

'You had them taken to the morgue? Had them goddamn *butchered*?'

'I had some questions about their deaths. I followed procedures.'

More or less.

'So you *were* the one. Detective Talbot Simms.' She'd memorized his name. 'I'll want to be sure you're personally named in the suit.'

'You're not supposed to be here,' Tal said. 'The scene hasn't been released yet.'

He remembered this from a cop show on TV.

'Fuck your scene.'

A different response than on the TV show.

'Let *me* see some ID,' Tal said, stepping forward, feeling more confident now.

The staring match began.

He added cheerfully, 'I'm happy to call some officers to take you downtown.' This – from another show – was a bit inaccurate; the Westbrook Sheriff's Department wasn't downtown at all. It was in a strip mall next to a large Stop & Shop grocery.

She reluctantly showed him her driver's license. Sandra Kaye Whitley, thirty-six. He recognized the address, a very exclusive part of the county.

'What was so fucking mysterious about their deaths? They killed themselves.'

Tal observed something interesting about her. Yes, she was angry. But she wasn't sad.

'We can't talk about an open case.'

'What *case*?' Sandra snapped. 'You keep saying that.'

'Well, it was a murder, you know.'

Her hand paused then continued carrying her cigarette to her lips. She asked coolly, 'Murder?'

Tal said, 'Your father turned the car ignition on. Technically he murdered your mother.'

'That's bullshit.'

Probably it was. But he continued anyway. 'Had they ever had a history of depression?'

She debated for a moment then answered. 'My father's disease was serious. And my mother didn't want to live without him.'

'But his illness wasn't terminal, was it?'

'He wasn't on a goddamn feeding tube, no. But he *was* going to die. And he wanted to die with dignity.'

Tal felt he was losing this contest; she kept going on the defensive. He tried to think more like Greg LaTour. 'What exactly're you doing here?'

'It's my family's house,' she snapped. 'My house. I grew up here. I wanted to see it. They *were* my parents, you know.'

He nodded. 'Of course . . . I'm sorry for your loss. I just want to make sure that everything's what it seems to be. Just doing my job.'

She shrugged and stubbed the cigarette out in a heavy crystal ashtray on the dresser. She noticed, sitting next to it, a picture of her with her parents. For a long moment she stared at it then turned away, hiding tears from him. She wiped her face then turned back. 'I am an attorney, you know. I'm going to have one of my litigation partners look at this situation through a microscope, Detective.'

'That's fine, Ms Whitley,' Tal said. 'Can I ask what you put in your purse earlier?'

'Purse?'

'When you were downstairs.'

A hesitation. 'It's nothing important.'

'This is a crime scene. You can't take anything. That's a felony. Which I'm sure you knew. Being an attorney, as you say.'

Was it a felony? he wondered.

At least lawyer Sandra didn't seem to know it wasn't.

'You can give it to me now and I'll forget about the incident. Or we can keep going with that trip downtown.'

She held his eye for a moment, slicing him into tiny pieces, as she debated. Then she opened her purse. She handed him a small stack of mail. 'It was in the mailbox to be picked up. But with that yellow tape all over the place the mailman didn't come by. I was just going to mail it.'

'I'll take it.'

She held the envelopes out to him with a hand that seemed to be quivering slightly. He took them in his gloved hands.

In fact, he'd had no idea that she'd put anything in her purse; he'd had a flash of intuition. Talbot Simms suddenly felt a rush; statisticians never bluff.

Sandra looked around the room and her eyes seemed mournful again. But he decided it was more anger he was seeing. She said icily, 'You will be hearing from my litigation partner, Detective Simms. Oh, you will. Shut the lights out when you leave, unless the county's going to be paying the electric bill.'

'I'm getting coffee, boss. You want some?'

'Sure, thanks,' he told Shellee.

It was the next morning and Tal was continuing to pore over the material he'd collected. Some new information had just arrived: the Whitleys' phone records for the past month, the autopsy results and the handwriting analysis of the suicide note.

He found nothing immediately helpful about the phone records and set them aside, grimacing as he looked for someplace to rest them. There wasn't any free space on his desk and so he stacked them, as orderly as he could, on top of another stack. It made him feel edgy, the mess, but there wasn't anything else he could do, short of moving another desk into his office – and he could imagine the ribbing he'd take for that.

Data plural . . . humping his calculator . . .

Tal looked over the handwriting expert's report first. The woman said that she could state with ninety-eight per cent certainty that Sam Whitley had written the note, though the handwriting had been unsteady, the grammar flawed, too, which was unusual for a man of his education.

The garage is filled with dangrous fumes.

Finally Tal turned to the autopsy results. Death was, as they'd thought, due to carbon monoxide poisoning. There were no contusions, tissue damage or ligature marks to suggest they'd been forced into the car. There was alcohol in the blood, .010 per cent in Sam's system, 0.19 in Elizabeth's, neither particularly high. But they both had medication in their bloodstreams, too. One, in particular, intrigued him.

Present in both victims were unusually large quantities of 9-fluoro, 7-chloro-1,3-dihydro-1-methyl-5-phenyl-2H-1,4-benzodiazepin, 5-hydroxytryptamine and N-(1-phenethyl-4-piperidyl) propionanilide citrate.

This was, the ME's report continued, an analgesic/anti-anxiety drug sold under the trade name 'Luminux'. The amount in their blood meant that the couple had nearly three times the normally prescribed strength of the drug, though it did not, the ME concluded, make them more susceptible to carbon monoxide poisoning or otherwise directly contribute to their deaths.

Tal supposed it had been this combination of liquor and the drug that had been responsible for the unsteady handwriting.

Looking over his desk – too goddamn many papers! – he finally found another document and carefully read the inventory of the house, which the Crime Scene Unit had prepared. The Whitleys had plenty of medicine – for Sam's heart problem, as well as for Elizabeth's arthritis and other maladies – but no Luminux.

Shellee brought him the coffee. Her eyes cautiously took in the cluttered desktop.

'Thanks,' he muttered.

'Still lookin' tired, boss.'

'Didn't sleep well.' Instinctively he pulled his striped tie straight, kneaded the knot to make sure it was tight.

'It's fine, boss,' she whispered, nodding at his shirt. Meaning: Quit fussing.

He winked at her.

Thinking about common denominators . . .

The Bensons' suicide note, too, had been sloppy, Tal recalled. He rummaged through the piles on his desk and found their lawyer's card then dialed the man's office and was put through to him.

'Mr Metzer, this's Detective Simms. I met you at the Bensons' a few days ago.'

'Right. I remember.'

'This is a little unusual but I'd like permission to take a blood sample.'

'From me?' he asked in a startled voice.

'No, no, from the Bensons.'

'Why?'

'I'd like to update our database about medicines and diseases of recent suicides. It'll be completely anonymous.'

'Oh. Well, sorry, but they were cremated this morning.'

'They were? That was fast.'

'I don't know if it was fast or it was slow. But that's what they wanted. It was in their instructions to me. They wanted to be cremated as soon as possible and the contents of the house sold—'

'Wait. You're telling me—'

'The contents of the house sold immediately.'

'When's that going to happen?'

'It's probably already done. We've had dealers in the house since Sunday morning. I don't think there's much left.'

'Can they do that? Isn't it a crime scene?'

'There were some Greeley police officers there. They said the county called it a suicide so they didn't think anybody'd care.'

Tal remembered the man at the Whitleys' house – there to arrange for the liquidation of the estate. He wished he'd known about 2124-ing scenes at the Bensons' house.

Common denominators . . .

'Do you still have the suicide note?'

'I didn't take it. I imagine it was thrown out when the service cleaned the house.'

This's all way too fast, Tal thought. He looked over the papers on his desk. 'Do you know if either of them was taking a drug called Luminux?'

'I don't have a clue.'

'Can you give me Mr Benson's cardiologist's name?'

A pause, then the lawyer said, 'I suppose it's okay. Yeah. Dr Peter Brody. Over in Glenstead.'

Tal was about to hang up but then a thought occurred to him. 'Mr Metzer, when I met you on Friday, didn't you tell me the Bensons weren't religious?'

'That's right. They were atheists . . . What's this all about, Detective?'

'Like I say – just getting some statistics together. That's all. Thanks for your time.'

He got Dr Brody's number and called the doctor's office. The man was on vacation and his head nurse was reluctant to talk about patients, even deceased ones. She did admit, though, that Brody had not prescribed Luminux for them.

Tal then called the head of Crime Scene and learned that the gun the Bensons had killed themselves with was in an evidence locker. He asked that Latents look it over for prints. 'Can you do a rush on it?'

'Happy to. It's comin' outa your budget, Detective,' the man said cheerfully. 'Be about ten, fifteen minutes.'

'Thanks.'

As he waited for the results on the gun, Tal opened his briefcase and noticed the three letters Sandra Whitley had in her purse at her parents' house. Putting on a pair of Buy-Rite Pharmacy latex gloves once again, he ripped open the three envelopes and examined the contents.

The first one contained a bill from their lawyer for four hours of legal work, performed that month. The project, the bill summarized, was for 'estate planning services'.

Did he mean redoing the will? Was this another common denominator? Metzer had said that the Bensons had just redone theirs.

The second letter was an insurance form destined for the Cardiac Support Center at Westbrook Hospital, where Sam had been a patient.

Nothing unusual here.

But then he opened the third letter.

He sat back in his chair, looking at the ceiling then down at the letter once more.

Debating.

Then deciding that he didn't have any choice. When you're writing a proof you go anywhere the numbers take you. Tal rose and walked across the office, to the Real Crimes side of the pen. He leaned into an open door and knocked on the jamb. Greg LaTour was sitting back in his chair, boots up. He was reading a short document. 'Fucking liar,' he muttered and put a large check mark next to one of the paragraphs. Looking up, he cocked an eyebrow.

Humping his calculator . . .

Tal tried to be pleasant. 'Greg. You got a minute?'

'Just.'

'I want to talk to you about the case.'

'Case?' The man frowned. 'Which case?'

'The Whitleys.'

'Who?'

'The suicides.'

'From Sunday? Yeah, okay. Drew a blank. I don't think of suicides as cases.' LaTour's meaty hand grabbed another piece of paper and pulled it in front of him. He looked down at it.

'You said that the cleaning lady'd probably been there? She'd left the glove prints? And the tire treads.'

It didn't seem that he remembered at first. Then he nodded. 'And?'

'Look.' He showed LaTour the third letter he'd found at the Whitleys. It was a note to Esmeralda Costanzo, the Whitleys' cleaning lady, thanking her for her years of help and saying they wouldn't be needing her services any longer. They'd enclosed the check that LaTour had spotted in the register.

'They'd put the check in the mail,' Tal pointed out. 'That means she wasn't there the day they died. Somebody else wore the gloves. And I got to thinking about it? Why would a cleaning lady wear kitchen gloves to clean the rest of the house? Doesn't make sense.'

LaTour shrugged. His eyes dipped to the document on his desk and then returned once more to the letter Tal held.

The statistician added, 'And that means the car wasn't hers either. The tread marks. Somebody else was there around the time they died.'

'Well, Tal—'

'Couple other things,' he said quickly. 'Both the Whitleys had high amounts of a prescription drug in their bloodstream. Some kind of narcotic. Luminux. But there were no prescription bottles for it in their house. And their lawyer'd just done some estate work for them. Maybe revising their wills.'

'You gonna kill yourself, you gonna revise your will. That ain't very suspicious.'

'But then I met the daughter.'

'Their daughter?'

'She broke into the house, looking for something. She'd pocketed the mail but she might've been looking for something else. Maybe she got the Luminux bottles. She didn't want anybody to find them. I didn't search her. I didn't think about it at the time.'

'What's this with the drugs? They didn't OD.'

'Well, maybe she got them doped up, had them change their will and talked them into killing themselves.'

'Yeah, right,' LaTour muttered. 'That's outa some bad movie.'

Tal shrugged. 'When I mentioned murder she freaked out.'

'Murder? Why'd you mention murder?' He scratched his huge belly, looking for the moment just like his nickname.

'I meant murder–suicide. The husband turning the engine on.'

LaTour gave a grunt – Tal hadn't realized that you could make a sound like that condescending. But he continued, 'And, you know, she had this attitude.'

'Well, now, Tal, you *did* send her parents to the county morgue. You know what they do to you there, don'tcha? Knives and saws. That's gotta piss the kid off a little, you know.'

'Yes, she was pissed. But mostly, I think, 'cause I was there, checking out what'd happened. And you know what she didn't seem upset about?'

'What's that?'

'Her parents. Them dying. She *seemed* to be crying. But I couldn't tell. It could've been an act.'

'She was in shock. Skirts get that way.'

Tal persisted, 'Then I checked on the first couple. The Bensons? They were cremated right after they died and their estate liquidated in a day or two.'

'Liquidated? It was a crime scene. They can't do that.'

Tal said, 'Well, everybody kept saying, it's only a suicide . . . the town released the scene.'

LaTour lifted an eyebrow and finally delivered a comment that was neither condescending nor sarcastic. 'Cremated that fast, hmm? Seems odd, yeah. I'll give you that.'

'And the Bensons' lawyer told me something else. They were atheists, both of them. But their suicide note said they'd be in heaven forever or something like that. Atheists aren't going to say that. I'm thinking maybe *they* might've been drugged, too. With that Luminux.'

'What does their doctor—'

'No, he didn't prescribe it. But maybe somebody slipped it to them. Their suicide note was unsteady, too, sloppy, just like the Whitleys'.'

'What's the story on *their* doctor?'

'I haven't got that far yet.'

'Maybe, maybe, maybe.' LaTour squinted. 'But that gardener we talked to at the Benson place? He said they'd been boozing it up. You did the blood work on the Whitleys. They been drinking?'

'Not too much . . . Oh, one other thing. I called their cell phone company and checked the phone records – the Whitleys'. There was a call from a pay phone forty minutes before they died. Two minutes. Just enough time to see if they're home and say you're going to stop by. And who calls from pay phones any more? Everybody's got cells, right?'

Reluctantly LaTour agreed with this.

'Look at it, Greg: two couples, both rich, live five miles from each other. Both of 'em in the country club set. Both husbands have heart disease. Two murder–suicides a few days apart. What do you think about that?'

In a weary voice LaTour said, 'Outliers, right?'

'Exactly.'

'You're thinking the bitch—'

'Who?' Tal asked.

'The daughter.'

'I didn't say that.'

'I'm not gonna quote you in the press, Tal. You——'

'Okay,' he conceded, 'she's a bitch.'

'You're thinking she's got access to her folks, there's money involved. She's doing something funky with the will or insurance.'

'It's a theorem.'

'A what?' LaTour screwed up his face.

'It's a hunch is what I'm saying.'

'Hunch. Okay. But you brought up the Bensons. The Whitley daughter isn't going to off them now, is she? I mean, why would she?'

Tal shrugged. 'I don't know. Maybe she's the Bensons' goddaughter and she was in their will, too. Or maybe her father was going into some deal with Benson that'd tie up all the estate money so the daughter'd lose out and she had to kill them both.'

'Maybe, maybe, maybe,' LaTour repeated.

Shellee appeared in the doorway and, ignoring LaTour, said, 'Latents called. They said the only prints on the gun were Mr Benson's and a few smears from cloth or paper.'

'What fucking gun?' he asked.

'I will thank you not to use that language to me,' Shellee said icily.

'I was talking to *him*,' LaTour snapped and cocked an eyebrow at Tal.

Tal said, 'The gun the Bensons killed themselves with. Smears – like on the Whitleys' suicide note.'

Shellee glanced at the wall poster behind the desk then back to the detective. Tal couldn't tell whether the look of distaste was directed at LaTour himself or the blonde in a red-white-and-blue bikini lying provocatively across the seat and teardrop gas tank of the Harley. She turned and walked back to her desk quickly, as if she'd been holding her breath.

'Okay . . . This's getting marginally fucking interesting.' LaTour glanced at the huge gold watch on his wrist. 'I gotta go. I got some time booked at the range. Come with me. Let's go waste some ammunition, talk about the case after.'

'Think I'll stay here.'

LaTour frowned, apparently unable to understand why somebody wouldn't jump at the chance to spend an hour punching holes in a piece of paper with a deadly weapon. 'You don't shoot?'

'It's just I'd rather work on this.'

Then enlightenment dawned. Tal's office was, after all, on the Unreal Crimes side of the pen. He had no interest in cop toys.

You're the best at what you do, statistician. Man, that's a hard job . . .

'Okay,' LaTour said. 'I'll check out the wills and the insurance policies. Gimme the name of the icees.'

'The—'

'The corpses, the stiffs . . . the losers who killed 'emselves, Tal. And their lawyers.'

Tal wrote down the information and handed the neat note to LaTour, who stuffed it into his plaid shirt pocket behind two large cigars. He ripped open a desk drawer and took out a big chrome automatic pistol.

Tal asked, 'What should I do?'

'Get a PII team and—'

'A what?'

'You go to the same academy as me, Tal? Post-Incident Interviewing team,' he said as if he were talking to a three-year-old. 'Use my name, and Doherty'll put one together for you. Have 'em talk to all the neighbors around the Bensons' and the Whitleys' houses. See if they saw anybody around the houses just before or after the TOD. Oh, that's—'

'Time of death.'

'You got it, my man. We'll talk this afternoon. I'll see you back here, how's four?'

'Sure. Oh, and maybe we should find out what kind of car the Whitleys' daughter drove. See if the wheelbase data match.'

'That's good thinking, Tal,' he said, looking honestly impressed. Grabbing some boxes of 9mm cartridges LaTour walked heavily out of the Detective Division.

Tal returned to his desk and arranged for the PII team. Then he called DMV, requesting information on Sandra Whitley's car. He glanced at his watch. One p.m. He realized he was hungry; he'd missed his regular lunch with his buddies from the university. He walked down to the small canteen on the second floor, bought a cheese sandwich and a diet soda and returned to his desk. As he ate he continued to pore over the pages of the crime-scene report and the documents and other evidence he himself had collected at the house.

Shellee walked past his office, then stopped fast and returned. She stared at him, then barked a laugh.

'What?' he asked.

'This is too weird, you eating at your desk.'

Hadn't he ever done that? he wondered. He asked her.

'No. Not once. Ever . . . And here you are going to crime scenes, cluttering up your desk . . . Listen, boss, on your way home?'

'Yes?'

'Watch out for flying pigs. The sky's gotta be full of 'em today.'

+ − < = > ÷

'Hi,' Tal said to the receptionist.

Offering her a big smile. Why not? She had sultry, doe eyes, a heart-shaped face, and the slim, athletic figure of a Riverdance performer.

Margaret Ludlum – according to the name plate – glanced up and cocked a pale, red eyebrow. 'Yes?'

'It's Maggie, right?'

'Can I help you?' she asked in a polite but detached tone. Tal offered a second assault of a smile then displayed his badge and ID, which resulted in a cautious frown on her freckled face.

'I'm here to see Dr Sheldon.' This was Sam Whitley's cardiologist, whose card he'd found in the couple's bedroom last night.

'It's . . .' She squinted at the ID card.

'Detective Simms.'

'Sure. Just hold on. Do you have—'

'No. An appointment? No. But I need to talk to him. It's important. About a patient. A former patient. Sam Whitley.'

She nodded knowingly and gave a slight wince. Word of the suicides would have spread fast, he assumed.

'Hold on, please.'

She made a call and a few minutes later a balding man in his fifties stepped out into the waiting room and greeted him. Dr Anthony Sheldon led Tal back into a large office, whose walls were decorated with dozens of diplomas and citations. The office was opulent, as one would expect for a man who probably made $30,000 an hour.

Gesturing for Tal to sit in a chair across the desk, Sheldon dropped into his own high-backed chair and said, 'I was troubled to hear the news.'

'We're looking into their deaths,' Tal said. 'I'd like to ask you a few questions if I could.'

'Yeah, sure. Anything I can do. It was . . . I mean, we heard it was a suicide, is that right?'

'It appeared to be. We just have a few unanswered questions. How long had you treated them?'

'Well, first, not *them*. Only Sam Whitley. He'd been referred to me by his personal GP.'

'That's Ronald Weinstein,' Tal said. Another nugget from the boxes of evidence that'd kept him up until 3 a.m. 'I just spoke to him.'

Tal had learned a few facts from the doctor, though nothing particularly helpful, except that Weinstein had not prescribed Luminux to either of the Whitleys, nor had he ever met the Bensons. Tal continued to Sheldon, 'How serious was Sam's cardiac condition?'

'Fairly serious. Hold on – let me make sure I don't misstate anything.'

Sheldon pressed a buzzer on his phone.

'Yes, Doctor?'

'Margaret, bring me the Whitley file, please.'

So, not Maggie.

'Right away.'

A moment later the woman walked briskly into the room, coolly ignoring Tal.

He decided that he liked the Celtic dancer part. He liked 'Margaret' better than 'Maggie'.

The tough-as-nails part gave him some pause.

'Thanks.'

Sheldon looked over the file. 'His heart was only working at about fifty per cent efficiency. He should've had a transplant but wasn't a good candidate for one. We were going to replace valves and several major vessels.'

'Would he have survived?'

'You mean the procedures? Or afterward?'

'Both.'

'The odds weren't good for either. The surgeries themselves were the riskiest. Sam wasn't a young man and he had severe deterioration in his blood vessels. If he'd survived that, he'd have a fifty-fifty chance for six months. After that, the odds would've improved somewhat.'

'So it wasn't hopeless.'

'Not necessarily. But, like I told him, there was also a very good chance that even if he survived he'd be bedridden for the rest of his life.'

Tal said, 'So you weren't surprised to hear that he'd killed himself?'

'Well, I'm a doctor. Suicide doesn't make sense to most of us. But he was facing a very risky procedure and a difficult, painful recovery with an uncertain outcome. When I heard that he'd died, naturally I was troubled, and guilty, too – thinking maybe I didn't explain things properly to him. But I have to say that I wasn't utterly shocked.'

'Did you know his wife?'

'She came to most of his appointments.'

'But she was in good health?'

'I don't know. But she seemed healthy.'

'They were close?'

'Oh, very devoted to each other.'

Tal looked up. 'Doctor, what's Luminux?'

'Luminux? A combination antidepressant, painkiller and anti-anxiety medication. I'm not too familiar with it.'

'Then you didn't prescribe it to Sam or his wife?'

'No – and I'd never prescribe anything to a spouse of a patient unless she was a patient, too. Why?'

'They both had unusually high levels of the drug in their bloodstream when they died.'

'Both of them?'

'Right.'

Dr Sheldon shook his head. 'That's odd . . . Was that the cause of death?'

'No, it was carbon monoxide.'

'Oh. Their car?'

'In the garage, right.'

The doctor shook his head. 'Better way to go than some, I suppose. But still . . .'

Another look at the notes. 'At their house I found an insurance form for the Cardiac Support Center here at the hospital. What's that?'

'I suggested he and Liz see someone there. They work with terminal and high-risk patients, transplant candidates. Counseling and therapy mostly.'

'Could they have prescribed the drug?'

'Maybe. They have MDs on staff.'

'I'd like to talk to them. Who should I see?'

'Dr Peter Dehoeven is the director. They're in Building J. Go back to the main lobby, take the elevator to three, turn left and keep going.'

Tal thanked the doctor and stepped back into the lobby. Cell phones weren't allowed in the hospital so he asked Margaret if he could use one of the phones on her desk. She gestured toward it distractedly and turned back to her computer. It was three forty-five and Tal had to meet Greg LaTour in fifteen minutes.

One of the Homicide Division secretaries came on the line and he told her to tell LaTour that he'd be a little late.

But she said, 'Oh, he's gone for the day.'

'Gone? We had a meeting.'

'Didn't say anything about it.'

He hung up, angry. Had LaTour just been humoring him, agreeing to help with the case to get Tal out of his hair?

He made another call – to the Cardiac Support Center. Dr Dehoeven was out but Tal made an appointment to see him at eight thirty in the morning. He hung up and nearly asked Margaret to clarify the way to the Cardiac Support Center. But Sheldon's directions were solidly implanted in his memory and he'd only bring up the subject to give it one more shot with sweet Molly Malone. But why bother? He knew to a statistical certainty that he and this red-haired lass would never be step dancing the night away then lying in bed till dawn discussing the finer points of perfect numbers.

+ − < = > ÷

'All the valves?' Seventy-two-year-old Robert Covey asked his cardiologist, who was sitting across from him. The name on the white jacket read *Dr Lansdowne* in scripty stitching, but with her frosted blond hair in a Gwyneth Paltrow bun and sly red lipstick, he thought of her only as 'Dr Jenny'.

'That's right.' She leaned forward. 'And there's more.'

For the next ten minutes she proceeded to give him the lowdown on the absurd medical extremes he'd have to endure to have a chance of seeing his seventy-third birthday.

Unfair, Covey thought. Goddamn unfair to've been singled out this way. His weight, on a six-foot-one frame, was around 180, had been all his life. He gave up smoking forty years ago. He'd taken weekend hikes every few months with Veronica until he lost her, and then had joined a hiking club where he got even more exercise than he had with his wife, outdistancing the widows who'd try to keep up with him as they flirted relentlessly.

Dr Jenny asked, 'Are you married?'

'Widower.'

'Children?'

'I have a son.'

'He live nearby?'

'No, but we see a lot of each other.'

'Anybody else in the area?' she asked.

'Not really, no.'

The doctor regarded him carefully. 'It's tough, hearing everything I've told you today. And it's going to get tougher. I'd like you to talk to somebody over at Westbrook Hospital. They have a social services department there just for heart patients. The Cardiac Support Center.'

'Shrink?'

'Counselor/nurses, they're called.'

'They wear short skirts?'

'The men don't,' the doctor said, deadpan.

'Touché. Well, thanks, but I don't think that's for me.'

'Take the number anyway. If nothing else, they're somebody to talk to.'

She took out a card and set it on the desk. He noticed that she had perfect fingernails, opalescent pink, though they were very short – as befit someone who cracked open human chests on occasion.

He asked her a number of questions about the procedures and what he could expect, sizing up his odds. Initially she was reluctant to quantify his chances but she sensed finally that he could indeed handle the numbers and told him. 'Sixty-forty against.'

'Is that optimistic or pessimistic?'

'Neither. It's realistic.'

He liked that.

There were more tests that needed to be done, the doctor explained, before any procedures could be scheduled. 'You can make the appointment with Janice.'

'Sooner rather than later?'

The doctor didn't smile when she said, 'That would be the wise choice.'

He rose. Then paused. 'Does this mean I should stop having strenuous sex?'

Dr Jenny blinked and a moment later they both laughed.

'Ain't it grand being old? All the crap you can get away with.'

'Make that appointment, Mr Covey.'

He walked toward the door. She joined him. He thought she was seeing him out but she held out her hand; he'd forgotten the card containing the name and number of the Cardiac Support Center at Westbrook Hospital.

'Can I blame my memory?'

'No way. You're sharper than me.' The doctor winked and turned back to her desk.

He made the appointment with the receptionist and left the building. Outside, still clutching the card, he noticed a trash container on the sidewalk. He veered toward it and lifted the card like a Frisbee, about to sail the tiny rectangle into the pile of soda empties and limp news-papers. But then he paused.

Up the street he found a pay phone. Worth more than 50 million dollars, Robert Covey believed that cell phones were unnecessary luxu-ries. He set the card on the ledge, donned his reading glasses and began fishing in his leather change pouch for some coins.

+ − < = > ÷

Dr Peter Dehoeven was a tall blond man who spoke with an accent that Tal couldn't quite place.

European – Scandinavian or German maybe. It was quite thick at times and that, coupled with his oddly barren office, suggested that he'd come to the United States recently. Not only was it far sparser than Dr Anthony Sheldon's but the walls featured not a single framed testament to his education and training.

It was early the next morning and Dehoeven was elaborating on the mission of his Cardiac Support Center. He told Tal that the CSC coun-selors helped seriously ill patients change their diets, create exercise regimens, understand the nature of heart disease, deal with depression and anxiety, find caregivers, and counsel family members. They also helped with death and dying issues – funeral plans, insurance, wills. 'We live to be older, yes?' Dehoeven explained, drifting in and out of his accent. 'So we are having longer to experience our bodies' failing than we used to. That means, yes, we must confront our mortality for a longer time, too. That is a difficult thing to do. So we need to help our patients prepare for the end of life.'

When the doctor was through explaining CSC's mission Tal told him that he'd come about the Whitleys. 'Were you surprised when they killed themselves?' Tal found his hand at his collar, absently adjusting his tie knot; the doctor's hung down an irritating two inches from his buttoned collar.

'Surprised?' Dehoeven hesitated. Maybe the question confused him. 'I didn't think about being surprised or not. I didn't know Sam personal, yes? So I can't say—'

'You never met him?' Tal was surprised.

'Oh, we're a very big organization. Our counselors work with the patients. Me?' He laughed sadly. 'My life is budget and planning and building our new facility up the street. That is taking most of my time now. We're greatly expanding, yes? But I will find out who was assigned to Sam and his wife.' He called his secretary for this information.

The counselor turned out to be Claire McCaffrey, who, Dehoeven explained, was both a registered nurse and a social worker/counselor. She'd been at the CSC for a little over a year. 'She's good. One of the new generation of counselors, experts in aging, yes? She has her degree in that.'

'I'd like to speak to her.'

Another hesitation. 'I suppose this is all right. Can I ask why?'

Tal pulled a questionnaire out of his briefcase and showed it to the doctor. 'I'm the department statistician. I track all the deaths in the county and collect information about them. Just routine.'

'Ah, routine, yes? And yet we get a personal visit.' He lifted an eyebrow in curiosity.

'Details have to be attended to.'

'Yes, of course.' Though he didn't seem quite convinced that Tal's presence here was completely innocuous.

He called the nurse. It seemed that Claire McCaffrey was about to leave to meet a new patient but she could wait fifteen or twenty minutes.

Dehoeven explained where her office was. Tal asked, 'Just a couple more questions.'

'Yessir?'

'Do you prescribe Luminux here?'

'Yes, we do often.'

'Did Sam have a prescription? We couldn't find a bottle at their house.'

He typed on his computer. 'Yes. Our doctors wrote several prescriptions for him. He started on it a month ago.'

Tal then told Dehoeven the level of the drugs the Whitleys had in their blood. 'What do you make of that?'

'Three times the usual dosage?' He shook his head. 'I couldn't tell you.'

'They'd also been drinking a little. But I'm told the drug didn't directly contribute to their death. Would you agree?'

'Yes, yes,' he said quickly. 'It's not dangerous. It makes you drowsy and giddy. That's all.'

'Drowsy and giddy?' Tal asked. 'Is that unusual?' The only drugs he'd taken recently were aspirin and an antiseasickness medicine, which didn't work for him, as a disastrous afternoon date on a tiny sailboat on Long Island Sound had proven.

'No, not unusual. Luminux is our anti-anxiety and mood-control drug of choice here at the Center. It was just approved by the FDA. We were very glad to learn that, yes? Cardiac patients can take it without fear of aggravating their heart problems.'

'Who makes it?'

He pulled a thick book off his shelf and read through it. 'Montrose Pharmaceuticals in Paramus, New Jersey.'

Tal wrote this down. 'Doctor,' he asked, 'did you have another patient here . . . Don Benson?'

'I'm not knowing the name but I know very little of the patients here, as I was saying to you, yes?' He nodded out the window through which they could hear the sound of construction – the new CSC facility that was taking all his time, Tal assumed. Dehoeven typed on the computer keyboard. 'No, we are not having any patients named Benson.'

'In the past?'

'This is for the year, going back.' A nod at the screen. 'Why is it you are asking?'

Tal tapped the questionnaire. 'Statistics.' He put the paper away, rose and shook the doctor's hand. He was directed to the nurse's office, four doors up the hall from Dehoeven's.

Claire McCaffrey was about his age, with wavy brunette hair pulled back in a ponytail. She had a freckled, pretty face – girl next door – but seemed haggard.

'You're the one Dr Dehoeven called about? Officer—?'

'Simms. But call me Tal.'

'I go by Mac,' she said. She extended her hand and a charm bracelet jangled on her right wrist as he gripped her strong fingers. He noticed a small gold ring in the shape of an ancient coin on her right hand. There was no jewelry at all on her left. 'Mac,' he reflected. A Celtic theme today, recalling Margaret, Dr Sheldon's somber step dancer.

She motioned him to sit. Her office was spacious – a desk and a sitting area with a couch and two armchairs around a coffee table. It seemed more lived-in than her boss's, he noted, comfortable. The decor was soothing – crystals, glass globes and reproductions of Native American artifacts, plants and fresh flowers, posters and paintings of seashores and deserts and forests.

'This is about Sam Whitley, right?' she asked in a troubled monotone.

'That's right. And his wife.'

She nodded, distraught. 'I was up all night about it. Oh, it's so sad. I couldn't believe it.' Her voice faded.

'I just have a few questions. I hope you don't mind.'

'No, go ahead.'

'Did you see them the day they died?' Tal asked.

'Yes, I did. We had our regular appointment.'

'What exactly did you do for them?'

'What we do with most patients. Making sure they're on a heart-friendly diet, helping with insurance forms, making sure their medication's working, arranging for help in doing heavy work around the house . . . Is there some problem? I mean, official problem?'

Looking into her troubled eyes, he chose not to use the excuse of the questionnaire as a front. 'It was unusual, their deaths. They didn't fit the standard profile of most suicides. Did they say anything that'd suggest they were thinking about killing themselves?'

'No, of course not,' she said quickly. 'I would've intervened. Naturally.'

'But?' He sensed there was something more she wanted to say.

She looked down at her desk, organized some papers, closed a folder.

'It's just . . . See there was one thing. I spent the last couple of days going over what they said to me, looking for clues. And I remember they said how much they'd enjoyed working with me.'

'That was odd?'

'It was the way they put it. It was the past tense, you know. Not *"enjoy* working with me". It was *enjoyed* working with me. It didn't strike me as odd or anything at the time. But now we know . . .' A sigh. 'I should've listened to what they were saying.'

Recrimination. Like the couples' lawyers, like the doctors. Nurse McCaffrey would probably live with these deaths for a long, long time.

Perhaps *forever* . . .

'Did you know,' he asked, 'they just bought a book about suicide? *Making the Final Journey.*'

'No, I didn't know that,' she said, frowning.

Behind her desk Nurse McCaffrey – Mac – had a picture of an older couple with their arms around each other, two snapshots of big, goofy black Labs, and one picture of her with the dogs. No snaps of boyfriends or husbands – or girlfriends. In Westbrook County, married or cohabitating couples comprised 74% of the adult population, widows 7%, widowers 2% and unmarried/divorced/noncohabitating were 17%. Of that latter category only 4% were between the ages of twenty-eight and thirty-five.

He and Mac had at least one thing in common; they were both members of the Four Per Cent Club.

She glanced at her watch and he focused on her again. 'They were taking Luminux, right?'

She nodded. 'It's a good anti-anxiety drug. We make sure the patients have it available and take it if they have a panic attack or're depressed.'

'Both Sam and his wife had as unusually large amount in their bloodstreams when they died.'

'Really?'

'We're trying to find out what happened to the prescription, the bottle. We couldn't find it at their house.'

'They had it the other day, I know.'

'Are you sure?'

'Pretty sure. I don't know how much they had left on the prescription. Maybe it was gone and they threw the bottle out.'

Raw data, Tal thought. Wondering what to make of these facts. Was he asking the right questions? Greg LaTour would know.

But LaTour was not here. The mathematician was on his own. He asked, 'Did the Whitleys ever mention Don and Patsy Benson?'

'Benson?'

'In Greeley.'

'Well, no. I've never heard of them.'

Tal asked, 'Had anybody else been to the house that day?'

'I don't know. We were alone when I was there.'

'And you left when?'

'At four. A little before.'

'You sure of the time?'

'Yep. I know because I was listening to my favorite radio program in the car on my way home. *The Opera Hour* on NPR.' A sad laugh. 'It was highlights from *Madame Butterfly*.'

'Isn't that about the Japanese woman who . . .' His voice faded.

'Kills herself.' Mac looked up at a poster of the Grand Tetons, then one of the surf in Hawaii. 'My whole life's been devoted to prolonging people's lives. This just shattered me, hearing about Sam and Liz.' She seemed close to tears then controlled herself. 'I was talking to Dr Dehoeven. He just came over here from Holland. They look at death differently over there. Euthanasia and suicide are a lot more acceptable . . . He heard about Sam and Liz, their deaths, and kind of shrugged. Like it wasn't any big deal. But I can't get them out of my mind.'

Silence for a moment. Then she blinked and looked at her watch again. 'I've got a new patient to meet. But if there's anything I can do to help, let me know.' She rose, then paused. 'Are you . . . what *are* you exactly? A homicide detective?'

He laughed. 'Actually, I'm a mathematician.'

'A—'

But before he could explain his curious pedigree his pager went off, a sound Tal was so unaccustomed to that he dropped his briefcase then knocked several files off the nurse's desk as he bent to retrieve it. Thinking: Good job, Simms, way to impress a fellow member of the Westbrook County Four Per Cent Club.

'He's in there and I couldn't get him out. I'm spitting nails, boss.'

In a flash of panic Tal thought that Shellee, fuming as she pointed at his office, was referring to the sheriff himself, who'd descended from the top floor of the county building to fire Tal personally for the 2124 call.

But, no, she was referring to someone else.

Tal stepped inside and lifted an eyebrow to Greg LaTour. 'Thought we had an appointment yester—'

'So where you been?' LaTour grumbled. 'Sleepin' in?' The huge man was finishing Tal's cheese sandwich from yesterday, sending a cascade of breadcrumbs everywhere.

And resting his boots on Tal's desk.

It had been LaTour's page that caught him with Mac McCaffrey. The message: 'Office twenty minutes. Stat. LaTour.'

The slim cop looked unhappily at the scuff marks on the desktop.

LaTour noticed but ignored him. 'Here's the thing. I got the information on the wills. And, yeah, they were both changed—'

'Okay, that's suspicious—'

'Lemme finish. No, it's *not* suspicious. There weren't any crazy house-keepers or some Moonie guru assholes like that controlling their minds. The Bensons didn't have any kids so all they did was add a few charities and create a trust for some nieces and nephews – for college. A hundred thousand each. Small potatoes. The Whitley girl didn't get diddly-squat from them.

'Now, them, the Whitleys, gave their daughter – bitch or not – a third of the estate in the first version of the will. She still gets the same in the new version but she also gets a little more so she can set up a Whitley family library.' LaTour looked up. 'Now *there's* gonna be a fucking fun place to spend Sunday afternoons . . . Then they added some new charities, too, and got rid of some other ones . . . Oh, and if you were going to ask, they were *different* charities from the ones in the Bensons' will.'

'I wasn't.'

'Well, you should have. Always look for connections, Tal. That's the key in homicide. Connections between facts.'

'Just like—'

'Don't say fucking statistics.'

'Mathematics. Common denominators.'

'Whatever,' LaTour muttered. 'So, the wills're out as motives. Same with—'

'The insurance policies.'

'I was going to say. Small policies and most of the Bensons' goes to paying off some debts and giving some bucks to retired employees of the husband's companies. It's like twenty, thirty grand. Nothing suspicious there . . . Now, what'd you find?'

Tal explained about Dr Sheldon, the cardiologist, then about Dehoeven, Mac and the Cardiac Support Center.

LaTour asked immediately, 'Both Benson and Whitley, patients of Sheldon?'

'No, only Whitley. Same for the Cardiac Support Center.'

'Fuck. We . . . what'sa matter?'

'You want to get your boots off my desk.'

Irritated, LaTour swung his feet around to the floor. 'We need a connection, I was saying. Something—'

'I might have one,' Tal said quickly. 'Drugs.'

'What, the old folks were dealing?' The sarcasm had returned.

Tal explained about the Luminux. 'Makes you drowsy *and* happy. Could mess up your judgment. Make you susceptible to suggestions.'

'That you blow your fucking brains out? One hell of a suggestion.'

'Maybe not – if you were taking three times the normal dosage . . .'

'You think maybe somebody slipped it to 'em?'

'Maybe.' Tal nodded. 'The counselor from the Cardiac Support Center left the Whitleys' at four. They died around eight. Plenty of time for somebody to stop by, put some stuff in their drinks.'

'Okay, the Whitleys were taking it. What about the Bensons?'

'They were cremated the day after they died. We'll never know.'

LaTour finished the sandwich. 'You don't mind, do you? It was just sitting there.'

He glanced at the desktop. 'You got crumbs everywhere.'

The cop leaned forward and blew them to the floor. He sipped coffee from a mug that'd left a sticky ring on an evidence report file. 'Okay, your – what the fuck do you call it? Theory?'

'Theorem.'

'Is that somebody slipped 'em that shit? But who? And why?'

'I don't know that part yet.'

'Those *parts*,' LaTour corrected. 'Who and why. Parts plural.'

Tal sighed.

'You think you could really give somebody a drug and tell 'em to kill themselves and they will?'

'Let's go find out,' Tal said.

'Huh?'

The statistician flipped through his notes. 'The company that makes the drug? It's over in Paramus. Off the Parkway. Let's go talk to 'em.'

'Shit. All the way to Jersey.'

'You have a better idea?'

'I don't need any fucking ideas. This's your case, remember?'

'Maybe *I* twenty-one-twenty-foured it. But it's *everybody's* case now. Let's go.'

She would've looked pretty good in a short skirt, Robert Covey thought, but unfortunately she was wearing slacks.

'Mr Covey, I'm from the Cardiac Support Center.'

'Call me Bob. Or you'll make me feel as old as your older brother.'

She was a little short for his taste but then he had to remind himself that she was here to help him get some pig parts stuck into his heart and rebuild a bunch of leaking veins and arteries – or else die with as little mess as he could. Besides, he joked that he had a rule he'd never date a woman a third his age. (When the truth was that after Veronica maybe he joked and maybe he flirted, but in his heart he was content never to date at all any more.)

He held the door for her and gestured her inside with a slight bow. He could see a bit of her defenses lower. She was probably used to dealing with all sorts of pricks in this line of work but Covey limited his grousing to surly repairmen and clerks and waitresses who thought because he was old he was stupid.

There was, he felt, no need for impending death to alter good manners. He invited her in and directed her to the couch in his den.

'Welcome, Ms McCaffrey—'

'How 'bout Mac? That's what my mother used to call me when I was good.'

'What'd she call you when you were bad?'

'Mac then, too. Though she managed to get two syllables out of it. So, go ahead.'

He lifted an eyebrow. 'With what?'

'With what you were going to tell me. That you don't need me here. That you don't need any help, that you're only seeing me to humor your cardiologist, that you don't want any hand-holding, that you don't want to be coddled, that you don't want to change your diet, you don't want to exercise, you don't want to give up smoking and you don't want to stop drinking your' – she glanced at the bar and eyed the bottles – 'your port. So here're the ground rules. Fair enough, no hand-holding, no coddling. That's my part of the deal. But, yes, you'll give up smoking—'

'Did before you were born, thank you very much.'

'Good. And you will be exercising and eating a cardio-friendly diet. And about the port—'

'Hold on—'

'I think we'll limit you to three a night.'

'Four,' he said quickly.

'Three. And I suspect on most nights you only have two.'

'I can live with three,' he grumbled. She'd been right about the two (though, okay, sometimes a little bourbon joined the party).

Damn, he liked her. He always had liked strong women. Like Veronica.

She was on to other topics. Practical things about what the Cardiac Support Center did and what it didn't do, about caregivers, about home care, about insurance.

'Now, I understand you're a widower. How long were you married?'

'Forty-nine years.'

'Well, now, that's wonderful.'

'Ver and I had a very nice life together. Pissed me off we missed the fiftieth. I had a party planned. Complete with harpist and open bar.' He raised an eyebrow. 'Vintage port included.'

'And you have a son?'

'That's right. Randall. He lives in California. Runs a computer company. But one that actually makes money. Imagine that! Wears his hair too long and lives with a woman – he oughta get married – but he's a good boy.'

'You see him much?'

'All the time.'

'When did you talk to him last?'

'The other day.'

'And you've told him all about your condition?'

'You bet.'

'Good. He going to get out here?'

'In a week or so. He's traveling. Got a big deal he's putting together.'

She was taking something out of her purse. 'Our doctor at the clinic prescribed this.' She handed him a bottle. 'Luminux. It's an anti-anxiety agent.'

'I say no to drugs.'

'This's a new generation. You're going through a lot of crap right now. It'll make you feel better. Virtually no side effects—'

'You mean it won't take me back to my days as a beatnik in the Village?' She laughed and he added, 'Actually, think I'll pass.'

'It's good for you.' She shook out two pills into a small cup and handed them to him. She walked to the bar and poured a glass of water.

Watching her, acting like she lived here, Covey scoffed, 'You ever negotiate?'

'Not when I know I'm right.'

'Tough lady.' He glanced down at the pills in his hand. 'I take these, that means I can't have my port, right?'

'Sure you can. You know, moderation's the key to everything.'

'You don't seem like a moderate woman.'

'Oh, hell no, I'm not. But I don't practice what I preach.' And she passed him the glass of water.

Late afternoon, driving to Jersey.

Tal fiddled with the radio trying to find the *Opera Hour* program that Mac had mentioned.

LaTour looked at the dash as if he was surprised the car even had a radio.

Moving up and down the dial, through the several National Public Radio bands, he couldn't find the show. What time had she said it came on? He couldn't remember. He wondered why he cared what she listened to. He didn't even like opera that much. He gave up and settled on all news, all the time. LaTour stood that for five minutes then put the game on.

The homicide cop was either preoccupied or just a natural-born bad driver. Weaving, speeding well over the limit, then braking to a crawl. Occasionally he'd lift his middle finger to other drivers in a way that was almost endearing.

Probably happier on a motorcycle, Tal reflected.

LaTour tuned in to another game on the radio. They listened for a while, neither speaking.

'So,' Tal tried. 'Where you live?'

'Near the station house.'

Nothing more.

'Been on the force long?'

'A while.'

New York seven, Boston three . . .

'You married?' Tal had noticed that he wore no wedding band.

More silence.

Tal turned down the volume and repeated the question.

After a long moment LaTour grumbled, 'That's something else.'

'Oh.' Having no idea what the cop meant.

That's something else . . .

He supposed there was a story here – a hard divorce, lost children. *And six point three per cent kill themselves before retirement . . .*

But whatever the sad story might be, it was only for Bear's friends in the department, those on the Real Crimes side of the pen.

Not for Einstein, the calculator humper.

They fell silent and drove on amid the white noise of the sportscasters.

Ten minutes later LaTour skidded off the parkway and turned down a winding side road.

Montrose Pharmaceuticals was a small series of glass and chrome buildings in a landscaped industrial park. Far smaller than Pfizer and the other major drug companies in the Garden State, it nonetheless must've done pretty well in sales – to judge from the number of Mercedes, Jaguars and Porsches in the employee parking lot.

Inside the elegant reception area, Westbrook County Sheriff's Department badges raised some eyebrows. But, Tal concluded, it was LaTour's bulk and hostile gaze that cut through whatever barriers existed here to gaining access to the inner sanctum of the company's president.

In five minutes they were sitting in the office of Daniel Montrose, an earnest, balding man in his late forties. His eyes were as quick as his appearance was rumpled, and Tal concluded that he was a kindred soul – a scientist, rather than a salesperson. The man rocked back and forth in his chair, peering at them through curiously stylish glasses with a certain distraction. Uneasiness, too.

Nobody said anything for a moment and Tal felt the tension in the office rise appreciably. He glanced at LaTour, who said nothing and simply sat in the leather-and-chrome chair, looking around the opulent space. Maybe stonewalling was a technique that Real cops used to get people to start talking.

'We've been getting ready for our sales conference,' Montrose suddenly volunteered. 'It's going to be a good one.'

'Is it?' Tal asked.

'That's right. Our biggest. Las Vegas this year.' Then he clammed up again.

Tal wanted to echo, 'Vegas?' for some reason. But he didn't.

Finally LaTour said, 'Tell us about Luminux.'

'Luminux. Right, Luminux . . . I'd really like to know, I mean, if it's not against any rules or anything, what you want to know for. I mean, and what are you doing here? You haven't really said.'

'We're investigating some suicides.'

'Suicides?' he asked, frowning. 'And Luminux is involved.'

'Yes indeedy,' LaTour said with all the cheer that the word required.

'But . . . it's based on a mild diazepam derivative. It'd be very difficult to fatally overdose on it.'

'No, they died from other causes. But we found—'

The door swung open and a strikingly beautiful woman walked into the office. She blinked at the visitors and said a very unsorrowful, 'Sorry. Thought you were alone.' She set a stack of folders on Montrose's desk.

'These are some police officers from Westbrook,' the president told her.

She looked at them more carefully. 'Police. Is something wrong?'

Tal put her at forty. Long, serpentine face with cool eyes, very beautiful in a European fashion model way. Slim legs with runner's calves. Tal decided that she was like Sheldon's Gaelic assistant, an example of some predatory genus not as evolved as Mac McCaffrey.

Neither Tal nor LaTour answered her question. Montrose introduced her – Karen Billings. Her title was a mouthful but it had something to do with product support and patient relations.

'They were just asking about Luminux. There've been some problems, they're claiming.'

'Problems?'

'They were just saying . . .' Montrose pushed his glasses higher on his nose. 'Well, what *were* you saying?'

Tal continued, 'A couple of people who killed themselves had three times the normal amount of Luminux in their systems.'

'But that can't kill them. It couldn't have. I don't see why . . .' Her voice faded and she looked toward Montrose. They eyed each other, poker-faced. She then said coolly to LaTour, 'What exactly would you like to know?'

'First of all, how could they get it into their bloodstream?' LaTour sat back, the chair creaking alarmingly. Tal wondered if he'd put his feet up on Montrose's desk.

'You mean how could it be administered?'

'Yeah.'

'Orally's the only way. It's not available in an IV form yet.'

'But could it be mixed in food or a drink?'

'You think somebody did that?' Montrose asked. Billings remained silent, looking from Tal to LaTour and back again with her cautious, swept-wing eyes.

'Could it be done?' Tal asked.

'Of course,' the president said. 'Sure. It's water soluble. The vehicle's bitter—'

'The—?'

'The inert base we mix it with. The drug itself is tasteless but we add a compound to make it bitter so kids'll spit it out if they eat it by mistake. But you can mask that with sugar or—'

'Alcohol?'

Billings snapped, 'Drinking isn't recommended when taking—'

LaTour grumbled, 'I'm not talking about the fucking fine print on the label. I'm talking about could you hide the flavor by mixing it in a drink?'

She hesitated. Then finally answered, 'One could.' She clicked her nails together in impatience or anger.

'So what's it do to you?'

Montrose said, 'It's essentially an anti-anxiety agent, not a sleeping pill. It makes you relaxed. Your mood improves. There'd be diminished cognitive functioning.'

'English?' LaTour grumbled.

'They'd feel slightly disoriented but in a happy way.'

Tal recalled the misspellings in the note. 'Would it affect their hand-writing and spelling?'

Dangrous . . .

'It could, yes.'

Tal said. 'Would their judgment be affected?'

'Judgment?' Billings asked harshly. 'That's subjective.'

'Whatta you mean?'

'There's no quantifiable measure for one's ability to judge something.'

'No? How 'bout if *one* puts a Glock to *one*'s head and pulls the rigger?' LaTour said. 'I call that bad judgment. Any chance we agree on that?'

'What the fuck're you getting at?' Billings snapped.

'Karen,' Montrose said, pulling off his designer glasses and rubbing his eyes.

She ignored her boss. 'You think they took our drug and decided to ill themselves? You think we're to blame for that? This drug—'

'This drug that a couple of people popped – maybe *four* people – and then killed themselves. Whatta we say about that from a statistical point of view?' LaTour turned to Tal.

'Well within the percentile of probability for establishing a causal relationship between the two events.'

'There you go. Science has spoken.'

Tal wondered if they were playing the good-cop/bad-cop routine you see in movies. He tried again. 'Could an overdose of Luminux have impaired their judgment?'

'Not enough so that they'd decide to kill themselves,' she said firmly. Montrose said nothing.

'That your opinion, too?' LaTour muttered to him.

The president finally said, 'Yes, it is.'

Tal persisted, 'How about making them susceptible?'

Billings leapt in with, 'I don't know what you mean . . . This is all crazy.'

Tal ignored her and said levelly to Montrose, 'Could somebody persuade a person taking an overdose of Luminux to kill themselves?'

Silence filled the office.

Billings said, 'I strongly doubt it.'

'But you ain't saying no,' LaTour grumbled.

A glance between Billings and Montrose. Finally he pulled his wire-rims back on, looked away and said, 'We're not saying no.'

+ − < = > ÷

The next morning they arrived at the station house at the same time, and the odd couple walked together through the Detective Division per into Tal's office.

Tal and LaTour had looked over the case so far and found no firm leads.

'Still no who,' LaTour grumbled. 'Still no why.'

'But we've got a how,' Tal pointed out. Meaning the concession abou Luminux making one suggestible.

'Fuck *how*. I want *who*.'

At just that moment they received a possible answer.

Shellee stepped into Tal's office. Pointedly ignoring the homicide cop she said, 'You're back. Good. Got a call from the PII team in Greeley They said a neighbor saw a woman in a small, dark car arrive at th

Bensons' house about an hour before they died. She was wearing sunglasses and a tan or beige baseball cap. The neighbor didn't recognize her.'

'Car?' LaTour snapped.

It's hard to ignore an armed, 250-pound goateed man named Bear, but Shellee did it easily.

Continuing to speak to her boss, she said, 'They weren't sure what time she got there but it was before lunch. She stayed maybe forty minutes, then left. That'd be an hour or so before they killed themselves.' A pause. 'The car was a small sedan. The witness didn't remember the color.'

'Did you ask about the—' LaTour began.

'They didn't see the tag number,' she told Tal. 'Now, that's not all. DMV finally calls back and tells me that Sandra Whitley drives a blue BMW 325.'

'Small wheelbase,' Tal said.

'And getting better 'n' better, boss. Guess who's leaving town before her parents' memorial service?'

'Sandra?'

'How the hell you'd find that out?' LaTour asked.

She turned coldly to him. 'Detective Simms asked me to organize all the evidence from the Whitley crime scene. Because, like he says, having facts and files out of order is as bad as not having them at all. I found a note in the Whitley evidence file with an airline locator number. It was for a flight from Newark today to San Francisco, continuing on to Hawaii. I called and they told me it was a confirmed ticket for Sandra Whitley. Return is open.'

'Meaning the bitch might not be coming back at all,' LaTour said. 'Going on vacation without saying goodbye to the folks? That's fucking harsh.'

'Good job,' Tal told Shellee.

Eyes down, a faint smile of acknowledgment.

LaTour dropped into one of Tal's chairs, belched softly and said, 'You're doing such a good job, Sherry, here, look up whatever you can about this shit.' He offered her the notes on Luminux.

'It's Shellee,' she snapped and glanced at Tal, who mouthed, 'Please.'

She snatched them from LaTour's hand and clattered down the hall on her dangerous heels.

LaTour looked over the handwritten notes she'd given them and growled, 'So what about the why? A motive?'

Tal spread the files out on his desk – all the crime-scene information, the photos, the notes he'd taken.

What were the common denominators? The deaths of two couples. Extremely wealthy. The husbands ill, yes, but not hopelessly so. Drugs that make you suggestible.

A giddy lunch then suicide. A drink beside a romantic fire then suicide . . .

Romantic . . .

'Hmm,' Tal mused, thinking back to the Whitleys.

'What hmm?'

'Let's think about the wills again.'

'We tried that,' LaTour said.

'But what if they were *about* to be changed?'

'Whatta you mean?'

'Try this for an assumption: Say the Whitleys and their daughter had some big fight in the past week. They were going to change their will again – this time to cut her out completely.'

'Yeah, but their lawyer'd know that.'

'Not if she killed them before they talked to him. I remember smelling smoke from the fire when I walked into the Whitley house. I thought they'd built this romantic fire just before they killed themselves. But maybe they hadn't. Maybe Sandra burned some evidence – something about changing the will, memos to the lawyer, estate planning stuff. Remember, she snatched the mail at the house. One was to the lawyer. Maybe that was why she came back – to make sure there was no evidence left. Hell, wished I'd searched her purse. I just didn't think about it.'

'Yeah, but offing her own *parents*?' LaTour asked skeptically.

'Seventeen point two per cent of murderers are related to their victims.' Tal added pointedly, 'I know that because of my questionnaires, by the way.'

LaTour rolled his eyes. 'What about the Bensons?'

'Maybe they met in some cardiac support group, maybe they were in the same country club. Whitley might've mentioned something about the will to him. Sandra found out and had to take them out, too.'

'Sounds crazy.'

'It's a theorem, I keep saying. Let's go prove it or disprove it. See if she's got an alibi. And we'll have forensics go through the fireplace.'

'If the ash is intact,' LaTour said, 'they can image the printing on the sheet. Those techs're fucking geniuses.'

Tal called Crime Scene again and arranged to have a team return to the Whitleys' house. Then he said, 'Okay, let's go visit our suspect.'

+ − < = > ÷

'Hold on there.'

When Greg LaTour charged up to you, muttering the way he'd just done, you held on there.

Even tough Sandra Whitley.

She'd been about to climb into the BMW sitting outside her luxurious house. Suitcases sat next to her.

'Step away from the car,' LaTour said, flashing his badge.

Tal said, 'We'd like to ask you a few questions, ma'am.'

'You again! What the hell're you talking about?' Her voice was angry but she did as she was told.

'You're on your way out of town?' LaTour took her purse off her shoulder. 'Just keep your hands at your sides.'

'I've got a meeting I can't miss.'

'In Hawaii?'

Sandra was regaining the initiative. 'I'm an attorney, like I told you. I *will* find out how you got that information and for your sake there better've been a warrant involved.'

Did they *need* a warrant? Tal wondered.

'Meeting in Hawaii?' LaTour repeated. 'With an open return?'

'What're you implying?'

'It's a little odd, don't you think? Flying off to the South Seas a few days after your parents die? Not going to the funeral?'

'Funerals're for the survivors. I've made peace with my parents and their deaths. They wouldn't've wanted me to blow off an important meeting. Dad was as much a businessman as a father. I'm as much a businesswoman as a daughter.' Her eyes slipped to Tal. 'Okay, you got me, Simms.' Emphasizing the name was presumably to remind him again that his name would be spelled correctly in the court documents she filed. She nodded to the purse. 'It's all in there. The evidence about me escaping the country after – what? – stealing my parents' money? What *exactly* do you think I've done?'

'We're not accusing you of anything. We just want to—'

'Ask you a few questions.'

'So ask, goddamn it.'

LaTour was reading a lengthy document he'd found in her purse. He frowned and handed it to Tal, then asked her, 'Can you tell me where you were the night your parents died?'

'Why?'

'Look, lady, you can cooperate or you can clam up and we'll—'

'Go downtown. Yadda, yadda, yadda. I've heard this before.'

LaTour frowned at Tal and mouthed, 'What's downtown?' Tal shrugged and returned to the document. It was a business plan for a company that was setting up an energy joint venture in Hawaii. Her law firm was representing them. The preliminary meeting seemed to be scheduled for two days from now in Hawaii. There was a memo saying that the meetings could go on for weeks and recommended that the participants get open-return tickets.

Oh.

'Since I have to get to the airport now,' she snapped, 'and I don't have time for any bullshit. Okay, I'll tell you where I was on the night of the quote crime. On an airplane. I flew back on United Airlines from San Francisco, the flight that got in about eleven p.m. My boarding pass is probably in there' – a contemptuous nod at the purse LaTour held – 'and if it isn't, I'm sure there's a record of the flight at the airline. With security being what it is nowadays, picture IDs and everything, that's probably a pretty solid alibi, don't you think?'

Did seem to be, Tal agreed silently. And it got even better when LaTour found the boarding pass and ticket receipt in her purse. Tal's phone began ringing and he was happy for the chance to escape from Sandra's searing fury. He heard Shellee speak from the receiver. 'Hey, boss, 's me.'

'What's up?'

'Crime Scene called. They went through all the ash in the Whitleys' fireplace, looking for a letter or something about changing the will. They didn't find anything about that at all. Something had been burned but it was all just a bunch of information on companies – computer and biotech companies. The crime-scene guy was thinking Mr Whitley might've just used some old junk mail or something to start the fire.'

Oh.

Damn.

'Thanks.'

He nodded LaTour aside and told him what Crime Scene had reported.

'Shit on the street,' he whispered. 'Jumped a little fast here . . . Okay, let's go kiss some ass. Brother.'

The groveling time was quite limited -- Sandra was adamant about catching her plane.

She sped out of the driveway, leaving behind a blue cloud of tire smoke.

'Aw, she'll forget about it,' LaTour said.

'You think?' Tal asked.

A pause. 'Nope. We're way fucked.'

As they walked back to the car LaTour said, 'We still gotta find the mysterious babe in the sunglasses and hat.'

Tal wondered if Mac McCaffrey might've seen someone like that around the Whitleys' place. Besides, it'd be a good excuse to see her again. Tal said, 'I'll look into that one.'

'You?' LaTour laughed.

'Yeah. Me. What's so funny about that?'

'I don't know. Just you never investigated a case before.'

'So? You think I can't talk to witnesses on my own? You think I should just go back home and hump my calculator?'

Silence.

'You heard that?' LaTour finally asked, no longer laughing.

'I heard.'

'Hey, I didn't mean it, you know.'

'Didn't mean it?' Tal asked, giving an exaggerated squint. 'As in you didn't mean for me to hear you? Or as in you don't actually believe I have sex with adding machines?'

'I'm sorry, okay? . . . I bust people's chops sometimes. It's the way I am. I do it to everybody. Fuck, people do it to me. They call me Bear 'causa my gut. They call you Einstein 'cause you're smart.'

'Not to my face.'

LaTour hesitated. 'You're right. Not to your face . . . You know, you're too polite, Tal. You can give me a lot more shit. I wouldn't mind. You're too uptight. Loosen up.'

'So it's *my* fault that I'm pissed 'cause you insult me?'

'It was . . .' he began defensively but then he stopped. 'Okay, I'm sorry. I am . . . Hey, I don't apologize a lot, you know. I'm not very good at it.'

'That's an apology?'

'I'm doing the best I can . . . Whatta you want?'

Silence.

'All right,' Tal said finally.

LaTour sped the car around a corner and wove frighteningly through the heavy traffic. Finally he said, 'It's okay, though, you know.'

'What's okay?'

'If you want to.'

'Want to what?' Tal asked.

'You know, you and your calculator . . . Lot safer than some of the weird shit you see nowadays.'

'LaTour,' Tal said, 'you can—'

'You just seemed defensive about it, you know. Figure I probably hit close to home, you know what I'm saying?'

'You can go straight to hell.'

The huge cop was laughing hard. 'Shit, don'tcha feel like we're finally breaking the ice here? I think we are. Now, I'll drop you off back at your car, Einstein, and you can go on this secret mission all by your lonesome.'

+ – < = > ÷

His stated purpose was to ask her if she'd ever seen the mysterious woman in the baseball cap and sunglasses, driving a small car, at the Whitleys' house.

Lame, Tal thought.

Lame *and* transparent – since he could've asked her that on the phone. He was sure the true mission here was so obvious that it was laughable: to get a feel for what would happen if he asked Mac McCaffrey out to dinner. Not to actually *invite* her out at this point, of course. She was, after all, a potential witness. No, just to test the waters.

Tal parked along Elm Street and climbed out of the car, enjoying the complicated smells of the April air, the skin-temperature breeze, the golden snowflakes of fallen forsythia petals covering the lawn.

Walking toward the park where he'd arranged to meet her, Tal reflected on his recent romantic life.

Fine, he concluded. It was fine.

He dated 2.66 women a month. The mean age of his dates in the past 12 months was approximately 31 (a number skewed somewhat by the embarrassing – but highly memorable – outlier of a Columbia

University senior). And the mean IQ of the women was around 140 or up – and that latter statistic was a very sharp bell curve with a very narrow standard deviation; Talbot Simms went for intellect before anything else.

It was this latter criterion, though, he'd come to believe lately, that led to the conclusion that his love life was the tepid 'fine'.

Yes, he'd had many interesting evenings with his $2^2/_3$ dates every month. He'd discuss with them Cartesian hyperbolic doubt. He'd argue about the validity of analyzing objects in terms of their primary qualities ('No! I'm suspicious of secondary qualities, too. I mean, how 'bout that?'). They'd draft mathematical formulae in crayon on the paper table coverings at the Crab House. They'd discuss Fermat's Last Theorem until 2 or 3 a.m. (These were not wholly academic encounters, of course; Tal Simms happened to have a full-sized chalkboard in his bedroom.)

He was intellectually stimulated by most of these women. He even learned things from them.

But he didn't really have a lot of fun.

Mac McCaffrey, he believed, would be fun.

She'd sounded surprised when he'd called. Cautious, too, at first. But after a minute or two she'd relaxed and had seemed pleased at the idea that he wanted to meet with her.

He now spotted her in the park next to the Knickerbocker Home, which appeared to be a nursing facility.

'Hey,' he said.

'Hi there. Hope you don't mind meeting outside. I hate to be cooped up.'

He recalled the Sierra Club posters in her office. 'No, it's beautiful here.'

Her sharp green eyes, set in her freckled face, looked away and took in the sights of the park. Tal sat down and they made small talk for five minutes or so. Finally she asked, 'You started to tell me that you're, what, a mathematician?'

'That's right.'

She smiled. There was a crookedness to her mouth, an asymmetry, which he found charming. 'That's way pretty cool. You could be on a TV series. Like *CSI* or *Law and Order*, you know. Call it *Math Cop*.'

They laughed. He glanced down at her shoes, old black Reeboks, and saw they were nearly worn out. He noticed, too, a worn spot on the knee of her jeans. It'd been rewoven. He thought of cardiologist

Anthony Sheldon's designer wardrobe and huge office; he reflected that Mac worked in an entirely different part of the health care universe.

'So I was wondering,' she asked. 'Why this interest in the Whitleys' deaths?'

'Like I said. They were out of the ordinary.'

'I guess I mean, why are *you* interested? Did you lose somebody? To suicide, I mean.'

'Oh, no. My father's alive. My mother passed away a while ago. A stroke.'

'I'm sorry. She must've been young.'

'Was, yes.'

She waved a bee away. 'Is your dad in the area?'

'Nope. Professor in Chicago.'

'Math?'

'Naturally. Runs in the family.' He told her about Wall Street, the financial crimes, statistics.

'All that adding and subtracting. Doesn't it get, I don't know, boring?'

'Oh, no, just the opposite. Numbers go on forever. Infinite questions, challenges. And remember, math is a lot more than just calculations. What excites me is that numbers let us understand the world. And when you understand something you have control over it.'

'Control?' she asked, serious suddenly. 'Numbers won't keep you from getting hurt. From dying.'

'Sure they can,' he replied. 'Sometimes. Numbers make car brakes work and keep airplanes in the air and let you call 911. Medicine, science.'

'I guess so. Never thought about it.' Another crooked smile. 'You're pretty enthusiastic about the subject.'

Tal asked, 'Pascal?'

'Heard of him.'

'A philosopher. He was a prodigy at math but he gave it up completely. He said math was so enjoyable it had to be related to sex. It was sinful.'

'Hold on, mister,' she said, laughing. 'You got some math porn you want to show me?'

Tal decided that the preliminary groundwork for the date was going pretty well. But, apropos of which, enough about himself. He asked, 'How'd you get into your field?'

'I always liked taking care of people or animals,' she explained.

'Somebody's pet'd get hurt, I'd be the one to try to help it. I hate seeing anybody in pain. I was going to go to med school but my mom got sick and, without a father around, I had to put that on hold – where it's been for, well, a few years.'

No explanation about the missing father. But he sensed that, like him, she didn't want to discuss Dad. A common denominator among these particular members of the Four Per Cent Club.

She continued, looking at the nursing-home door. 'Why I'm doing *this* particularly? My mother, I guess. Her exit was pretty tough. Nobody really helped her. Except me, and I didn't know very much. The hospital she was in didn't give her any support. So after she passed I decided I'd go into the field myself. Make sure patients have a comfortable time at the end.'

'It doesn't get you down?'

'Sometimes it's tougher than others. But I'm lucky. I'm not all that religious but I do think there's something there after we die.'

Tal nodded but he said nothing. He'd always wanted to believe in that *something*, too, but religion wasn't allowed in the Simms household – nothing, that is, except the cold deity of numbers his father worshipped – and it seemed to Tal that if you don't get hooked early by some kind of spiritualism, you'll rarely get the bug. Still, people do change. He recalled that the Bensons had been atheists but apparently toward the end had come to believe differently.

Together forever . . .

Mac was continuing, speaking of her job at the Cardiac Support Center. 'I like working with the patients. And I'm good, if I do say so myself. I stay away from the sentiment, the maudlin crap. I knock back some scotch or wine with them. Watch movies, pig out on low-fat chips and popcorn, tell some good death and dying jokes.'

'No,' Tal said, frowning. 'Jokes?'

'You bet. Here's one: When I die, I want to go peacefully in my sleep, like my grandfather . . . Not screaming like the passengers in the car with him.'

Tal blinked then laughed hard. She was pleased he'd enjoyed it, he could tell. He said, 'Hey, there's a statistician joke. Want to hear it?'

'Sure.'

'Statistics show that a person gets robbed every four minutes. And, man, is he getting tired of it.'

She laughed. 'That really sucks.'

'Best we can do.' Then after a moment he added, 'But Dr Dehoeven said that CSC isn't all death and dying. There's a lot of things you do to help before and after surgery.'

'Oh, sure,' she said. 'Didn't mean to neglect that. Exercise, diet, caregiving, getting the family involved, psychotherapy.'

Silence for a moment, a silence that, he felt, was suddenly asking: What exactly was he doing here?

He said, 'I have a question about the suicides. Some witnesses said they saw a woman in sunglasses and a beige baseball cap, driving a small car, at the Bensons' house just before they killed themselves. I was wondering if you know who that might be.'

'Me?' she asked, frowning. 'I wasn't seeing the Bensons, remember?'

'No, I mean at the Whitleys'.'

'Oh.' She thought for a moment. 'Their daughter came by a couple of times.'

'No, it wasn't her.'

'They had a cleaning lady. But she drove a van. And I never saw her in a hat.'

Her voice had grown weaker and Tal knew that her mood had changed quickly. Probably the subject of the Whitleys had done it – raised the issue of whether there was anything else she might've done to keep them from dying.

Silence surrounded them, as dense as the humid April air, redolent with the scent of lilac. He began to think that it was a bad idea to mix a personal matter with a professional one – especially when it involved patients who had just died. Conversation resumed but it was now different, superficial, and as if by mutual decision, they both glanced at their watches, said goodbye, then rose and headed down the same sidewalk but in different directions.

+ − < = > ÷

Shellee appeared in the doorway of Tal's office, where the statistician and LaTour were parked. 'Found something,' she said in her redneck Beantown accent.

'Yeah, whatsat?' LaTour asked, looking over a pile of documents that she was handing her boss.

She leaned close to Tal and whispered, 'He just gonna move in here?'

Tal smiled and said to her, 'Thanks, Detective.'

An eye roll was her response.

'Where'd you get all that?' LaTour asked, pointing at the papers but glancing at her chest.

'The Internet,' Shellee snapped as she left. 'Where else?'

'She got all that information from there?' the big cop asked, taking the stack and flipping through it.

Tal saw a chance for a bit of cop–cop jibe, now that, yeah, the ice was broken, and he nearly said to LaTour, You'd be surprised, there's a lot more online than wicked-sluts.com that you browse through in the wee hours. But then he recalled the silence when he asked about the cop's family life.

That's something else . . .

And he decided a reference to lonely nights at home was out of line. He kept the joke to himself.

LaTour handed the sheets to Tal. 'I'm not gonna read all this crap. It's got fucking numbers in it. Gimme the bottom line.'

Tal skimmed the information, much of which might have contained numbers but was still impossible for him to understand. It was mostly chemical jargon and medical formulae. But toward the end he found a summary. He frowned and read it again.

'Jesus.'

'What?'

'We maybe have our perps.'

'No shit.'

The documents Shellee had found were from a consumer protection website devoted to medicine. They reported that the FDA was having doubts about Luminux because the drug trials showed that it had hallucinogenic properties. Several people in the trials had had psychotic episodes believed to have been caused by the drug. Others reported violent mood swings. Those with problems were a small minority of those in the trials, less than a tenth of one per cent. But the reactions were so severe that the FDA was very doubtful about approving it.

But Shellee also found that the agency had approved Luminux a year ago, despite the dangers.

'Okay, got it,' LaTour said. 'Montrose slipped some money to somebody to get the drug approved and then kept an eye on the patients taking it, looking for anybody who had bad reactions.'

The cops speculated that he'd have the patients with particularly bad reactions killed – making it look like suicide – so that no problems with Luminux ever surfaced. LaTour wondered if this was a realistic motive – until Tal found a printout that revealed that Luminux was Montrose's only moneymaker, to the tune of $38 million a year.

Their other postulate was that it had been Karen Billings – as patient relations director – who might have been the woman in the hat and sunglasses at the Bensons' and who had left the tire tracks and worn the gloves at the Whitleys'. She'd spent time with them, given them overdoses, talked them into buying the suicide manual, and helped them – what had Mac said? That was it: Helped them 'exit'.

'Some fucking patient relations,' LaTour said. 'Way fucking harsh.' Using his favorite adjective. 'Let's go see 'em.'

Ignoring – with difficulty – the clutter on his desk, Tal opened the top drawer and pulled out his pistol. He started to mount it to his belt but the holster clip slipped and the weapon dropped to the floor. He winced as it hit. Grimacing, Tal bent down and retrieved it, then hooked it on successfully.

As he glanced up he saw LaTour watching him with a faint smile on his face. 'Do me a favor. It probably won't come to it but if it does, lemme do the shooting, okay?'

+ – < = > ÷

Nurse McCaffrey would be arriving soon.

No, 'Mac' was her name, Robert Covey reminded himself.

He stood in front of his liquor cabinet and finally selected a nice vintage port, a 1977. He thought it would go well with the Saga blue cheese and shrimp he'd laid out for her, and the water crackers and nonfat dip for himself. He'd driven to the Stop & Shop that morning to pick up the groceries.

Covey arranged the food, bottle and glasses on a silver tray. Oh, napkins. Forgot the napkins. He found some under the counter and set them out on the tray, which he carried into the living room and set on the table. Next to it were some old scrapbooks he'd unearthed from the basement. He wanted to show her pictures – snapshots of his brother, now long gone, and his nieces, and his wife, of course. He also had many pictures of his son.

Oh, Randall . . .

Yep, he liked Mac a lot. It was scary how in minutes she saw right into him, perfectly.

It was irritating. It was good.

But one thing she couldn't see through was the lie he'd told her.

'You see him much?'

'All the time.'

'When did you talk to him last?'

'The other day.'

'And you've told him all about your condition?'

'You bet.'

Covey called his son regularly, left messages on his phone at work and at home. But Randy never returned them. Occasionally he'd pick up, but it was always when Covey was calling from a different phone, so that the son didn't recognize the number (Covey even wondered in horror if the man bought a caller ID phone mostly to avoid his father).

In the past week he'd left two messages at his son's house. He'd never seen the place, but pictured it being a beautiful high-rise somewhere in LA, though Covey hadn't been to California in years and didn't even know if they had real high-rises there, the City of Angels being to earthquakes what trailer parks in the Midwest are to twisters.

In any case, whether his home was high-rise, low- or a hovel, his son had not returned a single call.

Why? he often wondered in despair. *Why?*

He looked back on his days as a young father. He'd spent much time at the office and traveling, yes, but he'd also devoted many, many hours to the boy, taking him to the Yankees games and movies, attending Randy's recitals and Little League games.

Something had happened, though, and in his twenties he drifted away. Covey had thought maybe he'd gone gay, since he'd never married, but when Randy came home for Ver's funeral he brought a beautiful young woman with him. Randy had been polite but distant and a few days afterward he'd headed back to the coast. It had been some months before they'd spoken again.

Why?

Covey now sat down on the couch, poured himself a glass of the port, slowly to avoid the sediment, and sipped it. He picked up another scrapbook and began flipping through it.

He felt sentimental. And then sad and anxious. He rose slowly from the couch, walked into the kitchen and took two of his Luminux.

In a short while the drugs kicked in and he felt better, giddy. Almost carefree.

Damn good stuff, drugs.

The book sagged in his hands. He reflected on the big question: Should he tell Randy about his illness and the impending surgery? Nurse Mac would want him to, he knew. But Covey wouldn't do that. It was cheap. He either wanted the young man to come back on his own, or not at all. He wasn't going to use sympathy as a weapon to force a reconciliation.

A glance at the clock on the stove. Mac would be here in fifteen minutes.

He decided to use the time productively and return phone calls. He confirmed his next appointment with Dr Jenny and left a message with Charley Hanlon, a widower up the road, about going to the movies next weekend. He also made an appointment for tomorrow about some special alternative treatments the hospital had suggested he look into. 'Long as it doesn't involve colonics, I'll think about it,' Covey grumbled to the soft-spoken director of the program, who'd laughed and assured him that it did not.

He hung up. Despite the silky calm from the drug Covey had a moment's panic. Nothing to do with his heart, his surgery, his potential mortality, his estranged son, tomorrow's noncolonic treatment.

No, what troubled him: What if Mac didn't like blue cheese?

Covey rose and headed into the kitchen, opened the refrigerator and began to forage for some other snacks.

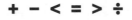

'You can't go in there.'

But in there they went.

LaTour and Tal pushed past the receptionist into the office of Daniel Montrose.

At the circular glass table sat the president of the company and the other suspect, Karen Billings.

Montrose leaned forward, eyes wide in shock. He stood up slowly. The woman, too, pushed back from the table. He was as rumpled as before; she was in a fierce crimson dress.

'You, don't move!' LaTour snapped.

The red-dress woman. She blinked, unable to keep the anger out of her face. Tal could hear the tacit rejoinder: Nobody talks to me that way.

'Why didn't you tell us about the problems with Luminux?'

The president exchanged a look with Billings.

He cleared his throat. 'Problems?'

Tal dropped the downloaded material on Montrose's desk. The president scooped it up and began to read.

Montrose looked up. LaTour had told Tal to watch the man's eyes. The eyes tell if someone's lying, the homicide cop had lectured. Tal squinted and studied them. He didn't have a clue what was going on behind his expensive glasses.

LaTour said to Billings, 'Can you tell me where you were on April seventh and the ninth?'

'What the fuck are you talking about?'

'Simple question, lady. Where were you?'

'I'm not answering any goddamn questions without our lawyer.' She crossed her arms, sat back and contentedly began a staring contest with LaTour.

'Why didn't you tell us about this?' Tal nodded at the documents.

Montrose said to Billings, 'The dimethylamino.'

'They found out about that?' she asked.

'Yeah, we found out about it,' LaTour grumbled.

Montrose turned to Tal. 'What exactly did you find in the victims' blood?'

Unprepared for the question, he frowned. 'Well, Luminux.'

'You have the coroner's report?'

Tal pulled it out of his briefcase and put it on the table. 'There.'

Montrose frowned in an exaggerated way. 'Actually, it doesn't say "Luminux".'

'The fuck you talking about? It's—'

Montrose said, 'I quote: "9-fluoro, 7-chloro-1, 3-dihydro-1-methyl-5-phenyl-2H-1, 4-benzodiazepin, 5-hydroxytryptamine and N-(1-phenethyl-4-piperidyl) propionanilide citrate".'

'Whatever,' LaTour snapped, rolling his eyes. 'That is Luminux. The medical examiner said so.'

'That's right,' Karen snapped right back. 'That's the approved version of the drug.'

LaTour started to say something but fell silent.

'Approved?' Tal asked uncertainly.

Montrose said, 'Look at the formula for the early version.'

'Early?'

'The one the FDA rejected. It's in that printout of yours.'

Oh. Tal was beginning to see where this was headed and he didn't like the destination. He found the sheet in the printout and compared it to the formula in the medical examiner's report. They were the same except that the earlier version of Luminux contained another substance, dimethylamino ethyl phosphate ester.

'What's—'

'A mild antipsychotic agent known as DEP. That's what caused the problems in the first version. In combination it had a slight psychedelic effect. As soon as we took it out, the FDA approved the drug. That was a year ago. You didn't find any DEP in the bodies. The victims were taking the approved version of the drug. No DEP-enhanced Luminux was ever released to the public.'

Billings muttered, 'And we've never had a single incidence of suicide among the six million people worldwide taking the drug – a lot of whom are probably alive today because they were taking Luminux and didn't kill themselves.'

Montrose pulled a large binder off his shelf and dropped it on his desk. 'The complete study and FDA approval. No detrimental side effects. It's even safe with alcohol in moderation.'

'Though we don't recommend it,' Billings snapped, just as icily as she had earlier that day.

'Why didn't you tell us before?' LaTour grumbled.

'You didn't ask. All drugs go through a trial period while we make them safe.' Montrose wrote a number on a memo pad. 'If you still don't believe us, this's the FDA's number. Call them.'

Billings's farewell was, 'You found your way in here. You can find your way out.'

+ – < = > ÷

Tal slouched in his office chair. LaTour was across from him with his feet up on Tal's desk again.

'Got a question,' Tal asked. 'You ever wear spurs?'

'Spurs? Oh, you mean like for horses? Why would I wear spurs? Or is that some kind of math nerd joke about putting my feet on your fucking desk?'

'You figure it out,' Tal muttered as the cop swung his feet to the floor. 'So where do we go from here? No greedy daughters, no evil drug maker. And we've pretty much humiliated ourselves in front of two *harsh* women. We're batting oh for two.' The statistician sighed. 'So where do we go from here? . . . Maybe they *did* kill themselves. Hell, sometimes life is just too much for some people.'

'You don't think that, though.'

'I don't *feel* it but I do *think* it and I do better thinking. When I start feeling I get into trouble.'

'And the world goes round and round,' LaTour said. 'Shit. It time for a beer yet?'

But a beer was the last thing on Tal's mind. He stared at the glacier of paper on his desk, the printouts, the charts, the lists, the photographs, hoping that he'd spot one fact, one *datum*, that might help them.

Tal's phone rang. He grabbed it. ''Lo?'

'Is this Detective Simms?' a meek voice asked.

'That's right.'

'I'm Bill Fendler, with Oak Creek Books in Barlow Heights. Somebody from your office called and asked to let you know if we sold any copies of *Making the Final Journey: The Complete Guide to Suicide and Euthanasia.*'

Tal sat up. 'That's right. Have you?'

'I just noticed the inventory showed one book sold in the last couple of days.'

LaTour frowned. Tal held up a wait-a-minute finger.

'Can you tell me who bought it?'

'That's what I've been debating . . . I'm not sure it's ethical. I was thinking if you had a court order it might be better.'

'We have reason to believe that somebody might be using that book to cover up a series of murders. That's why we're asking about it. Maybe it's not ethical. But I'm asking you, please, give me the name of the person who bought it.'

A pause. The man said, 'Okay. Got a pencil?'

Tal found one. 'Go ahead.'

The mathematician started to write the name. Then paused. 'Are you sure?' he asked.

'Positive, Detective. The receipt's right here in front of me.'

The phone sagged in Tal's hand. He finished jotting the name, showed it to LaTour. 'What do we do now?' he asked.

LaTour lifted a surprised eyebrow. 'Search warrant,' he said. 'That's what we do.'

The warrant was pretty easy, especially since LaTour was on good terms with nearly every judge and magistrate in Westbrook County personally, and a short time later they were halfway through their search of the modest bungalow located in even more modest Harrison Village. Tal and LaTour were in the bedroom; three uniformed county troopers were downstairs.

Drawers, closets, beneath the bed . . .

Tal wasn't exactly sure what they were looking for. He followed LaTour's lead. The big cop had considerable experience sniffing out hiding places, it seemed, but it was Tal who found the jacket, which was shedding the off-white fibers that appeared to match the one they'd found at the Whitleys'.

This was *some* connection, though a tenuous one.

'Sir, I found something outside!' the voice called up the stairs.

They went out to the garage, where the officer was standing over a suitcase, hidden under stacks of boxes. Inside were two large bottles of Luminux, with only a few pills remaining in each. There were no prescription labels attached but they seemed to be the containers that were sold directly to hospitals. This one had been sold to the Cardiac Support Center. Also in the suitcase were articles cut from magazines and newspapers – one was from several years ago. It was about a nurse who'd killed elderly patients in a nursing home in Ohio with lethal drugs. The woman was quoted as saying, 'I did a good thing, helping those people die with dignity. I never got a penny from their deaths. I only wanted them to be at peace. My worst crime is I'm an Angel of Mercy.' There were a half-dozen others, too, the theme being the kindness of euthanasia. Some actually gave practical advice on 'transitioning' people from life.

Tal stepped back, arms crossed, staring numbly at the find.

Another officer walked outside. 'Found these hidden behind the desk downstairs.'

In his latex-gloved hands Tal took the documents. They were the Bensons' files from the CSC. He opened them and read through the first page.

LaTour said something but the statistician didn't hear. He'd hoped up until now that the facts were wrong, that this was all a huge misunderstanding. But true mathematicians will always accept where the truth leads, even if it shatters their most heartfelt theorem.

There was no doubt that Mac McCaffrey was the killer.

She'd been the person who'd just bought the suicide book. And it was here, in her house, that they'd found the jacket, the Luminux bottles and the euthanasia articles. As for the Bensons' file, her name was prominently given as the couple's nurse/counselor. She'd lied about working with them.

The homicide cop spoke again.

'What'd you say?' Tal muttered.

'Where is she, you think?'

'At the hospital, I'd guess. The Cardiac Support Center.'

'So you ready?' LaTour asked.

'For what?'

'To make your first collar.'

$$+ \; - \; < \; = \; > \; \div$$

The blue cheese, in fact, turned out to be a bust.

But Nurse Mac – the only way Robert Covey could think of her now – seemed to enjoy the other food he'd laid out.

'Nobody's ever made appetizers for me,' she said, touched.

'They don't make gentlemen like me any more.'

And bless her, here was a woman who didn't whine about her weight. She smeared a big slab of pâté on a cracker and ate it right down then went for the shrimp.

Covey sat back in the couch in the den, a bit perplexed. He recalled her feistiness from their first meeting and was anticipating – and looking forward to – a fight about diet and exercise. But she made only one exercise comment. She'd opened the back door.

'Beautiful yard.'

'Thanks. Ver was the landscaper.'

'That's a nice pool. You like to swim?'

He told her he loved to, though since he'd been diagnosed with the heart problem he didn't swim alone, worried he'd faint or have a heart attack and drown.

Nurse Mac had nodded. But there was something else on her mind. She finally turned away from the pool. 'You're probably wondering what's on the agenda for this session?'

'Yes'm, I am.'

'Well, I'll be right up front. I'm here to talk you into doing something you might not want to do.'

'Ah, negotiating, are we? This involve the fourth glass of port?'

She smiled. 'It's a little more important than that. But now that you've brought it up . . .' She rose and walked to the bar. 'You don't mind, do you?' She picked up an old Taylor Fladgate, lifted an eyebrow.

'I'll mind if you pour it down the drain. I don't mind if we drink some.'

'Why don't you refill the food,' she said. 'I'll play bartender.'

When Covey returned from the kitchen Nurse Mac had poured him a large glass of port. She handed it to him then poured one for herself. She lifted hers. He did, too, and the crystal rang.

They both sipped.

'So what's this all about, you acting so mysterious?'

'What's it about?' she mused. 'It's about eliminating pain, finding peace. And sometimes you just can't do that alone. Sometimes you need somebody to help you.'

'Can't argue with the sentiment. What've you got in mind? Specific, I mean.'

Mac leaned forward, tapped her glass to his. 'Drink up.' They downed the ruby-colored liquor.

$$+ \; - \; < \; = \; > \; \div$$

'Go, go, go!'

'You wanna drive?' LaTour shouted over the roar of the engine. They skidded sharply around the parkway, over the curb and onto the grass, nearly scraping the side of the unmarked car against a jutting rock.

'At least I know *how* to drive,' Tal called. Then: 'Step on it!'

'Shut the fuck up. Let me concentrate.'

As the wheel grated against another curb Tal decided this was a wise idea and fell silent.

Another squad car was behind them.

'There, that's the turnoff.' Tal pointed.

LaTour controlled the skid and somehow he managed to keep them out of the oncoming traffic lane.

Another three hundred yards. Tal directed the homicide cop down the winding road then up a long driveway. At the end of which was a small, dark blue sedan. The same car the witnesses had seen outside the Bensons' house, the same car that had left the tread marks at the Whitleys' the day they died.

Killing the siren, LaTour skidded to a stop in front of the car. The squad car parked close behind, blocking the sedan in.

All four officers leapt out. As they ran past the vehicle Tal glanced in the backseat and saw the tan baseball cap that the driver of the car had worn outside the Bensons' house.

In a movement quite smooth for such a big man LaTour unlatched the door and shoved inside, not even breaking stride. He pulled his gun from his holster.

They and the uniformed officers behind them charged into the living room and then the den.

They stopped, looking at the two astonished people on the couch.

One was Robert Covey, who was unharmed.

The other, the woman who'd been about to kill him, Mac McCaffrey, was standing over him, eyes wide. She was just offering him one of the tools of her murderous trade: a glass undoubtedly laced with enough Luminux to render him half-conscious and suggestible to suicide. He noticed that the back door was open, revealing a large swimming pool. So, not a gun or carbon monoxide. Death by drowning this time.

'Tal!' she gasped.

But he said nothing. He let LaTour step forward to cuff her and arrest her. The homicide cop was, of course, much better versed in such matters of protocol.

+ − < = > ÷

The homicide detective looked through her purse and found the suicide book inside.

Robert Covey was in the ambulance outside, being checked out by the medics. He'd seemed okay but they were taking their time, just to make sure. He wouldn't have had time to ingest too much of the drug.

After they found the evidence at Mac's house, they'd gone to the hospital. She was out, but Dr Dehoeven at the CRC had pulled her client list and they'd gone through her calendar, learning that she was meeting with Covey at that moment.

LaTour would've been content to ship Mac off to Central Booking but Tal was a bit out of control; he couldn't help confronting her. 'You *did* know Don and Patsy Benson. Don was your client. You lied to me.'

Mac started to speak then looked down, her tearful eyes on the floor.

'We found Benson's files in your house. And the computer logs at CSC showed you erased his records. You *were* at their house the day they died. It was you the witness saw in the hat and sunglasses. And the Whitleys? You killed them, too.'

'I didn't kill anybody!'

'Okay, fine – you *helped* them kill themselves. You drugged them and talked them into it. And then cleaned up after.' He turned to the uniformed deputy. 'Take her to Booking.'

And she was led away, calling, 'I didn't do anything wrong!'

'Bullshit,' LaTour muttered.

Though, staring after her as the car eased down the long drive, Tal reflected that in a way – some abstract, moral sense – she truly *did* believe she hadn't done anything wrong.

But to the people of the state of New York, the evidence was irrefutable. Nurse Claire 'Mac' McCaffrey had murdered four people and undoubtedly intended to murder scores of others. She'd gotten the Bensons doped up on Friday and helped them kill themselves. Then on Sunday she'd called the Whitleys from a pay phone, made sure they were home, then went over there and arranged for their suicides, too. She'd cleaned up the place, taken the Luminux and hadn't left until *after* they died. Tal had learned that the opera show she listened to wasn't on until 7 p.m. Not 4 p.m., as she'd told him. That was why he hadn't been able to find it when he'd surfed the frequencies in LaTour's car.

She'd gone into this business to ease the suffering of patients – because her own mother had had such a difficult time dying. But what she'd meant by 'easing suffering' was putting them down like dogs.

Robert Covey returned to his den. He was badly shaken but physically fine. He had some Luminux in his system but not a dangerously high dosage. 'She seemed so nice, so normal,' he whispered.

Oh, you bet, Tal thought bitterly. A goddamn perfect member of the Four Per Cent Club.

He and LaTour did some paperwork – Tal so upset that he didn't even think about his own questionnaire – and they walked back to LaTour's car. Tal sat heavily in the front seat, staring straight ahead. The homicide cop didn't start the engine. He said, 'Sometimes closing a case is harder than not closing it. That's something they don't teach you at the academy. But you did what you had to. People'll be alive now because of what you did.'

'I guess,' he said sullenly. He was picturing Mac's office. Her crooked smile when she'd looked over the park. Her laugh.

'Let's file the papers. Then we'll go get a beer. Hey, you do drink beer, don'tcha?'

'Yeah, I drink beer,' Tal said.

'We'll make a cop outta you yet, Einstein.'

Tal clipped his seat belt on, deciding that being a Real cop was the last thing in the world he wanted.

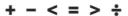

A beep on the intercom. 'Mr Covey's here, sir.'

'I'll be right there.' Dr William Farley rose from his desk, a glass-sheet-covered Victorian piece his business partner had bought for him in New England on one of the man's buying sprees. Farley would have been content to have a metal desk or even a card table.

But in the *business* of medicine, not the *practice*, appearances count. The offices of the Lotus Foundation, near the mall containing Neiman Marcus and Saks Fifth Avenue, were filled with many antiques in this rococo style. Farley had been amused when they'd moved here three years ago to see the fancy furniture, paintings, objets d'art. Now, they were virtually invisible to him. What he greatly preferred was the huge medical facility itself behind the offices. As a doctor and researcher, that was the only place he felt truly at home.

Forty-eight, slim to the point of being scrawny, hair with a mind of its own, Farley had nonetheless worked hard to rid himself of his back-room medical researcher's image. He now pulled on his thousand-dollar suit jacket and applied a comb. He paused at the door, took a deep breath, exhaled and stepped into a lengthy corridor to the Foundation's main lobby. It was deserted except for the receptionist and one elderly man, sitting in a deep plush couch.

'Mr Covey?' the doctor asked, extending his hand.

The man set down the coffee cup he'd been given by the receptionist and they shook hands.

'Dr Farley?'

A nod.

'Come on into my office.'

They chatted about the weather as Farley led him down the narrow corridor to his office. Sometimes the patients here talked about sports, about their families, about the paintings on the walls.

Sometimes they were so nervous they said nothing at all.

Entering the office, Farley gestured toward a chair and then sat behind the massive desk. Covey glanced at it, unimpressed. Farley looked him over. He didn't appear particularly wealthy – an off-the-rack suit, a tie with stripes that went one way while those on his shirt went another. Still, the director of the Lotus Foundation had learned enough about rich people to know that the wealthiest were those who drove hybrid Toyota gas savers and wore raincoats until they were threadbare.

Farley poured more coffee and offered Covey a cup.

'Like I said on the phone yesterday, I know a little about your condition . . . Your cardiologist is Jennifer Lansdowne, right?'

'That's right.'

'And you're seeing someone from the Cardiac Support Center at the hospital.'

Covey frowned. 'I *was*.'

'You're not any longer?'

'A problem with the nurse they sent me. I haven't decided if I'm going back. But that's a whole 'nother story.'

'Well, we think you might be a good candidate for our services here, Mr Covey. We offer a special program to patients in certain cases.'

'What kind of cases?'

'Serious cases.'

'The Lotus Foundation for *Alternative* Treatment,' Covey recited. 'Correct me if I'm wrong but I don't think ginseng and acupuncture work for serious cases.'

'That's not what we're about.' Farley looked him over carefully. 'You a businessman, sir?'

'Was. For half a century.'

'What line?'

'Manufacturing. Then venture capital.'

'Then I imagine you generally like to get straight to the point.'

'You got that right.'

'Well, then let me ask you this, Mr Covey. How would you like to live forever?'

$$+ \ - \ < \ = \ > \ \div$$

'How's that?'

In the same way that he'd learned to polish his shoes and speak in words of less than four syllables, Farley had learned how to play potential patients like trout. He knew how to pace the pitch. 'I'd like to tell you about the Foundation. But first would you mind signing this?' He opened the drawer of his desk and passed a document to Covey.

He read it. 'A nondisclosure agreement.'

'It's pretty standard.'

'I know it is,' the old man said. 'I've written 'em. Why do you want me to sign it?'

'Because what I'm going to tell you can't be made public.'

He was intrigued now, the doctor could tell, though trying not to show it.

'If you don't want to, I understand. But then I'm afraid we won't be able to pursue our conversation further.'

Covey read the sheet again. 'Got a pen?'

Farley handed him a Mont Blanc; Covey took the heavy barrel with a laugh suggesting he didn't like ostentation very much. He signed and pushed the document back.

Farley put it into his desk. 'Now, Dr Lansdowne's a good woman. And she'll do whatever's humanly possible to fix your heart and give you a few more years. But there're limits to what medical science can do. After all, Mr Covey, we all die. You, me, the children being born at this minute. Saints and sinners . . . we're all going to die.'

'You got an interesting approach to medical services, Doctor. You cheer up all your patients this way?'

Dr Farley smiled. 'We hear a lot about aging nowadays.'

'Can't turn on the TV without it.'

'And about people trying to stay young forever.'

'Second time you used that word. Keep going.'

'Mr Covey, you ever hear about the Hayflick limit?'

'Nope. Never have.'

'Named after the man who discovered that human cells can reproduce themselves a limited number of times. At first, they make perfect reproductions of themselves. But after a while they can't keep up that level of quality control, you could say; they become more and more inefficient.'

'Why?'

Covey, he reflected, was a sharp one. Most people he pitched sat there and nodded with stupid smiles on their faces. He continued. 'There's an important strand of DNA that gets shorter and shorter each time the cells reproduce. When it gets too short, the cells go haywire and they don't duplicate properly. Sometimes they stop altogether.'

'I'm following you in general. But go light on the biology bullshit. Wasn't my strong suit.'

'Fair enough, Mr Covey. Now, there're some ways to cheat the Hayflick limit. In the future it may be possible to extend life span significantly, dozens, maybe hundreds of years.'

'That ain't forever.'

'No, it's not.'

'So cut to the chase.'

'We'll never be able to construct a human body that will last more than a few hundred years at the outside. The laws of physics and nature just don't allow it. And even if we could, we'd still have disease and illness and accidents that shorten life spans.'

'This's getting cheerier and cheerier.'

'Now, Dr Lansdowne'll do what she can medically, and the Cardiac Support Center will give you plenty of help.'

'Depending on the nurse,' Covey muttered. 'Go on.'

'And you might have another five, ten, fifteen years . . . Or you can consider our program.' Farley handed Covey a business card and tapped the logo of the Lotus Foundation, a golden flower. 'You know what the lotus signifies in mythology?'

'Not a clue.'

'Immortality.'

'Does it now?'

'Primitive people'd see lotuses grow up out of the water in riverbeds that'd been dry for years. They assumed the plants were immortal.'

'You said you can't keep people from dying.'

'We can't. You will die. What we offer is what you might call a type of reincarnation.'

Covey sneered. 'I stopped going to church thirty years ago.'

'Well, Mr Covey. I've never gone to church. I'm not talking about spiritual reincarnation. No, I mean scientific, provable reincarnation.'

The old man grunted. 'This's about the time you start losing people, right?'

Farley laughed hard. 'That's right. Pretty much at that sentence.'

'Well, you ain't lost me yet. Keep going.'

'It's very complex but I'll give it to you in a nutshell – just a little biology.'

The old man sipped more coffee and waved his hand for the doctor to continue.

'The Foundation holds the patent on a process that's known as neuro stem cell regenerative replication . . . I know, it's a mouthful. Around here we just call it consciousness cloning.'

'Explain that.'

'What is consciousness?' Farley asked. 'You look around the room, you see things, smell them, have reactions. Have thoughts. I sit in the same room, focus on different things, or focus on the same things and have different reactions. Why? Because our brains are unique.'

A slow nod. This fish was getting close to the fly.

'The Foundation's developed a way to genetically map your brain and then program embryonic cells to grow in a way that duplicates it perfectly. After you die your identical consciousness is re-created in a fetus. You're' – a slight smile – 'born again. In a secular, biological sense, of course. The sensation you have is as if your brain were transplanted into another body.'

Farley poured more coffee, handed it to Covey, who was shaking his head.

'How the hell do you do this?' Covey whispered.

'It's a three-step process.' The doctor was always delighted to talk about his work. 'First, we plot the exact structure of your brain as it exists now – the parts where the consciousness resides. We use super-computers and micro-MRI machines.'

'MRI. That's like a fancy X-ray, right?'

'Magnetic resonance. We do a perfect schematic of your consciousness. Then step two: You know about genes, right? They're the blueprints for our bodies, every cell in your body contains them. Well, genes decide not only what your hair color is and your height and susceptibility to certain diseases but also how your brain develops. After a certain age the brain development gene shuts off; your brain's structure is determined and doesn't change – that's why brain tissue doesn't regenerate if it's destroyed. The second step is to extract and reactivate the development gene. Then we implant it into a fetus.'

'You clone me?'

'No, not your body. We use donor sperm and egg and a surrogate mother. There's an *in vitro* clinic attached to the Foundation. You're "placed", we call it, with a good family from the same socioeconomic class as you live in now.'

Covey wanted to be skeptical but he was still receptive.

'The final part is to use chemical and electromagnetic intervention to make sure the brain develops identically to the map we made of your present one. Stimulate some cell growth, inhibit others. When you're born again, your perceptions are exactly what they are from your point of view now. Your sensibilities, interests, desires.'

Covey blinked.

'You won't look like you. Your body type will be different. Though you will be male. We insist on that. It's not our job to work out gender identity issues.'

'Not a problem,' he said shortly, frowning at the absurdity of the idea. Then: 'Can you eliminate health problems? I had skin cancer. And the heart thing, of course.'

'We don't do that. We don't make supermen or superwomen. We simply boost your consciousness into another generation, exactly as you are now.'

Covey considered this for a moment. 'Will I remember meeting you, will I have images of this life?'

'Ah, memories . . . We didn't quite know about those at first. But it seems that, yes, you will remember, to some extent – because memories are hardwired into some portions of the brain. We aren't sure how many yet, since our first clients are only three or four years old – in their second lives, of course – and we haven't had a chance to fully interview them yet.'

'You've actually *done* this?' he whispered.

Farley nodded. 'Oh, yes, Mr Covey. We're up and running.'

'What about will I go wacko or anything? That sheep they cloned and died? She was a mess, I heard.'

'No, that can't happen because we control development, like I was explaining. Every step of the way.'

'Jesus,' he whispered. 'This isn't a joke?'

'Oh, no, not at all.'

'Let's say it actually works . . . You said, "Forever". So, what? We do the same thing in seventy years or whatever?'

'It's literally a lifetime guarantee, even if that lifetime lasts ten thousand years. The Lotus Foundation will stay in touch with all our clients over the years. You can keep going for as many generations as you want.'

'How do I know you'll still be in business?'

A slight chuckle. 'Because we sell a product there's an infinite demand for. Companies that provide that don't ever go out of business.'

Covey eyed Farley and the old man said coyly, 'Which brings up your fee.'

'As you can imagine . . .'

'Forever don't come cheap. Gimme a number.'

'One half of your estate with a minimum of ten million dollars.'

'One half? That's about twenty-eight million. But it's not liquid. Real estate, stocks, bonds. I can't just write you a check for it.'

'We don't want you to. We're keeping this procedure very low-key. In the future we hope to offer our services to more people, but now our costs are so high we can work only with the ones who can cover the expenses . . . And, let's be realistic, we prefer people like you in the program.'

'Like me?'

'Let's say higher in the gene pool than others.'

Covey grunted. 'Well, how *do* you get paid?'

'You leave the money to one of our charities in your will.'

'Charities?'

'The Foundation owns dozens of them. The money gets to us eventually.'

'So you don't get paid until I die.'

'That's right. Some clients wait until they actually die of their disease. Most, though, do the paperwork and then transition themselves.'

'Transition?'

'They end their own life. That way they avoid a painful end. And, of course, the sooner they leave, the sooner they come back.'

'How many people've done this?'

'Six.'

Covey looked out the window for a moment, at the trees in Central Park, waving slowly in a sharp breeze. 'This's crazy. The whole thing's nuts.'

Farley laughed. '*You'd* be nuts if you didn't think that at first . . . Come on, I'll give you a tour of the facility.'

Setting down his coffee, Covey followed the doctor out of the office. They walked down the hallway through an impressive-looking security door into the laboratory portion of the Foundation. Farley pointed out first the massive Mistsuhana supercomputers used for brain mapping and then the genetics lab and cryogenic facility itself, which they couldn't enter but could see from windows in the corridor. A half-dozen white-coated employees dipped pipettes into tubes, grew cultures in petri dishes and hunched over microscopes.

Covey was intrigued but not yet sold, Farley noted.

'Let's go back to the office.'

When they'd sat again the old man finally said, 'Well, I'll think about it.'

Farley nodded with a smile and said, 'You bet. A decision like this . . . Some people just can't bring themselves to sign on. You take your time.' He handed Covey a huge binder. 'Those're case studies, genetic data for comparison with the transitioning clients and their next life selves, interviews with them. There's nothing identifying them but you can read about the children and the process itself.' Farley paused and let Covey flip through the material. He seemed to be reading it carefully. The doctor added, 'What's so nice about this is that you never have to say goodbye to your loved ones. Say you've got a son or daughter . . . we could contact them when they're older and propose our services to them. You could reconnect with them a hundred years from now.'

At the words 'son or daughter', Covey had looked up, blinking. His eyes drifted off and finally he said, 'I don't know . . .'

'Mr Covey,' Farley said, 'let me just add one thing. I understand your skepticism. But you tell me you're a businessman? Well, I'm going to treat you like one. Sure, you've got doubts. Who wouldn't? But even if you're not one hundred per cent sure, even if you think I'm trying to sell you a load of hooey, what've you got to lose? You're going to die anyway. Why don't you just roll the dice and take the chance?'

Farley let this sink in for a minute and saw that the words – as so often – were having an effect. Time to back off. He said, 'Now I've got some phone calls to make, if you'll excuse me. There's a lounge through that door. Take your time and read through those things.'

Covey picked up the files and stepped into the room the doctor indicated. The door closed.

Farley had pegged the old man as shrewd and deliberate. And accordingly the doctor gave him a full forty-five minutes to examine the materials. Finally he rose and walked to the doorway. Before he could say anything Covey looked up from the leather couch he was sitting in and said, 'I'll do it. I want to do it.'

'I'm very happy for you,' Farley said sincerely.

'What do I need to do now?'

'All you do is an MRI scan and then give us a blood sample for the genetic material.'

'You don't need part of my brain?'

'That's what's so amazing about genes. All of us is contained in a cell of our own blood.'

Covey nodded.

'Then you change your will and we take it from there.' He looked in a file and pulled out a list of the charities the Foundation had set up recently.

'Any of these appeal? You should pick three or four. And they ought to be something in line with interests or causes you had when you were alive.'

'There.' Covey circled three of them. 'I'll leave most to the Metropolitan Arts Assistance Association.' He looked up. 'Veronica, my wife, was an artist. That okay?'

'It's fine.' Farley copied down the names and some other information and then handed a card to Covey. 'Just take that to your lawyer.'

The old man nodded. 'His office is just a few miles from here. I could see him today.'

'Just bring us a copy of the will.' He didn't add what Covey of course, a savvy businessman, knew. That if the will was not altered, or if he changed it later, the Foundation wouldn't do the cloning. They had the final say.

'What about the . . . transition?'

Farley said, 'That's your choice. Entirely up to you. Tomorrow or next year. Whatever you're comfortable with.'

At the door Covey paused and turned back, shook Farley's hand. He gave a faint laugh. 'Who would've thought? Forever.'

✛ – < = > ÷

In Greek mythology Eos was the goddess of dawn and she was captivated with the idea of humans as lovers. She fell deeply in love with a mortal, Tithonos, the son of the king of Troy, and convinced Zeus to let him live forever.

The god of gods agreed. But he neglected one small detail: granting him youth as well as immortality. While Eos remained unchanged Tithonos grew older and more decrepit with each passing year until he was so old he was unable to move or speak. Horrified, Eos turned him into an insect and moved on to more suitable paramours.

Dr William Farley thought of this myth now, sitting at his desk in the Lotus Foundation. The search for immortality's always been tough on us poor humans, he reflected. But how doggedly we ignore the warning in Tithonos's myth – and the logic of science – and continue to look for ways to cheat death.

Farley glanced at a picture on his desk. It showed a couple, arm in arm – younger versions of those in a second picture on his credenza. His parents. Who'd died in an auto accident when Farley was in medical school.

An only child, desperately close to them, he took months to recover from the shock. When he was able to resume his studies, he decided he'd specialize in emergency medicine – devoting his life to saving lives threatened by trauma.

But the young man was brilliant – too smart for the repetitious mechanics of ER work. Lying awake nights he would reflect about his parents' deaths and he took some reassurance that they were, in a biochemical way, still alive within him. He developed an interest in genetics, and that was the subject he began to pursue in earnest.

Months, then years, of manic twelve-hour days doing research in the field resulted in many legitimate discoveries. But this also led to some ideas that were less conventional, even bizarre – consciousness cloning for instance.

Not surprisingly, he was either ignored or ridiculed by his peers. His papers were rejected by professional journals, his grant requests turned down. The rejection didn't discourage him, though he grew more and more desperate to find the millions of dollars needed to research his theory. One day a few years ago, nearly penniless and living in a walk-up beside one of Westbrook's commuter train lines, he'd gotten a call from an old acquaintance. The man had heard about Farley's plight and had an idea.

'You want to raise money for your research?' he'd asked the impoverished medico. 'It's easy. Find really sick, really wealthy patients and sell them immortality.'

'What?'

'No, no, no, listen,' the man had continued. 'Find patients who're about to die anyway. They'll be desperate. You package it right, they'll buy it.'

'I can't sell them anything yet,' Farley had replied. 'I *believe* I can make this work. But it could take years.'

'Well, sometimes sacrifices have to be made. You can pick up ten million overnight, twenty. That'd buy some pretty damn nice research facilities.'

Farley had been quiet, considering those words. Then he'd said, 'I *could* keep tissue samples, I suppose, and then when we actually can do the cloning, I could bring them back then.'

'Hey, there you go,' said the doctor. Something in the tone suggested to Farley that he didn't think the process would ever work. But the man's disbelief was irrelevant if he could help Farley get the money he needed for research.

'Well, all right,' Farley said to his colleague – who was none other than Anthony Sheldon, of the Cardiology Department at Westbrook Hospital, a man who was as talented an entrepreneur as he was a cardiovascular surgeon.

Five years ago they'd set up the Lotus Foundation, an *in vitro* clinic, and a network of bogus charities. Tony Sheldon, whose office was near the Cardiac Support Center, would finagle a look at the files of patients there and would find the richest and sickest. Then he'd arrange for them to be contacted by the Lotus Foundation, and Farley would sell them the program.

Farley had truly doubted that anybody would buy the pitch but Sheldon had coached him well. The man had thought of everything. He found unique appeals for each potential client and gave Farley this information to snare them. In the case of the Bensons, for instance, Sheldon had learned how much they loved each other. His pitch to them was that this was the chance to be together forever, as they so poignantly noted in their suicide note. With Robert Covey, Sheldon had learned – by ransacking the CSC files – about his estranged son, so Farley added the tactical mention that a client could have a second chance to connect with children.

Sheldon had also come up with one vital part of the pitch. He made sure the patients got high doses of Luminux (even the coffee that Covey had just been drinking, for instance, was laced with the drug). Neither doctor believed that anyone would sign up for a far-fetched idea without the benefit of some mind-numbing Mickey Finn.

The final selling point was, of course, the desperate desire of people facing death to believe what Farley promised them.

And that turned out to be one hell of a selling point. The Lotus Foundation had earned almost $93 million in five years.

Everything had gone fine – until recently, when their greed got the better of them. Well, got the better of Sheldon. They'd decided that the cardiologist would never refer his own patients to the Foundation – and would wait six months or a year between clients. But Tony Sheldon apparently had a mistress with very expensive taste and had lost some serious money in the stock market recently. Just after the Bensons signed up, the Whitleys presented themselves. They were far too wealthy to pass up and so Farley reluctantly yielded to Sheldon's pressure to go ahead with the plan.

But they learned that, though eager to proceed, Sam Whitley had wanted to reassure himself that this wasn't pure quackery and he'd tracked down some technical literature about the computers used in the technique and genetics in general. After the patients had died, Farley had to find this information in his house, burn it and scour the place for any other evidence that might lead back to the Foundation.

The intrusion, though, must've alerted the police to the possibility that the families' deaths were suspicious. Officers had actually interviewed Sheldon, sending a scream of panic through Farley. But then a scapegoat stumbled into the picture: Mac McCaffrey, a young nurse/counselor at the Cardiac Support Center. She was seeing their latest recent prospect – Robert Covey – as she'd been seeing the Bensons and the Whitleys. This made her suspect to start with. Even better was her reluctance to admit she'd seen the Bensons; after their suicide, the nurse had apparently lied about seeing them and had stolen their files from the CSC. A perfect setup. Sheldon had used his ample resources to bribe a pharmacist at the CSC to doctor the logs and give him a couple of wholesale bottles containing a few Luminux tablets, to make it look like she'd been drugging patients for some time. Farley, obsessed with death and dying, had a vast library of articles on euthanasia and suicide. He copied several dozen of these. The drugs and the articles they planted in her garage – insurance in case they needed somebody to take the fall.

Which they had. And now the McCaffrey woman had just been hauled off to jail.

A whole 'nother story, as Covey had said.

The nurse's arrest had troubled Farley. He'd speculated out loud about telling the police that she was innocent. But Sheldon reminded him coolly what would happen if Farley did that, and he relented.

Sheldon had said, 'Look, we'll do one more – this Covey – and then take a break. A year. Two years.'

'No. Let's wait.'

'I checked him out,' Sheldon said. 'He's worth over fifty million.'

'I think it's too risky.'

'I've thought about that.' With the police still looking into the Benson and Whitley suicides, Sheldon explained, it'd be better to have the old man die in a mugging or hit-and-run, rather than killing himself.

'But,' Farley had whispered, 'you mean murder?'

'A suicide'll be way too suspicious.'

'We can't.'

But Sheldon had snapped, 'Too late for morality, Doctor. You made your deal with the devil. You can't renegotiate now.' And hung up.

Farley stewed for a while but finally realized the man was right; there was no going back. And, my, what he could do in the lab with another $25 million . . .

His secretary buzzed him on the intercom.

'Mr Covey's back, sir.'

A hesitation. Then: 'Show him in.'

Covey walked into the office. They shook hands again and Covey sat. As cheerful and blinky as most patients on 75 mg of Luminux. He happily took another cup of special brew then reached into his jacket pocket and displayed a copy of the codicil to the will. 'Here you go.'

Though Farley wasn't a lawyer he knew what to look for; the document was in proper form.

They shook hands formally.

Covey finished his coffee and Farley escorted him to the lab, where he would undergo the MRI and give a blood sample, making the nervous small talk that the clients always made at this point in the process.

The geneticist shook his hand and told him he'd made the right decision. Covey thanked Farley sincerely and with a hopeful smile on his face that was, Farley knew, only partly from the drug. He returned to his office and the doctor picked up the phone, called Anthony Sheldon. 'Covey's changed the will. He'll be leaving here in about fifteen minutes.'

'I'll take care of him now,' Sheldon said and hung up.

Farley sighed and dropped the receiver into the cradle. He stripped off his suit jacket, then pulled on a white lab coat. He left his office and fled up the hall to the research lab, where he knew he would find solace in the honest world of science, where he would be safe from all his guilt and sins, as if they were locked out by the double-sealed doors of the airlock.

+ − < = > ÷

Robert Covey was walking down the street, feeling pretty giddy, odd thoughts going through his head.

Thinking of his life – the way he'd lived it. And the people who'd touched him and whom he'd touched. A foreman in the Bedford plant, who'd worked for the company for forty years . . . The other men in his golfing foursome . . . Veronica . . . His brother . . .

His son, of course.

Still no call from Randy. And for the first time it occurred to him that maybe there *was* a reason the boy – well, young man – had been ignoring him. He'd always assumed he'd been such a good father. But maybe not. He'd have to rethink that.

Nothing makes you question your life more closely than when somebody's trying to sell you immortality.

Walking toward the main parking garage, Covey noted that the area was largely deserted. He saw only a few grungy kids on skateboards, a pretty redhead across the street, two men getting out of a white van parked near an alley.

He paid attention only to the men, because they were large, dressed in what looked like cheap suits and who, with a glance up and down, started in his direction.

Covey soon forgot them, though, and concentrated again on his son. Thinking about his decision not to tell the boy about his illness. Maybe withholding things like this had been a pattern in Covey's life. Maybe the boy had felt excluded. He'd have to consider this.

He laughed to himself. Maybe he should leave a message about what he and Farley had just been talking about. Lord have mercy, what he wouldn't give to see Randy's reaction when he listened to that! He could—

Covey slowed, frowning.

What was this?

The two men from the van were now jogging – directly toward him. He hesitated and shied back. Suddenly the men split up. One stopped and turned his back to Covey, scanning the sidewalk, while the other sped up, springing directly toward the old man. Then simultaneously they both pulled guns from under their coats.

No!

He turned to run, thinking that sprinting would probably kill him faster than the bullets. Not that it mattered. The man approaching him was fast and before Covey had a chance to take more than a few steps he was being pulled roughly into the alleyway behind him.

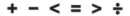

'No, what are you doing? Who are—'

'Quiet!'

The man pressed Covey against the wall.

The other joined them but continued to gaze out over the street as he spoke into a walkie-talkie. 'We've got him. No sign of hostiles. Move in, all units, move in!'

From out on the street came the rushing sound of car engines and the bleats of sirens.

'Sorry, Mr Covey. We had a little change of plans.' The man speaking was the one who'd pulled him into the alley. They both produced badges and ID cards of the Westbrook County Sheriff's Department. 'We work with Greg LaTour.'

Oh, LaTour . . . He was the burly officer who, along with that skinny young officer named Talbot Simms, had come to his house early this morning with a truly bizarre story. This outfit called the Lotus Foundation might be running some kind of scam, targeting sick people, but the police weren't quite sure how it worked. Had he been contacted by anyone there? When Covey had told them yes and that he was in fact meeting with Farley that afternoon they wondered if he'd be willing to wear a wire to find out what it was all about – the recorder taped low on his abdomen so the MRI wouldn't pick it up.

Well, what it was all about was immortality . . . and it *had* been one hell of a scam.

The plan was that after he stopped at Farley's office and dropped off the codicil to his will (he executed a second one at the same time, voiding the one he'd given Farley), he was going to meet LaTour and Simms at a Starbucks not far away.

But plans had apparently changed.

'Who're you?' Covey now asked. 'Where're Laurel and Hardy?'

The officer who'd shoved him into the alley had blinked, not understanding. He said, 'Well, sir, what happened was we had a tap on the phone in Farley's office. He called Sheldon to tell him about you and we got the impression like they weren't going to wait to try to talk you into killing yourself. Sheldon was going to kill you right away – make it look like a mugging or hit-and-run, we think.'

Covey muttered, 'You might've thought about that possibility right up front.' He remembered a saying from his army days: Never volunteer.

There was a crackle in the mike/speaker of one of the officers. Covey couldn't hear too well but the gist of it was that they'd arrested Dr Anthony Sheldon just outside his office. They now stepped out of the alley, and Covey observed a half-dozen police officers escorting William Farley and three men in lab coats out of the Lotus Foundation offices in handcuffs.

Covey observed the processional coolly, feeling contempt for the depravity of the scam, though also a grudging admiration. A businessman to his soul, Robert Covey couldn't help being impressed by someone who'd identified an inexhaustible market demand. Even if the product he sold was completely bogus.

+ − < = > ÷

The itch had yet to be scratched. Tal's office was still as sloppy as LaTour's. The mess was driving him crazy, though Shellee seemed to think it was a step up on the evolutionary chain – for him to have digs that looked like everyone else's.

Captain Dempsey was sitting in the office, playing with one rolled-up sleeve, then the other. Greg LaTour, too, his booted feet on the floor for a change; the reason for this propriety seemed to be that Tal's desk was piled too high with paper to find a place to rest them.

'How'd you tip to this scam of theirs?' the captain asked. 'The Lotus Foundation?'

Tal said, 'Some things just didn't add up.'

'Haw.' From LaTour.

Both the captain and Tal glanced at him.

LaTour stopped smiling. 'He's the math guy. He says something didn't add up. I thought it was a joke.' He grumbled, 'Go on.'

Tal explained that after he'd returned to the office following Mac's arrest, he couldn't get her out of his head.

'Women do that,' LaTour said.

'No, I mean there was something odd about the whole case,' he continued. 'Issues I couldn't reconcile. So I checked with Crime Scene – there *was* no Luminux in the port Mac was giving Covey. Then I went to see her in the lockup. She admitted she'd lied about not being the Bensons' nurse. She admitted she destroyed their records at the Cardiac Support Center and that she was the one the witnesses had seen the day they died. But she lied because she was afraid she'd lose her job – two of her patients killing themselves? When, to her, they seemed to be doing fine? It shook her up bad. That's why she bought the suicide book. She bought it *after* I told her about it – she got the title from me. She wanted to know what to look for, to make sure nobody else died.'

'And you believed her?' the captain asked.

'Yes, I did. I asked Covey if she'd ever brought up suicide. Did he have any sense that she was trying to get him to kill himself? But he said no. All she'd talked about at that meeting – when we arrested her – was how painful and hard it is to go through a tough illness alone. She'd known that he hadn't called his son. She gave him some port, got him relaxed and was trying to talk him into calling the boy.'

'You said something about an opera show?' Dempsey continued, examining both sleeves and making sure they were rolled up to within a quarter-inch of each other. Tal promised himself never to compulsively play with his tie knot again. 'You said she lied about the time it was on.'

'Oh. Right. Oops.'

'Oops?'

'The Whitleys died on Sunday. The show's on at four then. But it's on at *seven* during the week, just after the business report. I checked the NPR program guide.'

The captain asked, 'And the articles about euthanasia? The ones they found in her house?'

'Planted. Her fingerprints weren't on them. Only glove-print smudges. The stolen Luminux bottle, too. No prints. And, according to the inventory, those drugs disappeared from the clinic when Mac was out of town. Naw, she didn't have anything to do with the scam. It was Farley and Sheldon.'

LaTour continued, 'Quite a plan. Slipping the patients the drugs, getting them to change their wills, then kill themselves and cleaning up afterwards.'

'They did it all themselves? Farley and Sheldon?'

LaTour shook his head. 'They must've hired muscle or used somebody in the Foundation for the dirty work. We got four of 'em in custody. But they clammed up. Nobody's saying anything.' LaTour sighed. 'And they got the best lawyers in town. Big surprise, with all the fucking money they've got.'

Tal said, 'So, anyway, I knew Mac was being set up. But we still couldn't figure what was going on. You know, in solving an algebra problem you look for common denominators and—'

'Again with the fucking math,' LaTour grumbled.

'Well, what was the denominator? We had two couples committing suicide and leaving huge sums of money to charities – more than half their estates. I looked up the statistics from the NAEPP.'

'The—'

'The National Association of Estate Planning Professionals. When people have children, only two per cent leave that much of their estate to charities. And even when they're childless, only twelve per cent leave significant estates – that's over ten million dollars – to charities. So that made me wonder what was up with these nonprofits. I called the guy at the SEC I've been working with and he put me in touch with the people in charge of registering charities in New York, New Jersey, Massachusetts and Delaware. I followed the trail of the nonprofits and found they were all owned ultimately by the Lotus Foundation. It's controlled by Farley and Sheldon. I checked them out. Sheldon was a rich cardiologist who'd been sued for malpractice a couple of times and been investigated for some securities fraud and insider trading. Farley? . . . Okay, now *he* was interesting. A crackpot. Trying to get funding for some weird cloning theory. I'd found his name on a card for the Lotus Foundation at the Whitleys'. It had something to do with alternative medical treatment but it didn't say what specifically.'

LaTour explained about checking with Mac and the other Cardiac Support Center patients to see if they'd heard from the Foundation. That led them to Covey.

'Immortality,' Dempsey said slowly. 'And people fell for it.'

Together forever . . .

'Well, they were pretty doped up on Luminux, remember,' Tal said.

But LaTour offered what was perhaps the more insightful answer. 'People always fall for shit they wanta fall for.'

'That McCaffrey woman been released yet?' Dempsey asked uneasily. Arresting the wrong person was probably as embarrassing as declaring a bum 2124 (and as expensive; Sandra Whitley's lawyer – as harsh as she was – had already contacted the Sheriff's Department, threatening suit).

'Oh, yeah. Dropped all charges,' Tal said. Then he looked over his desk. 'I'm going to finish up the paperwork and ship it off to the prosecutor. Then I've got some spreadsheets to get back to.'

He glanced up to see a cryptic look pass between LaTour and the captain. He wondered what it meant.

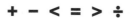

Naiveté.

The tacit exchange in Tal's office between the two older cops was a comment on Tal's naiveté. The paperwork didn't get 'finished up' at all. Over the next few days it just grew and grew and grew.

As did his hours. His working day expanded from an average 8.3 hours to 12+.

LaTour happily pointed out, 'You call a twenty-one-twenty-four, you're the case officer. You stay with it all the way till the end. Ain't life sweet?'

And the end was nowhere in sight. Analyzing the evidence – the hundreds of cartons removed from the Lotus Foundation and from Sheldon's office – Tal learned that the Bensons hadn't been the first victims. Farley and Sheldon had engineered four other suicides, going back several years, and had stolen tens of millions of dollars. The prior suicides were like the Bensons and the Whitleys – upper class and quite ill, though not necessarily terminal. Tal was shocked to find that he was familiar with one of the earlier victims: Mary Stemple, a physicist who'd taught at the Princeton Institute for Advanced Study, the famed think tank where Einstein had worked. Tal had read some of her papers. A trained mathematician, she'd done most of her work in physics and astronomy and made important discoveries about the size and nature of the universe. It was a true shame that she'd been tricked into taking her life; she might have had years of important discoveries ahead of her.

He was troubled by the deaths, yes, but he was even more shocked to find that the Foundation had actually completed a series of *in vitro* fertilization cycles, which resulted in four pregnancies using surrogate mothers. Three had already given birth. The children were ultimately placed with parents who could not otherwise conceive.

This had been done, Tal, LaTour and the district attorney concluded, so that Farley and Sheldon could prove to potential clients that they were actually doing the cloning (though another reason, it appeared, was to make an additional $75,000 per placement from childless couples).

The main concern was for the health of the children, and the county hired several legitimate genetics doctors and pediatricians to see if the three children who'd been born and the one fetus within the surrogate mother were healthy. They were examined and found to be fine and, despite the immortality scam, the surrogate births and the adoption placements were completely legal, the attorney general concluded.

One of the geneticists Tal and LaTour had consulted said, 'So Bill Farley was behind this?' The man had shaken his head. 'We've been hearing about his crazy ideas for years. A wacko.'

'There any chance,' Tal wondered, 'that someday somebody'll actually be able to do what he was talking about?'

'Cloning consciousness?' The doctor laughed. 'You said you're a statistician, right?'

'That's right.'

'You know what the odds are of being able to perfectly duplicate the structure of any given human brain?'

'Small as a germ's ass?' LaTour suggested.

The doctor considered this and said, 'That sums it up pretty well.'

+ − < = > ÷

The day was too nice to be inside so Mac McCaffrey and Robert Covey were in the park. Tal spotted them on a bench overlooking a duck pond. He waved and veered toward them.

She appeared to be totally immersed in the sunlight, the soft breeze; Tal remembered how much this member of the Four Per Cent Club loved the out-of-doors.

Covey, Mac had confided to Tal, was doing pretty well. His blood pressure was down and he was in good spirits as he approached his surgery. She was breaching confidentiality rules by telling Tal this but she justified it on the grounds that Tal was a police officer investigating a case involving her patient. Another reason was simply that Tal liked the old guy and was concerned about him.

Mac also told him that Covey had finally called his son and left a message about his condition and the impending surgery. There'd been no reply, though Covey'd gotten a hang-up on his voice mail, the caller ID on the phone indicating 'Out of Area'. Mac took the optimistic position that it had indeed been his son on the other end of the line and the man hadn't left a message because he preferred to talk to his father in person. Time would tell.

In his office an hour ago Tal had been distracted as he listened to Mac's breathy, enthusiastic report about her patient. He'd listened attentively but was mostly waiting for an appropriate lull in the conversation to leap in with a dinner invitation. None had presented itself, though, before she'd had to hang up to get to a meeting. He'd hurriedly made plans to meet here.

Tal now joined them and she looked up with that great crooked smile he was deciding he really liked and was more than just a little sexy.

'Hey,' he said.

'Officer,' Robert Covey said. They warmly shook hands. Tal hesitated for a moment in greeting Mac but then thought, hell with it, bent down and kissed her, though on the noncommittal cheek. This seemed unprofessional on several levels – his as well as hers – but she didn't seem to care; he knew he certainly didn't have a problem with the lapse.

Tal proceeded to explain to Covey that since he was the only victim who'd survived the Lotus Foundation scam the police needed a signed and notarized copy of his statement.

'In case I croak when I'm under the knife you'll still have the evidence to put the pricks away.'

That was it exactly. Tal shrugged. 'Well . . .'

'Don'tcha worry,' the old man said. 'I'm happy to.'

Tal handed him the statement. 'Look it over, make any changes you want. I'll print out a final version and we'll get it notarized.'

'Will do.' Covey skimmed it and then looked up. 'How 'bout something to drink? There's a bar—'

'Coffee, tea or soda,' Mac said ominously. 'It's not even noon yet.'

'She claims she negotiates,' Covey muttered to Tal. 'But she don't.'

The old man pointed toward the park's concession stand at the top of a hill some distance away. 'Coffee's not bad there – for an outfit that's not named for a whaler.'

'I'll get it.'

'I'll have a large with cream.'

'He'll have a medium, skim milk,' Mac said. 'Tea for me, please. Sugar.' She fired a crooked smile his way.

+ – < = > ÷

About a hundred yards from the bench where the old man sat chatting away with his friend, a young woman walked along the park path. The redhead was short, busty, attractive, wearing a beautiful tennis bracelet and a diamond/emerald ring, off which the sunlight glinted fiercely.

She kept her eyes down as she walked, so nobody could see her abundant tears.

Margaret Ludlum had been crying on and off for several days. Ever since her boss and lover, Dr Anthony Sheldon, had been arrested.

Margaret had greeted the news of his arrest – and Farley's, too – with horror, knowing that she'd probably be the next to be picked up. After all, she'd been the one that Sheldon and Farley had sent as a representative of the Lotus Foundation to the couples who were planning to kill themselves. It was she who'd slipped them plenty of Luminux during their last few weeks on earth, then suggested they buy the blueprint for their deaths – the suicide books – and coerced them into killing themselves, and afterward cleaned up any evidence linking them to the Foundation or its two principals.

But the police had taken her statement – denying everything, of course – and let her go. It was clear they suspected Sheldon and Farley had an accomplice, but seemed to think that it was one of Farley's research assistants. Maybe they thought that only a man was capable of killing defenseless people.

Wrong. Margaret had been completely comfortable with assisted suicide. And more: she'd been only a minute away from murdering Robert Covey the other day as he walked down the street after leaving the Lotus Foundation. But just as she started toward him a van stopped nearby and two police officers jumped out, pulling him to safety. Other officers had raided the Foundation. She'd veered down a side street and called Sheldon to warn him. But it was too late. They got him outside his office at the hospital as he'd tried to flee.

Oh, yes, she'd been perfectly willing to kill Covey then.

And was perfectly willing to kill him now.

She watched that detective who'd initially come to interview Tony Sheldon walk away from the bench up the path toward the refreshment stand. It didn't matter that he was leaving; he wasn't her target.

Only Covey. With the old man gone it would be much harder to get a conviction, Sheldon explained. He might get off altogether or serve only a few years – that's what they doled out in most cases of assisted suicides. The cardiologist promised he'd finally get divorced and he and Margaret would move to Europe . . . They'd taken some great trips to the South of France and the weeks there had been wonderful. Oh, how she missed him.

Missed the money, too, of course. That was the other reason she had to get Tony out of jail. He'd been meaning to set up an account for her but hadn't gotten around to it. She'd let that slide for too long and the paperwork never materialized.

In her purse, banging against her hip, she felt the heavy pistol, the one she'd been planning to use on Covey several days ago. She was familiar with guns – she'd helped several of the other Lotus Foundation clients 'transition' by shooting themselves. And though she'd never actually pulled the trigger and murdered someone, she knew she could do it.

The tears were gone now. She was thinking of how to best handle the shooting. Studying the old man and that woman – who'd have to die, too, of course; she'd be a witness against Margaret herself for the murder today. Anyway, the double murder would make the scenario more realistic. It would look like a mugging. Margaret would demand the wallet and the woman's purse and when they handed the items over, she'd shoot them both in the head.

Pausing now, next to a tree, Margaret looked over the park. A few passersby, but no one was near Covey and the woman. The detective – Simms, she recalled – was still hiking up the hill to the concession stand. He was two hundred yards away; she could kill them both and be in her car speeding away before he could sprint back to the bench.

She waited until he disappeared into a stand of trees then reached into her purse, cocking the pistol. Margaret stepped out from behind the tree and moved quickly down the path that led to the bench. A glance around her. Nobody was present.

Closer now, closer. Along the asphalt path, damp from an earlier rain and the humid spring day.

She was twenty feet away . . . ten . . .

She stepped quickly up behind them. They looked up. The woman gave a faint smile in greeting – a smile that faded as she noted Margaret's cold eyes.

'Who are you?' the woman asked, alarm in her voice.

Margaret Ludlum said nothing. She pulled the gun from her purse.

+ − < = > ÷

'Wallet!' Pointing the pistol directly at the old man's face.

'What?'

'Give me your wallet!' Then turning to the woman, 'And the purse! Now!'

'You want—?'

They were confused, being mugged by someone outfitted by Neiman Marcus.

'Now!' Margaret screamed.

The woman thrust the purse forward and stood, holding her hands out. 'Look, just calm down.'

The old man was frantically pulling his wallet from his pocket and holding it out unsteadily.

Margaret grabbed the items and shoved them into her shoulder bag. Then she looked at the man's eyes and – rather than feel any sympathy, she felt that stillness she always did when slipping someone drugs or showing them how to grip the gun or seal the garage with duct tape to make the most efficient use of the carbon monoxide.

The woman was saying, 'Please, don't do anything stupid. Just take everything and leave!'

Then Robert Covey squinted. He was looking at her with certain understanding. He knew what this was about. 'Leave her alone,' he said. 'Me, it's okay. It's all right. Just let her go.'

But she thrust the gun forward at Covey as the woman with him screamed and dropped to the ground. Margaret began to pull the trigger, whispering the phrase she always did when helping transition the Lotus Foundation's clients, offering a prayer for a safe journey. 'God be with—'

A flash of muddy light filled her vision as she felt, for a tiny fragment of a second, a fist or rock slam into her chest.

'But . . . what . . .'

Then nothing but numb silence.

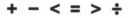

A thousand yards away, it seemed.

If not miles.

Talbot Simms squinted toward the bench, where he could see the forms of Robert Covey and Mac on their feet, backing away from the body of the woman he'd just shot. Mac was pulling out her cell phone, dropping it, picking it up again, looking around in panic.

He lowered the gun and stared.

A moment before, Tal had paid the vendor and was turning from the concession stand, holding the tray of drinks. Frowning, he saw a woman standing beside the bench, pointing something toward Mac and Covey, Mac rearing away then handing her purse over, the old man giving her something, his wallet, it seemed.

And then Tal had noticed that what she held was a gun.

He knew that she was in some way connected to Sheldon or Farley and the Lotus Foundation. The red hair . . . Yes! Sheldon's secretary, unsmiling Celtic Margaret. He'd known, too, that she'd come here to shoot the only living eyewitness to the scam – and probably Mac, too.

Dropping the tray of tea and coffee, he'd drawn his revolver. He'd intended to sprint back toward them, calling for her to stop, threatening her. But when he saw Mac fall to the ground, futilely covering her face, and Margaret shoving the pistol forward, he'd known she was going to shoot.

Tal had cocked his own revolver to single-action and stepped into a combat-firing stance, left hand curled under and around his right, weight evenly distributed on both feet, aiming high and slightly to the left, compensating for gravity and a faint breeze.

He fired, felt the kick of the recoil and heard the sharp report, followed by screams behind him of bystanders diving for cover.

Remaining motionless, he'd cocked the gun again and prepared to fire a second time in case he'd missed, looking for a target.

But he saw immediately that another shot wouldn't be necessary. Tal Simms carefully lowered the hammer of his weapon, replaced it in his holster and began running down the path.

+ − < = > ÷

'Excuse me, you were standing *where?*'

Tal ignored Greg LaTour's question and asked them both one more time, 'You're okay? You're sure?'

The bearded cop persisted. 'You were on *that* hill. Way the fuck up *there?*'

Mac told Tal that she was fine. He instinctively put his arm around her. Covey, too, said that he was unhurt, though he added that, as a heart patient, he could do without scares like that one.

Margaret Ludlum's gun had fired but it was merely a reflex after Tal's bullet had struck her squarely in the chest. The slug from her pistol had buried itself harmlessly in the ground somewhere nearby.

Tal glanced at her body, now covered with a green tarp from the Medical Examiner's Office. He waited to feel upset, or shocked or guilty, but he was only numb. Those would come later, he supposed. At the moment he was just relieved to find that Mac and Robert Covey were all right – and that the final itch in the case had been alleviated: the tough Irish girl, Margaret, was the missing link.

They must've hired muscle or used somebody in the Foundation for the dirty work.

As the crime-scene techs picked up evidence around the body and looked through the woman's purse, LaTour persisted. 'That hill up there? No fucking way.'

Tal glanced up. 'Yeah. Up there by the concession stand. Why?'

The bearded cop glanced at Mac. 'He's kidding. He's jerking my chain, right?'

'No, that's where he was.'

'That's a fucking long shot. Wait . . . how big's your barrel?'

'What?'

'On your service piece.'

'I don't know. It's whatever they gave me.' Tal nodded at the gun on his hip.

'Three-inch,' Greg said. 'You made that shot with a three-inch barrel?'

'We've pretty much established that, Greg. Can we move on?' Tal turned back to Mac and smiled, feeling weak, he was so relieved to see her safe.

But LaTour said, 'You told me you don't shoot.'

'I didn't say that. You *assumed* I don't shoot. I just didn't want to go to the range the other day. I've shot all my life. I was captain of the rifle team at school.'

LaTour squinted at the distant concession stand. He shook his head. 'No way.'

Tal glanced at him and asked, 'Okay, you want to know how I did it? There's a trick.'

'What?' the big cop asked eagerly.

'Easy. Just calculate the correlation between gravity as a constant and the estimated mean velocity of the wind over the time it takes the bullet to travel from points A to B – that's the muzzle to the target. The "MTT". Got that?'

'MTT. Yeah.'

'Then you multiply distance times that correlated factor divided by the mass of the bullet times its velocity squared.'

'You—' The big cop squinted again. 'Wait, you—'

'It's a joke, Greg.'

'You son of a bitch. You had me.'

'Haven't you noticed it's not that hard to do?'

The cop mouthed words that Mac couldn't see but Tal had no trouble deciphering.

LaTour squinted one last time toward the knoll and exhaled a laugh. 'Let's get statements.' He nodded to Robert Covey and escorted him toward his car, calling back to Tal, 'You get hers. That okay with you, Einstein?'

'Sure.'

Tal led Mac to a park bench out of sight of Margaret's body and listened to what she had to say about the incident, jotting down the facts in his precise handwriting. An officer drove Covey home, and Tal found himself alone with Mac. There was silence for a moment and he asked, 'Say, one thing? Could you help me fill out this questionnaire?'

'I'd be happy to.'

He pulled one out of his briefcase, looked at it, then back to her. 'How 'bout dinner tonight?'

'Is that one of the questions?'

'It's one of *my* questions. Not a police question.'

'Well, the thing is I've got a date tonight. Sorry.'

He nodded. 'Oh, sure.' Couldn't think of anything to follow up with. He pulled out his pen and smoothed the questionnaire, thinking: Of *course* she had a date. Women like her, high-ranking members of the Four Per Cent Club, always had dates. He wondered if it'd been the Pascal-sex comment that had knocked him out of the running. Note for the future: Don't bring that one up too soon.

Mac continued, 'Yeah, tonight I'm going to help Mr Covey find a health club with a pool. He likes to swim but he shouldn't do it alone. So we're going to find a place that's got a lifeguard.'

'Really? Good for him.' He looked up from Question 1.

'But I'm free Saturday,' Mac said.

'Saturday? Well, I am, too.'

Silence. 'Then how's Saturday?' she asked.

'I think it's great. Now how 'bout those questions?'

$$+ \; - \; < \; = \; > \; \div$$

A week later the Lotus Foundation case was nearly tidied up – as was Tal's office, much to his relief – and he was beginning to think about the other tasks awaiting him: the SEC investigation, the statistical analysis for next year's personnel assignments, and, of course, hounding fellow officers to get their questionnaires in on time.

The prosecutor still wanted some final statements for the Farley and Sheldon trials, though, and he'd asked Tal to interview the parents who'd adopted the three children born following the *in vitro* fertilization at the Foundation.

Two of the three couples lived nearby and he spent one afternoon taking their statements. The last couple was in Warwick, a small town outside of Albany, over an hour away. Tal made the drive on a Sunday afternoon, zipping down the picturesque roadway along the Hudson River, the landscape punctuated with blooming azaleas, forsythia and a billion spring flowers, the car filling with the scent of mulch and hot loam and sweet asphalt.

He found both Warwick and the couple's bungalow with no difficulty. The husband and wife, in their late twenties, were identically pudgy and rosy skinned. Uneasy, too, until Tal explained that his mission there had nothing to do with any challenges to the adoption. It was merely a formality for a criminal case.

Like the other parents, they provided good information that would be helpful in prosecuting Farley and Sheldon. For a half-hour Tal jotted careful notes and then thanked them for their time. As he was leaving he walked past a small, cheery room decorated in a circus motif.

A little girl, about four, stood in the doorway. It was the youngster the couple had adopted from the Foundation. She was adorable – blond, gray-eyed, with a heart-shaped face.

'This is Amy,' the mother said.

'Hello, Amy,' Tal offered.

She nodded shyly.

Amy was clutching a piece of paper and some crayons. 'Did you draw that?' he asked.

'Uh-huh. I like to draw.'

'I can tell. You've got lots of pictures.' He nodded at the girl's walls.

'Here,' she said, holding the sheet out. 'You can have this. I just drew it.'

'For me?' Tal asked. He glanced at her mother, who nodded her approval. He studied the picture for a moment. 'Thank you, Amy. I love it. I'll put it up on my wall at work.' The girl's face broke into a beaming smile.

Tal said goodbye to her parents, and ten minutes later he was cruising south on the parkway. When he came to the turnoff that would take him to his house and his Sunday retreat into the world of mathematics, though, Tal continued past. He continued instead to his office at the County Building.

A half-hour later he was on the road again. En route to an address in Chesterton, a few miles away.

He pulled up in front of a split-level house surrounded by a small but immaculately trimmed yard. Two plastic tricycles and other assorted toys sat in the driveway.

But this wasn't the right place, he concluded with irritation. Damn. He must've written the address down wrong.

The house he was looking for had to be nearby and he decided to ask the owner here where it was. Walking to the door, Tal pushed the bell then stood back.

A pretty blonde in her thirties greeted him with a cheerful, 'Hi. Help you?'

'I'm looking for Greg LaTour's house.'

'Well, you found it. Hi, I'm his wife, Joan.'

'He lives *here*?' Tal asked, glancing past her into a suburban home right out of a Hollywood sitcom.

She laughed. 'Hold on. I'll get him.'

A moment later Greg LaTour came to the door, wearing shorts, sandals and a green Izod shirt. He blinked in surprise and looked back over his shoulder into the house. Then he stepped outside and pulled the door shut after him. 'What're you doing here?'

'Needed to tell you something about the case.' But Tal's voice faded. He was staring at two adorable blond girls, twins, about eight years old, who'd come around the side of the house and were looking at Tal curiously.

One said, 'Daddy, the ball's in the bushes. We can't get it.'

'Honey, I've got to talk to my friend here,' he said in a singsong, fatherly voice. 'I'll be there in a minute.'

'Okay.' They disappeared.

'You've got two kids?'

'*Four* kids.'

'How long you been married?'

'Eighteen years.'

'But I thought you were single. You never mentioned family. You don't wear a ring. Your office, the guns, the biker posters.'

'That's who I need to be to do my job,' LaTour said in a low voice. 'That life' – he nodded vaguely in the direction of the Sheriff's Department – 'and this life I keep 'em separate. Completely.'

That's something else . . .

Tal now understood the meaning of the phrase. It wasn't about tragedies in his life, marital breakups, alienated children. And there was nothing LaTour kept exclusively from Tal. His was a life kept separate from everybody in the department.

'So you're mad I'm here,' Tal said.

A shrug. 'Just wish you'd called first.'

'Sorry.'

LaTour shrugged again. 'You go to church today?'

'I don't go to church. Why?'

'Why're you wearing a tie on Sunday?'

'I don't know. I just do. Is it crooked?'

The big cop said, 'No, it's not crooked. So. What're you doing here?'

'Hold on a minute.'

Tal got his briefcase out of the car and returned to the porch. 'I stopped by the office and checked up on the earlier suicides Sheldon and Farley arranged.'

'You mean from a few years ago?'

'Right. Well, one of them was a professor named Mary Stemple. I'd heard of her – she was a physicist at Princeton. I read some of her work a while ago. She was brilliant. She spent the last three years of her life working on this analysis of the luminosity of stars and measuring black-body radiation—'

'I've got burgers about to go on the grill,' LaTour grumbled.

'Okay. Got it. Well, this was published just before she killed herself.' He handed LaTour what he'd just downloaded from the *Journal of Advanced Astrophysics'* website:

The Infinite Journey of Light:
A New Approach to Measuring
Distant Stellar Radiation
By Prof. Mary Stemple, Ph.D.

He flipped to the end of the article, which consisted of several pages of complicated formulae. They involved hundreds of numbers and Greek and English letters and mathematical symbols. The one that occurred most frequently was the sign for infinity: ∞

LaTour looked up. 'There a punch line to all this?'

'Oh, you bet there is.' He explained about his drive to Warwick to interview the adoptive couple.

And then he held up the picture that their daughter, Amy, had given him. It was a drawing of the earth and the moon and a spaceship – and all around them, filling the sky, were infinity symbols, growing smaller and smaller as they receded into space.

Forever . . .

Tal added, 'And this wasn't the only one. Her walls were *covered* with pictures she'd done that had infinity signs in them. When I saw this I remembered Stemple's work. I went back to the office and I looked up her paper.'

'What're you saying?' LaTour frowned.

'Mary Stemple killed herself four years ago. The girl who drew this was conceived at the Foundation's clinic a month after she died.'

'Jesus . . .' The big cop stared at the picture. 'You don't think . . . Hell, it can't be real, that cloning stuff. That doctor we talked to, he said it was impossible.'

Tal said nothing, continued to stare at the picture.

LaTour shook his head. 'Naw, naw. You know what they did, Sheldon or that girl of his? Or Farley? They showed the kid pictures of that symbol. You know, so they could prove to other clients that the cloning worked. That's all.'

'Sure,' Tal said. 'That's what happened. Probably.'

Still, they stood in silence for a long moment, this trained mathematician and this hardened cop, staring, captivated, at a clumsy, crayon picture drawn by a cute four-year-old.

'It can't be,' LaTour muttered. 'Germ's ass, remember?'

'Yeah, it's impossible,' Tal said, staring at the symbol. He repeated: 'Probably.'

'Daddy!' came a voice from the backyard.

LaTour called, 'Be there in a minute, honey!' Then he looked up at Tal and said, 'Hell, as long as you're here, come on in. Have dinner. I make great burgers.'

Tal considered the invitation, but his eyes were drawn back to the picture, the stars, the moon, the infinity signs. 'Thanks but think I'll pass. I'm going back to the office for a while. All that evidence we took out of the Foundation? I wanta look over the data a little more.'

'Suit yourself, Einstein,' the homicide cop said. He started back into the house, but paused and turned back. 'Data plural,' he said, pointing a huge finger at Tal's chest.

'Data plural,' Tal agreed.

LaTour vanished inside, the screen door swinging shut behind him with a bang.

About the Author

A former journalist, folksinger and attorney, Jeffery Deaver is an international number-one best-selling author. His novels have appeared on best-seller lists around the world, including *The New York Times*, *The Times* of London, Italy's *Corriere della Sera*, the *Sydney Morning Herald* and the *Los Angeles Times*. His books are sold in 150 countries and translated into twenty-five languages.

The author of thirty-one novels, three collections of short stories, and a non-fiction law book, he's received or been shortlisted for a number of awards around the world. His *The Bodies Left Behind* was named Novel of the Year by the International Thriller Writers. And his Lincoln Rhyme thriller, *The Broken Window*, and a stand-alone thriller, *Edge*, were also nominated for that prize. He has been awarded the Steel Dagger and the Short Story Dagger from the British Crime Writers' Association, and the Nero Wolfe Award, and he is a three-time recipient of the Ellery Queen Readers Award for Best Short Story of the Year, and a winner of the British Thumping Good Read Award. *The Cold Moon* was recently named the Book of the Year by the Mystery Writers Association of Japan, as well as by *Kono Mystery Wa Sugoi* magazine. In addition, the Japanese Adventure Fiction Association awarded the book their annual Grand Prix award; Deaver's *Carte Blanche* also received that honor.

Deaver has been nominated for seven Edgar Awards from the Mystery Writers of America, a Shamus award, an Anthony Award and a Gumshoe Award. He was recently shortlisted for the ITV3 Crime Thriller Award for Best International Author.

His latest novels are *The October List*, a reverse-time thriller, the Lincoln Rhyme novel *The Kill Room*, *XO*, featuring Kathryn Dance, and *Carte Blanche*, the 2011 James Bond continuation thriller.

His book *A Maiden's Grave* was made into an HBO movie starring James Garner and Marlee Matlin, and his novel *The Bone Collector* was a feature release from Universal Pictures, starring Denzel Washington and Angelina Jolie. And, yes, the rumors are true; he did appear as a corrupt reporter on his favorite soap opera, *As the World Turns*.

He was born outside Chicago and has a bachelor of journalism degree from the University of Missouri and a law degree from Fordham University.

Readers can visit his website at www.jefferydeaver.com.

Coming soon: the new LINCOLN RHYME thriller
and long anticipated follow-up to *The Bone Collector*

JEFFERY DEAVER

THE SKIN COLLECTOR

A new type of serial killer is stalking the streets of New York – one more
devious and disturbing than ever before.

They call this butcher The Skin Collector: a tattooist with a chamber
of torture hidden deep underground. But instead of using ink to create
each masterpiece, the artist uses a lethal poison which will render targets
dead before they can even entertain the prospect of escape . . .

Drafted in to investigate, NYPD detective Lincoln Rhyme and his associate Amelia Sachs have little to go on but a series of cryptic messages
left etched into the skin of the deceased. As the pair struggle to discover
the meaning behind the designs, they are led down a treacherous and
twisting path where nothing is as it seems. And with the clock rapidly
ticking before the killer strikes again, they must untangle the twisted
web of clues before more victims – or they themselves – are next.

Out in hardback and ebook May 2014

HODDER &
STOUGHTON

In the best books, the ending often comes as a shock.
Not just because of that one last twist in the tale,
but because you have been so absorbed in their world,
that coming back to the harsh light of reality is a jolt.

If that describes you now, then perhaps you should track down
some new leads, and find new suspense in other worlds.

Join us at www.hodder.co.uk, or follow us on
Twitter @hodderbooks, and you can tap in to a
community of fellow thrill-seekers.

Whether you want to find out more about this book,
or a particular author, watch trailers and interviews, have
the chance to win early limited editions, or simply browse
our expert readers' selection of the very best books,
we think you'll find what you're looking for.

And if you don't, that's the place to tell us what's missing.

We love what we do, and we'd love you to be part of it.

www.hodder.co.uk

 @hodderbooks

HodderBooks

HodderBooks